Pavel Kornev

THE ILLUSTRIOUS

thank you for being
my Reader!
Without you Books
ARE Nothing!
PAVEL KORNEV

SUBLIME ELECTRICITY
Book One

Magic Dome Books

The Illustrious
(The Sublime Electricity Book #1)
Copyright © Pavel Kornev 2016
Cover Art © Vladimir Manyukhin 2016
Translator © Andrew Schmitt 2016
Editor: Barbara D. Jenkins
Published by Magic Dome Books, 2017
All Rights Reserved
ISBN: 978-80-88231-30-1

TABLE OF CONTENTS:

IN THIS WORLD, THERE WERE no Dark ages; they were called Bloody instead. In this world, the skies were once obscured by the wings of the fallen, striking fear into the hearts of mankind. In this world, science has freed society of its shackles, and the Second Empire, the empire of humanity, stretches from sea to sea. In this world, combat steamships furrow the waters, armored trains await their hour, and army dirigibles float through the heavens. And yet, the delicate balance this world has achieved hangs by a thread. The age of steam is on its way out, and the era of the Sublime Electricity is just beginning. In this time of dramatic transition, even the tiniest deviation in course could topple the world into a vortex of chaos.

"I will cut out my own heart.
I will give my heart to you!"

Phillip August, Steamfonia

PART ONE

THE FALLEN

A Titanium Blade and the Power of Imagination

1

IS IT TRUE THAT ALL WHICH is born to crawl cannot fly? Indeed!

People simply were not made for flight, so any attempt at it is doomed to end in a fall. And the faster the ascent, the more disastrous the consequences. Consider, for example, *the fallen...*

I OPENED MY EYES. I immediately slammed them shut, but it was too late. When I opened them again, I caught a glimpse of the gray-smoke-shrouded sky spinning and whirling above me, creating the illusion that I was lying on a rescue raft in the middle of a giant whirlpool. The mere thought of having to stand to my feet was painful, though, so I stayed where I was, sprawled out in a cowardly fashion on top of the rubbish pile that broke my fall.

I took a timid breath, and my ribs were instantly pierced by a sharp pain. But, when I inhaled a second time, the unpleasant sensations were already on the decline, letting me know that I had been lucky enough to get away with nothing more than a bruise to the back. No pieces of brick, nor broken bottles, as luck would have it, were to be found among the trash heap that took me in its sweet embrace.

That brightened my mood. Overall, I still wasn't feeling too great, considering the circumstances of my fall but, nevertheless, I did have something to be happy about.

I opened my eyes again.

Gloomy building walls rose up all around me, giving the impression that I was at the bottom of a deep well. Above them loomed a gray sky, hostile and ugly like everything else around. Suddenly, the darkness grew even thicker, foreshadowing the coming of an army dirigible. Its cabin was lined with tightly battened-down square weapons hatches. After that, I saw the tail stabilizers, keel, and Gatling-gun barrels, reflecting back a solar sheen. But next thing I knew, all trace of the airship was gone, as if it had never been there at all.

No matter! It wasn't as if I'd tumbled out of the cabin of that flying monster. Not at all: I had been sent on a short flight out the snarling maw of a shattered second-story window.

Though, to be frank, saying I was "sent" is rather overstating it.

"Leopold!" the echo of a far off scream rolled over the courtyard. I heard a booming clatter, and a moment later, the voice was closer: "Leo! Curses, where are you?!"

The beam of an electric torch swept over the area; its bright light ran across the walls, sidled off in my direction and went out. Only when my eyes began getting reaccustomed to the darkness did I see a short constable step into the courtyard. He was wearing a police-issue cloak and service cap. His high-caliber lupara was giving me an ugly snarl with the muzzle-end of its quadruple barrels.

"Don't point that thing at me!" I demanded, frowning in annoyance.

Ramon Miro dallied for a moment, then tucked his weapon into the crease of his left elbow.

"Are you alright?" he asked, looking around apprehensively.

"I will be," I answered tersely but concisely.

"Are you sure?" My hulking black-haired partner doubted, extending his free hand.

I batted it away, irritated. Mustering my strength, I rolled over onto my side, and even managed to lift myself up on an elbow before hearing the jingle of broken glass ring out above me.

A round-faced gentleman of middling years wearing a three-piece gray suit and an equally unassuming bowler appeared behind the glass-shard-toothed smile in the window. With the handle of his cane, he knocked yet another piece of broken glass from the frame, then looked at me, his face acquiring an expression of extreme disapproval.

"What happened to that damned succubus,

Leo?" asked Inspector White.

I turned my head, first in one direction, then the other, surveying the entire garbage mound I was sprawled out on and smirked unhappily.

"Well... I can say for sure that I don't see her here, inspector."

"Detective Constable Orso!" Robert White rapped off, letting me know that jokes were entirely unwelcome. "Answer me now. Where the hell is she?!"

"I don't know," I then confessed. "It's just... I don't remember much after being thrown out that window."

"A particularly regrettable turn of events," the inspector winced, retreating from the window.

I lied back down and sighed helplessly, then looked up at Ramon and asked:

"Well, what are you staring at?"

The constable gave an ambiguous snort and turned away. On his imperturbable ruddy face there was not a sliver of emotion, but his ostentatious indifference could not deceive me – my colleague's disappointment could be felt almost physically.

No matter! There's still the boss to appease...

I sat up among the rubbish and suddenly turned my head. I hadn't yet managed to come to my senses in earnest. Nevertheless, the back door swung open, and Inspector White appeared on a high staircase.

"Leo," he said with uncharacteristic tenderness, looking around the darkened courtyard with a fastidious grimace. "Leo, what the devil happened here?"

I didn't rush to answer. I first stood to my feet and pulled my split-end telescoping stun baton toward me by its rubber-coated cord, then shrugged my shoulders ambiguously.

"A real calamity," I announced when the extended pause became entirely indecent in length.

"Is that right?" The inspector snorted, and his gray eyes drained of their color, losing the last trace of their already faded shade.

The *Illustrious* Robert White possessed a *talent* that was exceedingly valuable in our line of work: he could smell lies. He couldn't always tell when he was being lied to but, like a trained bloodhound, he could easily sniff out the conscious intention to mislead when being spoken to. His very, very useful *talent* was left to him by his parents, who had marked themselves with the blood of *the fallen...*

That was the very reason I didn't even try to wheedle, and simply lifted my stun baton.

"The shock is weak," I told the inspector.

"You don't say?" asked Robert White, perplexed.

Just then, two constables wearing police-issue cloaks walked up to us with their new-fashioned semi-automatic carbines at the ready. The gun's box magazines stuck up in a way that gave them a silly appearance, but people who really knew guns weren't bothered by that in the least; in small skirmishes, the short-barreled Madsen-Biarnoff rifle spoke for itself quite eloquently.

"I think there's something wrong with the electric jar," I posited, not paying any mind to the skeptical gazes of my colleagues.

"You've got something wrong with your head, Leo!" the red-headed constable squealed out just then.

"No, no, Jimmy!" intervened the other young man, his teeth brown from chewing tobacco. He immediately clarified his observation, though: "His problem is that he's got messed-up arms."

The red-head laughed with a satisfied look:

"Billy, old boy! I see no reason why both couldn't be true at the same time!"

"I think you've hit the nail on the head there, Jimmy! In his case, they seem to amplify one another!"

I didn't get offended; Jimmy and Billy were

notorious wisecrackers. Just give them something to mock, and they're off to the races. But the inspector wanted explanations, so my idea to give Billy a jab with my stun baton and put a cork in his yapper doing so seemed like killing two birds with one stone.

So I did just that.

A blinding flash of sparks blazed forth. The constable jumped back jerkily and rubbed his chest.

"Have you gone totally batty?" he bared his teeth.

"Forget it!" I said, waving it off and turning to the inspector. "Like I said, the shock is weak!"

Infernal creatures were particularly sensitive to electricity, but a zap as weak as I was packing would do nothing to stun a succubus or any other hell-spawn for that matter.

Robert White came down the stairs, his cane hanging from his arm, and set about unhurriedly packing his pipe with strong Persian tobacco.

"This morning, you should have been checking the shock instead of reading your yellow rags!" He reproached me.

"But I checked it three times! It was working just fine!"

"Come then, give it here," the inspector demanded, taking the electric jar that I'd pulled from my pocket and looking at the little label on its base. "Des Prez Electric?" He read out and flared up: "Leo, where'd you dig this clunker up from?!"

I answered with the pure truth:

"I got it from our stockroom."

"Curses!" The inspector cried, ripping the cord out in a fit of anger and tossing the electric jar onto the rubbish heap. "Leo, we'd been tracking that beast for two weeks! Two weeks! And it all came to naught because of this piece of junk!"

"But..."

"Silence!" Robert White demanded and set about taking furious puffs on his pipe. "Ramon!" He raised his voice after a few deep draws. "Who manufactured the electric jar in your lupara?"

His gun, with four short ten-caliber barrels, was manufactured by Heim, and used electrically ignited rounds as ammunition. After a cursory glance at its folding stock, the constable reported back:

"Edison Electric Lights, inspector!"

"Do you see, Leo?" My superior scolded. "Remember that for the future: only Edison Electric Lights will do, Tesla forgive me! Do you understand?"

"Yes, sir."

"And by the way, why did you go in without waiting for the others?"

"The door was open. I decided to do some reconnaissance."

"Oh you did? And where'd that get you?" The inspector frowned, shrugging his shoulders in annoyance and starting off out of the courtyard. "Let's go!" he called, but immediately stopped us and patted down his pockets: "Jimmy, where are my gloves?"

"I don't know, inspector," the constable answered, poking his partner in the side. "Billy, where are the inspector's gloves?"

"What are you asking me for?" he snarled, looking around.

"Forget it!" Robert White called for order, creeping under the archway.

Jimmy and Billy sized me up with unkind gazes and rushed off after our boss; I wiped the dirt from my back and shuffled off behind them. Ramon Miro was walking next to me in silence, trying to match my uneven gait.

It should be said that the Catalan constable was a surprisingly taciturn man. Incidentally, he was only Catalonian on his father's side. His mother's origins were among the natives of the New World. As a matter of fact, in temperament, Ramon had more in common with his mother's people than his Mediterranean father's.

Just then, a terrified rat jumped up from under our feet. Ramon just kicked it away with the tip of his boot and kept walking calmly. I went over the heap of rubbish lying in the entryway and ducked my head to avoid the soot-coated underside of the arch.

Being tall isn't nearly as glamorous as some envious pip squeaks suppose. It just is what it is.

That silent courtyard was replaced by another, just as dirty and unsightly as the one that came before it. From there, we emerged onto an unpeopled alley and stopped to wait for further orders from the inspector. He unhurriedly tapped his pipe out on the wall of the building, fished a silver pocket-watch out of his vest and pursed his lips, deep in thought.

Taking advantage of the moment of peace, I stomped the rest of the trash off my rubberized cloak, folded the telescoping stun baton back up and took my round tinted glasses from my breast pocket. I clipped them onto my nose and finally felt comfortable again.

Unlike the inspector, I didn't enjoy attracting the attention of locals with my unnaturally colorless eyes. That was why I found it impossible to bear looking directly at someone when talking. Of course, there was also the fact that I didn't especially enjoy people in general. They are usually so obtuse!

"Let's get back to the Box!" Robert White decided just then and, waving his cane unevenly and even nervously, he began walking toward the nearest Metro station.

New Babylon was a surprising city! It was always awake and alive, day or night. Here, the wonderful and the horrible were so closely intertwined as to be indistinguishable. And there were no angles or sharp edges, either. It was all just shades and blurred half-tones blending seamlessly into one another.

Ancient palaces, their marbled siding having long since grown dark with soot, butted up against new buildings, which were still clean, though their plainness detracted from any beauty that could have lent them. Avenues, wide in the downtown, got lost in a rat's nest of little winding streets in the outskirts, though it wasn't clear exactly how. Age-old trees in the Emperor's Park were thick with rustling foliage, but their leaves were more-often-than-not yellow and dying from the constant smog. The azure waters of the harbor rolled into shore in unctuous breaks, and the endless sky was constantly packed tight with clouds of smoke from factory smokestacks.

That's how everything was in New Babylon. Even the granite sett paving stones were reddish, not because of the stone's natural coloration, but because they were now permanently stained with the blood of *the fallen...*

New Babylon was the capital of the Second Empire; at once the heart of government and an ulcer, eating it from the inside.

THE NARROW LITTLE STREET with soot-covered walls, interspersed with the odd hazy rectangular window led us out to an intersection. There, I could see smokestacks, mountainous and crested with long clouds of smoke. Fortunately, the wind was carrying the fumes away from the suburbs today, so it was less smoggy than usual.

Soon, we'd left the shanties behind. The street grew wider, and the stench of reeking factory runoff began drifting up from the grates of the storm drains. We were now going downhill and, a few blocks later, we were nestling up to Yarden Embankment. The silvery expanse of water was shackled by a railroad bridge that stretched from one bank to the other; clumsy tugs and barges looked like toy boats on the backdrop of its pillars, making all the freight dirigibles drifting into port also look less striking than they were.

"Hurry up!" The inspector rushed us along.

I placed my palm on my forehead, noticed a wisp of smoke crawling slowly in our direction and increased my pace, rushing after the others.

With our heels clacking on the paving stones of the embankment, we paraded to the train station past the fence and the ticket booths. Fortunately, we didn't have to wait in their never-ending lines. Once on the platform, it was too crowded to even push our way through the workers from the surrounding factories. Thankfully, the grubby proles gave a wide berth to our well-armed division, no prodding necessary.

A powerful whistle blew, and a gargantuan train rolled in under the awning, enshrouded in clouds of white steam. The room suddenly filled with the smoke pouring from its stacks. With a metallic clang, the brakes screeched to a halt. The train stopped, and its passengers gushed out onto the platform, pushing against the working rabble on their way home after the night shift.

The inspector was in no mind to knock elbows with commoners, and took a decisive step into a first class train-car; we all followed behind our boss. At the entrance, Robert White used his cane to shoo the conductor, who was taken aback at his lack of manners, then took a seat next to the window, looking collected. There weren't enough places for the rest of us to sit but, that didn't stop the Metro attendant from practically having a fit while the distinguished public looked askance at us with barely restrained indignation.

Two short horn-blows rang out. The train shook, and columns and dejected fences began flittering by out the window, gradually increasing their speed. Soon, the tracks dove into a tunnel, and the train bolted beneath the earth, leaving the hustle and bustle of the streets with all their speed-demon cabbies and day-dreaming pedestrians somewhere far, far above us. Now, the train was flying along at full steam, shaking us around mercilessly. We had to latch firmly onto the handrail and clench the back of the nearest seat just to remain standing.

A few minutes later, the steam train slowed its pace and, with a deafening blast of its horn, rolled out of the tunnel onto the platform of an underground station lit only by the uneven flame of gas jets. Some got out, some came in, and the train rolled onward.

The Metro was great! Nothing could compare with it. Not steam trams, and not the new-fangled self-propelled carriages. It did make a lot of smoke, though – it was impossible to breathe...

Three stations later, we got off the train and walked up onto the street. The colossal Newton-Markt was towering over us on the opposite side of the square. The inspector could only stand to look peevishly at the marble columns of its portico before walking off in the opposite direction.

"I need to wet my whistle," he grumbled, having gotten wind of our inquisitive looks with his back.

No one objected.

And what was there to object to? After such a major fiasco, returning to the Box, as everyone called police headquarters, was something none of us wanted. And me least of all.

WE USUALLY GOT DRINKS at *Archimedes' Screw*, a small public house, known for its huge selection of Flemish beers and primarily law-enforcement clientele.

"Morning edition here!" burst out from the hoarse throat of a boy holding a thick packet of newspapers near the door. "Tensions rising in the Sea of Judea! More troop movements in Alexandria! Get yours here! Only in the Saturday edition! Split in the ranks of the Sublime Electricity! Tesla versus Edison! Full-page article!"

Robert White threw the lad a ten-centime coin, grabbed an edition of the *Atlantic Telegraph* and walked into the bar.

"Hello, Almer!" He said, greeting the bar's corpulent owner, and taking a seat at his regular place by the window. "The usual."

The fat Fleming took out a small decanter of red port and placed it in front of the inspector. After that, he poured a glass of white for Jimmy and Billy, who retired to a far-away corner with their drinks, a plate of bread, and a few slices of spicy pork terrine.

When Ramon Miro walked away with a glass of white wine, which he drank fairly diluted with soda water, I took a seat on a high stool and leaned against the bar on my elbows.

"Lemonade?" sighed the barkeep.

"Lemonade," I confirmed, looking with no particular interest over the array of beer bottles, each bearing a technicolor label tied around its neck with thick twine and a wax-sealed cap.

"I can't stand this new trend!" Almer shook his head. "Soon, people will be drinking beer mixed with lemonade!"

"Ugh! No thank you," I chuckled in reply.

"They will, though. Mark my words!" the proprietor announced confidently and set off for the ice-cellar. Soon, he was back with a condensation-covered pitcher of lemonade. He set it before me and pieces of ice started jingling around joyfully in it.

I filled my tall glass, took a few sips and nodded:

"Great!"

Almer took the praise as a matter of course and set about drying one of the beer mugs with a towel.

"I can never recall you ever having ordered a real drink," he said, not stopping what he was doing.

"That's right. I've never touched the stuff," I confirmed.

"Surprising."

"Why's that? I would've thought it commonplace."

"For a moral-crazed reductionist, sure," the Fleming said with a smirk, "but you'd have an easier time finding a churchgoing hooker than a constable that doesn't drink."

"Alcohol gives me sleeping problems," I explained my refusal, not especially bending the truth.

The owner of the establishment burst out in booming laughter:

"Do you think many of your colleagues are concerned with such trifles?"

I just shrugged my shoulders, not planning on disputing his assertion. To be perfectly honest, I personally knew people, who could only be stopped from drinking by a shot to the head, preferably from a high-caliber rifle.

Talking with my drunk colleagues sober didn't make me feel any less close to them, though. After all, people are usually pretty open and honest after a few drinks.

Alcohol allows people to forget about their fears, at least for a time. Who was I to judge?

I took the pitcher of lemonade and slid off the chair, intending to join Ramon, but I was suddenly called over by the inspector, who was leafing through the newspaper.

"Leopold!" He said, not tearing himself from his reading. "Won't you join me?"

Curses! That was the last thing I needed!

I swore mentally and, in no particular hurry, walked up to the table, taking a seat opposite my boss. After I'd filled my glass with lemonade, Robert White twirled his fingers before his face and asked:

"Would you please remove your glasses?"

After completing his request, I breathed out onto the round black lenses, wiped them with a linen cloth and placed them on the edge of the table. After that, I finished the lemonade and shifted my gaze to a blueprint for an Archimedes' screw that was pinned to the wall, one of many.

"You don't ever look people in the eyes, do you Leo?" the inspector asked unexpectedly. "Is that right?"

"As a rule, I do not," I confirmed, turning my gaze back from the yellowing drawing to my superior officer. I evaluated the cut of his made-to-order suit, his ideally cropped hair, and the fanciful pattern on his silken handkerchief.

I did not look him in the eyes, though.

Between the inspector's eyes, there was a deep wrinkle. He finished his fortified red wine, wiped his thin pale lips with a napkin and, only after completing the procedure, said:

"I know of your *illustrious talent.* I'm sure it isn't easy looking in peoples' eyes, if all you see is fear."

"There's little to enjoy in it," I answered. "Looking into someone's eyes is still climbing into someone's soul, after all. I prefer... to keep my distance."

"That won't work on me."

"Keeping my distance?" I joked.

"Climbing into the soul," Robert White answered, totally serious. He then wiped his chin and remarked in contemplation: "It was supposed that your *talent* would be a bit more useful around here..."

More useful? His words gave me a nasty impression.

Sure, my *talent* could have been of more use at work, but I simply couldn't bear digging around in others' fears, allowing them into my own head and bringing them to life. Though I could do it without any particular strain, actually using my *talent* left me feeling like I'd just had a wallow in a mud puddle.

Then again, this conversation wasn't about my delicate psyche...

"Inspector!" I shuddered. "With the succubus..."

"Listen to me, Leopold!" Robert drummed his fingers on the edge of the table, calling for silence. "This isn't about the succubus! You just aren't getting it! You aren't settling into the job! You cannot work with people and you don't want to. In our line of work, that is half the battle. What made you want to become a policeman in the first place? You could've been a librarian!"

"I need to pay the bills somehow," I made away with a half-truth, as usual.

If the inspector noticed my understatement, he didn't make it known.

"Well, alright, people!" He frowned, getting to the main point. "This city is so packed with thieves, they're like sardines in a can. Arresting burglars, robbers and murderers has been business as usual for a long time. Separatists and Anarcho-Christians? That whole restless brotherhood is of little interest to anyone. And the inspector general wouldn't even give you a hand-shake for catching an Egyptian agent. Infernal creatures, though – that's serious business! That's how you get on the front page of newspapers. We'd been tracking that succubus for two weeks, Leo. For two weeks, we've been ignoring all other assignments! And now, that's all down the drain. All because of you."

Trying to justify myself would have been at the very least stupid, which is why I fixed my gaze on my glass and jingled around the pieces of ice that remained.

"I thought it was a coincidence!" the inspector continued his excoriation. "A simple coincidence! But I read the papers and I realized: no, it is no coincidence. Point blank, Leo, you've been nothing but trouble."

"What do you mean?" I grew confused, thrown off by the unexpected turn.

Robert White slid the morning edition of the *Atlantic Telegraph* to me and hinted:

"The society page."

I took a look at the headline he was pointing at and winced dolefully but, all the same, read the article in its entirety, only sighing afterward:

"What a pest..."

Robert White took the newspaper, shuddered, sitting up straight, and read aloud:

"The famous New-Babylon poet Albert Brandt, in conversation with our correspondent, alluded to the fact that he has recently written a poem for his good friend, the Viscount Cruce, dedicated to his beloved, the *Illustrious*

Elizabeth-Maria N." The inspector pressed the newspaper to the table with his palm and burned me with his hateful gaze. "Well, Viscount Cruce, what do you think the *Illustrious* Elizabeth-Maria N.'s father will do to you after reading that little tidbit?"

"Hold up!" I jumped in. "You aren't understanding this right at all!"

"Is that so?" the inspector screwed up his face skeptically. "You don't have to have the wisdom of Solomon to guess what it's talking about. A blue-eyed, red-headed girl by the name 'Elizabeth-Maria N.!' Do you know many people, who fit that description? I know only one! And that is the daughter of Inspector General von Nalz! Curses! That geezer caught many of *the fallen* himself! Rumor has it that he smeared himself with their blood from head to toe! And now, he is striving with every bone in his body to get his dear little daughter married off to the nephew of the Minister of Justice. If this whole thing goes belly-up over one little article..."

"You've got it all wrong..."

"No, I don't!" Robert White frowned. "If this goes badly, the old man will challenge you to a duel, and he will kill you. It wouldn't be the first time for him. And, Leo, whether you know it or not, he would have every right to do so." The inspector finished his port and threw himself back into his chair. "I personally would like to just wash my hands of this, and would do so with the greatest of pleasure. The problem is that the incident will reflect deplorably on my career."

"It's just a coincidence," I repeated obstinately. "They aren't connected..."

"Come off it!" Snapped my boss. "Your excuses won't change a thing. By midday, even the floor-polishers in headquarters will know about your affair with the inspector general's daughter. The old man won't even be listening!"

"I could..."

"There's nothing you can do," the inspector cut me off, but immediately snapped his fingers. "Actually, there is! Disappear for a week. Two would be better. Hand in your weapons, don't come in to work. After that, we can decide how to proceed."

I was categorically not in favor of whatever he meant by "proceed," but any attempt to convince my boss to try another way was sure to fail. He'd already made up his mind. An unpleasant sour sensation appeared in my mouth. My eyes began to sting from the injustice of being.

Albert! What a bastard you are! Well, who was it that got your tongue wagging?

"Now make yourself scarce," the inspector ordered, putting up his newspaper to block me out.

I made no effort to carry out that order quickly. I felt like a beaten dog, which was very unpleasant. In a pitiful attempt to retain my last shred of dignity, I first finished my lemonade, only standing from the table after I was done. I then took my rubberized cloak down from the hook and turned to the bartender:

"Almer, put it on my tab."

"So soon?" confirmed the quirky Fleming, who knew our employees' payment schedules at least as well as our actual accountant.

I waved farewell to everyone, went out onto the street, and looked up at the sky. In it, there were scant clouds mixed in with wisps of smoke from factory smokestacks. I started shouting curse words helplessly. Next, I snapped my dark glasses to my nose in a habitual motion and started off toward the Newton-Markt.

I'll hand in my weapons and change clothes at the same time.

Even though, as a detective constable I was not required to come to work in police uniform like most rank-and-file, I usually did not abuse that privilege. They didn't give me a stipend to clean or mend my own clothes, and the Viscount Cruce hadn't had much money lying around as of late.

A stiff wind roared up from the Viscount

Cruce's pockets, as a matter of fact. My home had been remortgaged three times, and the only thing allowing me to look on the future with even cautious optimism was the fund I had been willed by my grandfather on my mother's side.

Why cautious, though? Because the current executor of the fund, my uncle the Count Kósice, was not exactly burning with desire to part with the twenty thousand francs of yearly income it provided him and was drawing out the procedure in various ways, keeping me from me from my rightful inheritance as long as he could. I had turned twenty-one a month ago, but the fiduciaries hadn't even yet managed to compose the asset register, which was to say nothing of material transfers. And it was totally unclear just how long it would be before that confusing procedure was completed. I doubted that my uncle would take it to the point of legal battles, but I was sure I wouldn't be able to avoid the remaining "charms" of splitting up the estate.

On the other hand, what did I need the money for now? I was lucky not to have just lost my head...

2

I ENTERED THE NEWTON-MARKT, the whole-block police headquarters building, through the back service entrance. I let an armored car pass by as it left the garage to the measured claps of a gunpowder engine before it rolled unhurriedly down the alley. I took a look around and ran up the stairs. I flung the door open confidently, nodding to the sleepy sentry on my way and walking through the empty halls into the armory.

There, I handed a sergeant my stun baton and took an electric jar from my pocket, still wrapped in this morning's edition of the *Atlantic Telegraph*. I threw the crumpled newspaper into the trash can. The item collector handed my things to the arsenal warden.

"Stun baton, one," and made a corresponding note in the registry. "Edison electric jar, one..." And immediately shuddered: "And where is the second one? The Des Prez?"

"Put it down under irrecoverable losses."

"And why on earth would I do that?"

"Any questions should be directed to Inspector White."

"Alright, we'll figure it out," the sergeant frowned, dipping his iron quill back into the inkwell.

I walked away to the table in the far corner and set two loaded cartridge clips on it, then took my Roth-Steyr from its holster, and removed the bolt all the way from the head, which was affixed with a titanium barrel extension. With its side stock open, I pressed the round eject button, collected the ammunition that flew out onto the table in an empty clip and turned to the sergeant.

"Semi-automatic Roth-Steyr pistol, model eighteen-seventy-four, one," the man grumbled. "Eight millimeter bullets, thirty. Is that all?"

"That's all," I answered and walked to the changing room. There wasn't a single living soul to be found there.

And that was to be expected. It was the dead middle of a shift right now. Our boys would still be out pounding pavement 'til nightfall.

I opened my locker with a certain amount of relief and kicked off my cloak, uniform and boots. I changed into a light-colored linen suit and a pair of lightweight half-boots, tied my neckerchief, and smoothed my hair before a mirror. Lastly, I took a cantankerous look at my reflection and donned my dark glasses.

Damn it! Damn all this inner turmoil! I need to live in the present.

After transferring a kerosene lighter and titanium-bladed jackknife from my uniform to my new clothes, I hesitated briefly, but still clipped my Cerberus holster to my belt. It was a thin and compact pistol. I slipped a backup clip with three ten-millimeter bullets into the pocket of my jacket.

This gun was an invention of the weapons genius Tesla. He had decided that the barrels should be a detachable cluster of cylinders, like a pepper-box. For that reason, the Cerberus wasn't, to put it lightly, known for its accuracy. That said, in close-range firefights, it was simply indispensable. Its firing mechanism used an electric igniter on a gunpowder round, which launched an aluminum-plated bullet. All those bells and whistles were to make sure this weapon would work against both malefics and hell-spawn, alike. Common weapons, due to peculiarities in their design, were of little use against them: over many centuries, evil spirits had managed to develop an invulnerability to iron, copper and even lead, while experienced conjurers had learned to put out the spark of a punched primer and hamper the complex trigger mechanisms in semi-automatic weapons with a single wave of the finger. For revolvers, shooting blanks at such monsters was also anything but a rarity.

The Cerberus, on the other hand, was a different story! Its electric jar and total lack of moving components left no chance for either malefics and infernal beasts to prevent a shot getting off. What was more, in comparison with my one-kilo Roth-Steyr, this pistol weighed practically nothing.

I took a light gray derby hat from the upper shelf of my locker, locked the door and left the changing room. On my way out, I ran into an unfamiliar gray-mustached sergeant, who was accompanied by two uniformed constables.

"Detective Constable Orso," the sergeant said as he walked, "follow me! The inspector general would like to see you."

My heart practically jumped out of my chest, and I took a heavy sigh in a none-too-successful attempt to calm myself down.

The experienced public servant noticed my utter bewilderment and clarified:

"Will you be coming with us, detective constable?"

"Naturally!" I squeezed out a sour smile with a bit of effort and repeated, this time more confidently: "Naturally!"

The sergeant nodded and headed for the stairs. The constables, though, let me go in front of them initially, but moved around behind shortly thereafter, forcing me with an artless maneuver to cast all thoughts of fleeing from my mind, panicked and disgraced.

Calm yourself!

Weren't you expecting this? Well, weren't you?

Yes, devil take me, I was! I was expecting this, but not so soon. The old man was most likely diabolically angry, if he had sent someone to keep watch for my return.

THE *ILLUSTRIOUS* FRIEDRICH VON NALZ was old, but not decrepit. Seven decades had done nothing to weaken this veteran of the force. In fact, they had only steeled him; the inspector general looked like a big, strong tangle of pine roots. And his eyes... his deep-set eyes shone back in the partial darkness like two angry flames, like flickering candles in the slits of a wrinkled jack-o-lantern.

His surprising longevity was simply astonishing. Most of those who had actually touched the blood of *the fallen* had long since bid this world farewell. After all, the Night of the Titanium Blades was fifty-three years ago – in December of the year eighteen hundred twenty-four after the Divine Retribution, or in usual parlance, of the Common Era.

Despite his advanced years, the *Illustrious* von Nalz was not only a leader of the metropolitan police, but also a member of dozens of clubs and charitable societies, and a man who started every morning with a review of the morning's papers, demonstrating an enviable working stamina. And now, there was a towering stack of newspapers on his table but, as could have been expected, he had stopped reading precisely upon reaching the *Atlantic Telegraph*.

Curses! Ugh, who asked Albert to stick his long tongue out!

When I arrived, Friedrich von Nalz tore himself from the paper and stretched his lips out in something resembling a smile.

"The Viscount Cruce! I don't believe I've ever had the honor of making your acquaintance..."

In reply, I could only lower my head.

The old man readjusted the cuff of his black uniform. His wrinkled wrist, which looked like a bone picked clean by vultures, was protruding just barely. He then asked me:

"Are you acquainted with my daughter, Viscount?"

"I was introduced to her at the autumn ball," I answered, struck with horror.

In the office, it became hot and stuffy all at once. And it had nothing at all to do with the fireplace. It hadn't been lit today. Hot air was emanating in waves from the old man sitting across the table from me. It was his *illustrious talent* revealing itself. I had already seen its terrible effects before, and I in no way wanted to become a victim. A few years ago, I had caught a glimpse of the dried-out mummy of an anarchist after he made an attempt on the inspector general's life. The sight of a man after being baked alive had left me sick for the rest of the day.

"You were introduced at the ball, and that was all?" clarified the *Illustrious* von Nalz, making no external signs of the rage seething inside himself.

"And that was all," I replied, diligently making sure not to make eye contact.

Just looking at him was very, very scary.

But then, the old man suddenly broke out laughing, crumpled the paper and threw it into the paper bin.

"You know, Viscount? I believe you. Implicitly," the inspector general surprised me with his unexpected proclamation. "I simply know my daughter too well. Elizabeth-Maria would never go for someone like you..." He cringed fastidiously and threw himself back into his high-backed armchair. "That isn't important! What is important is that your loose-lipped rhyme-peddler's idle talk will start rumors. And I cannot have that..."

"Inspector general!" I tried making an excuse. "They were talking about a different Elizabeth-Maria! Not your daughter! It's just a coincidence!"

But Friedrich von Nalz could only shake his head, sending another wave of transparent heat wafting toward me.

"Viscount! I can imagine you in the role of a secret admirer, but never that of a lover," the old man cut-in with cold ruthlessness. "Don't lower yourself to such base lies."

"My fiancée is named Elizabeth-Maria Nickley. Her family is from Ireland. She's named after her grandmother on her mother's side. I am preparing to present her at tomorrow's ball."

The inspector general started to think, as if solving a complicated charade, then nodded.

"That would be nice," he said slowly, with detachment, but immediately turning his eyes on me in rage. "Just know, Viscount, that if you drag some cheap actress down there and bring shame on my daughter, I will destroy you myself, myself! I will make the blood boil in your veins and cook you alive!"

"I assure you, inspector general, it will not come to that!"

"If the poem was in fact intended for my daughter, it would be best for you to admit it, here and now," continued the *Illustrious* von Nalz, already absolutely calm. "In that case, I would have to challenge you to a duel, though at least you would die with dignity. And not in such torment..."

"There's no reason for..."

"You could, it stands to reason, hide, but I do not advise that at all. I really do not."

"I wasn't even thinking of it!"

"Get out of my face," the highly placed officer then rasped, ending my hearing.

With a furious speed, I jumped out into the reception. The air there seemed simply icy by comparison. A trickle of cold sweat started running down my back. Somehow, I slowed my panicked breathing and went down to the first floor, but before I'd managed to close the entrance behind me, I was called out to again.

"Detective constable!"

I gave a surprised shudder and turned to see a constable getting up from his desk with an envelope in his hands.

"Correspondence for you!" he said.

I took the unexpected letter and nodded:

"Thank you," and went out into the colonnade-enclosed portico courtyard, where ancillary workers were trying without particular success to wash away the soot that had accumulated last winter on the white marble of our Themis statues.

With a heavy sigh, I lowered myself onto one of the benches placed around the fountain and took a look inside the thick paper envelope addressed to me only by name, no address, stamps or mention of who'd sent it. After giving an uncomprehending snort, I took my jackknife from my pocket, cut open the seal and shook out a laconic invitation to visit the Witstein Banking House to discuss the issue of my gaining access to my inheritance.

I reread the letter two times and furrowed my brow in consternation. My attorney hadn't managed to beat any paper from my fund in the past month, so why then would my uncle move the situation forward so easily? And what did the Witstein Banking House have to do with my inheritance? The Kósice family had never had many dealings with the Judean community.

After looking at my massive timepiece, new-fashioned, meaning it was worn on the arm, I decided I still had time to visit the Banking House before it closed for lunch, and if I didn't make it, no matter, I could wait. I didn't have anything planned for today that couldn't be rescheduled anyway.

I jammed the envelope in my jacket pocket, and left of police headquarters' courtyard. Then, in no particular hurry, I stepped off down Newtonstraat toward Ohm Square.

For the beginning of April, today was shaping up to be an unusually humid day, and the sun hanging over the roofs of the houses was heating up the city everywhere I went, like a steak thrown into a smoking pan. Even the black clouds billowing on the horizon were no guarantee that the freshness of evening would soon be arriving; most likely, they would simply disperse over the ocean.

Ducking away from the muggy air, I turned down a sycamore alley and began walking further into the shade of the trees. Five minutes later, I came out onto the rear of Ohm Square and happened upon a mercilessly smoking steam tram. I was barely able to grab onto the handrail before its iron wheels started clanking around the bend where the rails had a juncture, causing the tram to rock palpably.

On the other side of the windows, buildings drifted by at a snail's pace. Puffs of smoke came into the open door from time to time, stinging my eyes unbearably. We couldn't even dream of the speeds of the Metro, though. To get from the nearest underground railroad station to the Judean Quarter, you'd have to spend no less than a quarter hour slogging through the confusing little side-streets of the old city.

And what was the point of that?

Bit by bit, my view of the city was

beginning to change as we left the newly constructed high-rises behind us. Dilapidated commercial buildings and office buildings with slanted roofs started closing in on one another while the tram traveled down the narrowing road. The tiny, damp alleys between buildings flickered by, and the steam tram rolled on.

Cabbies looked on with unhidden disapproval at the passengers now filling the tram-car to the brim. Their horses were sneezing and shaking their heads, caught in the smoke trail the tram was leaving behind. A few times, we were passed by open self-propelled carriages, their chauffeurs wearing leather jackets, leggings and goggles that covered half the face. The carriages shot off into the distance, but the loud chirruping of their gun-powder engines continued to carry down the street for some time.

When we reached Mendeleev Boulevard, I jumped out of the steam tram and swerved off the sidewalk into a passage between two buildings, both scuffed and uncared-for with narrow windows on the second story and above. I got a bit lost in the back alleys and soon came out onto a large thoroughfare. The nearest building on it was sporting a fresh sign: Mihelson Street.

The first floors of the solid stone building were occupied by many shops and stalls, but it all looked like one solid mass now, with the storefronts shuttered behind security doors in preparation for nightfall. Based on my impression, it seemed as if one of the liveliest trading streets of the Judean neighborhood had suddenly died out. I walked a whole block, and not a single living soul crossed my path.

Only on the corner next to a barber shop did I see someone: a long figure standing motionless in a long-skirted black frock and hat to match.

Sliding my gaze over the dispassionate peyos- and beard-framed face, I walked alone up the stairway of the detached three-story building with a solid signboard reading Witstein Banking House and pulled the door handle toward me.

It didn't yield. I jostled it – still stuck.

Then I gave a few hits of the knocker on the iron sheet door, waited a few minutes and again pulled on the handle, but suddenly froze, struck by an unexpected thought.

"Saturday!" I slapped my palm on my forehead. "Today is Saturday!"

Shabbos!

In our enlightened society, any manifestation of religious thought was viewed in a dim light, and all forms of mysticism were mercilessly rooted out and eliminated. Orthodox Judeans, though, had been steadfast in bearing the incessant accusations of the reductionists. As a matter of course, these threats were rarely acted on: the buoyant financials of the group allowed them to grease the right wheels of the state apparatus if need be, so any talk about massacring them remained just that – talk.

Though science had completely extricated religion from mainstream society, our top power brokers had a healthy pragmatism and held holy the principle of "render unto Caesar that which is Caesar's." Money was the lifeblood of the Empire, and everything else came second.

I took a tin of sugar drops from my pocket and threw the first one I happened upon into my mouth.

So then, today is Saturday; the Banking House is closed. Tomorrow as well. Sunday is an official day off.

What a shame.

At that very moment, a covered wagon rolled through the intersection with a screech. The driver, his cap thrown down over his eyes, was hurrying the truck into the barber shop's back courtyard, and the lanky Judean was rushing to open the gates. As soon as the cart was out of view, the gate closed just as quickly.

Very interesting.

I took a quizzical look around, then pressed down a button on my wristwatch, setting a countdown, and tossed another sugar drop into my mouth.

I can wait...

THE CART ROLLED BACK OUT onto the street twenty minutes later, but this time, the haulers were obviously straining themselves, and the cart was leaving a dust cloud in its wake. The lanky man stood in front of the gate and tried to unlock the entrance to the barber shop, but the key just didn't want to turn in the lock; he even had to remove his thick canvas gloves and hold them under his armpit.

I popped another sugar drop into my mouth, slipped the tin into my jacket's side pocket and stepped across the road.

"My good man!" hailed the Judean, standing up in the middle of the carriageway.

The lanky one turned, shot me a worried glance and croaked:

"We're closed!"

"I'm not here for that! Can you tell me where the nearest Metro station is?"

"Over there," the lanky barber waved me down the street with his left arm; his right arm, bearing an old bluing tattoo, he jammed into his frock pocket, acting casual.

I bowed my head slightly and pressed the very tips of my fingers to my derby hat.

"Thank you," I smiled and walked off in the direction he pointed, not asking him to specify the route.

After all, that wasn't why I was asking.

3

I FOUND ROBERT WHITE in *Archimedes' Screw*; based on his untied neckerchief, he clearly hadn't limited himself to just the one little decanter of port. That said, the inspector's drinking had done nothing to improve his mood.

Some people are like that – they know perfectly well that they have no business drinking, but they still drink, and when they do, it doesn't make them feel relieved, just all the gloomier. Robert was definitely one of those types so, before my boss had time to open his mouth and have me thrown out by the scruff of my neck, I decisively took a seat opposite him and, without delay, announced:

"A bank robbery is being planned."

"I told you to bugger off," the inspector mumbled, letting my words pass by unheard, as expected.

"I did what you ordered," I reminded him, removing my dark glasses and, exerting a certain amount of effort to look my boss in the eyes. "Inspector, bank robberies are serious business."

"And what of it?" Robert White frowned skeptically. My confidence hooked him in, though. His fire-filled eyes went dull, taking on a colorless-gray shade. "Tell me about it!" He gasped with a wave of his hand.

"I think there's trouble brewing at the Witstein Banking House."

"You think so? What gave you that revelation?"

I gave a two-word description of what I'd seen in the Judean Quarter and, when the inspector fell into deep contemplation, I turned and called a server over. It was lunch time, and my boss was now being waited on by a pair of nimble girls.

"Saturday," Robert White muttered. "An Orthodox Judean cannot work on Saturday, right? So then he must have not been working. Or does opening and closing a gate count as work? Perhaps they're just doing some repairs?"

"So you're saying the Judean brought in outside workers?" I snorted, filling my glass from the pitcher of lemonade placed on the table. "He'd never hear the end of it! No, I do not think this man is part of Judean society."

"You're thinking again," White screwed up

his face.

"The tattoo," I reminded him. "There was a snake on his right fist. Or a long fish, I couldn't quite tell."

"And what of it?"

"Orthodox Judeans are forbidden from getting tattoos. 'You shall not make gashes in your flesh for the dead, or incise any marks on yourselves.'"

The inspector stared at me with unhidden surprise.

"You know the Torah?"

"No, I just know a lot about tattoos."

"Even if that is so, what makes you so sure that the bank is their target?"

"What other options are there? On one side, there's a grocer's stall, and on the other there's a shoemaker's. It's got to be the bank."

Robert White finished his port, and barked with his whole throat, drowning out the din that had been ruling over the pub:

"Jimmy!"

The red-head hurriedly stood from his corner table and walked up to us.

"Yes, inspector?" He uttered ponderously, readjusting his uniform. The constable was a bit sotted, but he could still stand up straight and wasn't wobbling.

"Take a seat!" Robert White ordered him,

and asked: "Have you heard any rumors recently about a bank robbery?"

"Nothing, total silence," the constable shook his head after a moment in thought.

"Can you tell me anything about a tall, hunchbacked Judean with a tattoo either of an eel or a snake on his right arm?"

This time, Jimmy answered without hesitation:

"Uri Katz, alias: 'the Loach.' He was sentenced to five years breaking rocks for robbing a store. He might already be out."

"Is that so?" The inspector said in surprise, then ordered: "Find out about him, Jimmy. And that's enough drinking. It's looking like we have plans tonight..."

I took advantage of the pause and took a few sips of my tomato soup. It was salty and hot.

WE MADE FOR THE CRIME SCENE with the city already enshrouded in twilight. We walked quietly and unnoticed, like spies from an enemy nation. Our field team was rolling down Newtonstraat, which was illuminated by streetlights. All you had to do was turn off it, though, and the murk grew impenetrable once again. The darkness was somehow dispersed by nothing but the meager light of the gas lamps, just having finished being lit by the lamplighters, who ambled with their ladders under-arm from post to post before themselves disappearing. In the dark alleyways of the older neighborhoods, Nix reigned unchallenged, despite the fact that every restaurant was adorned with a flickering lamp, and dull beams of light shot out from the odd slit in cracked blinds.

Jimmy was driving the carriage; he had lit the kerosene lamp, but it wasn't lighting our path so much as it was advertising our coming in the darkness. Without it, we might just run into someone or run over a drunk laying in the street. We also, naturally, were carrying electric torches, but using them would have been equivalent to loudly announcing that a police division was rolling down the street.

And there was no reason to do that. Now, our carriage was visually indistinguishable from a private car. Jimmy had even changed his uniform out for a pair of scuffed-up trousers and a checkered jacket, while the others were hiding inside the vehicle from the immodest gazes of passers-by.

Robert White was sitting on a bench, straight as a bayonet. Only his fingers running incessantly over the top of his electric torch betrayed his discomfort. Ramon set his still-unloaded lupara butt-first on the ground, leaned on it and started dozing off. Billy, though, was holding onto the semi-automatic carbines left near the wall, one for him and another for his partner, chewing measuredly on a wad of tobacco, which occasionally gave his already high-cheekbone-d face, with its wide slit of a frog-like mouth, a totally grotesque appearance.

I took the tin from my pocket and threw a sugar-drop into my mouth; it was mint flavor.

"You'll ruin your teeth," Billy smirked with an uncommon calm, like a neurotic after taking opiated patent medicine.

"Look at your own," I retorted, pulling a face.

There was no tooth powder in the world that could get rid of the brownish shade left by tobacco, but aficionados of the simple pleasure were left with no other choice since the manufacturer of patented rubber chewing gum had ceased operation due to lack of raw materials. And there was no reason to expect the rubber supply problem to improve in the next few weeks: the plantations in Ceylon and Zuid-India couldn't satisfy all the demand, and there was no discussion at all of renewing trade with the Aztecs. What was more, if there was another flare-up in the Sea of Judea, merchant vessels would have to be sent all the way around Africa, because the military fleets of Great Egypt and Persia were capable of covering both the Red Sea and the Persian Gulf. Even air-superiority wouldn't be able to provide adequate support to the merchant fleet, in that our dirigibles would need to stay within range of our fortresses on the north of the Island of Arabia.

Billy just chuckled at my remark, opened the curtain and spit onto the street. Ramon took a look over his shoulder, shuddered, chasing off his sleepiness, and snapped open the barrels of his lupara. After that, he removed a solid round from his bandoleer with a lead slug in an aluminum jacket and slipped it into one of the chambers in a well-practiced motion.

There was no need for such a powerful weapon when arresting every-day burglars, but you never knew who you'd end up coming across on the dark little streets of our restless city. Regardless, fifty grams of white-hot death could bring down even a demon; not for long, but it was something.

The main disadvantages of this four-barreled monster, produced at the Heim Weapons Manufactory, were its strong recoil and considerable weight. In our division, the only one who could handle one comfortably was Ramon.

Just then, a distinctive knock came on the wall, and the flickering of the kerosene lamps was immediately extinguished; Ramon loaded his last round and hurried to click the barrels shut.

"Are we close by?" He clarified.

"We are," the inspector said and, after throwing back the tails of his cloak, checked to make sure his six-chambered Hydra would come easily out of its holster.

The Cerberus's older brother looked like a many-barreled revolver and was renowned for three reasons: its extreme resistance to malefic spells and the otherworldly attacks of infernal creatures – after all, electricity is stronger than magic! – and its unwieldiness and overly time-consuming reloading procedure. For those reasons, the Hydra did not enjoy particular popularity among policemen. And I generally shared the opinion that it would have been better if the engineers of the Tesla Weapons Factories had stopped at the three-shot Cerberus.

Our carriage began slowing its pace, and then the inspector commanded Billy:

"You, guard the exit. Stay on Mihelson Street."

The constable flung open the doors, handed the second carbine to Jimmy and jumped out onto the paving stones, fading away instantly into the darkness of the night. The red-head took out his rifle, placed it on his knees, put out the kerosene lamp and pulled back on the reins, slowing the horses' gait even further.

I placed my dark glasses into my breast

pocket and unbuttoned the clasp on my holster. I pulled out my Roth-Steyr and placed a round in the barrel. But when the carriage turned at the intersection, leaving the barber shop behind, I was first to jump from the running boards and dart off to the gates. In one moment, I slipped between them, flicked the latch and cracked the gate open, letting Inspector White and Ramon Miro into the alley.

Jimmy turned the carriage toward the next building over and stayed sitting in the driver's seat, carbine in hand; keeping watch suited him just fine.

"Over here!" I called the inspector after me, and he immediately hissed back:

"No noise!"

My boss did not turn his electric torch on, and we had to make our way to the barber shop's back alley in the pitch black. Devil take this new moon...

Fortunately, the dark wasn't quite as impenetrable in the back courtyard, so we were able to find the door just by crawling over the junk and construction debris that was strewn everywhere.

"Keep quiet!" Robert White warned again when I put my pistol back in its holster and slipped the crowbar I'd brought with between the door and its jamb.

I cautiously pushed, and the door gave a barely audible creak, then opened. Ramon, his lupara at the ready, was first to step over the threshold. The inspector slipped in after him and hurriedly flicked the switch of his torch.

A bright beam ran across the back room of the barber shop – there was no one there.

"Leo, check the room and wait here," Robert White ordered. "Ramon, let's go to the second floor. And keep qu-i-et!"

I set my crowbar down on the buffet, held my pistol in two hands and walked down the corridor, trying my best not to upset any of the creaky floorboards. I looked beyond the curtain, and saw the silhouettes of two empty armchairs – it was clear! I turned into the back room to wait for my coworkers to come back down from the second floor.

"Clear," I sounded off when the inspector was coming back down from the residential area above.

"Nobody up there either," Robert White grumbled. "I hope you haven't led us on a wild goose chase..."

"They must be in the basement!" I retorted.

"Let's search the stairs," the inspector decided, shining his light out on the doors that went back into the entryway.

Behind one was the cleaning room, and the

second led us into a room with piles of bags, stuffed full and covered in dust. They almost occupied the entire space. The only part free was a narrow passage next to the wall.

I took out my knife. With a quiet flick, I unfolded its blade and carefully cut into the plain fabric; dirt poured out.

"Bingo!" I then sighed, not hiding my relief.

"They're in the basement!" The inspector came to life. "We'll catch them red handed!"

We carefully made our way along the passage to a dark hole in the floor and surrounded it, not having any idea what to do from there. After some brief thought, the inspector nudged Ramon in the shoulder and pointed at the floor.

"Come on, then!"

The constable got down on his knees, placed his lupara on the dusty boards and tried to see what was underneath.

"There's a light on," he informed us almost instantly.

"Keep quiet! You'll spook them!" Robert White gasped with zeal, finally having forgotten all his doubts about me.

As a matter of fact, leaving the light on in the basement of the barber shop was not at all the behavior you'd expect from a pious Judean.

"Let's go! Let's go!" the inspector

commanded. "Faster!"

Ramon rolled down first. I darted off after him without delay, despite the fact that I was usually not too fond of basements. They scared me so badly that I got an uncomfortable chill; they made me feel ants on my back and started my knees shaking involuntarily.

But what could I do?

Push on!

Practically stepping on the constable's heels, I ran into a small closet, practically half-way filled up by a huge pile of dirt. Here as well, there were fragments of wall lying everywhere. At the table, in a circle of light coming from a "bat" that hung down from the ceiling, sat the lanky Judean from earlier, his bald head no longer hidden under a black hat.

Having heard the sound of our footsteps, he set a mug down on the table and turned, but when he saw the lupara barrels pointed at him, he froze, not wanting to do anything stupid.

"Hands up!" Ramon ordered under his breath, and the man obeyed.

I walked around the pile of hauled-in dirt, stepped over the upturned cart and took a seat next to the opening in the torn-down wall. I carefully looked at the wooden-beam-reinforced entrance hole. There was only one thing back there: darkness.

"Clear," I reported to Ramon.

"Inspector!" He called to our boss, not turning his weapon nor his persistent gaze away from our captive.

Robert White went down into the basement in no particular hurry, walked up to the table and picked up the strange-looking pistol that was lying on it. With its bent grip and open cock-hammer, the back part of this strange weapon was reminiscent of a revolver, while the front part of the device was a copy of the Mauser K63, with the one difference being that, here, the magazine was removable.

"Bergman, number five!" The inspector announced, adding tellingly: "A total greenhorn."

He turned the weapon over in his hands and pointed the barrel at our captive, feigning that it was on accident.

"Who else is in on this?" Robert White asked, playing with his thumb on the cock hammer.

The lanky man swallowed loudly and hurried to answer:

"No one."

"Two others? Three?" Robert clarified, his eyes becoming whiter than chalk and more transparent than the freshest spring water.

"No one!" our detainee once again lied.

The inspector, in a rough motion, tore off

one of the man's fake payos, then the other and, with unhidden grief in his voice, said:

"Why are you lying to me, Uri?"

He shivered, but found himself not strong enough to tear his gaze from the eyes of my *illustrious* commander. He tried to turn his head, but was not able and, somehow all at once, collapsed.

"Two," the criminal admitted.

"Are they armed?"

"Yes."

"Ramon, go look for them," White then ordered the constable.

"On your knees!" The inspector commanded. "Hands together on the back of your head!"

Inspector White nodded in satisfaction, set the pistol on the table and walked up to me.

"What's going on with you, Leo?"

I looked into the darkness of the passageway and gave an involuntary shiver:

"Just a touch of claustrophobia." I then asked: "Inspector, shall we call Jimmy and Billy?"

"We'll manage without them," my boss cut me off, turned up the regulator on his electric torch to full power and took his Hydra from its holster. "Let's go!" he ordered, the bright ray of light sliding over the wooden construction beams and stopping on a dirt wall.

I, with a heavy sigh, crawled into the tunnel, doubled over and, pistol in hand, began moving forward. The inspector tried to light the way, but it did no good, the beam often falling only on the back of my uniform.

Not able to restrain myself, I turned and suggested:

"Let me hold it!"

After that, torch in hand, I got to the point where the tunnel turned to one side and discovered that the robbers had encountered some old stonework there. They hadn't managed to make it through with a direct route, and had to make a turn to the right.

And it was no surprise – New Babylon was almost two thousand years old; there was history no matter where you dug in this city. And though old buildings were being demolished constantly to make room for new ones, the old foundations were typically left below the earth, newer and newer buildings rising up above them.

This was no a city; it was an archeologist's wildest dream. But, given that, trying to dig tunnels was often a ruinous undertaking. Now, it was clear where the whole colossal pile of dirt had come from.

I crept up closer to the turn and licked my dried-out lips.

I was afraid. Very afraid, in fact. In the

darkness, the burglars could simply be hiding with their pistols drawn or even...

"Leo!" The inspector pulled me out of my thinking.

His bark shook away my pent-up consternation, replacing it with annoyance and shame; I felt as if I had been caught doing something unseemly.

I cannot bear basements!

And despite my lame-brained premonition, I stepped around the corner. I walked at a crouch, torch held high over my head and pistol drawn, but it just led to another hallway dug out along the stone wall.

"It smells bad in here, inspector," I whispered.

White reacted as if he didn't hear me.

"Move it!" He hissed at my back.

I ducked down so I wouldn't bump my forehead on a ceiling board, and resumed my movement. I made it to the next turn and took a cautious look around the corner, not noticing anything suspicious. But after I took one more step, my leg immediately caught on an overturned stone from the old wall. I was lucky not to have tripped.

As it turned out, the burglars had been lucky enough to discover a slit in the unfortunate wall, and they had widened it in the hope of cutting a path through the deserted catacombs the easy way. But these fairly heavy stones, unlike soil, were quite difficult to haul out, so they had simply tossed them away from the wall in a semi-circle pattern.

Then I hesitated. The history of the Judean Quarter wasn't very well understood. These robbers may have simply hit upon a plague-stricken burial ground, or something worse.

"Faster!" The inspector hurried me along once again.

He had every intent of covering up the morning's fiasco by catching a dangerous gang, so there was nothing left for me to do than obey the order and crawl into the opening in the partially excavated wall. Beyond it, the corridor darkened. And now, it really wasn't a tunnel anymore, but a proper corridor.

"Be careful," I warned the inspector, stepping very carefully on the uneven soil- and stone-covered floor.

In trying to make their work easier, the bandits had thrown the loose soil they removed all around, and now my shoes were becoming deeper and deeper immersed in the crumbly mass with every step.

Gasping out a soundless curse, I set off in search of the wrongdoers, but soon stopped at a fork in the path.

"Right?" I turned to ask my boss's opinion.

The floor was fairly well-trod. There was clearly just one set of tracks going to the left and it turned around fairly quickly. In the other direction, however, a fully-fledged path had been worn in.

The inspector elbowed up to me, looked down at the floor and agreed.

"Right!"

Lighting the path with the electric torch, I walked on. Robert White was wheezing loudly behind me, and all that remained for me was to hope that the barrels of his Hydra were pointed at the floor, and not aimed right at my loins.

An uneven floor, a slight descent – should I warn my boss?

"Faster!" the inspector hurried me along once again.

I got distracted by his nervous whispering and slapped my forehead on a stone ledge under the ceiling.

"Damn!" I whispered, crouching down on my haunches from the unexpected pain.

My thoroughly peeved boss took the torch and, not waiting for me to follow, stomped off decisively down the hallway.

"Stop!" I gasped to his back, finding the derby hat that had been knocked off my head and hurrying after him. But before I'd managed to catch up, Robert White had already found a room with stone columns holding up a high ceiling.

"Uri?" came an uncomprehending shout. "Uri, you putz, what the devil'd you limp down here for?!"

The inspector's arm shot up, putting the caught-unawares criminal right in the sights of his Hydra and commanded:

"Hands up! Drop your weapon!"

In reply, the distinct clink of a hammer being pulled back rang out. And it came from the opposite corner, the one behind the inspector!

"You first!" the second burglar exclaimed hoarsely, stepping out from behind the stone column with a pistol in his hands.

In an instant, his partner filled with enthusiasm and pulled his pocket Colt.

"Gotcha, piggy!" he grinned.

The inspector turned out not to have been prepared for this turn of events and froze in confusion. I, though, did not hesitate.

I stepped out from the corridor and shouted:

"Police!" And, to enhance the effect, fired a shot up into the ceiling.

In response, a pair of shots clapped out; *Robert White* sank down into a pile of rubble, his chest shot through. *Detective Constable Orso* dropped his smoking pistol and fell to the floor like a sack of potatoes. There was a black hole gaping in his forehead. He died instantly. The inspector, though, was scraping his feet on the stones, not having any desire to kick the bucket himself. Blood was bubbling up between his lips. The stubborn man was still trying to gather his strength and reach his pistol.

Before he could, though, I shot him through the head. I simply raised my Roth-Steyr, aimed it, and pulled the trigger. Just like at the firing range.

"Shit," gasped Inspector White.

"Shit," I agreed, pulling a tin of sugar-drops from my pocket and sending the first candy I happened upon down my throat with a trembling hand.

Robert shined his light at the robber on the pile of rubbish. He had returned to his true appearance after death. Robert then shined his torch on the man's partner. Death had returned him to his original body as well.

"How the hell?! How'd you do that?" The inspector demanded an answer, mechanically patting his chest and finding it utterly unharmed. "How did you force them to kill each other?"

I shrugged my shoulders, faking ambivalence.

"They were afraid. They were afraid of a police raid, afraid of a cave-in, and afraid of being shot in the back by an untrustworthy partner. I simply took advantage of their fears, and got them to see something that was not there. That is my *talent*, as you know."

"But I saw it, too!" Robert White bellowed, the volume of his breathing drawing attention to its unevenness. "Curses! I saw you shoot me! You! Me!"

"Fear is inside all of us," I stated calmly. "You can't be telling me you never considered the possibility that you could be wounded, or even die, right? I'm sure you're afraid of that, just like everyone else. It's one of the hazards of the profession."

"Do you mean to tell me that you are capable of changing reality itself with the power of your thoughts?"

"More like the power of my imagination. I have an extremely active imagination." I looked at the shot-through robber and shook my head. "And no, I do not have the power to change reality. I only gave it a slightly different face, that's all."

I said nothing about how exactly my *talent* was fed by others' fears. If I had, the conversation may have gone too far; being accused of black magic was serious, even for an *illustrious* gentleman such as myself.

The inspector just shook his head and placed his pistol in the holster. I followed his example and asked:

"What now?"

"I don't know," Robert White answered, shining his torch all around the underground room. "I don't see a hole leading into the bank."

"Maybe they hadn't dug it out yet?"

"Or maybe it's in a different room," the inspector decided, calling me after him: "Let's go! We can send all this dog's meat to the morgue in the morning."

Leaving the stiffs on the bloodied floor, we turned back toward the fork in the path and walked off down the second corridor. Soon, Robert White slowed his pace and raised his torch, aiming its bright beam into the black maw of an empty door-frame. The darkness immediately dashed off into the corners of the small room with a high cupola-ed roof, revealing rows of dusty, sculpted-stone benches.

"Check them!" the inspector ordered.

After the recent incident, the desire to crawl headfirst into a new mystery had diminished a good amount.

Before stepping inside, I took my Roth-Steyr from its holster just in case, but I didn't need it: in the small room there was neither any person, nor any exit.

A dead-end.

A dead-end, sure, but what kind of room was it?

"Strange..." I muttered, returning my pistol to its holster.

"What's up there?" The inspector elbowed his way past me and scanned from side to side with his torch. "It looks like an abandoned chapel," he declared, deeming it, "old news."

"That could very well be," I nodded and agreed. "Would you be so kind as to point your torch over there, though?!" I asked my boss, indicating the place at the end of the room where, according to my suppositions, there had once been an altar.

Robert White swept the beam of his torch along the far wall and turned back around to leave.

"Let's go!" He called, but I couldn't even get a single word out. It felt like I was having an epileptic seizure.

And I might as well have been. Because a *fallen one* had cast its gaze on me.

Right then and there, he looked at me, and his bottomless eyes sucked into themselves all the darkness, rage and injustice of this world; all that and a bit more.

And there's quite a lot of that around, mind

you.

My reality started blurring...

MY CONSCIOUSNESS RETURNED from a punch straight to the shoulder.

"Detective constable!" The inspector's roar burst into my oblivion. "Eyes open, now!"

I greedily sucked down some air and crawled away to the nearest bench. I sat on the floor next to it and leaned on it back first. I started massaging my temples with my palms in a pitiful attempt to stop my much-suffering head from exploding.

"What's going on with you, Leo?" Robert White got down on his haunches and touched my shoulder with his fingers. "What happened?!"

"A *fallen one*," I exhaled. "There..."

The inspector turned to the far wall, then stared at me with unhidden annoyance.

"Are you stark raving mad, Leo?" He wondered acridly. "That's nothing but a statue!"

"Not at all! That is a *fallen one*! I'm telling you!"

Robert White gave a quizzical snort and shined his torch on the wall again.

"That is a statue," he declared after a short break, not quite as certain this time. "A strange statue..."

The quality of the sculpture did, in fact,

reflect how wrong he was. It was sculpted down to the smallest detail, as if every fiber, hair and wrinkle were carved into its marble skin, but only above the belt. Its legs were hidden in the wall. Beyond that, it didn't look like it was being held in the wall, it simply made a smooth transition into the unified whole of the wall, as if the *fallen one* had been bursting out toward freedom, and only something minor had stopped it from escaping its stony prison.

"Do you not feel that, inspector?" I asked, overcoming my weakness and leaning more upright against the bench. I got up from the floor and repeated my question: "Do you not feel that?"

I was trying not to look at the *fallen one* another time if I didn't have to. To be perfectly honest, I tried not looking at all. The *fallen one*, even in this stony form, weighed on me with a sensation of limitless power and a pronounced otherworldliness. Every feature of its stony face reflected its perfection but, all together, it formed something so ideal that nothing human remained in its frozen mask whatsoever.

Ideal without the slightest flaw.

A dead ideal.

And that ideal weighed down on me.

"Do I not feel what?" Robert White seethed with anger. "You are stark raving mad, Leo!"

"You're *illustrious*, though! You cannot tell

me you don't feel that!"

The inspector burned a hole in me with his hateful gaze, approached the statue and placed his palm decisively on its stone chest. I unintentionally followed him with my eyes, not noticing how my attention had once again been seized by the marble sculpture; it held me completely. The *fallen one* increased in dimension, filling the whole space. Its stone wings, spread in different directions, and began glowing from the inside with an amber light, which only made it seem darker in the chapel. And the eyes... Its black eyes were no longer dead; they were now filled with a boundless darkness. Darkness and something else, like scornful incomprehension.

Its supernatural willpower was again pressing me down into the floor like an unseen hand. It reached my head. With a gust of transparent wind, it upended my memories. I tried to reach the exit, but my hands and feet were numb. I really don't know how it all would have ended if the torch hadn't burnt out. Its wire started smoking, and the room began filling with the smell of burning rubber. The caustic stench helped me master the ghastly apparition, throw off my consternation and flee back into the corridor.

Robert White jumped out behind me,

pulled back on my legs, and pressed me to the wall with his elbow.

"What the devil was that?!" growled the inspector, spittle flying from his lips.

"That was a *fallen one*!" I shouted, tearing my boss's arm from me and carefully, following the wall, continuing away from the ghastly chapel. "I don't know how it was turned into stone, but that is a genuine *fallen one*! We must tell the authorities. We must plug up this tunnel system before he makes it out to freedom!"

"Come off it!" The inspector gave me a jerk. "Even if that is so, how many decades has he been down here collecting dust? How many centuries? He can't escape, Leo! There's no way."

"I could have returned him to life. And if I could have, that means others can as well!"

Robert White even took a step back.

"You've gone mad!" he announced.

"No!" I assured my boss. "That's all my *talent*, my cursed imagination! It's enough for me to simply imagine him free! Do you understand? If I simply imagine it, he will burst out of his stone prison! Freeing him would be easy. Too easy. We need to plug the chapel up!"

"What are you on about?!" The inspector walked up to me again and shook me sharply by the shoulders. "You've always spoken of fear! Of the fact that others' fears could feed your *talent* and give it power!

The fallen are that very power! A pure, totally unclouded power!

Infernal creatures are simply energy incarnated into the material world. They generously shared their power with the mortals who swore allegiance to them and began to act as generators for even more power, but they didn't create electricity, they created death, sorrow and destruction.

In the end, the malefics were forced to settle accounts with these hell-spawn at the cost of their own souls and many others' lives. My *talent*, though, allows me to use the power of these otherworldly creatures directly, because fear and deadly horror walk hand-in-hand with them.

But that *fallen one* was too strong. It weighed down on me with an unearthly grandeur and rage. It forced all images from my head except its own. I was merely a tool to it, and I was capable of breaking the curse and turning its stone firmament into living flesh; to it, I was a mindless 'skeleton key' and nothing more.

Giving impetus to such an unnatural metamorphosis would be certain to fry my consciousness, but why should *the fallen* mind that? Tools do tend to break, right?"

All my admonishments did not seem to be

convincing to Robert White.

"That's enough!" he ordered.

"No, it's not enough, inspector!" Having forgotten my place, I walked up to the man. "Do *the fallen* not hold sway over forces that go beyond the limits of human understanding? Curses! Just remember what they did to the Arabian Peninsula! They simply ripped a fair chunk of it off and chucked it half a world away into the Atlantic Ocean! They needed only a single day to create Atlantis, just one day!"

"That's all hogwash!" Robert White cut me off, pushing my back against the wall. "I'm the final say in all matters, got it? Not a word to anyone. Not Jimmy, not Billy and not Ramon. Not a living soul, do you understand, Leo? That is an order!"

"Yes sir," I grudgingly agreed to keep my silence.

"Then let's go."

Robert White headed for the exit, and I shuffled off in his wake, asking:

"Was its heart beating? Inspector, did you feel its heart beating? You did, didn't you?"

The inspector stopped with a fateful sigh and looked at the palm he had placed on its stone heart.

"It was beating!" He suddenly confirmed. "It was beating, Leo. But be nice and hold your tongue. Alright?"

"Alright," I relented, not wanting to get into a senseless squabble with my boss. I guess I'd just have to deal with this.

"Feel free to check, I can handle it," Robert White promised.

And I believed him. He could handle it. The inspector knew where his interests lie. He wasn't that kind of person.

WHEN WE GOT OUT of the tunnel into the barber shop's basement, Ramon Miro was standing against the opposite wall with his weapon drawn, simultaneously watching over the hole and our captive.

"What happened to you two?!" He asked in agitation, lowering his lupara. "I heard gun shots!"

"Nothing happened to us," the inspector answered calmly and took the pistol lying on the table. "Nothing at all," he repeated, shooting our kneeling captive in the back of the head.

Uri fell awkwardly on his side. A very thin trickle of blood ran down his cheek onto the dirty floor. Then Robert threw the pistol back and let out another gasp:

"Nothing!"

"What devilry was that?!" Ramon marveled. "Inspector, what's going on?!"

White grabbed the constable under the arm and dragged him to the stairs.

"Ramon!" He spoke didactically. "Do you have hearing problems? Can you not hear me? Nothing happened and nothing is happening! Nothing! You weren't here at all, Ramon. Leave it to me."

"How do you mean...?" What the constable tried to do was turn to look at the executed man, but the inspector held him in place and pushed him back toward the exit.

"Leave this all to me," White declared. "Get out! And send Jimmy!"

So we went. We came up from the basement in silence, striding wordlessly through the empty rooms. Only when we'd reached the dead darkness of the back courtyard did the constable decide to express the doubts that had beset him.

"Has the inspector decided to clear out the bank himself?" he asked directly.

"No," I refuted his theory. My colleague was clearly expecting something more concrete, though, so I shared a partial truth: "Ramon, you should know that complications of a certain nature have arisen, and our boss has taken them... let's say, a bit too close to heart."

"Is that right?" my hulking partner stared at me with unhidden suspicion, beginning to suspect that he was being tricked.

"That's exactly right" I affirmed. "The robbers didn't even make it to the vault. Don't worry."

"Ah, then what is it to me? The inspector knows best," Ramon shrugged his shoulders and headed off to find Jimmy.

I nodded and went after him.

To you, it's nothing, and to me it's nothing.

We don't have so many responsibilities. Let the higher-ups deal with the headache.

How could I have been so naïve?

4

RAMON AND I SET OFF back toward our respective homes. The constable left his lupara in his work locker and was now empty-handed, but he walked with such gloomy focus that it seemed he had a heavy pack on his back. I had no doubt that he was now tormented by doubts on the reason for the inspector's order. We couldn't discuss it though, as questioning orders from the higher-ups was something this hulk was not planning to do.

And neither was I.

Now perhaps Ramon, ignorant of the real

facts, was filled with lingering doubts. I though, on the other hand, knew too much. And the fact that lots of knowledge can bring lots of sorrow is something that smart people noticed a long time ago.

I wasn't feeling any less sick either, so we walked in silence.

Right after the Dürer-Platz, the constable took a left and trod down the hill to Little Catalonia; I was going in the opposite direction. Up the winding slope of the hill, the street began rising to Calvary. The dense urban development was soon behind me. Mountainous fences now extended along the road, hiding the estates of retired army officers, diplomats and ministerial civil servants from the immodest gazes of passers-by.

The city had long surrounded Calvary on all sides but, for some reason, Calvary had never expanded vertically, with the exception of the two-hundred-and-two-meter-high open-work iron tower erected on the very peak of the hill a few years before the overthrow of *the fallen*. At night, its signal light was turned on, and lighting often struck it, not only during thunderstorms, but also in clear skies.

When Gustav Eiffel saw this rusted monstrosity, he became obsessed with the idea of outdoing it and, by some unfathomable miracle, not only received his monarch's approval, but also sold the design to the Paris city council. Admittedly, he must be given his dues for his talent as an architect – the new three-hundred-meter tower, based on post cards I'd seen, looked somewhat more elegant than its predecessor.

Roads had only started being built up the hill a quarter century ago, which is when one of the plots ended up in my grandfather's possession. Not Count Kósice, who never even had enough to rub two sticks together his whole life, but retired Imperial Army Colonel Peter Orso, my grandfather on my father's side.

Our property was located on the outskirts. It was truncated on two sides by steep slopes, and the third was lined with the rustling leaves of a small thicket. I can't say for sure if my grandfather chose such a secluded place on purpose or not, but we weren't often pestered by our neighbors. No one came around at all, to be honest; even tax inspectors just looked the other way.

They had for the last sixteen years in any case...

WHEN I BEGAN TO HEAR the gurgling of a fast stream in front of me, I turned toward the curb to face a small pile of stones, taking the one on top. After that, I walked up the steep bridge and sent a heavy stone flying at full speed into an eye that was shining back at me from beneath it with a fell light.

The beast roared up, and quieted down, then the pair of eyes retreated.

I have no idea what kind of creature lived down there, but it wasn't fond of this kind of treatment.

It would have been wise to solve the problem once and for all, but the retirees who lived around here had long since lost their former influence, and all their complaints usually slipped past the ears of the city government unnoticed. None of the clerks were too eager to be the one to pursue an unknown creature at night, and even those local inhabitants who loved boasting of their African safaris did nothing but give mere promises to dig their old weapons out of their closets. And they were right: it wasn't yet clear who would be hunting whom.

What was more, the unknown creature hadn't actually caused any problems. At least, that's the opinion our community treasurers were inclined toward after familiarizing themselves with a few estimates from professional exterminators.

Past the bridge, the road began twisting up to the top of the hill, and a few turns later, you could already see a stone fence with denuded blackening tree branches behind it.

That was my destination.

The oil lamp near the gate, as usual, wasn't lit, but you could still clearly make out a black square containing a diagonal crimson cross on the doors – the quarantine symbol of the Diabolic Plague, discolored and flaking.

Without pulling the bell cord, I moved the iron hasp from in front of the key hole, and opened the lock with my key. The gate swung open. To the screech of its rusty hinges, I clapped it shut behind me and headed for the night-darkened giant of my three-story manor straight through my dead garden.

The dried-out trees surged up to the sky, their twisted branches and black leaves stretching out in all directions. Dried grass stuck up from the earth in brittle gray spears.

The manor itself looked just as dead as the garden. There were no lights on, and no smoke coming from the pipes. Not a single sound could be heard. When I was five years old, one horrible night, death had visited our estate. Everything had died. Only my father and I had survived. Though, as for my father, his survival had only been partial; something cracked inside him and burned out forever. He could no longer stay for long in one place, and didn't allow himself to accrue possessions or personal attachments.

And, like a shark, he stayed in constant motion. In his head, not moving was equivalent to death.

And, when the inspector asked what the devil had made me seek employment with the police, I hadn't been totally frank with him. I mean, I really did have to pay bills, but the true reason was my aspiration to discover those who had cursed this place and all its inhabitants. And it had been done so artfully that the curse could still kill sixteen years later.

Curses...

I sighed and threw my head back to the sky. There were dull stars shining back like pieces of worn glass. The curse usually pricked the back of my head with an uncomfortable cold, weighed down on my heart, and ran up my spine, but did no actual harm to me.

Why? I do not know. Despite how much I had racked my brains over the topic, I still hadn't figured it out. And figuring out what had attracted this sorrow to my home in the first place had also come to naught; even having access to the police archive, which I had received with the rank detective constable, hadn't helped at all. There simply wasn't even a shred of information in the investigation reports; and there hadn't been any real evidence as such, either.

Diabolic Plague, they said, and that was

that.

And I retreated; I had no time to waste on stirring up the past. I simply waited until I came of age, comforting myself with the fact that my family's money would allow me to not work and dedicate myself to seeking the truth.

But now I do not know, oh I do not know...

I shrugged my shoulders, walked onto the porch and swung open the unlocked door. I threw my derby hat on a rack in the entryway. The small flame of a kerosene lamp flickered in the dark corridor.

"Is everything alright, Viscount?" wondered a lank middle-aged man in an old-fashioned frock coat.

"Completely, Theodor," I laughed. "Couldn't be better."

Theodor Barnes was my butler. He had served the Kósice family for his entire life, as his father and grandfather had served my ancestors before him. He was even present for some of the first memories I had.

"Is there anything you require?"

"No, thank you," I shook my head, but immediately snapped my fingers and corrected myself: "No, wait! Prepare the room on the third floor. We're expecting guests. A guest..."

Theodor was a butler by family trade; he could bite the bullet like no other, and usually didn't allow himself any expressions of strong emotion, but this time had gotten to him.

"What, excuse me?" Barnes clarified, not able to hide his amazement. "But, how do you mean...?"

I gave my servant a reassuring clap on the shoulder, throwing out frivolously:

"Just trust me," and headed for my bedroom.

I immediately turned the gas fixture there on, took off my jacket, pants and shirt, put them in the wardrobe, and unloaded my Roth-Steyr. But the Cerberus I did not unload, placing it near my wrist chronometer on the bedside table.

Then, I lit the night light, checked to see if the blinds were shut and, only after that, put out the gas light.

Funny?

I do not know, I do not know.

Life had taught me not to ignore my fears, no matter how contrived they may have seemed.

The night light must be on, the blinds must be closed, and a loaded pistol must be lying on my bedside table.

Period.

A RESTLESS BEAM OF SUN, having discovered a crack in my aging blinds, stole into my bedroom and went straight into my eyes, heralding the morning.

I turned over on my other side, but immediately got myself together and, unlike before, didn't keep snoozing. I splashed along the cold floor with my bare feet, swung open the windows one after the other and, just in case, took a persnickety look at the thickened boards of the blinds for fresh scratches.

But no – new ones hadn't appeared.

Morning freshness frolicked into the room, filling it completely; I went back to throw on a robe, then turned to a window facing East. From the hillock, an indescribable view of the old neighborhoods of the city was revealed, showing a plethora of steeple-roofs, gilded towers, palaces and gardens. Much farther away loomed the grayness of the factory outskirts; there were a great many smokestacks stretching out toward the sky there and freight dirigibles drifted lazily in the black clouds of smoke they expelled.

They say, once, in clear weather, you could see the ocean from the top of Calvary. But now, clear days in New Babylon were harder to come by than pearls in a cesspool. Smoke, char and smog rolled over the city from all sides.

No matter! I shrugged my shoulders and walked away to the bedside table. I snapped the chronometer bracelet to my wrist and set about getting dressed. In my head, though, like a broken gramophone record, one word kept turning over, again and again: "Sunday. Sunday. Sunday!"

Ball!

At four o'clock P.M., the ball would start, and if something went wrong there...

I didn't even want to think what could happen.

Straining my will, I forced myself to forget the ominous presentiments and headed for the bathroom.

"Is the room ready?" I asked Theodor who happened to be going the opposite direction.

"Yes sir, Viscount," the butler confirmed, slickening down his pitch black mutton chops. "What is the news from the New World?"

"Same as before," I said. "Houston is embattled. There is currently trench warfare raging on all fronts."

"The Aztecs just won't settle down, eh?" Theodor shook his head and hazarded: "Would you like to take a look at the guest room?"

"That won't be necessary," I refused and went down to the first floor.

My gut was crying out in hunger, but I wasn't in the habit of eating breakfast at home. On weekends, I usually dropped into the Italian taverna close by, where I had a line of credit.

And, in that my normal order of the day had already gone down the drain, all that was left was to swallow my spit in expectation of this evening's reception.

I took a vexed look at my timepiece and, there in the entryway, the bell clanged.

"Oh!" My butler said pointedly, not taking even one step back.

The news of the guest arriving simply knocked the man sideways. However, it also set my nerves indescribably more on edge. In much knowledge, there was much sorrow, that was true.

Nevertheless, I did nothing to display my agitation.

"Leave that to me, Theodor," I said, calling off my servant. I then left the house and hurried to the gates. As I walked, I clipped my glasses to my nose. The dark round eyepieces returned my confidence in my own abilities to me all at once.

The doubts left me; I swung the door open decisively and smiled to a young girl with fire-red hair, proper features on her pretty round face and the colorless-glowing eyes of the *illustrious*. The guest's figure was covered up by a long cloak, but I still knew that the body beneath it could teach a lesson to Aphrodite herself. She had taught thighs, an hourglass figure and a high chest...

"Elizabeth-Maria!" I smiled with all the cordiality I could muster, driving away the vision rising up before my eyes. "Words cannot express how glad I am that you found it possible to accept my invitation..."

"Leopold, you were extremely convincing," the girl burst out laughing, handing me her voluminous traveling bag. "You simply gave me no choice!"

"I hope I haven't spoiled your plans..."

"Not at all, I assure you!"

Her snow-white teeth flashed a smile and, with a certain share of deprivation, I decided that only her thin pale lips were keeping Elizabeth-Maria from being counted among the city's great beauties. But I didn't stress my attention on that and hurriedly stepped back to the side, letting my guest enter:

"Come in, I beg you!"

The girl stepped past the fence, cast her gaze on the dead garden and couldn't resist a bemused observation:

"How sweet..."

In the morning sun, the black trees didn't look nearly as ominous as they did in the dead of night, but I still thought it necessary to correct my guest:

"Original. Unusual. Provocative. But in no way sweet."

Elizabeth-Maria cast her attentive gaze on me and nodded slowly:

"As you say, Leopold."

We walked up onto the porch and entered the house. There, I handed her traveling bag to my butler and introduced my guest to my servant.

"This is Theodor, if you have any questions, you need only ask him. Unfortunately, I must take my leave. It's time for work."

"I am at your service, madam," my butler announced ceremoniously, accepting the girl's cloak.

Elizabeth-Maria smiled favorably in reply, removed her hat, and shook out a thick shock of hair.

"Leopold, you can't tell me you plan on leaving me alone so soon, right?" she cooed. "We could..."

I swallowed nervously and hurried to take the situation under control, or more accurately, took the girl under the arm and led her to the guest room.

"The ball is at four," I reminded my guest. "I need to go pick up my suit from the tailor's. And your evening dress..."

"Don't worry about that, dear," the girl answered and stopped opposite the fireplace, her attention caught by a saber hanging on the wall.

"To Captain Orso for personal valor. Zuid-India, October thirtieth, eighteen thirty-seven from K. N." Elizabeth-Maria looked closely at the engraving on the blade. "Is this your father's weapon?" she turned to me.

"My grandfather's," I shook my head. "He distinguished himself in the assault of Batavia. He was given the rank of captain there and made a hereditary noble."

"Yes, that's right!" the girl realized. "Year thirteen after the founding of the Second Empire! Forty years ago. That's a long time."

"My grandfather retired at the rank of colonel. He's the one who built this house..."

But Elizabeth-Maria wasn't interested in the history of my estate. With acute fascination, she continued to look at the saber and, as she did it, something uncharacteristically inappropriate was throbbing in her shimmering maidenly eyes.

"Blood," she whispered. "This saber has taken a rich harvest..."

"My grandfather was the best saber-man in his regiment," I told her. Then I was shaken by an inexplicably returning lack of confidence, and said: "Theodor will show you to your room. I will see you at lunch."

"As you say, Leopold," the girl nodded and unexpectedly asked: "Is the saber sharpened?"

"It would assume so," I sighed and turned away to my butler who was standing in the door watching us with unhidden amazement. "Theodor!" I raised my voice, attracting the attention of my servant who had grown unaccustomed to having guests in recent years.

He shuddered, lifted the traveling bag and turned to the girl, saying:

"Follow me, madam."

Elizabeth-Maria walked into the guest room; on the stairs, she slightly lifted the skirts of her dress, looking uncharacteristically elegant.

My heart clenched up. A chill rolled over me; a strange mixture of desire, relief, fear and contempt filled my soul. But I did not indulge the self-flagellation, instead grabbing my derby hat from the rack and jumping headlong away from my house.

While I was walking to the gates, I saw the rusted top of the tower looming on the summit of the hill. Now, you couldn't see the blinking navigation signal on top of the rusty finger cascading up into the sky, causing mixed feelings. Its sheer decrepitude was impressive, but it simultaneously weighed on you with its power. Like something forgotten, something from an entirely different era. And I couldn't even say if it was from the past or the future...

It would seem that I should have grown accustomed to this view long ago, but no – I still felt ants on my skin for what must have been the thousandth time.

When the gate swung open, an envelope that had been stuffed into the crack fell under my feet. There were no stamps on it, and it had nothing written on the outside. I looked quizzically at the desolate street, picked it up and folded the titanium blade out of my jackknife. I cut open the seal, familiarized myself with the laconic missive and cursed fatefully.

Inspector White had set our meeting for midday, and I wasn't at all sure that I would be available by that time. And what was more, I wasn't sure that I wanted to see the inspector today anyway.

I cursed out again, this time louder and started walking down the hillock. Crossing the bridge, I couldn't resist looking down, but there was nothing there, just water babbling and jumping between the rocks.

I LEFT THE TAILOR'S WITH A RENTED three-piece suit, unbearably fashionable and just as unbearably gaudy. Unfortunately, I also left with an empty wallet. I didn't have any money left, even for lunch, but that fact was no longer capable of spoiling my mood.

If something went wrong this evening, hopelessness would be the least of my problems. To be more accurate, it wouldn't even have been a problem.

And in fact, what does a corpse need money for, anyway?

Also, there was still the inspector. What the devil did he need from me on the weekend?!

Having shifted the bag containing my old suit into my left hand, I clinked two coins together, slipped the shimmering change back into my pocket and walked over to the Yarden Embankment. This Sunday morning, it turned out to be impossible to even elbow your way through the loitering city-dwellers, and I soon grew sick of intercepting the gazes of people whose eyes I'd caught: chic ladies, their no-less-gauche gentlemen and the street traders. Then I turned down Des Cartes street, and miscalculated once again: the normally empty little street was plugged up by a motley public, sorrowful and quiet. And only the whooping of the boy handing out leaflets carried over the crowd, flying out like the screeching of a seagull over a desolate sea coast.

"Six-blade shoe polisher here! Patented design!" chirruped the grimy little boy, sticking his advertising in the faces of passers-by. "Just one turn of the handle! Shine guaranteed! Easier than ever before!"

I took the rumpled paper and held it up to the boy.

"What is the meaning of this public demonstration?" I asked him.

"Some famous conductor is being buried," he answered airily. "He lost his favorite baton and the freak popped his neck in a noose."

People began staring at us, but that didn't embarrass the boy whatsoever.

"Choked with a rope, the dummy," he continued, sharply throwing his thumb upward. "His head popped off."

"I see," I nodded and stepped out of the way.

From behind, I was overtaken by a scream:

"Steam iron! Lighten your wife's load! Gets rid of wrinkles fast!"

And the quiet hum of the honorable public, which slowly moved to the Imperial Theater, covered up the rage-filled squabbling of the two boys competing for territory.

And that scene encompassed New Babylon: another's death here wasn't even worth a minute of silence.

Nothing was, for that matter.

And it never had been.

I threw the advertisement into the first trash-can I came across, turned down the neighboring street, looked at my watch and increased my pace.

The Imperial Theater was hidden from view, and the street curved in an arc, taking me to a stone-block paved square. In the middle of it, there was a pigeon-shit covered monument of the great trinity – Ampère, Ohm, and Volt.

But then, the lyceum of the Sublime Electricity, rushing up to the heavens in two steel masts, was a place those flying vandals kept a wide berth from. And it was no wonder. Around the huge copper balls, which crowned the elegant constructions, there were wavering halos of electric current. From time to time, they lit up in blinding sparks, which caused a distinctive clicking to ring out over the square, but only those who were visiting from the provinces tucked their heads between their shoulders in fear. City-dwellers sitting on the open verandas of the many cafes didn't even look away from their newspapers.

The huge Nicola Tesla coil must have used a simply monstrous amount of energy, which was always a riddle to me: why would these learned men waste electricity so wantonly day after day, and month after month? Simply to demonstrate their greatness? And only now, when the manmade lightning was circling directly over my head, did I truly feel the power of science in full measure.

Immeasurable power was the true thing that Nicola Tesla's creation embodied.

Power and safety.

The energy bubbling around could blow any infernal creature to smithereens, and dissolve its remains into ash. Any, even the most powerful demon, would burn here in a few short seconds' time in the blessed flame of electrical discharge; it wouldn't be some mere dash into the underworld with a slightly singed pelt, this creature would be annihilated once and for all.

There is no protection from electricity. Electricity is stronger than magic!

The sett tiles under my feet were slightly trembling, shaking in time with the powerful steam generator in the lyceum's basement. In a strange way, that shivering gave me confidence. I removed my derby cap from my head, went into the complex and took a look around the room, which was filled with bright electric light. The inspector didn't catch my eye. To the sound of the lecture coming over the loudspeaker plates, I had to set out in search of a boss I wasn't even sure had been here today.

I found him in the western wing of the complex. With one leg thrown carelessly over the other, Robert White was sitting back in a wooden bench and, with a helpless look, gazing into a battle painting titled "The Great Maxwell kills a *Fallen One*." I did nothing to distract the inspector from his thoughts, taking a seat next to him in silence and listening to the lecture.

"We all live in a surprising time. A time of change!" Carried out from the slightly creaking speakers. "The old world is in its death throes. The era of steam is coming to an end, and the era of electricity will soon be upon is! But, as man came to this earth writhing and screaming, so the labor pains of progress are rattling the present, giving birth to conflicts. The greatest minds of our time, Nicola Tesla and Thomas Edison have disputes on the course of electricity's development. But don't believe the sensationalist newspapermen smacking their lips, and writing in words the average person doesn't know. The truth is born in disputes! Remember! Direct current or alternating, it doesn't matter. It's all electricity! Sublime Electricity! Knowledge in its purest form!"

Here the inspector turned to me and asked:

"You do know the story of Maxwell, right Leopold?"

"Who hasn't heard of the great Maxwell and the demon?!" I grew surprised.

"The *fallen one*," my boss corrected me. "Maxwell made his *fallen one* obey."

"And what of it?"

"I mean that I do not want to spend my whole life stagnating in anonymity!" Robert White's eyes glimmered in rage. "I don't want the next quarter century to be spent busting my butt, just to make it to senior inspector. And that's the best case scenario! That's if some greenhorn with a high-ranked friend doesn't get it before me! And now, a chance to blow that endless circle up has presented itself, see?"

"I'm afraid I don't," I replied with a confused tone.

But I did understand. I understood it all. And I could feel that understanding jabbing into my chest like a jagged shard of ice. But I didn't want to hear what else the inspector had to say.

The inspector, though, wasn't at all stopped by that.

"The *fallen one* in that basement," he said slowly, looking at his right palm, "he was real and everything you said was true. I sensed his heartbeat. I felt a living heart in a marble sculpture!"

"And what of it?"

"If he escapes..." Robert White whispered, but immediately corrected himself: "If you free him, we could both become powerful beyond our wildest dreams!"

"No! He would simply turn us to ash on the spot!" I objected, not having tried to persuade the man that I was incapable of freeing the *fallen one* from its stone prison.

Robert White just broke into laughter.

"*The fallen* have long lost their power," he declared flippantly. "For the first thousand years, their rule was undivided and unchallenged but, the longer they went, the more they lost their rage. *The fallen* ceased to be Divine Retribution, and got carried away playing ruler. Some considered themselves leaders of the world, and some thought themselves anchorites. Finally, they became nothing more than a shadow of their former selves. Our fathers and grandfathers on the Night of the Titanium Blades poured their blood over the entirety of Atlantis and another half the world as well, so you can't seriously think that we won't be able to handle one lone *fallen one*, right?"

"Sure, we'll handle it, but what then?" I grimaced. "We will control the *fallen one* jointly, and make it obey us. But just think, how will society look on this? Well, I can tell you! The Empress will order us skinned alive, quartered and roasted over a low flame, and that, they say, is extremely unpleasant!"

"I'm glad to see you've retained your sense of humor, Leo," the inspector glanced at me unkindly with his colorless eyes. "As for that old nag, you don't need to worry. She's just the

Emperor's widow, and the Crown Princess is a constantly ill little girl. People need a strong hand! The old aristocracy spent centuries licking the paws of *the fallen*, they'll have to obey – servility is in their blood."

I didn't share my boss's confidence on that. When, sixteen years ago, after the Emperor's death, his own brother, the great Duke of Arabia stopped short in his claim to the throne, he and all his close relatives were cut down at once by a flu from Africa. Few doubted that her Imperial Majesty's hand was mixed up in such a sudden end.

After all, he was her brother-in-law! But us? The inspector and I were simply dust under her feet!

For that reason, I said with as much confidence as I could muster:

"The old aristocracy has long lacked any influence."

"That is precisely why they will support us!" Robert White gave his answer with fanatical confidence. "I'm not such an idiot that I would start an open rebellion, but the power of even one *fallen one* would be enough to change the balance!"

"I don't like that," I admitted honestly.

"Me neither," nodded the inspector appeasingly. "But we can't just let this chance slip through our fingers." He shook his head and again started staring at his open palm. "I felt his heart beating. They turned him into stone, but they couldn't kill him. I sensed his power, I touched it..."

"If your right hand tempts you, cut it off," I said in a detached manner, looking at Maxwell lashing a *fallen one* with an electric whip; sputtering fire was shooting off in all directions, as well as pieces of snow-white feathers. "The *fallen one* is tempting you, inspector."

"Hold your tongue!" Robert White threw in sharply. "It wasn't for nothing that I set our meeting here precisely! My mind is free. Spells and curses cannot touch us in this place!"

"As you say."

"So, are you gonna help or not?"

"I don't like this," I repeated stubbornly.

"You prefer to vegetate on twenty thousand a year in income when you could be rising to the very top?"

"Rising to heaven, more like," I snorted. "But we don't believe in such fairy tales, do we? Though we do have firm evidence that hell exists. And that's exactly where we'll be going if you don't smarten up."

"Nonsense!" The inspector cut me off. "So, yes or no?"

"I need to think about it."

"Make the right choice," Robert White made a wry face, stood up from the bench and stepped off toward the exit; his cane was quivering in his hand like the tail of a disgruntled cat.

I picked up the newspaper he'd left behind, and shuffled off after him on my wobbly legs. I came out of the gates of the lyceum. In a stand on the corner I bought a gas water with raspberry syrup. I sucked down the cup in one gulp, and only then somewhat came to my senses.

To say that my boss's unexpected proposition had knocked me off course is to say nothing. In fact, it scared me. It scared me so bad I was hiccupping. After all, these were in no way empty fantasies, no – Robert White made a habit of getting what he wanted. Also, he could hardly have invented a crazier plot than returning a *fallen one* to life and forcing it to serve him. Even in stone statue form, that *fallen one* weighed down with its power. But if all its energy were to escape...

I shrugged my shoulders and continued into a cafe, its overhang lit up with the uneven flickering of fifty electric bulbs. The cafe was even named for it – *The Bulb*.

Inside, it was absolutely packed with adepts of the Sublime Electricity; the reductionists were having lunch, leafing through thick scientific almanacs, arguing until hoarse, and discussing the latest scientific trends, but I was able to get through into a relatively quiet corner, under a comfortable and not quite so bright bulb.

Basically, the place was quiet, but only relatively.

Yablochkov! Lodygin! Tesla! Edison!

Amperes, volts, generators, circuits, charges!

Electricity!!!

I had already looked everywhere for a somewhat calmer place to sit. Oh well. Just then, a waiter walked up to my table.

"I'll have a scoop of ice cream," I asked, remembering my empty wallet just in time.

"Anything else?"

"No thank you," I refused, putting up the newspaper as a shield.

As luck would have it, the front page was "decorated" with a photograph of a lank old lady with two light-struck eyes – the photographic film had proven incapable of containing the gaze of her Imperial Majesty – Empress Victoria.

I gave a shudder. That sweet old aunty wouldn't even hesitate to feed to her hunting hounds whatever remained of me after the interrogation. That was precisely how this all would end, there wasn't even the slightest doubt. And that was if the *fallen one* didn't eat my soul first!

Did I even have to say that I didn't consider the inspector's proposal seriously, and wasn't preparing to? I only had to come up with a way to refuse my boss and not make a deadly enemy in the process.

Should I tell Department Three?

I knew quite a few people who hated snitches deep down, and even announced that for all to hear but, thanks to their opportunistic interests, would denounce their colleagues or acquaintances at the first chance. I was not preparing to snitch myself, though.

Snitching is like the boomerang used by the aboriginals of Zuid-India; you wouldn't have time to come to your senses before it comes back and smacks you in the head. It would be one man's word against another's, and who would be believed in the end: the inspector or the detective constable? No, the balance of power was definitely not in my favor.

"Your order!" The waiter announced and placed a little dish of ice cream before me. He did not hurry on further.

I dug a few fifty-centime coins from my pocket, tossed them on the table and dived back into reading, trying to come away from these unhappy thoughts with something.

But I didn't.

Would Empress Victoria be finishing her visit to Paris, restored after last winter's flooding, and returning to New Babylon? On the landing pad, would her Imperial Highness Crown Princess Anna be there to meet her grandmother? Was the fifteenth birthday of the heir to the throne coming up?

And what did I care?

I was only concerned with the inspector's request and... the ball.

I scooped a bit of the vanilla ice cream into my dessert spoon and nodded.

Right, the ball!

Problems must be dealt with in order of their significance. And, if Inspector General von Nalz roasts a certain detective constable over a low flame, Robert White's intention to get the same one involved in unpleasant business would already have utterly no meaning.

Do I have to answer the inspector?

Curses! I'll have to worry about that this evening!

I glanced at my watch, set the newspaper down, shoveled down my ice cream in double time, and stood up from the table. I grabbed the bag with my old suit and, with relief, left the overly noisy institution.

Amperes, volts, lumens...

Phooey!

I HAD TO BORROW SOME MONEY from Ramon Miro for a cab; luckily, he wasn't so small-minded as to refuse his colleague, just asking with a smirk:

"I wonder if your yearly salary will cover your debts, or not?"

"I'll dig you up a tenner somehow," I answered, hiding the pair of rumpled bank notes in my wallet. I said nothing of the fact that, with interest, my debts had already piled up to thirty thousand francs.

"You can take it from your advance," the constable reminded me.

"I can take it from my advance." I agreed and set off to find a carriage suitable for my next appearance.

My income from the inheritance fund would be going in its entirety to paying back debts for the first year or two, so the perspective of losing my detective constable's salary had pushed me into a very natural depression. But not going because of that would be playing right into the inspector's hand! Life is more valuable...

I ROLLED HOME in an open carriage. It was nothing luxurious, but completely appropriate to the occasion. The cabby's livery was decked out in shining laces cleaner than a general's uniform.

"Wait here," I ordered him, opened the gate

and went into my home. And there, I whistled in surprise, having discovered Elizabeth-Maria in a pink satin dress, draped in lace, beads and sequins.

"Is it time yet?" The girl wondered, trying on a hat in the mirror. Her miniature reticule was waiting on the rack.

"It's time," I affirmed.

My guest walked up to me and took me by the arm.

"Then let's go!"

I slid my glasses down to the very tip of my nose and looked at the girl above their dark lenses. While I'd been gone, she had applied subtle make-up and, now, with lipstick, her lips no longer seemed withered and thin.

"Is something the matter, Leopold?" Elizabeth-Maria smiled charmingly, doubtlessly satisfied with the effect she'd achieved.

"You are simply charming," I answered, returning my glasses to their place.

We came down from the porch and walked through the dead black garden to the gates.

"How romantic!" Unexpectedly, the girl began laughing uncontrollably, plucking a blackened carnation from its stalk, dead like everything else around. Her graceful fingers nimbly broke the brittle stem off and stuck the flower into the buttonhole of my jacket. "There. Now that's much better!"

I sighed hopelessly and requested:

"Don't do that anymore."

"Why not?"

"They don't grow back."

"Oh, Leo!" my guest shook her head. "Do you also find dead flowers beautiful? You and I are so alike..."

I swung open the gate, helped the girl into the carriage and, only after we'd pulled away, expressed:

"That is not the issue. I simply remember when these flowers were still alive. Their value to me is as mementos, and not in their, as you put it, 'beauty...'"

"You must value what you have, not look into the past," Elizabeth-Maria reproached me. "I advise you to live in the present day, dear..."

"As you say."

"Or has this house made its mark on you?" the girl continued cooing. "Your butler is also strange. It's simply impressive, his composure. I've never seen the like."

"He's just old school," I once again let out a couple words, not wishing to speak about Theodor.

"Is something bothering you, Leopold?" Elizabeth-Maria took a closer look at me.

"What do you think?" I looked gloomily at her through the dark lenses of my glasses.

The girl only started laughing carelessly.

"Everything will be alright!"

"Let's hope so," I snorted, not sharing anything on the inspector's request.

I didn't even want to think about that, to say nothing of actually discussing it.

Soon, the narrow little streets of the old town were behind us, and our wheels stopped bouncing around on the uneven tiles. But the jostling was replaced by smog that stretched out over the street. The smoke from the factory outskirts made my throat itch. Elizabeth-Maria just kept silent, covering her face with a perfumed kerchief.

It grew easier only when the carriage turned onto Newtonstraat and the colossus of the police headquarters was looming in front of us. There was a whole file of carriages lined up in front of the central entrance; cabbies were dropping off passengers and immediately leaving, so I came to an agreement with our driver on where exactly he would be meeting us after the end of the reception, jumped out onto the sidewalk and pulled my companion after me by the arm. And when she stepped down from the running board, I pushed down the last remnants of doubt and led Elizabeth-Maria down to the flung-wide doors of the Newton-Markt.

The dress shirt on my back was soaked through with sweat. My mouth had gone dry, and the little hammers of an approaching headache were starting to pound in my temples. But I just smiled and looked around imperturbably. I handed my invitation to the steward standing in the doorway with a look of complete and total carelessness; I simply handed him the triangle of chalk paper and headed directly into the room where we normally held our staff meetings.

Now I could hear snippets of music coming from it, and Elizabeth-Maria slightly shifted her pace to fit the rhythm of the joyful melody. I couldn't even dream of such grace, so I simply walked through the corridor and greeted my acquaintances, who I came across from time to time. I didn't converse with anyone. The most I did was trade a few meaningless sentences for a few seconds.

I saw the inspector general standing near the entrance. The old bobby was busy speaking with a tall fat man and a doughy young boy in a shamelessly fancy suit but, when I approached, he immediately left the Minister of Justice and his nephew and made way for us.

"Viscount!" he faded into a smile. "Won't you introduce me to your companion?"

I swallowed nervously and smiled with great difficulty:

"Inspector general, my bride the *Illustrious* Elizabeth-Maria Nickley. Elizabeth-Maria, the head of the metropolitan police, Inspector General von Nalz."

"Viscount!" Friedrich von Nalz erupted into laughter, his eyes glimmering with colorless flame. "No need for such pomp! Everyone here today is a friend or sympathizer. No titles!"

"As you say... Friedrich," I bowed my head slightly.

"Come on in! Come on!" the inspector general allowed, then and returned to the conversation I'd interrupted. And I led Elizabeth-Maria into the room.

"That was the meeting you were so apprehensive about?" She whispered to me.

"Apprehensive? Me? Where'd you get that from?"

Then the girl got up on tip-toe and very quietly exhaled into my ear:

"I could smell your fear, Leo. And I still can. Why?"

"Nothing to be surprised at," I smiled light-heartedly. "He's just an overly talkative person by nature, and that makes me devilishly uncomfortable. I cannot bear being the center of attention."

"As you say," smiled Elizabeth-Maria craftily, not continuing to insist

I simply shrugged my shoulders and sent the girl to the buffet table at the far wall.

"Would you like to dance?" Elizabeth-Maria asked in surprise. "Listen, such music!"

"I can't hear. A bear stepped on my ear," I got out of it with a saying that I had heard quite often from my father.

"You're just..."

"And I didn't have time to eat lunch."

"Now that's a good reason!" the girl laughed uncontrollably.

In the end, before all the formal pandemonium began at the tables, I managed to scarf down my tenth canape, then sauntered around the room holding a glass of soda water. Elizabeth-Maria limited herself to a glass of cherry juice.

"Pretty much the same as blood," she told me.

"Only sour."

"I meant color-wise."

"Arterial is brighter, and venous is darker."

"You're unbearable!"

"Nerves," I sighed and, as Elizabeth-Maria was becoming an object of discussion, I began introducing the girl to my colleagues. And it would've all been hollow interaction, but then

Inspector White appeared.

"Leopold!" He smiled as if nothing had happened. "Let me steal your treasure away for a few dances!"

"Naturally, inspector!" I allowed without the slightest hesitation.

I wasn't planning on dancing today in any case.

At that moment, the orchestra on the improvised stage began playing a new melody. Robert and Elizabeth-Maria joined the dancing couples, and I headed back for the buffet tables, making an effort to avoid running into anyone I knew.

It's nothing! But I couldn't hide.

"She is pretty, though," rang out from behind my back. "And, they say, she looks somewhat like me."

I turned sharply and found myself face to face with the inspector general's daughter. Elizabeth-Maria von Nalz noticeably surpassed my companion in height, so our eyes were hardly on the same level. Mine, colorless-light, and hers light-gray, with blindingly orange sparkles. They were the kind of eyes one wanted to look into until the end of time.

"Few could compare with your beauty, my *illustrious* lady," I answered with an awkward compliment. Not having mastered my temptation,

I pulled off my dark glasses.

According to rumor, the *Illustrious* Ms. von Nalz's talent was the ability to bewitch people with a glance, but I wasn't at all worried by that now.

"What a flatterer you are, Viscount!" the inspector general's daughter shook her head.

"I may be a flatterer," I shrugged my shoulders, "but not in this case. And, as the chance has presented itself, I would like to offer you my most sincere apology for the deplorable incident with the paper. Believe me, I had no idea that poets could be so unrestrained."

The daughter of the inspector general just laughed uncontrollably.

"Think nothing of it!" she declared, twirling a reddish lock of hair around her finger. "I even found it flattering, being the main character in a story in the society pages. And it was so fun to see daddy get mad..."

Fun? Not so much for me.

I smiled sourly:

"I'm glad everything worked itself out."

"I'm sure that tomorrow, this misunderstanding will be the farthest thing from anyone's mind," the girl noted frivolously and got curious: "Viscount, do you really know Albert Brandt? He is called the most mysterious poet in modern times! How did you ever make his acquaintance?"

"The thing is..." I faltered, not able to keep my gaze from her dazzling feminine eyes and, much to my own surprise, answered with the pure truth: "It was in Athens, if memory serves..."

"In Athens?"

The pressure in my temples became unbearable. I replied:

"Yes," but immediately found the power to correct myself: "Or in Angora, I don't remember for certain. Albert got into a difficult position, and I did him a small service. And, since then, we talk."

"How interesting!" the inspector general's daughter gasped. "Have you done a lot of traveling?"

Instead of answering, I suggested:

"Elizabeth-Maria, why don't we continue this discussion over a dance? Maybe. You know, now that it wouldn't cause idle gossip..." and was struck by my own bravery in waiting for an answer.

"Naturally, Viscount!"

We joined the spinning couples in a waltz. I began leading the girl and immediately realized that Elizabeth-Maria danced incomparably better than me and, in order not to fall face-first into the mud once and for all, I would have to distract my partner with conversation.

And not step on her feet. Just make sure not to step on her feet...

"My mother died when I was five," I told the girl, "and that nearly killed my father."

"I'm very sorry..."

"I cannot recollect exactly, but I seem to remember us spending a certain period of time going from place to place after that. Around six months."

"Surely, you toured the whole Empire in that time!"

"No, not the whole Empire," I laughed uncontrollably, masking my nervousness. "But I did get to see quite a lot."

"And where did you like it most?"

I answered without hesitation:

"New Babylon, the heart of the Empire."

I did not share my impression that it was an ulcer eating the Empire from the inside, though.

"And your friend, Albert?" Elizabeth-Maria wondered. "Is he really as strange as they say?"

"No stranger than the other bohemians," I answered with a meaningful and even mysterious air. "Have you read about the conductor who took his own life after losing his wand?"

"Yes, simply horrible!"

At that moment, the music went silent, and I had to step back from the girl.

"It was nice to meet you, Viscount," Elizabeth-Maria smiled goodbye, walking away with the light step of a dancer.

Her breathtaking eyes paused on me, leaving me stunned, and I squeezed out:

"You too. You too..."

It grew dry in my mouth. I wanted to wet my throat unbearably, but before I'd had time to reach the buffet tables, I was grabbed by Robert White.

"Have you thought over my proposal?" asked my boss.

"No."

"You still haven't?"

"No, inspector," I shook my head and put my dark glasses on. "And I will not."

"As you say," Robert White shrugged his shoulders with surprising nonchalance and did not try to convince me. "But let's talk tomorrow when our minds are fresh. Promise me you'll think about it."

"I will," I promised.

"Don't come to work. I'll come to meet you," the inspector warned, giving a salute with his glass and heading back homeward.

Curses! His last remark had hit me right in the Achilles' heel. If the inspector doesn't have a change of heart about firing me, I'd be just as likely to see my advance as my own ears. After all, he definitely wouldn't change his mind...

I cursed silently once again and someone took me by the elbow.

"Leopold, is everything quite alright?" asked Elizabeth-Maria, *my* Elizabeth-Maria.

"Yes."

"You're breathing like a spooked horse."

"It's stuffy in here," I said, looking all around absent-mindedly. "Let's go get some fresh air."

The girl, after dancing, wasn't panting in the slightest. The blue vein on her neck didn't even start beating more rapidly, but I was obviously not doing well. My heart was pounding, and for some reason, it was uneven.

"You wanted to suck all the life out of the party?"

"Not a bad idea, don't you think?"

"If you're already finished..."

"Yes, we can leave."

We headed for the exit, but in the door we were intercepted once again by the inspector general.

"My *Illustrious* Mademoiselle," the ghastly old man smiled, "allow me to have a brief word with your handsome cavalier..."

Friedrich von Nalz and I walked over to a flung-open window and there the inspector general spent some time in silence looking at the row of electric torches illuminating the night outside.

"I am impressed, Viscount," he said some time later. "You are quite the shrewd young man."

"Thank you..."

"But!" The inspector general turned unexpectedly sharply, and I felt like I'd been doused in boiling water from head to toe. "In the future, keep your distance from my daughter! Get that straight!"

"There's no need for this warning whatsoever," I assured the man, making an effort to stop myself from taking a step back.

"Wonderful..." the old man uttered with detachment. His eyes gradually grew dim. He nodded a few times, as if agreeing with his own thoughts, and returned to the ball room.

I followed him with a steadfast gaze, then extended my hand to the approaching Elizabeth-Maria and, with her in tow, headed for the exit.

"What did he want from you?" the girl wondered when we'd gone out onto the street.

"Not going into particulars," I chuckled, "the inspector general told me that I'm lucky to have you."

"Can't argue with that!" Elizabeth-Maria laughed uncontrollably, sincerely and rollickingly.

I wiped off the perspiration that had started forming on my forehead and led the girl down the electric-light-ensconced sidewalk. We found our cabby waiting just where we'd left him. Together with the shadows, an uncomfortable chill had swept in, and Elizabeth-Maria, sensitive to the cold, wrapped herself in a weightless mantle.

"Will you stay with me for a few days?" I asked, helping the girl into the carriage.

The question cheered her up, and she laughed uncontrollably again:

"Naturally, dear. I am yours to command."

"That is excellent."

I threw myself into the back of the seat and closed my eyes. The future, as before, was making me weary. It was too indistinct. And though now I didn't have to be afraid of the inspector general's wrath, the threat of losing my soul scared me no less.

The reductionists were free to sound off on the Sublime Electricity and push their pens in libraries, trying to acquire their sacral *knowledge*, but I wasn't so naive. The underworld existed, I didn't have to doubt that, and I absolutely did not want to take up residence there. But now, everything in my life was leading to that.

And losing my salary, when compared with

that, somehow didn't seem so worrying.

Some things cannot be bought with money.

WHEN WE GOT HOME, night had already fallen completely over the city. Walking among the houses, it was mute and inky black but, from the hill, one could see just how spotty the night's hold over this city really was. Part of New Babylon, had in fact capitulated without a fight and would be immersed in darkness until the very morning, but other neighborhoods were yellow with the uneven light of gas torches and, over the very center, the light was silver with the luster of electric bulbs. And everywhere around, there were the flashing spots of navigation signals when you looked up.

"What a breath-taking place," Elizabeth-Maria said, lifting herself up on my hand and getting out of the carriage. "From up here, you can see the evanescence of being perfectly."

I didn't respond to her remark in any way, and led the girl into my house. I handed my guest over to the butler who'd come out to meet us, myself going up into my bedroom. Once there, I untied my neckerchief with relief.

And that was how that crazy day ended. Just like that...

I folded my jacket, vest and pants carefully,

stored them in their bag and placed the bag by the door so I could have it back to the tailor's first thing tomorrow. After that, I shed my dress shirt, stood next to the full-length mirror and took a skeptical look at my reflection.

The first thing that caught my eye was that I was thin. Thin and lanky like a pole.

There was no challenge at all in counting my ribs.

Gangly? No, just thin. And though my father never stopped harping on about how "if bones remain, flesh will grow," I still didn't believe that in the slightest. I was a thin person, period.

And also, just not a very handsome man. The lines of my face were too sharp. My nose was overly long; my uneven teeth did nothing to add to my attractiveness, either.

But in general, there was nothing special. Just an ordinary young man twenty-one years from birth. Although, no, not ordinary. I would be ordinary if not for my eyes.

The piercing gaze of my withered-light *illustrious* eyes caused fear, at times even in me.

No one could grant the title of *illustrious*. You could only be born *illustrious*, or become *illustrious*. To be more accurate, you used to be able to become *illustrious*. All *the fallen* have long been destroyed, and no one will ever again have the chance to bathe themselves in their cursed blood.

But had they really all been destroyed? I remembered the underground chapel in the Judean Quarter, and my mood instantly went sour like milk over a flame. It would have seemed worse, but it would have been naive to suppose that I had truly reached the very bottom. An infernal, bottomless abyss.

The inspector would never let up...

"That's the ticket!" whistled out suddenly from behind my back.

I turned to Elizabeth-Maria, who was frozen in the doorway with an irritated frown on her face.

Curses! There didn't used to be any reason to lock the bedroom at all...

But the girl had already stepped foot into my room, not at all embarrassed that I was standing in front of the mirror wearing nothing but underwear.

"A blank cross!" she whispered dumbfounded. Her thin small fingers slid along my spinal column. "Down your whole back. Did it hurt to get the tattoo?"

"Go away," I snapped, but it was in vain.

Elizabeth-Maria stepped away from the mirror and took an evaluating look at my nearly-naked form before her.

"An eight-pointed star on your heart, a fish to the right," she continued enumerating my tattoos, "a chain around the neck, and a Chi Rho on your spine, on your arm, though..." She took a closer look at what was written. The tattoo wrapped around my right bicep a few times, but the letters were too small for her to really make sense of. "Is that Latin?" she then asked.

"Pater Noster," I clued her in, and the girl involuntarily took a step back.

"Leopold, you're just full of surprises!" Elizabeth-Maria shook her head. "But by the fires of hell, why? Why'd you get more inked up than an Egyptian sailor?"

"My dad didn't always explain the reasons for his actions," I answered calmly and took the robe thrown on the bed.

"Original," the girl noted, frustrated. "It can't be that you never asked him about it, right?"

"He didn't want to talk about it."

"You didn't argue?"

"That wouldn't have been too smart."

"Surprising!" the girl shook her head, then tossed a red lock of hair from her face and said with a thoughtful smile: "But you know, there's something of a lack of symmetry with the left arm."

"My dad had some plans for it," I

confirmed, pulling on the belt of the robe. "And now, if you're not opposed, I would like to get some sleep."

Elizabeth-Maria got closer and whispered:

"Shall I stay?"

"No!" I cut her off very sharply, but did not apologize. "Please don't."

"Not today," the girl agreed and finally left me in peace.

I locked the door, lit my night light and checked all the shutters. After that, I put out the gas lamps and lay down in my bed. I began mentally sorting through the events of the past day, trying to restore in my memory the face of the inspector general's daughter, but all that remained of her image were orange sparks in a pair of gray eyes and the light aroma of perfume. And her voice.

To its captivating sounds, I slipped into a restless slumber.

5

I SLEPT BADLY. I would constantly wake up from rustling and creaking sounds, then drift into a half-sleep a bit later, but soon I would just be awoken again. Dreams and reality were so seamlessly interwoven that I was often not quite sure which of the two I was in.

That was why, after falling asleep once again and discovering an unfamiliar man on a stool in a dark corner, I was not at all surprised. Though the bedroom door was locked from the inside and the shutters were down over the windows, wood and iron, sadly, are not capable of stopping quite everyone.

"Mr. Orso," the man in the third-rate dress of a shopkeeper or a modest clerk said with unhidden reproach. "I advise you to consider Inspector White's request with a bit more understanding. You owe him a lot. Also, the inspector doesn't forget his friends. Jimmy and Billy haven't even been with him a year. He dragged them out of such a hole that it's scary to even imagine. If the inspector goes to the top, you go to the top too. His success is your success..."

"Go to hell!" I cursed him, turning to my other side.

"It is very impolite to turn your back to someone, Mr. Orso!" My uninvited guest got offended and, jumping up from the stool, began to pace about the room from corner to corner. "The inspector will get what he wants no matter what. You know that, and he knows that. So why complicate things? Why bring it to such an extreme? To pacify a *fallen* is make yourself like Maxwell himself. Wouldn't that be quite the gripping adventure?! Think about it!"

"Maxwell died a horrible death," I mumbled to myself under my breath, pulling my comforter over my head.

"The inspector won't just let this go!" the stranger broke into a scream, which was followed by a deafening clap. Knick-knacks went flying around the room, and the shutters flew open outward, their bolts broken.

I sat up in bed and picked at my left ear with my pinky finger, but that didn't make it ring any less.

Curses, how importune!

The door had been bashed open. I threw off my comforter and undid the latch; Elizabeth-Maria burst into the bedroom wearing nothing but a nightie, carrying a heavy candlestick in her hand.

"What's happening?" she shouted out, having noticed the burst of noise caused by my uninvited guest.

"I had a visit from a Mare last night," I chuckled, throwing on my robe. "Just a Mare, that's all."

"A simple nightmare?" the girl stared at me in amazement. "That was all from just a normal nightmare?"

"Not a totally normal one, but basically,

yes," I confirmed clearing my throat pointedly.

Elizabeth-Maria turned to the butler who was running in to see what the sound was from, lowered her eyes to her semi-transparent clothing, but was not at all embarrassed by that and left my bedroom in no particular hurry and with an unflinching sense of her own virtue.

"We'll have to get new windows put in, Theodor," I then sighed.

"No matter, Viscount," my servant reassured me. "There's plenty of glass left over from last time."

"And clean up in here," I asked him, carefully stepping around the junk lying around on the floor. I quickly gathered an armful of clothes and headed to the bathroom to get myself in order.

There I looked in the mirror, and it must be said that my reflection did not make me happy. The capillaries in my eyes had burst, and the normally colorless luster of my eyes had been replaced with a clearly glowing red shade.

Nothing scary, mind you. This was basically why I wore dark glasses.

After taking my brush and tin of tooth powder from the shelf, I rid myself of the unpleasant aftertaste in my mouth, got dressed right in the bathroom and returned to my butler, already in full dress as he cleaned up my bedroom.

"I don't need to go to work today. I'm just taking the suit back and returning home," I told him. I then took the paper bag lying against the wall and walked to the stairway, but Elizabeth-Maria intercepted me midway.

"Is there even anything edible here?" she looked out of her room, this time wrapping herself in a long robe for decorum's sake.

"I'll try to rustle something up," I promised, not having the faintest idea where to get the money to buy provisions.

"Would you like me to come with you?"

"It wouldn't be any fun," I waved her off and ran down to the first floor. I got to the gate, turned and began chuckling unhappily, looking over my gloomy estate.

There was one definite upside to the curse: despite the mortgage and heap of overdue payments, none of my creditors even considered taking my home to cover them. And those who did get that idea...

What can I say? The Diabolic Plague isn't the kind of disease you can cure with a couple of aspirin pills.

I WENT TO THE TAILOR'S on foot; I didn't have the money for a steam trolley today, to say nothing of the Metro. That said, I had no reason to rush, so

I walked the familiar streets in no particular hurry, wondering which of my few acquaintances would agree to lend me twenty or thirty francs for an indefinite period of time.

The only person who came to mind was Albert Brandt, but seeing him was the last thing I wanted.

After returning my suit, I stood on the atelier's porch, took out my tin of sugar drops and tossed a raspberry one into my mouth.

"Horrible catastrophe in Paris!" came the sudden wail of a boy walking up from the corner and waving a fresh paper. "The great Santos-Dumont is dead! Aeroplane crash! Powder engine explosion! Horrible catastrophe in Paris!"

The boy's yelling was so catching, that I dug around in my pockets for a few nickels to buy a paper out of pure curiosity. Unfortunately, I discovered that doing so would have cleaned out my wallet entirely, so I turned away and walked off down the street.

Horrible catastrophe? Ha! It would be simply impossible to think up a catastrophe more horrible than the dire financial straits I now found myself in.

Where could I scare up money? Where?!

Unexpectedly, I remembered my recent invitation to the Witstein Banking House and snapped my fingers.

That's right! Today is Monday, the bank is open, and where there's a bank, there's money. So that's where I went.

Once there, I saw a man sitting on the bench outside. He lowered his newspaper and smiled, having noticed my unfeigned amazement.

"Take a seat, Leopold," Inspector White offered. "I hope you've had enough time to think over my proposal?"

I stood opposite my boss and nodded:

"I have. And I will not do it."

Robert White didn't even bat an eyelash.

"May I inquire, what your reason is?" he asked quickly after hearing my refusal.

"I do not want that beast to devour my soul."

"Don't worry, you'll do just fine."

"Do just fine? A *fallen one* has as much power as one hundred tons of dynamite! I don't even want to get near it!"

"You'd be missing the chance to make something of your pointless life!"

"Sorry, inspector. You'll have to make do without me."

And, not wanting to hear out any more justifications, I turned around and walked in the opposite direction.

Robert White did nothing to stop me. He didn't even move from his place. He just stayed there, sitting on the bench. But I could feel his gracious smile burning into my back. And that smile made me feel very unwell on a deep level.

I didn't go to the bank; I went straight home. But it was too late...

MY PRESENTIMENTS HADN'T betrayed me. I only had to go through the gate to see that the door had been left wide open.

Theodor had never allowed himself such carelessness!

I took my Cerberus from my pocket, and undid the safety as I ran up onto the porch. I jumped into the house and immediately saw a rifle casing fly out from under my feet. It hit the skirting board and rolled in place.

"Shit!" I cursed in a fit of anger, standing over the body of my butler, his forehead blackening from a bullet hole with blood still oozing out of it. I picked up a business card that had been left on Theodor's chest, read the laconic missive on the other side and was once again unable to stop myself from cursing.

"You know where," read the words on Inspector White's business card. There was nothing else on it, but that was all I needed.

I did know where. And I also knew that the inspector wouldn't leave me alone until he got what he wanted.

Should I take this to Department Three?

With no thought in mind but that, a nervous smirk ripped itself from me.

Not an option. It would be nice, but it's not an option.

After casting the rumpled business card aside, I took a look at my butler and shook my head.

"Alright, Theodor," I sighed, cracking the bones in my fingers, "let's start over from the beginning."

And I forced myself to see what was really lying there on the floor, and not in the self-deceived reality of my imagination.

And the image of my butler began changing and losing human form. His singed skin stretched out over sharp cheekbones. His empty eye sockets collapsed. His lips stretched out into stripes of gray skin, exposing a set of yellow teeth, and his skull was crowned with locks of gray hair. The only thing that didn't change at all was the hole in the forehead. The bullet hole was in the here and now.

A fist came out of the sleeve unexpectedly and shook. His fingers started scraping on the oak parquet. His feet rolled up the floor into a pair of clean slippers, and then I put the undead man in his place:

"Patience, Theodor! Patience."

My butler had not, in fact, survived the night this house was visited by the curse. But he hadn't fully died, either. Theodor was a man of honor. His sense of duty was stronger than death, and that played an evil joke on him – all these years, he had remained locked inside his own dead body, like a criminal on death row. The old man with a sickle could come for him any day, but was taking his time, either intending to exasperate this impudent fellow, peeved at being made to wait, or not knowing which side to approach the stubborn man from. But me...

I remembered the living Theodor too well for him to come back as a taciturn undead. After all, I didn't have to revive the corpse, it was enough to simply imagine him alive and add the slightest bit of force to my remembrances.

And where could I get that force, if my talent drew power from fear?

From fear, where else? And it wasn't even that imagining living in the manor alone made me shake in horror. What helped me most was an inordinate fear of death.

Not mine, Theodor's. He was afraid to be resurrected, because the ersatz life I'd gifted him was inevitably doomed to end in yet another death. A moment of agony is equally horrible to the living as it is for those who merely think themselves living. It doesn't matter what height you fall from, if the pit below is bottomless.

And it was precisely that deadly horror I was playing on. I just had to use my emotions to add a small modicum of reality to it, and Theodor grabbed onto my memories, pulled them on like a mask, and began to jerkily twist his legs. His heart then started beating and his body warped, returning unnaturally from the kingdom of the dead.

I felt a slight head spin and leaned on the wall; my vision suddenly grew clear, and the ringing in my ears ceased. My dead butler didn't constantly need help. He had more than enough power of his own. The sensation of owing was what kept him from the grave. That feeling beat like his heart's otherworldly twin, and I had only to give him the initial impulse to embody this power in images impressed in his memory, nothing more. For a person with such a vivid imagination, that isn't hard.

It's no Christ and Lazarus, just an *illustrious* aristocrat with an uncommon *talent* and his servant, who is trapped in a state somewhere between life and death.

"Thank you, Viscount," Theodor exhaled, confidently standing to his feet and telling me: "They've taken your guest."

"Who?" I asked, already knowing the answer.

"Two boys, a red-head and another with brown hair. The brown haired one chewed tobacco."

"I see," I sighed and went up to my bedroom.

Jimmy and Billy would pay dearly for sneaking into my house. It didn't matter what killed them, me or the curse; in any case, they wouldn't survive the night. The inspector must have known about that when he sent them after Elizabeth-Maria.

In the bedroom, I grabbed the Roth-Steyr from my bedside table and pulled the head of the bolt all the way back; a moment later, the bolt had returned to its place, a round having chambered with a juicy metallic clang. Fastening my pistol holster onto my belt, I buttoned my suspenders. Without them, I risked being caught with my pants down. I checked the Cerberus in my jacket pocket and went down to the first floor.

"And don't forget to clean up my bedroom," I reminded my butler, who was fixing his mutton chops in front of the mirror.

"Of course not, Viscount," Theodor nodded, his facial expression now so neutral that you would never suspect he had been lying on the floor with a hole in his head just five minutes earlier.

Although, the bullet going through his

head wasn't the worst he'd had to live through, or to be more accurate, not live through. The Diabolic Plague didn't kill quite as mercifully as fifteen grams of lead and copper.

6

I REACHED THE JUDEAN QUARTER on foot. I walked without too much hurry, already thinking over my next steps. Again and again, I would choose words and arguments capable of solving the issue with no bloodshed. But, to be honest, I already had no hope that such an outcome was even possible.

Inspector White never stopped half way, but I wasn't planning on going on his mission and betting my own soul in someone else's game.

Elizabeth-Maria?

Oh sure, the inspector knew perfectly how to catch someone alive. But he made a big mistake when he decided that he would be able to force me to dance to his tune so easily.

And through the flap of my jacket, I felt for my pistol holster.

We'll see yet who comes out on top. We'll see...

AS COULD HAVE BEEN EXPECTED, the barber shop greeted me with a locked door. I stood on its porch, observing the day-to-day life of the local inhabitants. Then, I cracked open the gate and began walking cautiously into the narrow passage between buildings. There, I removed my dark glasses and took a listen, but I couldn't hear anything clearly in the indistinct din.

I started getting scared. Scared and very lonely.

But not for long. Feeling the weight of the Roth-Steyr in my hand allowed me to get myself together and return my confidence in my own powers.

The inspector needed me, but I didn't need him.

Quite a small advantage.

There was no one in the back yard. With a pistol in my hand, I approached the flung-wide doors of the barber shop and looked inside. There was no one there.

I threw a sugar-drop into my mouth at random. It was lemon. The only lemon drop in the whole tin. A bit of luck.

"How sour..." I frowned, carefully crossing the threshold.

Trying not to make a sound, I reached the stairs down to the basement and froze, not knowing whether to keep going.

"You know where," I heard the note repeated in my head. And I actually did know; know that I could never force myself to take the next step.

If I am fated to die a death not my own, it will happen in a basement.

What makes me so sure? Just a feeling. It's not for nothing that I cannot bear these dark holes...

Then again, I had Elizabeth-Maria waiting down below, which meant I had nothing to be afraid of this time.

Onward!

I dried my sweat-covered face with my handkerchief and began going down the stairs, doing nothing to try to mask my arrival. It would have been pointless anyway. I figured I'd never catch my colleagues unawares, so there was no reason to even try.

And I was right – as soon as I'd taken a step into the kerosene-lamp-lit basement, a cry immediately rang out:

"Hands!" and Jimmy stepped out of the dark corner with his carbine at the ready.

Billy emerged from somewhere else on the other side and demanded:

"Pistol! On the ground! Now!"

I let their orders go in one ear and out the other.

"Where's the girl?" I asked, my Roth-Steyr still gripped tight in my lowered hand.

Jimmy cleared his throat, spit his phlegm under my feet and whispered:

"If you don't stop pointing that thing..."

"Stop!" his partner brought him down a peg. On his round face, there was an incomprehensible half-smile half-smirk playing around. "Stop, Jimmy! Don't rush it. And you, Leo, don't go looking for trouble. Let's start over from the beginning."

Billy seemed far too cool-headed for the situation he was in; that put me off guard and made it hard to concentrate. It made for a big contrast with his red-headed friend standing opposite him. Jimmy was positively squirming up the wall.

"As far as I'm concerned, this guy's already in hell!" he exclaimed. "If he makes a move, I'll put a hole right through him!"

"And what would the inspector say about that?" I asked with a smirk, curious.

"I'd say that with your leg shot through, you'd become a good bit more talkative!" rang out then from a hole in the wall. A moment later, Inspector White stepped out of the darkness that grew there. He was holding Elizabeth-Maria in front of himself, pressing the barrels of his Hydra to the girl's head to stay on the safe side. "Don't do anything stupid, Leo. Drop your pistol. I just wanna have a chat."

"My dear, how are you feeling?" I asked, ignoring the inspector.

"I could be better," said Elizabeth-Maria pointedly, pulling at the belt of the robe she'd been dragged out of the house in. "But you could fix this all easily..."

"Enough chit-chat!" Jimmy cut the girl off, sneezed, turned his head from side to side and demanded: "Weapon! On the ground! Chop chop!"

"Inspector," I tried to appeal to the voice of reason. "I suggest we all go our separate ways as friends. You don't force me to free the *fallen one*, and I won't tell the administration. If you want, I'll quit my job. We'll just go our separate ways, like ships passing in the night."

"No, Leo." Robert White could only laugh in reply. "I'm not missing my chance!"

All his immovability turned out to have been put on. In fact, he was trembling worse than Jimmy, who couldn't find his place and could have burst out at any second. Billy seemed like a hermit who'd achieved enlightenment in comparison.

What was up with him? He should have been shaking from the Diabolic Plague already!

"You are possessed!" I turned to the inspector again. "The *fallen one* has gotten inside your head! And he's spinning you around however he likes, can't you see?"

"Leopold," my boss only smiled in reply, "would you like me to have Jimmy shoot you through the leg?"

"It's long overdue!" The red-headed constable grinned with a satisfied look.

"Do you know what your problem is, Jimmy?" I then sighed. After he gave a confused smirk, I said: "Your problem is that you're already dead. And Billy's dead too. You really shouldn't have sneaked into my house!"

"Don't force my hand, Leo," Robert White said with a threatening tone. "You'd better not make me..."

I turned to him and grinned back:

"It is you, Robert, who are forcing my hand. I could easily imagine your premature end!"

"Nonsense!" the inspector furrowed his brow. "I have no fear of death! What I'm really afraid of is obscurity! Your talent is powerless to harm me. You can't do a thing, Leo! Not a thing!"

"Are you sure of that?" I asked. "I beg to differ, inspector! For example, I could imagine that it is now deep in the night."

"And you think that would scare me?"

"Not you. And not scare. Jimmy, Billy, are you listening? It's already night. Deep in the night!"

The red-headed constable immediately started into a heart-rending cough, leaned against the wall and started just crawling along the floor. But it was as if Billy simply hadn't heard me. He was staring at his friend looking baffled when he asked:

"Jimmy, what is this? Jimmy!"

"Do you see what it's like to have a fire inside you?" I said, intensifying the curse. "It's burning straight through you, trying to burst out!"

With horror, Jimmy stared at his palms – they began to light up crimson with an internal glow, as if the constable had placed a powerful electric torch behind them. That then gave way to pustules that began quickly forming on the burn sites. Not only on his arms, but on his neck and face as well. The red-head was cowering in terrifying spasms and began rolling around the floor in an epileptic fit. Next, his body started glowing all over in a blinding luster and went limp. His corpse, cooked from the inside, was lying spread-eagle on the well-trodden earth.

But it wasn't I who killed him, not at all. The constable's innards had been devoured by the curse. My imagination had only given a slight nudge to the gaunt knacker. He was already racing to hell by the time I got to him.

Billy was a tougher nut to crack, though.

He sat down next to his friend, made sure of his death, then, as if in slow motion, got up from his knees and suddenly threw up his carbine.

"God damn..."

A shot rang out and a shower of blood started pumping from Billy's head. A few seconds later, the constable collapsed next to his dead colleague.

"Damned morphine addict!" cursed Inspector White, finally aiming the smoking Hydra away from Elizabeth-Maria. He ended up pointing it at me, though. "Drop your pistol, Leo! Or, I swear, I'll put a hole in your knee!"

Morphine! But of course! The constable's calm demeanor and immunity to fear were caused by a drug! He didn't even feel pain!

"Drop it now!" Robert shouted out again, and it became clear that if I delayed even a brief second longer, he would simply shoot me in the leg.

I laid my Roth-Steyr on the floor, slowly pushed it away with the tip of my shoe and reminded him:

"We could still go our separate ways..."

"I've already sacrificed my men," Robert mumbled in a deadened voice and shook his left arm, unfolding his pocketknife in a blistering motion. "Think what I could do to your bride. But, in order not to draw out this farce, I'll count.

And when I get to three, either you give me the right answer, or..."

"Finish. You have my permission," I winced and turned my head from side to side, chasing away the image of the girl, all lovely and fragile.

"What?" The inspector was taken aback as he suddenly felt his fist being stroked by the graceful fingers of Elizabeth-Maria.

His hand, sliced off by her claws, plopped onto the floor together with the pistol. Robert White tried to get away from the succubus and even managed to get a swipe in with his knife, but the infernal creature, in a motion untraceable by the human eye, got up close to him and gave him a sharp cut from bottom to top! He was ripped apart from groin to throat, gutted like a dead fish.

His blood gushed out, and the inspector fell to his knees. The succubus slid over to him on her back. She clenched her long fingers around his neck, so her sharp nails pierced the skin and, drop by drop, she began squeezing the last traces of life from her victim.

I didn't turn away and watched until the very end. I had killed the inspector, after all. I did it, no one else.

Did I feel bad for him?

I do not know. We live in a cruel world, and its main rule is kill or be killed. Mercy? Mercy is for the weak...

Then the succubus left the lacerated body in peace and, with a light dancing step, headed toward me. There was not even a trace left of the once sweet Elizabeth-Maria: her face had lengthened and become pale-white, her eyes had fallen in and were burning in the vermilion flames of the underworld. Her thin lips no longer covered up the razor-sharp teeth that filled up her mouth, either. Her blood-spattered robe flew further open with every step she took, revealing the taught skin over her ribs and a pair of small breasts with black pimples instead of nipples. Her thin fingers remained as graceful as ever, but now they were crowned with long nails of an unpleasant-steely color.

Well, they would have been that color if it weren't for the blood on them...

"Scram!" I commanded the infernal beast, throwing my jacket on the table and beginning to roll back my shirt sleeves. "You are free! Go back to the underworld!"

"My sweet Leo," the succubus laughed quietly and licked a droplet of blood from her upper lip with her split-end tongue. "It can't be that you no longer need my services, right? Believe me, I have a lot I could teach you..."

"To hell with you!" I burst into a scream. "You cannot break our agreement!"

"Stupid," the otherworldly creature shook her head. "You're so hopelessly in love with your Elizabeth-Maria. You spend so much time daydreaming of her, but she'll never be yours. I could be, though. Just imagine me..."

"Get away!" I sharply threw in, taking out my knife with a meaningful look.

The infernal creature, took a step back upon seeing the titanium blade, but immediately got herself together and reminded me:

"Leo, you cannot harm me. Do not forget, we have an agreement..."

"It didn't even enter my thoughts," I grinned, picking up one of the kerosene lamps and hurrying for the gap in the far wall. "Scram!" I shouted, before lowering my head and vanishing into the hole.

It wasn't a good idea to have dealings with a succubus, but to be honest, I simply wasn't left with any other choice than to cut a deal with her. I really had been so hopelessly stupid as to try to make an impression on the inspector general's daughter, and had turned for help to my poet friend. As any normal person could have predicted, he blew my secret around the whole town.

If the real truth had gotten out, Friedrich von Nalz would have barbecued me low and slow!

And I found a way out. With my *talent,*

otherworldly creatures were like soft clay. I could mold them into whatever I needed. And thus I had molded this succubus into a sweet-looking girl, my bride. When I came upon her, I was already anticipating the inspector general's reaction, so I suggested we make a deal. But now, it had all gone too far...

"You're gonna miss me, Leo!" I heard a silvery smile behind my back.

I didn't answer, though. I got to the fork in the path and turned to the underground chapel. I set my weapon down on one of the stone benches, straining to hold back a tremble when uneven glimmers began appearing on the stone-sculpture *fallen one.*

Sculpture? It surely wasn't that...

The winged creature, half-buried-in a wall, was hanging over me, pressing down with its dead majesty, trying to slowly but irreversibly burst out into reality from the bottomless pit he had been confined to years and years ago. The snow-white marble began glowing from the inside and started turning into flesh. His wings erupted in the finest hair of even rows of silver feathers. His chest shuddered as if straining to take a breath.

Then I hurriedly cast my gaze to the floor, and bit my lip until it bled, cleansing my consciousness of the mental effects of the stone-entombed creature. Fortunately, the *fallen one* did not manage to latch into my consciousness, and its luster slightly diminished.

When the shadows in the chapel grew thick once again and were just barely being held back by the dull light of the kerosene lamp, I walked up close to the sculpture, placed my palm on its stone chest and felt it. That's it! I felt a few heart beats!

With every bump, I could feel the blade of someone else's will being driven deeper and deeper into my mind; the *fallen one* had removed all my mental blocks in a rapid tsunami, demanding he be freed from his stony prison at once. But now, there was no need for that. I myself wanted to become the very key to unlock the door for him and release him into our reality.

Intoxicated with power, I dreamed of the majesty of those whose wings had once covered the horizon, blotted out the sun and turned day into night from horizon to horizon. I dreamed of their power and might. I thirsted to be like them...

Oh, right!

Scorching razors of pain dug into my head. The aftershocks of a greatness unknown to humankind practically knocked me from my feet with a crashing swell. Any contraction of my heart was answered with the strike of a blacksmith's hammer in my hand, still pressed to its marble chest.

And the *fallen one* awoke! His consciousness had just burst forth from the unfathomable abyss, while his body had already begun casting off its stone fetters. Starting from its left palm, a blinding light began shining forth from the whole sculpture. The metamorphosis my imagination started began turning the snow-white marble into flesh that burned with a fierce flame.

The statue shook. A spider web of cracks began running along the walls, floor and ceiling; my clenched-shut eyes were shaking, preparing to reveal the horrifying gaze of the *fallen* creature, but I did not wait for that, instead jerking my burning palm away from the statue and striking it with my knife.

I struck it, and the thin titanium blade slipped easily between his ribs!

The floor under my feet began to waver. The cracks began widening. A shard of stone wriggled out of the ceiling. The *fallen one* was cowering in agony. Boiling blood was gushing from the wound onto his fingers. With an incendiary flame, it flowed down his arm, but I kept widening the cut more and more, mangling its yielding flesh with my weapon.

The fallen are invulnerable, sure! Copper,

bronze, silver, obsidian, tempered steel and lead couldn't harm them whatsoever. But titanium...

Titanium was unknown to *the fallen*. They had no defense against it! In pure form, titanium was discovered at the very end of their lengthy reign. And, at that time, scientists were no longer rushing to share their discoveries with their immortal sovereigns.

The Night of Titanium Blades was a night they were not fated to survive...

I struck him again with my sharp blade. Then again, and again.

His caustic blood flowed down my arms. And it wasn't even blood, but pure, unclouded power! It made my skin burn in unbearable pain; my knife slipped out of my numbed fingers, but nothing could stop me now. I stuck both my hands into the horrible wound, felt the jerkily beating heart and ripped it out of his chest in one motion. The *fallen one* winced. His metamorphosis was interrupted before it could finish, and in one moment his body turned to ash.

Stones were falling from the ceiling, and I shot off out of the chapel. Just after I'd leaped out into the hall, behind me rushed a frightening cloud of dust-saturated air. Clenching the bright beaming heart in my hand, I charged down the tunnel, but, fortunately, the only thing to collapse was the chapel. The supports down the tunnel held out and were left with nothing but thin streams of sand that accumulated in places.

But I still didn't slow down at all, and when I got to the hole into the basement, I almost fell. The last thing I wanted was to be entombed under a heap of stones holding a singed heart that wouldn't stop pounding, pounding and pounding, driving me mad with its fell impropriety.

"Ugh, no thank you," I muttered and suddenly turned to stone, noticing the infernal creature looking out for me at the exit.

The succubus tore herself from counting the bank notes that had been taken from the inspector's leather wallet and smiled craftily:

"Leo, my boy, why do you look so surprised? We did have an agreement, after all, didn't we? You can't really have been hoping to get away from your other half so... easily, right? Please, let's have a bit more fun! We'll have a wildly good time; don't you dare doubt it!"

PART TWO

MUSE

Sublime Electricity and A Full-Aluminum Jacket

1

HAPPY PEOPLE ARE ALL ALIKE, but every unhappy person is unhappy in their own way.

That is what they say, right?

Oh well, nothing to be surprised by. The average person's dreams are impossibly ephemeral: self-sufficiency, love, and longevity. Power.

Fears are something else entirely. As a rule, people have a perfect understanding of what exactly they're afraid of. And those things are not banal, or common to everyone, either. No, every one of us has, concealed within ourselves, our very own unique flaw.

I personally, since childhood, could not bear basements, especially the icehouse cum cellar of my father's estate.

It was cold and dark with piles of dirty-gray ice everywhere. The flame of a kerosene lamp couldn't even try to drive off the darkness; the flame would tremble into nothing behind the glass, like a little fiery moth trapped in a jar, while evil shadows encroached from all sides. But at the entrance, the door was thickened and unwieldy, totally frosted over from the inside.

If you were behind that, it wouldn't matter how loud you screamed, or strained your vocal cords. You'd never get help, and I was feeling just such an urge to slam it shut. And not just to slam it, but to get a lock for it, fill it with nails and hang something unwieldy over it.

A nice heavy safe? Yes, a safe would do the trick...

Elizabeth-Maria could feel my pensive gaze with her back and turned around.

"Leo!" the girl frowned and shook her head in reproach. "You can't possibly have thought some old door would hold me back, could you?"

And she was right: putting my trust in oak boards and cold iron would have been at the very least naive on my part. I sighed hopelessly and began descending the hoar-frost coated steps. In one hand, the dull light of a kerosene lamp was shimmering, and in the other, there was a friction-top glass jar glowing. And though they didn't especially do much against the darkness, I couldn't even imagine walking around my basement without any light. Too scary.

"Leo!" the girl hurried me along, taking the box of fresh provisions to the very farthest corner. "What's taking you so long?"

"I'm coming! Coming!" I called back in annoyance and finally stepped onto the stone floor.

Along all the walls, there towered piles of ice chunks, which had yet to thaw out since being placed there fifteen years earlier. And the cold that reigned down here penetrated my jacket, forcing me to give a nervous burning shiver. Elizabeth-Maria on the other hand, wearing her light around-the-house frock, didn't seem to mind the frost one bit.

"What's it like down there?" I asked the succubus, much to my own surprise.

"Cold," the girl replied, but immediately turned to me and clarified: "Wait, down where? What do you mean, Leo?"

"Hell! By 'down there,' I meant 'hell.'" I squeezed out a nervous smile with my completely numb lips.

The succubus started laughing uncontrollably.

"My boy," she shook her head, drying the tears that had come into the corners of her eyes. "Try explaining what the Universe is to an ant! Tell a fish about outer space! If you can get them to understand you, come back to me and ask about the underworld. I mean no offense, but the human brain simply isn't capable of containing such knowledge. Everything in good time. Take that as a given."

I got into a huff and couldn't resist an evil grin:

"It probably wouldn't be nice to be trapped in the body of an ant. What do you think?"

Elizabeth-Maria thought, then nodded.

"That would impose certain limits, yes," she agreed.

"So then, could it be that you are not currently in proper form to envision the underworld yourself?" I continued, doing nothing to hide my malevolence. "Incarnation in this world did not deprive *the fallen* of their supernatural essence. Just with their presence, they were able to change the laws of reality, but you... You're still just a human."

"You can't make me angry," the succubus smiled, having unraveled my simple trick. "Leo, dear! I will not break the agreement, nor harm you. Ever."

"Forever is a very long time," I smirked. "Why not go back to the underworld right now?"

"Pish," Elizabeth-Maria screwed up her face, "coming back without any worthy trophies is bad form, my dear."

"While you're with me, you're not hunting for people. The agreement..."

"I wasn't even thinking of it," the succubus assured me. "Why take the risk, allowing you to jump off the hook? The soul of an *illustrious* gentleman pays back any waiting with interest."

I scraped my teeth in impotent rage.

"And also," the girl pressed up practically against my skin, "I do not think the waiting will be quite as long as you do."

"We'll see!" I grinned in response, placing the jar on the floor. Beams of bright light began issuing forth through the frosty glass.

The measured beats of the *fallen one*'s heart stopped causing pain in my scorched hands, but right after I began scooping the sharp, cold shards aside, my fingers immediately lost any sensitivity. Nevertheless, I dug quite deep into the packed pile of frozen chunks before placing the jar in it and covering it from the top with more ice.

Elizabeth-Maria threw a lock of her red hair from her forehead and warned:

"In that we cannot afford to hire a cook, I'll have to prepare it myself..."

"Have you eaten your fill of human meat?" I snapped, filling the pail with broken ice and heading for the stairs.

"I had to take advantage of the opportunity," Elizabeth-Maria shrugged her shoulders and laughed uncontrollably: "Broaden your horizons, Leo, while you still have the chance! It will have a very positive effect on the value of your soul..."

I stopped on the top stair, intending to quip back, but nothing smart came to mind, so I simply waved my hand and left the basement. My glasses were immediately covered with condensation; I removed them and stuck them into my breast pocket.

The girl came out after me, squeezing a paper bag in her hands, and shouted:

"Don't be late for dinner."

"I hope you haven't wasted all the money on provisions." I admonished her, dropping the basement door in place.

"And what if I have? You are the one who demanded I not touch the dead man's wallet, isn't that right?"

"I've had a change of heart."

"Have a look at the desk by the entry," Elizabeth-Maria then hinted.

In a small vase on the upper floor, I discovered a pair of rumpled twenties and a brand new ten; I popped them into my wallet with my stiff fingers, went into the cleaning room and, plugging the down pipe with a wooden stopper, emptied the bucket of ice into the sink. After that, I removed my jacket, rolled up my shirt sleeve and assessed the damage to my arms. On my skin, from my hands to my elbows, the crimson pustules of the Diabolic Plague had broken through. Their luster was no dimmer than the flame of a kerosene lamp, but they burned worse than even that.

Curses!

In its time, the Diabolic Plague had done in

practically half of the first generation of *illustrious*, and it was hardly possible that anyone in the Empire had ever had to go through an attack of it two times!

I turned on the water, stuck my *fallen-burned* fingers under the taught stream and caught my breath with relief. After that, I lowered my arms into the ice bath and spent some time standing in that position, feeling the burning sensation overcome by acute bone pain.

Good!

Rolling my sleeves back down as I walked, I headed for the bedroom, took my police-issue Roth-Steyr from my bedside table, stuck it into its holster and clipped it to my belt. I did not want to carry anything too heavy if I didn't have to, but all rules both written and unwritten indicated that my pistol was to have been returned to the armory the day before yesterday, so the earlier I did it the better.

"I'm going to have a peek at the grocer's," I warned my butler, having come down into the entryway, "if I buy anything, I'll send it by errand boy."

"As you say, Viscount," Theodor nodded.

Simply nodded, taking what he'd heard into account, and that was all.

To be honest, he sometimes made me feel beside myself. Not alive, not dead – how did

Theodor occupy his days? Why had he still not yet left this world? What was holding him here? The fact that he gave his word to my parents? Or was it the guilt of feeling indebted? It could even have just been a banal fear of death.

I shook my head, took out my tin and tossed back a mint sugar drop.

At that moment, Elizabeth-Maria came out of the kitchen, noticed the tin of sweets and wondered:

"May I, Leo?"

"Be my guest."

The girl popped a candy into her moth, rolled it around with her tongue and admitted with surprise:

"It's tasty," then melted into a malignant smile: "Do you have any blood flavored ones?"

"Curses!" I exclaimed and jumped out onto the street, slamming the door behind me thunderously. At the gates, I raked a thick plug of correspondence from my post box, primarily bills, split the envelopes between my pockets and walked down through the Italian quarter. I walked into a grocer's stall on the outskirts, left the owner a list of purchases and money, then called on the local baker, and after his cinnamon-scented shop, I headed for a two-story estate with a new banner on the side reading "Colonial Goods."

After pushing the door aside, I stepped across the threshold to the melodic ring of a bell and greeted the lanky black-haired boy on the other side of the counter.

"Good morning, Antonio!"

"Mr. Orso!" the roguish-looking clerk lit up, wiped his palm on a once-white apron and bent down over the counter toward me. "It's been some time since we've seen one another!"

I squeezed his outstretched hand and inquired:

"How's business?"

Antonio could only smile carelessly in reply:

And in fact, the owner of this little shop had no cause to complain about lack of customers: goods from both Indias, the South-African colonies and the New World were in unceasing demand.

"What type of tea do you recommend?" I wondered, pondering over the glass jars of spices, salt, sugar, coffee beans and tea leaves sitting on the shelves.

"Tea again?" Antonio winced disapprovingly and got a bottle of grappa out from under the counter. "Would you take a small glass?"

"No thank you," I refused.

The trader filled a glass, poured the grape liquor down his throat and shook his head. He begrudgingly hid the bottle under the counter and sighed:

"Leopold, I'd think you were a Londoner! Tea, tea and only tea! Try some coffee!"

"Coffee is bad for the heart and it'll make your teeth dark. That's what they say in all the magazines."

"Nonsense!" Antonio objected. "I'd think you were an Italian!"

"Antonio," I sighed, "but you know I'm not Italian."

"Enough bullshitting! Leo, look at yourself! You and I could be brothers!"

A certain similarity between us could in fact be seen, but the fact remained that there were no Italians among my ancestors. It was just that, my grandfather, on being ennobled, had decided that Piotr Orso sounded nicer than Piotr Medved and later, that same Russian officer in the Imperial army took an Irish woman as a bride, and into the world came Boris Orso, my father.

His mother's side of the family had old aristocratic origins, going back to the first days of the rise of Atlantis, which meant that my family genealogy contained more than enough Romans.

"Sure, we may as well be brothers!" I laughed uncontrollably. "I need tea! And don't even offer me any of that fancy stuff from the

Celestial Kingdom. Regular black tea will do just fine."

My grandfather had given me my love of tea; my father preferred vodka.

"Black tea?" Antonio sighed, scratching the back of his curly-haired head in deepest thought. "What about some high-mountain Ceylon? Or some Kenyan? The Kenyan is even better – it might even be – the last harvest."

"Egypt?" I guessed.

"Sure, but if the war starts, there will be no one around to harvest it," Antonio sighed, placing two jars in front of me and removing their fast-tightened tops to allow me to take a whiff.

"Ceylon," I decided a little while later. "As usual."

The trader placed some heavy weights in one of the scale's baskets, put a little paper bag on the other and set about filling it with the heavy tea.

"Four and a half francs," Antonio announced the price, setting the measuring spoon aside.

"That's for how much?" I clarified.

"One pound."

"One pound? Antonio, what time-period do you live in? Ounces, inches, pints! That's all last century! Believe me, Imperial Measurement Units are much more convenient."

"Oh, that garbage!" the trader waved it off. "I don't want to fill my head up with difficult calculations! My grandfather weighed in pounds, my father weighed in pounds, and I, Antonio..."

"Hold on! But isn't the price on the jar shown per kilogram?" I interrupted the man. "Ten and a half francs per kilogram of tea, isn't that right?"

"Drop it, Leo! It's too hard for me!"

"What are you talking about, Antonio?! It's actually quite simple. The length of the equator is forty thousand kilometers; thus one meter is..."

"And why forty thousand exactly?"

"Why not? The important thing is having a standard."

"Leopold," Antonio sighed hopelessly, "enough of the brain-busting! Tell me straight: what do you want?"

One pound of tea wasn't four and a half francs, just four francs twenty centimes, but it wouldn't have been polite for me to nickel and dime the man, so I didn't point out the inaccuracy in his calculations, just asked:

"Would you please weigh me out a half kilo."

The trader rolled his eyes, muttered an indecipherable curse under his breath, changed out one weight for another, and filled the bag up with his tea-measuring spoon.

"Are you satisfied?" he asked, lining up the arrows.

"So I pay four seventy-five, right?"

"Yes!"

With a smile, I threw a ten-franc note on the counter, and when Antonio began taking my change from the cash register, I asked quietly:

"You don't have anything else to offer me?"

The trader shot his attentive gaze over me, and just as quietly asked:

"How much?"

"One."

Then Antonio laid a bar before him in a plain paper wrapper and quickly covered it with a five-franc coin. I carelessly swept the change into my pocket and warned him:

"Give the tea to Mario. He will send an errand-boy."

"Deal. Good luck, Leopold!"

"Have a nice day, Antonio."

Exiting onto the street, I slid the loop of my dark glasses down to the very tip of my nose and took a careful look around. I didn't notice anything suspicious, so I freed the brown bar from its wrapper and popped it into my mouth.

Bliss! A pure, not at all cloudy bliss!

Curses, how little a person needs to be happy!

Just a couple grams of chocolate! Yes,

chocolate. The contraband delicacy, the trafficking of which, until recently threatened a huge fine and, for some, a prison sentence.

Chocolate itself didn't contain anything illegal, but by some quirk of fate, the cacao tree was found exclusively in territory under Aztec control, and any trade with these blood-thirsty savages was intercepted immediately after combat measures started in Texas again. In the Old World, chocolate trees were cultivated in sub-equatorial Africa, but candy and tobacco products made in Great Egypt had been forbidden for two decades already.

I stood still for some time, enjoying the taste of the treat, then I cast off the stupor and stepped off toward the nearest steam-trolley station. It was a money-saving move, but if I went everywhere on foot, I'd have been sewing patches into my soles and fixing my heels until I was frail. Footwear was not issued by the police, after all.

2

THE STEAM-TRAM LINE that went nearest the Italian quarter traced the outlines of the factory outskirts; in the windless weather, the smoke climbed along the earth in an impenetrable canopy, forcing me from time to time to hack and cough in an attempt to clear my raw throat and clean my watering eyes. And today, the street was covered by a stretched-out gray haze; the factory buildings got lost in it, as if in a cloud, and only their heightened smoke-stacks could be seen, looming somewhere above me like ships that had sunk in shallow water. Along the rails, there stretched-out warehouses and storage facilities, and only when we turned out to the river to the sound of steel wheels were they replaced with residential houses.

Right after Brown Bridge, the steam tram sharply decreased its pace, from then on crawling at the speed of an unhurried snail.

And that was no wonder – any large city is defined by its orderless, if not to say chaotic street traffic, and New Babylon was no exception in that regard. Carriages with arrogant drivers and clueless pedestrians, unhurried carts and racing self-propelled carriages, people on horseback and bicyclists filled the streets, scurrying from side to side and stepping on one another's toes, creating small jams where there was nothing to warn of their appearance.

And right now, when a wagon driver was thrown off by an unforeseen delay, he pulled on the handle under the ceiling, making a rolling hum sound. The horse next to him got startled by the steam-trolley and hit its cart on the carriage next to it. The driver of the impacted carriage gave a spirited flick of his switch to the nag. Its owner couldn't bear someone treating his horse that way and replied with whip strike on the man.

A squabble ensued. A pair of horse-riding constables set off for the small disturbance.

I looked with sadness at the plugged up transport artery "clot" and hopped over to the bridge, having made up my mind to go the rest of the way on foot. I passed the steam trap, walked in front of a pair of horses tied to a carriage and walked along the sidewalk, elbowing my way through the crowd of onlookers. I spotted a public thoroughfare, weaved under the ropes hanging low from the weight of the wet laundry, and soon came out onto a side ally that looked deserted and calm.

However, on the ground, it became apparent that it was nothing of the sort!

"Hey mister, wanna buy a watch?" shouted out a boy, rummaging through a trash heap.

I walked by in silence.

"I'll sell it cheap!" The little beggar scurried after me, waving a belt of wristwatches.

"Not interested," I tossed out curtly, not reducing my pace.

Watch theft, which thieves had begun to

live on immediately after the invention of the pocket watch, had received a second birth as soon as the fashion for wristwatches came around. And counting on catching someone with such a primitive trap was something only a jackass urchin would do.

"They're silver!" said the grubby boy, not even considering backing down, holding a rather large cap on his head, which was slipping around as he ran, sometimes over his eyes, and sometimes over the back of his head.

"Stop it!" I ordered, and two shadows immediately stepped out of a back alley to meet me.

"You're being rude, mister!" a meaty, broad-shouldered boy of imposing dimensions reproached me in a cracking voice.

"That's not nice," agreed a different boy who, while not as strong, was clearly somewhat more imaginative, in that he reinforced his words with a wag of his weighty finger. "And he's wearing glasses..."

My hand outstretched, I caught the boy who had been flittering around my legs by the collar, gave him a kick in the butt and sent him back to his partners in crime. He didn't even have time to squeal in surprise. He simply threw up his hands and sprawled out in the dirt.

"What a creep!" the husky one shouted, but

in an instant bit his tongue as soon as my service whistle appeared in my hand. "Well well..."

A sharp whistling shot through the alley and the under-aged robbers blew away like wind.

I didn't dally on the dead little street either; the locals here weren't fond of police, and some do-gooder could easily toss a basin of soapy water out the window at me, or dump out a trash can on my head. And I really didn't need to go tempting fate again. Some underage little animals might stick you in the back with a knife with the same ease their dads displayed sucking down a beer over lunch.

New Babylon was a harsh city.

I knew that not only from the rumors.

NOT FORGETTING TO WATCH my back and sides, I walked a few blocks and, as soon as I was able, turned onto a lively boulevard. From there I went down an imperceptible passageway between buildings with walls burning out in the sun. The winding narrow little street was snaking constantly, sometimes curving around high-fenced yards, sometimes bending in arcs, and occasionally becoming a downright foot-path, dirt and all, but in the end it led me to a neighborhood populated by natives of Greece and the Southern Balkans.

Next to the little shops and tavernas on the

first floors, there were dried out stools right in the road. In places, they had barrels and folding tables pushed up to them. Rarely, I would see housewives walking the opposite direction, usually weighed down by a bunch of young children. Hiding here and there in the shadows from the midday heat, there were gray-haired old geezers.

The rest of the neighborhood seemed to have died out. Empty tables were collecting dust under faded storefront banners. Chairs placed against the walls were anticipating the coming of evening, and windows were darkened with pulled-down blinds. Most establishments here opened their doors only with the coming of evening and worked all night straight through to the last client. Most, but not all.

The Charming Bacchante cabaret was hidden on the narrow little embankment of an unnamed canal. Under its awning, there were a few bohemian-looking gentleman sitting and enjoying themselves. Some, with deliberately bored looks on their faces, were smoking cigarettes and drinking strong black coffee; others, despite the fairly early hour, had chosen absinthe instead.

Art people, what good are they?! Bohemians!

But the lank Chinese man sitting on his

haunches near the next building over had absolutely nothing to do with the creative workshop. The tools of his trade were not a brush and paints, but gloves and bludgeons.

I knew him. He worked as an enforcer for Mr. Chan the moneylender.

When I showed up, the man stood to his feet and, probing his fabric cap as he walked, stomped out to meet me without particular hurry. After taking a few steps, he slapped a shabby hat on his head and, without the slightest accent, said:

"Mr. Chan wants his money."

"He'll get it," I assured the enforcer.

"Time's up."

"I've had problems. Mr. Chan will get everything to the last centime soon."

"Mr. Chan's patience isn't unlimited," the cutthroat warned, giving a mockingly flippant bow and walking off down the embankment.

I followed him with my gaze and shook my head.

Getting into debt with a Chinese moneylender was first-order idiocy, but how was I to know that this sweet old man would start clambering for my part of the family fortune with such desperate tenacity?

I shrugged my shoulders in annoyance, walked between the tables and flung open the cabaret door. A floor-cleaner turned and opened her eyes in amazement; I placed my pointer finger to my lips and told her:

"Not a sound."

The lady of indeterminate age, wearing a recently-washed robe, nodded obediently and turned back to her former occupation; a security guard took a hesitant peek out of his room, but, thinking correctly, decided not to interfere in the quarrels of the *illustrious* and ducked back inside.

I went calmly up the wide stairway with carved bannisters to the second floor, walked to the end of the corridor and, without knocking, flung open the door of the rented apartment.

In the room, a thick dimness reigned, and wisps of aromatic smoke were lingering. All the windows were drawn with thick curtains, and only the edge of one window had been left slightly uncovered just so the dim light would fall on the book in the hands of an imposing gentleman of thirty years with a sand-colored mustache and a carefully-groomed beard. The dressers and desk in the far corner got lost in the shadows.

The person whose apartment this was tore himself from the pipe of the hookah sitting on the floor when I appeared, took a breath and said in a well-delivered baritone:

"Leopold, my friend, I wholeheartedly share

your annoyance, but allow..."

I was in no mood to allow him anything.

"You'd better shut up!" I demanded, cutting off his explanation mid-way through.

"That is extremely rude on your part!" Albert Brandt feigned indignation. The man was a talented poet, a good friend and a lousy scum-bag. "Leopold, your actions..."

I cast the pillow that happened to be under my hand at him and repeated:

"That's enough!" Then I lied down on the ottoman and stared at the ceiling. "When you talk like *that*, I want to pop my own ear drums."

The poet gave a rollicking laugh, cleared his throat and said, back in his normal voice, gruffly and with a slight strain:

"I always forget you've lost your hearing." His eyes went dim, losing their luster in the semi-darkness of the apartment like two swamp fires.

Albert was talented not only as a composer of poems; when he began to recite his verses, the impressionable ladies fell into ecstasy from just the sound of his captivating voice. That was how his natural talent was revealed, his *illustrious talent*.

If he wanted, the poet could convince anyone of anything, even a *fallen one*.

"I may have lost my hearing, but you've lost

your conscience, Albert," I declared, making myself a bit more comfortable. "You're a scoundrel. A scoundrel and a dishonest person. Do you know why I didn't come shake your hand? I'm afraid I would lose control, and end up giving you a wallop to the snout!"

And, it must be said, my declaration was only partially exaggerated. I really was very, very upset with my old friend. I was trying not to show that, though, hiding my offense behind overly sharp words.

"You're overdramatizing things as usual, Leopold," the poet reproached me, got up from the couch and pulled at the belt of his eastern-style robe.

"Is that so?" I was taken aback, taking a second pillow from under my head and tossing it at the poet. "I almost got roasted because of your loose lips!"

Albert hit back the pillow with a lazy movement and drew the curtain the rest of the way, finally plunging the apartment into complete darkness. After that, he walked up to the bar and poured himself a glass of wine.

"Gosh, I didn't foresee particular complications," he shrugged his shoulders. "And that is so, Leo! Nothing bad did happen to you, in the end, isn't that right?"

"Nothing bad, you say?" I objected, fighting

back the desire to give the man a few punches to the ear. "Albert, you were asked to write poems, nothing more! Why the devil did you talk about that to a newspaperman?! After all, you knew perfectly well that the father of my beloved wouldn't let such a rumor go unpunished!"

The poet turned returned to the couch and collapsed with a glass of wine among a great many pillows.

"Your beloved, Leo? I didn't mishear?" He snorted. "Did the *Illustrious* Elizabeth-Maria von Nalz know about your feelings? No? Did you plan on explaining yourself at all? Or were you planning to send my poems in an anonymous letter?"

I kept silent, as that was precisely what I had been intending to do.

My silence turned out to be more eloquent than any words, and the poet waved it off, practically spilling his wine on the floor.

"Leopold! You must stop hiding your feelings. You cannot allow your easily-embarrassed nature to take over..."

"What the devil are you talking about embarrassment for?!" I exploded. "Albert, a month from now, she will be marrying the nephew of the Minister of Justice! What was left for me to do?"

"Drop it, Leo! Do you love her?"

"I do!"

"So, tell her. Fight for your love!"

"You don't understand a thing..."

Albert finished his wine and asked:

"How much time have you wasted on this? Six months?"

"That's about right." I laid back on the ottoman and stared at the ceiling again. "The chance will never present itself. And you ruined everything. You don't even know what unpleasant things you dragged me into."

"Blaming others for your own problems is a natural defensive reaction of the psyche, but if you choose that route, you'll never overcome your own weaknesses," the poet retorted without missing a beat. "Leopold, I know you well. I understand how hard it is for you to make friends. Yes, I did wrong when I decided to prod you along, but my intentions were good! You should have gathered the bravery long ago to tell her how you feel!"

"Does that mean I'm at fault for all this?"

"Who else would be?" Albert grew surprised.

"You're such a creep!" I exclaimed. "A conscienceless scumbag!"

"Tell me honestly: would you have ever gotten up the nerve to tell her how you felt if I hadn't pushed you?"

"Are you my psychiatrist?" I snapped.

"I just wanted to help!"

"Well, stop it. What we talk about is for our ears only. It's like you decided to help me treat a migraine by getting me beheaded, see? What if I inform on your lampoons of her Imperial Majesty? I'd be doing it out of concern for your predilection for alcohol, of course. At the work camp you'll have no choice but to part with that pernicious little habit!"

"I'll think about it," promised the poet, capitulating suspiciously quickly somehow. Usually, he didn't miss the chance to argue, but today, he was looking unusually scatter-brained; it seemed as if his thoughts were straying somewhere very, very far away.

Albert took a puff on the hookah's mouthpiece, fell limply onto the pillow and released a long stream of aromatic smoke toward the ceiling, adding to the cloud already hovering at the top of the room.

"It's too smoky," I complained. "Smoke outside, smoke in here..."

Atypically, my friend didn't react to my declaration in any way. He spent some time in silence lying on the couch, then suddenly raised himself up on one shoulder and asked:

"Would you care for a bit of lemon sharbat?"

"I wouldn't say 'no,'" I decided, though I did begin to suspect that there may have been some hidden purpose to his initially innocent-seeming offer.

Albert jerked on the bell cord, calling a servant, and took a puff on the hookah pipe once again. He wasn't looking in my direction, merely smiling mysteriously, clearly fostering some kind of rotten scheme in his mind.

A few minutes later, the door creaked, and I turned around and shuddered at the sight of shadows creeping into the room. But I wasn't able to pop my glasses down from my nose before the fleshless figure stepped out of the electric light at its back and revealed a short, well-built girl, black-haired and sweet looking.

"Sir," she bowed over the ottoman and extended me a small wooden tray with a crystal pitcher and a high glass.

"Thank you," I called back after a second of hesitation, accepting the refreshment.

The girl, leaving a subtle floral aroma in her wake, walked over to the poet's couch. There, she turned around graciously, and on the backdrop of the curtained window, her classical profile could be seen clearly, with a proper little nose and a high forehead. Her body, though, remained hidden by a floor-length dress.

"Albert, dear, would you like anything

else?" the girl wondered with an entrancing voice.

"No, my love," the poet answered, dismissing his new flame with a wave of the hand, "you may go..."

She, slightly pumping her thighs, walked out into the corridor.

"She's beautiful, isn't she?" the poet smiled dreamily. "You should hear how she sings! And see how she dances! A real treasure!"

I filled my high glass with the turbid drink and asked:

"And just where did you dig up a treasure like her?"

A rollicking laugh could be heard in the corridor.

"I come from Helicon!" the girl looked back toward us. "It's in Boeotia, a charming place! You should be sure to visit it. The views..."

"Kira!" the Poet hissed at his girlfriend; she faltered and hurried to close the door behind her.

I finished my lemon sharbat and nodded:

"Excellent."

"I asked her to make it without vodka, just for you," Albert said and sighed. "Well, what do you think of my she-devil? My world in a viewing glass..."

"My friend," I shook my head, "it's time for you to settle down. Fickleness in your relationships doesn't lead to anything good."

"Whatever do you mean!?" The poet objected. "Women love me. What am I supposed to do with that?"

"That is a problem, yes," I nodded and took a seat on the ottoman. "One of your admirers, I'm reminded, even wanted to eat you alive."

Albert gave an uncomfortable shiver.

"The deaf witch!" he cursed out, and took a seat on the couch. "That crazy enchantress practically killed me, Leo. What was the name of the whorehouse...?"

"Athens," I offered, standing to my feet and walking over to the poet's desk.

Unlike before, there were no work notes, rough drafts or loose paper on it whatsoever. Even the waste paper basket was totally empty. The only thing in it was a dark loose ash. I pulled in air through my nose and decided that the smoke hovering around the apartment might not all be from the hookah. Perhaps, it was mostly from this other source.

It smelled like burned paper, and that couldn't be covered up, even by the heavy aroma of fragrant tobacco.

"By the way, Leopold," the poet suddenly shuddered, "what wind blew you into that whorehouse? How old were you, fifteen?"

"Fourteen."

"Isn't that a bit young for a night out

chasing whores?"

"I was looking for my father," I said, opening the sideboard. In the bar, I discovered a few bottles of strong alcohol: rum, vodka, calvados and absinthe. There was no wine at all.

"You were looking for your father?" The poet grew surprised. "Is that so?"

"Yes."

"What on earth for?"

"I was afraid he'd do something stupid," I answered, cracking open the blinds. Under the window, I saw five empty bottles. I then found myself suddenly overcome by the impression that the furniture wasn't in the right place.

"What are you looking for?" Albert asked in surprise, filling his glass once again.

"Nothing now," I answered, drinking the last of my sharbat.

The poet took a few greedy gulps and asked:

"Do you miss him?"

"My father?" I asked in confusion, caught off guard by the unexpected question. "It was never calm with him," I said after a short wait, "but yes, I do miss him.

After my mother's death, my father tore off into a crazy mad dash that lasted ten years. We didn't often stay in one place longer than six months, but we never left New Babylon, as if we were trapped in a gigantic whirlpool.

Who was he running from? From his past? Or from himself and his own fears?

I still do not know. I didn't think about these kind of things back then."

"Was it hard to return to a home that had stood empty for so many years?" Albert asked, looking pensively into the far corner. His glass had run dry, but it seemed he hadn't even noticed. "To start a new life..."

"Albert!" I brought my friend down a peg. "Have you been bitten by some kind of exotic fly?"

"I'm fine!" he waved it off, setting his glass on the floor and interlacing his fingers. "It's all because of the Spring. Something always goes wrong in the Spring. Heat. Sun. The days grow longer, the sun comes up earlier, it grows dark later. I feel like I'm in prison here! If it weren't for Kira, I'd have gone mad long ago..."

Thanks to one of the wonderful hereditary diseases found in the *illustrious*, Albert couldn't bear direct sunlight. Of course, would be hard to imagine any creative type getting out of bed at sunrise, even under threat of being shot. So I reminded him:

"The whole night is at your disposal."

"The night, yes," Albert nodded, but somehow anxiously. "My apologies, Leopold. It's all this Springtime blues."

I doubted that.

"You burned your manuscripts and lapped up all the wine you had in your bar cabinet. Correct me if I'm wrong, but you usually write when you drink."

"I tried!" Albert shouted, upset. He shrugged his shoulders, wrapped himself in his robe and repeated: "I tried! All these days I tried... It's just that nothing comes to mind! My muse has left me..."

"Balderdash!"

"Balderdash," the poet nodded and led his finger over the scar that was peeking up from under his short reddish beard. "And yet, still true. I feel full of mediocrity. And all over some little bauble! It's stupid, it's horribly stupid..."

I shifted my chair away from the desk toward the table, took a seat on it and demanded:

"Tell me."

"You'll never believe it. You'll think I've lost my mind."

"I have a vivid imagination."

Albert folded, then raised his left arm with a crooked pinky and asked:

"You haven't noticed?"

I shook my head.

"No," but immediately corrected myself: "The ring!"

"It was a class ring," the poet corrected me. "The class ring of my student brotherhood."

"Did you lose it?"

"Did I lose it?" Albert cringed. "Leo, look at my finger! They broke it on the day I joined the brotherhood! My pinky healed back crooked, so to take the class ring off, I'd have to break it again. Curses! I couldn't even pawn this little trinket when I was dying of a hangover without a centime in my wallet!"

"And you don't remember where it went?"

"Naturally, I don't remember! A few days ago, I woke up, and it wasn't there. I've checked everything top to bottom three times. Three times, Leo! I moved all the furniture, looked in every nook and cranny! But nothing. I asked Kira to look; she didn't find it either, and neither did my servants."

"Well, how could you with it so dark in here?!"

"Don't take me for an idiot, Leo!"

"Do you think it was stolen?"

"How? How could they do that without cutting off my finger?"

"Was the class ring valuable?"

"A class ring? Are you kidding? When it was new, I think it cost five francs."

"Then why is it so important to you?" I asked, not understanding a thing. "What are you so upset over?"

Albert looked my way unhappily in reply, sank down back-first into his pillow and went silent.

"That class ring was given to me at sixteen. A few hours after that, I fought in my first and last duel. That's where my pinky got broken and my mug got fixed up," the poet answered after a long pause, rubbing the scar that gave definition to his left cheek. "And that very evening, I lost my innocence to the daughter of the doctor who stitched my wounds! An absolute hell-cat! When I wrote my first poem, my class ring was on my finger. That is even more serious than the doctor's daughter! I've worn it for half of my life, do you understand, Leo? I cannot get by without it. I cannot do anything more without it. I simply cannot."

"It will pass."

"I feel like I've lost a finger!"

"Not the biggest loss."

"Get away!"

Albert flung a pillow at me, but I was on my guard and gave slight duck. The pillow landed in a tube full of umbrellas, tipping it over on its side with a crash.

"Curse me!" The poet gasped.

"Shall we go for a walk this evening?" I suggested, trying to distract my friend from his intense thinking.

"I do not want to," Albert refused and suggested: "You can go. Ask Kira," but immediately sat up on his elbow. "Stop, Leo! You're a policeman, after all, so you find the ring!"

"You're drunk, my friend," I sighed, taking the half-empty bottle of wine near the couch and stashing it away in the bar cabinet. "Hire a private detective."

"Do you trust those impostors? They'd hang me out to dry for the newspapermen!"

"You'll know how it feels to be in my skin one day."

"From a business perspective – it's easy," Albert frowned. "But just imagine how much a detective would ask for if he found it! I'd be in his hands!"

"Make an agreement with a respectable agency."

"They're all the same," the poet waved it off, noting with surprising sobriety: "Also, it would be no challenge to simply find a similar-looking class ring in a pawnshop, but I don't need someone else's class ring. I need that very one. That's it, Leo. Will you help me?"

I looked at my friend's sorrowful face and relented.

"Alright, but now I need to go to work. I'll

come by this evening and take a look around."

"You're a true friend, Leo! I've been feeling so sick since this morning, I'm at my wit's end, but then I had a talk with you, and it took a load off my mind!" Albert took a nip on the hookah, but immediately shuddered and reminded me: "Just don't forget to send Kira! She calms me down."

"So that's what you're calling it now?"

"Don't be vulgar. Her love is the only thing I've got left..."

"Oh well," I frowned and walked out the door.

I found Kira on the first floor. The girl was looking closely at a hand-held mirror and quietly singing an unfamiliar melody.

"Albert called for you," I said, putting on my derby hat.

"That's how it goes!" the girl laughed uncontrollably. "He doesn't let me out of his sight for a minute!"

"But that's a good thing, isn't it?" I snorted and went out onto the street without waiting for an answer.

The poet's new girlfriend caused an incomprehensible vexation in me.

3

THE POLICE HEADQUARTERS BUILDING was overwhelming. With its tabernacle roof and stone gutters, it towered confidently over the suburban homes, making you feel like a single gear in the huge mechanism of the state apparatus. In total, the Newton-Markt occupied a whole block and was a true labyrinth of stairs, internal courtyards, corridors and offices. But there were also cramped chambers, damp interrogation rooms and underground vaults for notorious recidivists.

If I were to be arrested for double murder and working with a demon, that's right where I'd be locked up, in the very deepest and darkest underground they could find.

I wouldn't like to find out what that's like...

"Fresh edition of *Capital Times*! Get your *Capital Times* here!" the boy began squealing, his cart tossing about on the uneven bridge. "Clashes on the Island of Arabia! Constantinople garrison on high alert! Get your newspaper here! Alexandria and Tehran holding negotiations on military alliance! The Imperial Navy has sent additional ships to the Sea of Judea!" The boy noticed my interest and immediately demanded: "Mister, don't you wanna buy a newspaper?!"

I waved him off and crossed the street to the Newton-Markt. There was something quivering repugnantly in my gut, but my resolve was steeling with every step.

They don't know about it. They don't know about it. They don't know about it.

But then came the treacherous voice of logic: They don't know about it *yet...*

On my way in, no one paid me any special mind. I calmly passed the guard checkpoint and walked up to the third floor. When I got there, who should I find waiting for me near Inspector White's office, but the chancellery clerk looking bored in a gray frock coat, starched dress shirt and a thin tie.

"Detective Constable Orso?" he shuddered at my appearance, extending me a sheet of paper. "Senior Inspector Moran would like to speak with you. Sign here, please."

The messenger was carrying a portable ink well and a pen with an iron quill; I placed my signature.

"Do you know the way?" the clerk then asked.

"No," I shook my head. "And Senior Inspector Moran, what division is he from?"

In the Metropolitan Police, there were no

less than two dozen senior inspectors, and I had never had the pleasure of hearing of Mr. Moran previously. The head of the Criminal Investigations Department was Maurice LeBrun, so if anyone was to lead the investigation on Robert White's disappearance, it would be him.

Or was this nothing at all to do with my ill-fated boss? Today, after all, was only Monday. They may not have even noticed he was missing yet.

The clerk then looked at me somehow strangely and set about packing his writing implements into a small case, though still deigning to answer:

"Senior Inspector Moran works in Department Three."

Department Three?!

The unpleasant news made my expression change involuntarily; the messenger even softened up and offered:

"Detective constable, would you like me to accompany you?"

"Would you be so kind?" I nodded and moved after the clerk, busting my brains over the reason for being called to Department Three, which was devoted not only to exposing spies, religious fanatics and malefics, but also to smoking out police officers who were sullying the reputation of their badge.

I did not want to be numbered among any of these categories, so, as I walked with my escort, I held a perturbed look on my face.

But life went on; disheveled paper-pushers ran about and smoked in their stables, constables crowded the dressing rooms after the end of the night shift, fettered arrestees walked out bowlegged. In the offices, there were printing machines chirruping, doors slamming, and some people braying away behind locked doors.

Everything was as it always was. All was right, but at the same time, something was off.

I walked into Department Three, which made me look scared.

My mental suffering didn't bother the clerk one bit as he confidently walked down the endless corridors, sometimes turning onto stairways or open galleries. A little while later, we found ourselves in the far wing of the Newton-Markt, and the next stairwell we found led to a locked door, before which two plainclothes officers and two constables with semi-automatic carbines in horizontal position were going about their work.

"Detective Constable Orso," my escort introduced me and headed off somewhere else.

The attendant opened a journal lying on the table, found the proper line and permitted me to enter:

"Come in, constable. Office number seven."

I tried not to expose my own sadness and headed off in search of the senior inspector. And though the room-numbering system was uncommonly confusing, I did not have to ask any Department Three employees for help. With an important look, I nodded my head at those I came across, and went onward confidently.

Finally, in a dead-quiet hall, a door caught my eye. It was adorned with an unevenly curved brass number seven.

"Come in!" I heard in reply to my cautious knock.

I took a step inside and instantly lost all of my ostentatious calm.

On the other side of the desk, there sat a middle-aged gentleman with the thin, pale face of a hereditary aristocrat. His pomaded hair, high, angular brows and thin lips overwhelmed me with how much he looked like a theater actor, but the gaze of his cold gray eyes left me without the slightest doubt in the professional sympathies of this apparent decadent.

I didn't know him. Another thing – the corpulent giant in the guest chair, sitting under a portrait of Isaac Newton, was Senior Inspector Maurice LeBrun, head of Criminal Investigations. And though, when compared with the elegant Mr. Moran, with his blood-soaked face and deeply receded hairline, he seemed like an unsophisticated street bully, it was not a good idea to underestimate my chief. He truly did have a bull-dog's grip.

"Detective Constable Orso," I introduced myself, having overcome my lack of confidence. "You wanted to see me?"

"Take a seat, constable," the man pointed to a free chair at the wall and returned to the conversation he was having previously. "Maurice, with all due respect, I cannot agree with that order. The New World colonies have always been defined by a good deal of freethinking, and the scourge of separatism did not pass them by, though that is a matter for the future. For now, the Aztecs are trying to cut them off from the gulf and break into California. There isn't even a mention of independence."

"Do you suppose, Bastian, that the Aztecs will not move in the foreseeable future?" LeBrun caught his idea.

"That reminds me!" the dandy went on.

"They say there have been thousands of unwilling sacrifices in Tenochtitlan recently. They must be planning something big..."

Bastian Moran shrugged in indifference:

"For now, that's all just rumors."

"But if not the New World, then what?" The senior inspector wondered. "The Russians?"

"The Russians?" Mr. Moran repeated absently, taking a pack of Chesterfields out of the upper drawer of his desk. He lit a cigarette, sat back in his chair and blew his smoke up toward the ceiling. "Russians are like leeches. They always want more. Their provinces stretch from the Black and Baltic seas to the Eastern Ocean, and still they demand special treatment! The Russians are dangerous, but now their hands are tied."

"The Celestial Kingdom?"

"And Japan," Bastian Moran nodded. "First, the loss of Korea and Manchuria, and now they risk losing the Trans-Siberian Magistrate as well. The funniest thing is that we'll still have to help them!"

LeBrun pulled an ivory mouthpiece from his pocket and began turning it between his fingers.

"Then who?" He finally asked. "Who is the greatest cause for concern? The English, dreaming of their former imperial glory? Austria-Hungary and Germany, which grow closer every day? Our unreliable Indian vassals? Just don't say France. I know the prevailing moods in Paris, and not just by rumor. I assure you that this affair will not go beyond talk for them. We French have grown terribly lazy in recent years."

Mr. Moran handed the cigarette pack to

LeBrun.

"Be my guest, Maurice."

"Ah, I'm afraid I'll have to decline," the head of the CID refused. "My family doctor says my cough is from too much smoking. I have to cut back."

"Balderdash!" Bastian Moran frowned, but didn't insist and threw the pack into the upper desk drawer. "As for your question, I'll tell you directly: I'm most worried about Egyptian intelligence activity."

"Are you serious?" LeBrun couldn't hold back his skeptical grin. "Spies? I thought those newsboys were just making a mountain out of a molehill."

"Nothing of the sort. Over the last month, the volume of diplomatic mail to the Egyptian Embassy has grown by an order of magnitude. The second secretary is famed for his splendid receptions. Everyone who's anyone in New Babylon attends. That man is connected with Egyptian intelligence, though. That's all no accident."

"I do not know, I do not know."

"I assure you, Maurice, it's all very serious. Alexandria and Tehran are conducting negotiations on a military alliance. Their goal is control over the Bosporus and Gibraltar. The threat of an attack on Constantinople is more real than ever. After Russia's deplorable defeats in the Far East, Persia began seriously planning on expanding its holdings into their Transcaucasian territories. And also, they have certain plans for India as well."

Maurice LeBrun threw up his hands:

"I won't argue, my dear Bastian. I won't argue. That's your matter. And also..." the head of the CID drove the point further, "there's no sense in overestimating the external threat and forgetting about internal enemies!"

"And no one was forgetting about them, Maurice. No one was forgetting," the man smiled and suddenly turned to me: "We aren't wasting too much of your time, are we constable?"

The question was given in a tone both harsh and cold, but I didn't even wince and gave a laconic military-style answer:

"No sir, senior inspector."

"Right now, in the middle of the work day, you don't have anything better to do?" Bastian Moran grew surprised, conceiving an incomprehensible game.

"None," I answered and thought it necessary to explain: "Inspector White gave me time off until the end of the week."

"To hear you tell it, it was a reward!" Maurice LeBrun quipped.

I went silent.

"You were, after all, suspended, isn't that so?" the head of Criminal Investigations frowned when he realized that he wouldn't be getting an answer to his unasked question.

"I didn't hear anything like that," I objected.

"But Inspector White didn't want to see you, right?" Bastian Moran clarified.

"That's right," I confirmed and prepared to inform them of the offense I had committed, but Moran managed to surprise me.

"And where, by the way, is the inspector today?" He asked.

"Inspector White?" I asked.

"Who else would we be talking about!?" Maurice LeBrun flared up. "Where is White? And please remove your eyepieces! Why do you hide your eyes like a guilty student?!"

I complied with the order, licked my dried-out lips and said carefully:

"Has the inspector not come in today?"

"He has not," Bastian Moran confirmed. "Do you know anything about that?"

"No," I assured the administrators and shuddered: "Could you please tell me why Department Three is interested in the inspector? Is he alright?"

The head of the CID let my reply go in one ear and out the other, continuing his interrogation:

"When did you last see Inspector White?"

"When did I see the inspector?" I repeated the question, gathering my thoughts. "On Saturday, lunch at *Archimedes' Screw...* Although, wait! We did talk at the ball on Sunday!"

"And that was all?"

"Yes. And?"

Bastian Moran lit another cigarette and frowned, releasing smoke:

"You have nothing else you want to tell us?"

"I'm afraid I don't understand your question, senior inspector," I answered.

Then Maurice LeBrun stood up from his chair and loomed over me with a threatening expression on his face.

"What do you know about the Witstein Banking House?" He growled.

I opened my mouth, not able to find the right words and kept silent.

"Constable?!" The head of the detective division frowned. "Cat got your tongue?"

"No sir," I answered, moving my gaze from the window to the portrait of Isaac Newton. "As far as I know, the Witstein Banking House is located in the Judean Quarter."

"And that is all you know of it?"

"In essence – yes..."

Bastian Moran shook his head and extinguished his cigarette at the bottom of a crystal ashtray that was already half full of butts.

"Constable, you don't want to tell us anything about the tunnels being dug under the bank?" he asked, looking at me with his cold gray eyes.

"Tunnels?" I exhaled, shaking from chill. "Ah, that's right, the tunnels! The thing about that was..."

"Answer the question, constable!" Maurice LeBrun roared, standing up behind my back. "What are you hiding from us?"

"Me? Nothing! But Inspector White..."

"Tell us!" Moran demanded. "Now!"

So I did. But, it's only logical that I told them only about the tunnels and the inspector's order to hold my tongue; I didn't share what I knew about yesterday's massacre.

"Amusing story," Bastian Moran snorted thoughtfully and sat back in his armchair.

"And the inspector's behavior didn't seem suspicious to you?" LeBrun sat on me. "Why did you not tell anyone about this incident? That is a direct violation of the protocol, constable! Three people have been killed!"

"Maurice, Maurice, there's no reason to get hot-headed. An order is an order," Moran suddenly supported me. "Detective Constable

Orso, what do you think, why are you here?"

"I have no idea," I admitted frankly, again turning to the window despite the fact there was absolutely nothing interesting out there.

Bastian Moran followed my gaze and smiled:

"You have no idea? And what if you really think about it?"

"Was there a bank robbery?" I supposed, and truly got lost in my guesses.

"And?"

"Inspector White released the robbers? Or..." I made a carefully calculated pause and jumped up from my seat. "Is the inspector alright?!"

LeBrun placed his palm on my shoulder and took a seat back in his chair with ease.

"So, you weren't with him?" He asked, looking me in the eyes.

"No!" I exclaimed. "Is the inspector alright?"

The head of Criminal Investigations spent some time boring into me with his steadfast gaze, then said:

"The inspector has been murdered. And two constables died with him."

"Curses!"

Bastian Moran kept on, and demanded an answer:

"Why did the inspector not take you with to

the arrest?"

"The inspector..." I licked my dried-out lips, "the inspector was mad at me..."

"Because of the succubus you let get away?" asked Moran, displaying his knowledge of the situation and sitting back deeply into his armchair once again. "Why then did he not bring Constable Miro? After all, he wasn't mad at him? Or was he?"

"I have no idea."

"Your awareness, constable, seems to be of an extremely limited character," the senior inspector noted poignantly, training his index finger at LeBrun. "And, by the way, my dear Maurice, neutralizing infernal creatures comes under the purview of Department Three. What gave Inspector White the right to waste work time searching for this beast?"

"I didn't know him very well..." mumbled the head of the CID, realizing that he was starting to act defensive, and slapping his palm on the table. "Excellent question, Bastian! I wish I had an answer to it! Constable, why the devil didn't the inspector tell anyone from Department Three about the succubus?!"

"Or about the alarming floater from three months ago?" added Bastian Moran, clearly enjoying the effect he was creating. "Just half a year ago, a neophyte malefic was shot and a poltergeist was dissolved at an arrest. And that's just scratching the surface of what he's done."

"Constable!" LeBrun looked at me menacingly. "What does all this mean? Be so kind as to answer!"

"I was just following orders," I uttered shortly, having decided to place all the blame squarely on the dead man's shoulders, all the more so given that I had, in fact, been following the inspector's command.

Maurice LeBrun took out a kerchief and wiped his sweat-covered face.

"Well, do you have any speculation on all that?" He sighed afterward. "You must have had some opinion!"

"I suppose that the inspector wanted to attract attention from the top brass."

Bastian Moran chuckled darkly:

"The only thing left to do is feel sorrow for the fact that he didn't achieve that while alive."

"I suggest we concentrate on what's important," the head of Criminal Investigations then declared, hurrying along the unpleasant topic. Next, he set about eliciting the details from me of the unsuccessful capture of the succubus, the discovery of the tunnels and the events that followed. I answered confidently to all the tricky questions, but when they started repeating themselves, I couldn't hold back and objected:

"Allow me to speak! What does the succubus have to do with this? After all, the inspector was only after the robbers!"

"Actually, constable, that's what we wanted to find out from you; what role did the succubus play in these events?" Bastian Moran flung open a folder that was lying on the table and said: "The coroner is sure that Inspector White was killed by a creature from the underworld!"

"Such coincidences do not happen!" Maurice LeBrun added weightily.

"That cannot be..."

"Look for yourself!"

I walked up to the table and turned the folder to me with photographs of the crime. Two robbers, shot, a dead Judean with false payos, Jimmy and Billy charred with bullets in their heads, and the tormented body of Robert White.

"That is simply impossible," I declared, trying not to overplay it. "I do not understand how such a thing could have happened! I simply do not understand..."

"For now, it is unclear whether the creature took possession of the inspector's service weapon and shot one of the constables itself, or if it took control of his mind and forced him to kill his own subordinate," said the head of the CID with an important look. "You'd better take a look at what became of the second constable! It looks like he was burned from the inside!"

"I suppose that must be some form of curse," inferred Bastian Moran, looking at me with a clever squint. "Do you have any thoughts on the matter, constable?"

"No," I answered, perhaps a bit more hurriedly than would have been natural, but no one was paying any attention to that anymore.

"You are relieved of duty until this investigation is over! Do not leave the city without getting permission first," Maurice LeBrun declared and waved his hands in annoyance: "But now, get out of my sight!"

"Yes sir," I nodded and hopped out the door. On my way, I wiped my sweat-covered face and hurried for the exit.

On the street I turned, cast my gaze at the dark colossus of the police headquarters and gave a cold-blooded shiver, thinking back on the details of the interrogation. And though my belt was being weighed down by my holster and service pistol as before, I decided to pay the arsenal a visit some other time.

"Damn it!" I just waved my hand and set off for *Archimedes' Screw*.

RAMON MIRO WAS SITTING at the bar, drinking white wine and leafing through a newspaper. He didn't glance in my direction, pretending not to notice me. But then, the constables that filled the public house suddenly fell silent, clearly letting me know that the news of the inspector's death had already flown around the whole Newton-Markt.

Not paying attention to my curiosity-stricken colleagues, I took a seat next to my partner and asked the barman:

"Almer, bring me a lemonade, if you'd be so kind."

The fat Fleming looked at me with unhidden doubt. I had to take out my wallet and stamp my last five-franc coin to the darkened boards of the bar. Almer shook it into the pocket of his apron, heading down to the icebox only after it had landed.

"Ramon, would you be so kind as to look away from your newspaper for a minute," I then asked my partner, knowing in advance that the stout man would just pretend to be engrossed in his reading, when he was actually using a very poorly thought-out method of drawing out an unpleasant conversation.

It simply couldn't be any other way – the *Atlantic Telegraph* article the constable had fixed his eyes on was on the funeral of a famous driver, and there was little that annoyed my coworker more than a society column.

Ramon, with a hopeless sigh, set the

newspaper aside and turned to me.

"Yes, Leo?"

I took a pitcher of lemonade from the Fleming who'd just returned from the icebox, filled my glass and, only after that, choosing my words carefully, said:

"Ramon, if you, despite the inspector's order, decided to inform the administration about the tunnels, why didn't you warn me first? You made me look like an idiot, whether you know it or not."

Instead of an answer, the constable swung his paper at me. At first, I didn't understand how the driver's suicide was related to us, then I saw the next headline over and cursed out soundlessly.

"Tragic Events in the Judean Quarter!" cried out the header of the article below.

What horrible luck!

You couldn't think up a more banal story if you tried. The barber shop having been closed for several days in a row put the neighbors on alert. They then decided to check on the owner, discovered a basement full of corpses and called the police.

"I thought you read the papers," Ramon admonished me.

"I do. Normally. Just not today," I

frowned. "Curses! They practically turned me inside out!"

"Did you try to weasel out of it?"

"I did, and how!"

"And how did it all end?"

"They put me on leave until the end of the investigation."

Ramon shook his head.

"So it turns out I'm still lucky," he chuckled. "I just told LeBrun everything right away."

"LeBrun?" I grew surprised. "He interrogated you?"

"Did he not interrogate you?"

"There was another man there also," I shook my head, not wanting to go into detail.

At that moment, the clocks had begun to strike twelve. Ramon Miro looked at them with annoyance, slipped off the high chair and finished his wine in a couple of gulps.

"Time for work," he said, fastening the copper buttons of his uniform.

"Where did they assign you off to?"

"Street patrol, where else?" the constable snorted, put on his service cap, and adjusted it by grabbing the peak.

"Be a friend and check out the pawn-shops," I then asked. "There's a trinket I want you to ask about down there."

"And what do I get out of it?"

"I'm sure I'm not going to get this for just ten francs, right?"

"Twenty."

"My top price is a fiver. You'll have to lounge about on the street with nothing to do otherwise!"

"Alright," the constable agreed, "I'll ask about it. What kind of trinket are we talking about?"

"Nothing special, a class ring from the student brotherhood of Munich University."

"I'll get on it right away," Ramon promised.

"Are you leaving your paper?" I asked, having finished my lemonade.

"Take it," the constable gave me permission and went out onto the street.

With the shift change, the number of free seats in the bar had grown a good deal, so I took the issue of the Atlantic Telegraph and carried my pitcher to a table by the window.

The sun outside was really baking. Shadows pressed up to the buildings like frightened dogs to their master's legs, and the wind that tore into the open window just barely moved the curtains. That at least teased a potential promise of coolness, rather than being able to truly chase off the heat that had rolled over the city. I did not want to go onto the street.

I filled my glass with lemonade again and thought about whether to order lunch, but I remembered my empty wallet just in time and decided to just wait for the dinner that Elizabeth-Maria was making.

I finished the lemonade and began looking into the correspondence I'd brought with me from home, but it didn't have too much variety. Everywhere bills, demands of payment, notices of rate increase and missed payment.

Francs, francs, francs! They were all that was on anybody's mind!

The golden calf had long held our world in bondage, and nobody, not the socialists, nor the anarchists had been able to unseat this wretched idol. Everyone needs money, and I was in no way an exception.

My mood was finally spoiled. Without giving them a thorough review, I sent the papers into the trash can, drained my glass of lemonade in a few gulps and set off for home.

4

BOREDOM IS A SCARY THING. Boredom day after day, and night after night can unravel a man. It eats away at his soul and deprives him of his taste for life.

When I was a child, I would sit for hours on the window sill looking out a spyglass at the rooftops of the city below. It wasn't the most fun activity for a four- or five-year-old child but, for me then, any opportunity to occupy myself with something was important: watching our chef work, chasing impudent jackdaws from the garden, playing chess with my imaginary friend, or even fixing the mechanism in my broken alarm clock.

My father would often disappear in the city. My mother was very ill. Servants bustled around the house, and I hadn't yet grown up enough for library books. I could only search out the odd picture book and leaf through my mom's favorite tome, *Alice's Adventures in Wonderland* with illustrations by John Tenniel.

Until I was five, I was left to my own devices, meaning I was locked behind the manor gates. It was no wonder that I knew every nook and cranny in the house and every bush in the garden. I invented hundreds of ways of having fun, but none of them could hold me for long. And that was when the boredom came. Sometimes, it bubbled up so much that I wanted to howl like a wolf.

Later, I considered those years the happiest of my life.

Why was I remembering this now?

This was all Senior Inspector Moran's fault. After talking with him, I wanted to lock myself in the library and not poke my nose out in the street. Not look anyone in the eye for a few weeks, not attract any attention; wait for the ripples on the water to settle.

But I didn't.

WHEN I GOT BACK HOME, Elizabeth-Maria was sitting on the lower step of my porch, snapping off the thick black blades of the aster leaves she'd ripped out of my flower garden one at a time.

"A letter came for you," she said, not looking up from her activity.

I took a piece of thick expensive paper from a sealed envelope and snorted in surprise. It was my uncle inviting me over for a visit.

What suddenly came over him?

Elizabeth-Maria squinted at me and asked:

"Would you like me to come with you?"

"No," I refused. "And don't spoil the flowers."

"The dead black flowers. Do you really like them?"

"I like things to be tidy."

The girl got up from the step and adjusted my neckerchief.

"Introduce me to your uncle. I'm quite sure

he'll grow more accommodating. He won't be able to stand his ground against my charms..."

"No."

The forthcoming conversation was definitely not going to be of the pleasant variety, and the last thing I wanted was to curse my own kin because a succubus wanted to play games.

"I'm bored!" Elizabeth-Maria complained.

"Read the papers," I offered, handing the girl the newspaper I'd brought with me from the bar. "We don't have such things in hell."

She pursed her lips but did not make a scene.

"Shall I set the table?" she merely asked, setting the newspaper aside.

I began to think whether I should drink some of the expensive tea first, but the country estate where my uncle spent a large part of his time was quite a long journey from here. In the end, I decided not to waste the time, and shook my head:

"Business first."

"Don't be late. There's ragout for dinner," the girl warned and added with an aspiration: "It'll be hot as fire!"

"I'm not making any promises," I answered dryly and walked to the gate.

Any time the succubus talked about food, I got a bad feeling that she was fattening me to slaughter.

Foolishness? I'd like to believe so.

A deal's a deal, so now either I get rid of her, or she gets my soul.

There was no third option.

THE NEW BABYLON CENTRAL Train Station was rightly considered a city within a city. The main building had a high glass cupola, administrative area, pedestrian bridges, boiler-houses, innumerable intersections, crossings and detours, guard houses, and rows of identical packhouses and coalhouses. In total, it took up the same area as a whole neighborhood. And if New Babylon seemed at times to me a hellish boiler-room, fueled by human beings from all over the world, the Central Train Station was its boiling point.

I bought a first class ticket thanks to Albert Brandt, who had lent me the money. Not in the habit of returning a debt before it came due, I stuck the change in my wallet, and went to find the schedule board, then headed for the platform my train would be departing from. I was quickly lured in by the aroma of fresh baked goods and coffee, but I held myself together and walked straight past. The train was supposed to arrive any minute, and the last thing I wanted to do was be late and spend another half hour in this bedlam. My head was already spinning as it was.

My father and I used to come here often; he would meet with his people, and I would stare out of the waiting room at the trains, eating profiteroles in the very same bistro I was now walking so hurriedly past. It was surprising, but the hustle and bustle here never bothered me before. Now, though, I was ready to climb up the walls just to get a bit further from this ceaselessly babbling throng.

But there were no less people on the platform. At the far end, there was turmoil purer than that in front of the ticket booth at a cinema on premier day; mountains of parcels and other freight towered over me, children ran by, and someone was crying uncontrollably. The passengers on the other side were all in worn and patchy clothes; sun-burnt, grubby and quarrelsome. The third-class tail cars were normally chalk-full, and the narrow benches along the sides could only provide consolation to a small cohort of travelers.

Nearer the middle of the platform, it was hard to even remember the earlier jostling. The public that gathered there was somewhat more dignified and respectable. Gentlemen in derby hats, black morning coats, perfectly ironed striped trousers and lacquered half boots were standing around ash-trays, smoking and conducting unhurried conversations about theater premiers, grain prices and the fate of the world. There were absolutely no ladies among this category of passenger.

Wooden benches with comfortable backs seemed a completely rational compromise between comfort and price to me, and I would have bought a second class ticket without fail if it weren't for the obtrusive traveling companions. All these insurance agents and salesmen had a passion as they loved to tell you, and I had no desire to work up a migraine hearing out their endless high-sounding nonsense and emitting no less banal thoughts in reply. It was better to overpay a bit.

I showed the attendant my first class ticket and walked through a gate to the soft seats that could fit just six passengers.

An aristocrat accompanied by either his daughter or young wife; a mustached soldier in an infantry uniform with a saber at his side; an important looking engineer in a company-issued pea-coat with an emblem composed of little gilded hammers and calipers; and a young couple – a lank emigrant from the New World and his giggly bride. They were all sizing me up with cautious gazes, and they all found me equally unfit for a casual conversation. Communication in the car was limited to polite nods and that fact left me beyond satisfied.

I didn't like meeting new people, and didn't seek it out. Actually, people in general... I didn't like.

Further on the voyage, a freight train thundered past, enshrouded in black smoke. Its cars were all of one type and could be distinguished from one another only by the letter combinations printed on them. Behind it dashed a postal express train, then – right on time – our train arrived.

The third-class passengers immediately crowded up to the very edge of the platform and, just as much as one, recoiled back when a drawn out honk rang out and their legs were shrouded with wisps of white steam. Salesmen and clerks on business, in no particular hurry, set about extinguishing their cigarettes and tapping out their pipes. My traveling companions, though, began giving orders to their baggage-handlers. I was first to walk through the invitingly flung-open doors of our car. I took a seat on my own, removed my derby hat and carelessly threw myself into the soft back of my seat.

Unlike the second class cars, which were split up into six-seat coupes, this Pullman car had a spacious salon with paintings on the walls, comfortable soft armchairs and couches. There were also separate rooms for passengers traveling significant distances, but the only long-distance passengers with us now were the couple.

Two short honks rang out in short order and the train slowly, without a single jerk, touched off on its way. The train rolled out from under the station's glassed-in cupola, and the wheels started beating out a happy refrain on the rail ties. Out the window, the reserve tracks swept by, followed by endless rows of packhouses; stewards began bringing around refreshing beverages and I picked out a lemon soda. When I glanced out the window again, the train station was already behind us. The train drove across the bridge and was now rolling through the factory outskirts.

No matter where you looked, the only thing around was gray fences, barbed wire, the gloomy hulks of workshops and smoke-besmirched pipes giving off wisps of stinking smoke. On the side tracks, from time to time, a steam train would pass with two or three freight cars, but as a passenger train, we had priority, so we shot ahead without stopping. Only when the endless factories were left behind us did the train slow its pace a bit, stopping at an open platform at the Western Train Station, which was decaying and badly cared-for.

No one came into the first-class car there.

After that, the train sped along the edge of

the Emperor's Park, quickly blew by the sickly green of its smog-tormented trees, and entered a kingdom of warehouses and offices. Between its buildings, you could see the silver expanse of the Yarden peeking out from time to time. After that, the rails were laid through the residential outskirts. The clanging of our wheels began echoing off walls with chipping whitewash, their shabby exteriors interspersed with smudgy windows.

The houses slightly thinned out. The train burst out of the city into a vast rural expanse and started consistently gaining speed, taking a run at a tangent track. First, villages were carried by the window, then they were replaced with small farms, gardens, pastures and meadows, cordoned off with short fences. On the horizon, there loomed groves of fruit trees. Small wetlands occasionally popped by with clean water glimmering between the tall bushes of bulrush, and the ribbons of shallow streams stretched among the sedges. There were cows wandering along the train tracks. White little sheep were also flickering by from time to time.

It was as if I had found myself in a different world. A patented pastoral.

OUR TRAIN WAS DRIVING through a field of yellow alfalfa flowers being grown for animal feed when it started to slow down. A piercing honk rang out. The breaks screeched. The car shook and the train came to a stop at a tiny station consisting of nothing but a couple administrative buildings and a lone angular warehouse.

I got up from my chair and the remaining passengers, were staring with unhidden surprise at the freak who was intending to actually get off the train out here in the sticks. That didn't get to me at all; with a proud and independent look on my face, I walked over to the exit, crossed the empty platform, passed the closed ticket counters and, once on the street, allowed myself a saddened sigh.

My uncle hadn't taken the pains to send a carriage.

No matter! Three kilometers wasn't such a great distance.

So I walked up to my family estate along the country road, while colorful chickens searched for grains and bugs in the dust I kicked up.

The sun, hanging at its apex, burned on my skin. Fifty steps later, I was already untying my neckerchief and unbuttoning the collar of my dress shirt, though that didn't bring me any particular relief. Then, having spit on the rules of common decency, I removed my jacket and threw it over a shoulder. The holster of my Roth-Steyr was pulling at my belt obnoxiously, but the road was empty, so there was no one around to worry about upsetting with my pistol.

And even if I did upset someone, what did I care?

The sight of the bright yellow alfalfa flowers was dizzying. The sun-warmed field gave forth surprising aromas, and this rural air was surprisingly easy to breathe. Grasshoppers chirped, lizards darted about quickly on the grass by the road, larks flittered by, and the shadows of vultures circling high above would occasionally glide over the road.

And no matter where you looked, all around there was a brilliant blue sky! No smog or smoke, just the unaltered heavens in their natural azure.

Was that a good thing? I would even say very good.

But, like a true city-dweller, it threw me off somewhat. And it wasn't from the fear of getting lost in the field: the only road lead directly to my family estate. What threw me off was the endlessness of this open space.

I wasn't used to that. The only time I had left New Babylon was when I was five and my mom wanted to pay respects to her family home. The meeting with my grandmother didn't go very well. Deep down, she thought my mother's marriage a bad match and treated her newly discovered relatives accordingly. So we didn't return until the death of the old Countess, nor afterward for that matter.

Far, far in the distance there loomed an olive grove. I looked at my timepiece and increased my pace. Sometime later, from behind the trees, we started to see the roofs of the tenant's house. It had one lone pipe coming from it, and there was a liquid stream of smoke rising up from that. In the bushes next to the road, sheep were getting tangled in the bluebells. From far off, you could hear a cow mooing. A chained up dog was yapping lazily behind the fence.

After the farm, the road went around an overgrown sludge pond and a shady forest stretched out from its edge. Also there, I could finally see the manor. Behind its tall fence, there grew a well-kept garden. Towering above the trees, I saw a three-story mansion that I recognized from pictures. Above it, though...

My breathing seized up from the disgrace and injustice of what I saw.

Behind the house, the Count had installed a docking tower, and now there was a dirigible slightly rocking in the air, cabled to the ground next to it! Its semi-rigid body was white and titanic. It had a spacious cabin, steering wheel, and the word "Syracuse" painted down one whole side. The flying machine did not impress with its dimensions like an army zeppelin, but it was perfectly well suited for flights to the continent.

Having your own dirigible. Just think!

And this is the guy who's been crying and moaning over twenty-thousand a year! I'm sure it costs him far more just to maintain this toy!

I removed my glasses and wiped my sweat-covered face.

Envy is bad. I knew that, probably better than anyone, but when looking at my own shoes, dirty and worn, I simply trembled in rage. I even had to stand in the shade of the trees and force myself to reduce the annoyance by taking a few deep breaths.

After that, I buttoned up my shirt, put on my jacket, tied my neckerchief and set off for the gate of the estate, looking collected and tranquil. But I was still just seething inside...

THE COUNT HAD NOT FORGOTTEN to inform his guardsmen of his nephew's upcoming visit, so I didn't have to introduce myself. A sunburnt old man in a straw hat came out to meet me in good time, making sure to swing open the gate in advance; I gave him a careless nod and walked down the shady alley. By the stables, I caught a glimpse of a two-horse black landau, and I was again struck with anger.

It can't have been so hard to send a carriage out for me, right? It wasn't like I'd invited myself. I was invited!

Admittedly though, it no longer mattered.

I walked up calmly to the porch of the manor and pressed the electric buzzer. A servant of the count had been trained to the point of instinct. Before the metallic buzzing had even started in the house, the door had already been opened by a red-cheeked young man in livery that was too tight at the shoulders. On it was the Kósice family crest: gray and green flowers. Without the lace ornamentation and flamboyant decorations normally found on such uniforms, it looked a bit like the man was wearing a military uniform.

"Come in. The count is waiting for you," the footman stated primly and gave a slight bow, but without a hint of subservience.

I hung my derby hat on the rack and, intensely aware of my alienation from rich society – which was to say nothing of my dirty shoes! – I headed for the guest room where I met a slightly older version of Theodor Barnes.

His resemblance to my butler was simply striking; only the wrinkles at the corners of the mouth and the early graying allowed me not to reveal my confusion and give a patronizing smile:

"Philipp! You and your brother are simply

identical! I am glad to see you in good health!"

"You are very kind," my uncle's butler answered dryly and continued: "The Count is expecting you in his office."

I walked to the stairs; the butler stopped me and flung the door open. Behind it, I saw the cage of a service elevator.

"The Count ordered his home equipped with the very newest in technology," Philipp told me with a barely noticeable hint of condescension.

To my mind, rearranging rooms into an elevator shaft had been brought only by my Uncle's ambition to shine with his own originality, but I kept that opinion to myself and walked inside in silence. Philipp walked behind me and moved the lever from number one right to three. Somewhere beneath me, I heard the clunking of mechanisms. The steam engine gave a measured snort, and the basket rose to the top floor quite smoothly indeed. The butler flung open the door there, letting me out into the corridor. He walked behind me, and opened the door opposite without knocking.

"Please."

"Thank you," I nodded carelessly and went into my uncle's office.

Count Kósice turned and pointed at me for the other man in the room.

"Mr. Levinson, this is the very young man we were speaking about."

"Nice to meet you," the chubby man smiled charmingly and introduced himself: "I have the honor of being the manager of the New-Babylonian branch of the Witstein Banking House and a junior partner in the firm. We wrote you last week."

I shook the man's outstretched hand and glanced expectantly at my uncle; the purpose it all slipped by me.

The Count caught my perplexed gaze, but was in no hurry to explain and suggested:

"Would you like some wine?"

"No, thank you," I declined decisively, despite the fact that my throat was still dry after my walk in the baking sun.

"If you have no objections, Count," the banker said softly, taking the initiative in his own hands, "I would prefer to get straight to business. The path was quite long and, as you know, time is money."

Mr. Levinson was a plump man with dark curly hair, a weighty nose and smart black eyes, but neither his mediocre appearance, nor his light tone could deceive me. He was demanding – demanding precisely! – that the Count come clean and that was just confusing the situation.

What could this conversation possibly be

about, if not inheritance? And, if it was about inheritance, what could the Witstein Banking House have had to do with it?

As far as I knew, the Kósice family had never had many dealings with the Judeans.

Having a guest make such a demand left the Count plainly ashamed. His broad face with its firm chin was practically split into separate halves, and my oh-so-dear uncle had to exert a certain amount of effort to maintain a composed appearance.

"To begin, allow me to familiarize you with a fairly interesting document," he suggested, walking up to the table and pressing a button on its edge. In the corridor, a metal bell buzzed out. A moment later, the door cracked open and the doorman peeked into the office, his fortress-like physique not even a smidgen smaller than that of the boy at the entrance.

"Have Philipp bring in the papers," my uncle ordered.

The servant nodded and hid in the corridor; then the Count turned to us and warned:

"I'm afraid you'll have to wait a bit."

I decided to give my tired legs a rest, sat down in an open armchair and glanced around at the office. It was a bit too snazzy and eclectic for my taste.

Though the awkward pomposity of his

gilded telephone, the extreme complexity of the clock's face on the fireplace shelf and the bulkiness of the Dictaphone for voice recording on wax rollers did somewhat harmonize with one another, the full plate armor and carved shield with family crest and crossed swords looked like true atavism in comparison. New-fangled family photographs on the wall were hung next to ancient portraits of esteemed ancestors. A stack of business papers and heap of telegraph print-outs were lying around on the newspaper table next to a huge, almost half-wall-length aquarium.

Either my uncle had a multi-faceted personality, or he simply didn't know what to do with himself and grasped frantically at one hobby after the next.

If I was a betting man, I'd pick the latter.

Count Kósice looked at me sourly, then turned to the banker who offered up a pocket watch and suggested:

"Mr. Levinson, if your time is limited, please, begin..."

He then opened his leather folder and took a few yellowed sheets out of it.

"Sixteen years ago, the Countess Kósice, née Victoria de Myrte, gave us a number of pieces of jewelry to store. In accordance with her will, they were to go to her daughter, the *Illustrious* Diana Orso. She did not make use of that right, though. What's more, until recently, she was officially registered as a missing person. Only at the end of the last month was her death registered in the proper fashion, making her heir the Illustrious Mr. Leopold Orso, who is present here."

The banker looked at me expectantly. I nodded.

In his day, my dad hadn't wanted to weigh himself down with official business, so I had to do a fair amount of running around to different authorities, filling out documents after his death; without a death certificate, I couldn't even dream of getting my inheritance.

"Unfortunately, his Grace's fiduciary was only able to inform us of your place of employment, Viscount," the banker continued. "We left a message, but before you got in touch with us, we got an offer on today's meeting."

I nodded again, this time with poorly concealed disappointment, because my dead grandmother's jewelry wouldn't be enough to solve all my financial problems.

Just then, the butler came into the office; the count accepted a folder from him, took a quick look inside and handed it to the banker with a self-satisfied smile.

"Mr. Levinson, I think you may find this

document of interest. Please familiarize yourself with it."

He took a monocle on a chain from his pocket, placed it in his eye and set about acquainting himself with the documents.

"This changes things," he replied some time later, stretching his words.

"Beyond all doubt!" smirked Count Kósice, taking the folder back.

Without asking permission, I took the papers and gave a very natural-looking, but feigned start. Atop the sparse pile of documents, there was a death certificate for Leopold Orso.

A certificate of my death, dated fifteen years ago? That simply cannot be!

"What the hell is this nonsense?" I voiced the thought that was slamming around in my head like a terrified bird.

The Count gathered the documents and stated coldly:

"This is a death certificate for my nephew, the *Illustrious* Leopold Orso."

"That's a dirty old forgery!"

"No, young man. I think it's more likely that we are now dealing with a surprisingly impudent impostor," my uncle objected.

"But you know me!"

"When my missing nephew resurfaced after ten years, it filled me with joy. I didn't look into the details! But your financial ambitions forced me to look at the situation in a different light. The investigation that followed showed that you couldn't possibly be the person you claim to be."

"Drop the act!"

But the Count didn't even listen to a single word.

"Philipp, show this young man to the door," he demanded in an icy tone.

"Stop!" I exclaimed, but it was to no effect. The butler had already pinched me up by the shoulder like a louse, and was dragging me out of the office. I thought it below me to try to escape, so I simply pointed at the aquarium:

"Philipp, look at the fish."

The butler mechanically followed my gesture, and his grasp immediately weakened.

"We're in a pond, Philipp. At the very bottom, among the seaweed and fish. Can you feel yourself running out of air? Your lungs are on fire, but you cannot inhale – the only thing around is water..."

The servant grew pale as chalk and hurtled himself headlong out of the office. I turned my head, cracking my neck bones, and when the pain in my eyes had passed, I warned my uncle, his palm already hovering over the call button.

"It's not worth it, Count. Think about your daughters. You still need to get them married off..."

But, as often happens when you try to play on the fears of a person you aren't well acquainted with, my words had the exact opposite of the effect I'd intended. At the mention of his daughters, Count Kósice abruptly lowered his palm, and the buzz of an electric bell rang out in the hallway.

"It would be best, if you left on your own!" my Uncle snapped.

I was not happy with the end of our conversation by any means, so I turned away from the entrance and unbuttoned my jacket. And when two lackeys burst into the office, I threw back my left coattail and smiled:

"Leave us, gentlemen."

My *talent* allowed me to turn people's own fears against them, but now I had decided to rely entirely on the good sense of the servants the Count had called.

And in fact, little awakens good sense in people as quickly as seeing a semi-automatic pistol holstered on an opponent's belt.

The lackeys exchanged glances and slowly walked back out the door. I moved my gaze over to my uncle and shook my head:

"Hmm. What are you hoping to achieve here?"

The Count was choking in rage and

demanded:

"Leave my home! This instant!"

"Not before you explain yourself!" I flared up in reply.

"You're demanding explanations?" Count Kósice narrowed his eyes disdainfully. "And who, exactly, are you to insist on explanations? My nephew, Leopold Orso, is dead. You're nothing but an impostor!"

"Do you think that little fabrication is going to stop me?"

"Fabrication? Prove it!"

"Prove that I am myself? We're getting into *Alice in Wonderland* territory here! And I know exactly which of us isn't being sensible right now!"

"Leave my home," the Count repeated, calmer this time, regaining his self-confidence.

I stared at him for several minutes, assessing the man, decided that there really wasn't anything else for us to talk about and set about buttoning up my jacket.

"We'll see each other again," I promised and went for the exit.

And just then, the banker started gathering his things.

"Leopold! Could I ask for a moment of your time...?"

"Mr. Levinson!" Count Kósice raised his

voice. "I am the only legal executor of property in this family. If you give any of my relative's valuables to this impostor, I'll have to sue you. Is that clear?"

"Oh, dear Count, don't burden yourself with such warnings. Our lawyers understand the law at least as well as your fiduciary," the banker smiled carelessly and hurried me along: "Let's not waste time. Even though more than enough has already been wasted..."

We left the office, walked past the high-strung lackeys and went down the stairs to the first floor. We were met there by Philipp with the whitish-green face of someone who'd just almost drowned. His constant gaze bore down on the back of my head, but all I could do was smile amicably to the butler, take my derby hat from the rack and leave the house.

"Allow me to take you," Mr. Levinson suggested, following behind me.

I had been waiting for just such an offer from the very start, so I immediately answered with agreement.

The banker ordered the roof of the landau folded up, then asked with curiosity:

"Perhaps, my question will seem tactless to you, Leopold, but what happened to the poor butler?"

"Nothing too bad," I smiled. "The poor guy

just felt as if he'd drowned."

"And you can do that to anyone?"

"No, Mr. Levinson. Naturally, I cannot."

"Just Isaac is fine."

"No, Isaac. That trick wouldn't have worked on anyone else."

"Would you allow me to inquire as to why?"

"When he was a child, Philipp almost drowned in a pond. He was just barely saved. His twin brother told me about it. Something like that would have to make a mark on a person. I simply made use of that knowledge, and that's all. It is my *talent*."

"Ah, so that's it!" the banker began smiling. "As far as I understood, you were also trying to poke at a sore place for the Count, then?"

"Unfortunately, I failed at that, though," I frowned, getting into the landau with the man.

We sat opposite one another. The driver gave the reins a shake and the carriage started off. The shock absorbers concealed the unevenness of the village road. The thick rubber wheels rolled easily over stones and potholes. The shaking could practically not be felt.

"Would you like some soda water?" the banker offered, opening a little drawer.

"I wouldn't refuse."

Mr. Levinson took out a soda fountain, and

filled a glass with water. It was sparkling in the sun. He extended the glass to me.

"We are returning to the city," the banker told me after that. "Will you be accompanying me, or getting out at the station?"

I took a few gulps, washing down the unpleasant aftertaste, tossed a mint-flavored sugar drop into my mouth and stated without innuendo:

"That depends on why you're so interested in me, Isaac."

"Whether you see it or not, Viscount," the banker smiled softly at me, "I was in an extremely ticklish situation. Under normal circumstances, you'd have received your deceased grandmother's valuables by the end of the day, but a death certificate – your death certificate! – bound my hands. The Count threatened to sue and, it should be said, he does have grounds."

"And what do we do now?"

"You'll have to get your death certificate annulled by a judge. Unfortunately, that process can take years and years."

"Curses!" I let out. "And all over some little fabrication!"

"There's hardly a way to prove that the document was made after the fact."

I nodded.

According to the Imperial Code of Justice

on Missing Persons, a person can only be declared dead if they've been missing for more than a year, so my uncle had had more than enough time to get the ill-fated evidence on absolutely legal grounds. And though he didn't deign to get it done as early as possible, I wouldn't be finding any real evidence of wrongdoing either.

"Leopold, is there anyone who knew you before..." Isaac stumbled but still continued, "the tragic event?"

"No," I shook my head. "The Count and Countess were bombed by anarchists; that happened not long before we were... cursed. All our servants died that very night, while my father met his end six years ago. And I returned only after that..."

"Any relatives from his side?"

"No one left," I assured the man. "Only my uncle, that son of a..."

"We won't have to rely on the Count's support," he smiled softly.

I winced and wondered again:

"Isaac, what is your interest in this?"

"Can you say how many debts you've accumulated?" The banker surprised me with an unexpected question. "I don't need an exact number, just an approximation."

"Thirty or forty thousand," I answered, in

that I didn't see it as especially secret information. "Definitely not more than forty."

"You accumulated that much debt in six years?" Mr. Levinson looked at me with respect. "What a talent you've got!"

All I could do was laugh.

"A large part of that was left to me by my father. And interest on that debt had also run up to a pretty respectable sum."

"It would do you no credit, but you could have refused to accept responsibility for his debts."

"That's actually not true. Dad had the custom of taking loans against my inheritance, and his partners," I sighed, "are not the kind to easily come to terms with losing so much."

"And you mortgaged your house, which is of no value, because of this quarantine, with the condition that you would pay it all back only after you get control over the family fund?"

"That's right."

"And because you hit twenty-one this year, creditors have started to express impatience, no?"

I nodded.

"Think," the banker said thoughtfully, "how would they react if the Count were to expose you as an impostor on the basis of the death certificate he is in possession of?"

"How would they react? Not well!" I snorted,

remembering the Chinese moneylender and frowning. "I've sprouted a couple new few gray hairs over this, you know..."

Mr. Levinson leaned back into the seat and spent some time distantly observing the bright yellow fields of alfalfa. On them, there were sharp breaks of wind chasing after waves of dark green.

"If the Banking House buys out your debts," he said a little while later, "let's say, for ten centimes on the franc, how would you think about that?"

"I would think," I laughed uncontrollably, "that you and I do have something to discuss after all!"

5

WHEN WE GOT BACK to town, evening was already coming. We had been *en route* for some time, but we had been made to wait at a train crossing for the unhurried caterpillar treads of an armored train to crawl past us out toward to the seaside, snarling in all directions with its cannon barrels, mortars and double-barreled AA machine guns.

But as for lost time, I had no regrets,

because Mr. Levinson was not only an interesting man to talk to, he was also a skilled financial consultant. Over the course of the trip, my debts, which had been sitting at forty thousand francs, managed to shrink to the utterly laughable sum of four thousand, and even the two thousand the banker asked in commission didn't seem too much, given the ticklish and confusing situation.

By the way, Isaac's main interest was not so much in receiving a one-time pay-off as it was in managing my assets after I inherited the family fund. And I was in no way opposed to that.

"If this is all ok with you," the banker announced near the end of the trip, "I propose we go to the bank and sign all the documents right now. We don't have time to waste after your uncle declares you an impostor."

"I do not object," I answered irresolutely.

The carriage was now rolling through the outskirts of New Babylon, and the driver was looking carefully from side to side, stopping the horses yet again as another dumb pedestrian ran across the carriageway. And at one of the intersections, he suddenly turned off a wide avenue and started the landau circling a dark manufacturing building with a forest of smoking pipes on the roof. After that, the road started descending and soon dove into a tunnel. On its walls, there were chains of electric lights stretching out from one end to the other.

The hoof-beat gave off a long echo inside. Eventually, though, we made it out to a dull spot of light at the exit. There, the landau had a near miss with a heavily-weighed-down cart and turned down an unfamiliar street where the acrid odor of smoke suddenly rolled down my throat and forced me to start coughing.

The banker covered the bottom of his face with a perfumed handkerchief in good time, then warned:

"The air will be getting cleaner soon."

And in fact, the gray behemoth warehouses were left behind us very quickly, and manors extended down along the roadside, as well as homes that had been split into offices. The asphalt pavement came to an end. The landau began shaking again on the uneven cobblestone causeway, and then the carriage entered the Judean Quarter and the driver stopped the horses directly opposite the bank. A watchman ran up from the porch, and hurried to fling open the gate. I was first to get out onto the sidewalk. There, I waited for Isaac Levinson and followed him into the manor.

The banker took a key ring from a homely gentleman of thirty years with a crimson birth mark on half of his left cheek and turned to me.

"We never stop working, Viscount!" he told

me with pride. "You will never be left to face your problems alone."

"Except on Saturday," I chuckled.

"Except on Saturday," Mr. Levinson confirmed. "Every other day, we're at your service." And he pointed at the man who had handed him the keys: "In my absence, important clients are received by Aaron Malk."

The plain man gave me a slight bow.

"Nice to meet you," I smiled in reply.

"Leopold, you'll come to see the value of working with us soon!" Mr. Levinson assured me, leading me to the second floor.

The banker's office was furnished so neutrally, that there was no interior detail that even gave away his nationality. It was just a regular old office.

"Don't worry. Filling out the papers won't take long. I took pains to order them filled out in advance," Isaac warned, stopping in the doorway and asking: "Wine, fruit?"

"Thank you, I don't need anything," I refused, took a seat in the guest chair and took the newspaper lying on the coffee table.

The editorial was, as I could have expected, devoted to yet another incident in the Sea of Judea. On the second page, some professor from the medical academy was expanding on a heart problem the heir to the throne was suffering from. And just after I turned the next page, the banker had returned with the papers.

He placed the weighty stack on the table and started looking into them, searching for inaccuracies.

"To be honest," I chuckled, "I never imagined my uncle would dig in so deeply over just twenty thousand francs of yearly income. For him, that must be so little..."

"You shouldn't say that" he shook his head, continuing to play solitaire with the contracts, instructions and declarations before him. "Count Kósice, like many other well-to-do dilettantes, has an inflated opinion of his own analytical abilities. Sharp changes in stock exchange quotation fairly frequently catch such individuals, I beg your forgiveness, with their pants down."

"So he's bankrupt?"

"I suppose that this twenty thousand in yearly income has long been part of his future income calculations," the banker decided, tearing himself from the papers and asking: "Would you like to see the inventory of the property we have been storing on your grandmother's behalf?"

"What's the point?" I sighed. I then practically jumped out of my chair, as I felt the whole building shake from basement to ceiling in a serious explosion.

The windows sputtered with shards. Paintings started swinging on the wall, and the clock fell over, shattering completely into pieces.

Somehow, I got out of the armchair and, on shaky legs, limped over to the window. I brushed the shards of glass from the wide window-sill, bent over, stepped out and looked at the street. I saw a man in a gas mask, armored cuirass, and a steel army helmet climbing out a hole in the wall. He flew headlong at an armored car on the street, then the building shook again in an even more powerful explosion, and wisps of orange flame began pouring out of the hole in the wall.

What the devil?!

What is happening? Do these robbers really plan to clear out the bank in the middle of the day?

As it turned out, no. The bomber didn't return to the hole in the wall; instead, he pulled a hand-held Madsen machine gun from the open door of the armored car, ran around the self-propelled carriage and laid it out on the sett street.

A long trill broke through the ringing in my ears; a moment later, two constables jumped out of the next alley over and a police carriage turned out behind them. And, as dryly as ever, his rapid fire kept sputtering away. Horses, retreating in a long line, were clogging up the causeway. The constables, caught unawares, threw themselves every which way. One hid behind a corner, while another stayed lying on the blood-soaked causeway.

From the other side, a police armored car rolled out onto the intersection; a think slash in one of its portholes glimmered with two sparks, but just then, another bandit appeared from who-knows-where with a hand-held mortar. A shot rumbled out with a boom. The explosion of the grenade ripped the armor sheet from the windshield, and the smoke-enshrouded self-propelled carriage drove off the street into the corner of the house opposite.

The mortarist strained to plunk down the lever again, turning the drum of the awkward weapon, and shot it a second time, but this time not at the armored car, but at the glass window of the barber shop. The grenade broke through it and tore inside. A mess of glass was spit out onto the street; a glass-riddled armchair bounced out.

I took my Roth-Steyr from its holster, popped in a bullet, and tried to aim, but my arms were beginning to tremble in anxiety. Just to be sure, I had to clench the grip with both hands, and even then, the recoil moved the barrel too much. My first shot missed its target.

The mortarist turned and threw up his head in confusion. I took advantage of the moment and plunged my finger down on the trigger again. The bullet pinged off the man's army helmet. The bandit just shook, then raised his hand mortar and aimed it at my window. In a panic, I opened fire in a disorganized fashion, unloading practically my whole magazine before one of the shots hit him in the shoulder, which was not protected by his armored cuirass.

The robber's shot-through arm couldn't hold his weapon, and its barrel fell to the earth, but the wounded bird himself suddenly darted off toward the wall. As soon as I stepped back in the window, with a roar, the back side of the armored car was facing me, revealing a six-barreled Gatling gun. Sparks flew from the contact points on my electric jar. The barrels began spinning and I climbed down from the window sill to the floor without slowing down.

"Get down! Quickly!" I shouted to Isaac Levinson, covering my head with my hands. Meanwhile, Isaac had just come to his senses and was shaking his head cluelessly, standing in the middle of the room.

The banker ducked under the table just as a taught lash of lead whipped against the windows. The high-caliber bullets instantly took what was left of the glass out of the frames and went straight through the wooden ceilings. The durable stone walls, though, were a harder nut to crack. We didn't get hit, but wood splinters and chips of white paint were falling on our heads.

After unloading my Roth-Steyr, I got the backup magazine out of my pocket, stuck it up to the lower edge of the ejection port, and pressed the rounds in with my thumb in a well-practiced motion, driving them into the pistol. I pulled out an emptied hunk of metal, and the bolt went back into place all on its own.

"Leopold!" Levinson suddenly shouted out to me, looking out from under the table. "Fire!" he pointed at the door, which had flames lapping up from behind it.

Ducking down as not to get caught by a stray ricochet, I crossed the office, grabbed the copper door handle and threw back my palm with a curse. My glove had protected my fingers from a burn, but the metal had heated up to a degree that seemed excessive.

What was happening?!

Deftly, I flung open the door and involuntarily covered my face from the fire that was smoking up into it. The whole corridor was in the embrace of the smoking flames, but neither fire nor black smoke could impede my view of the figure standing at the stairwell in a long dress with a shiny coating of aluminum foil, a steel helmet and a gas mask with glass eye slots.

When I appeared, the arsonist lifted the nose-piece of his backpack flamethrower and a stream of liquid flame rolled out of it down the corridor. I managed to slam the office door shut before it came inside, though.

The fire outside roared up and fell silent; then I threw the pistol and took a few shots in a row through the thick oak paneling, not so much in hopes of hitting the man as hoping to stop him from coming any closer and burning us alive.

"What's out there?!" Isaac screamed in fear after the shooting had quieted down. "Who were you shooting at?"

Ignoring his outburst, I cracked the door slightly and peeked out into the corridor; the fire on the other side was so fierce that I had to take an immediate step back.

The flames flared up very quickly. Any delay threatened a torturous, fiery death, but could we really jump out of the window with the bandits still firing on it?!

Could we run out into the corridor and make it down the stairs? What about the flame-thrower?

I turned around toward the banker and asked him:

"Is there any exit from here other than the stairs?"

"Wouldn't it be easier..."

"No, devil! It wouldn't!"

"The back door is at the far end of the corridor," Isaac hinted. Not able to hold back any longer, he burst out to a scream again: "What is happening, Viscount?!"

I could hear unconcealed fear in his voice. I too felt gob-smacked by sheer terror. I wanted to just cower under the table and close my eyes as tightly as possible. Instead, I walked up to the banker and shook him by the shoulder.

"Calm down!" I bellowed at his reddened face. "Have you got any soda water?"

"Soda water?" Isaac was taken aback, but immediately got himself together and ran up to the bar. "Yes!"

"Bring it to me! Quickly!"

The banker flung open the little cabinet, filled to the brim with all kinds of bottles and got a bubbly soda fountain hose out from it. I then ripped the curtain down from one of the windows and threw it on the floor.

"Pour it here!" I commanded the banker. I then ripped down a second one and hurried him along: "Faster! Soak them both!"

Streams of gasified water slopped out onto the firm fabric, and when the soda fountain ran dry, we wrapped ourselves from head to toe and walked up to the door.

"No need to turn at all!" Isaac warned. "The

back door to the stairs is straight down the corridor."

"Keys?" I outstretched my arm.

"That door is never locked. We only lock the entrance!"

"Then follow me!" I commanded, first to jump out into the hallway.

At once, it became unbearably warm and stuffy. Air came into my lungs like superheated sand. Flames lapped at my legs. It felt like I'd just woken up in a forge. I had to walk blind, feeling for the walls and Mr. Levinson, but without the wet curtains, the fierce flames would have been searing out my eyes and burning through my skin to the bone.

After running into an unexpected obstacle, I first froze in horror, then remembered, flung open the door and burst out onto the top stair of the back door; Isaac Levinson came out after me, ripped the smoking fabric off himself and plopped down on his knees in a heart-rending coughing fit. And though we had left the fire on the other side of the door, wisps of smoke were already starting to creep in, and there was simply no air to breathe.

With the handle of my pistol, I bashed in a very thin window; we got up close to it, breathed in deeply and the banker pulled me down the stairs.

"This way!"

But there was such a fierce fire spreading from the first floor that it immediately became clear to me that monkeying around down there was equivalent to suicide.

"Let's jump for it!" I commanded and flung open the glass-shard filled window frame.

"We'll have a nasty fall!" Isaac grew alarmed.

I didn't listen though, climbed up onto the window sill and looked down. The ceilings in this building were, in fact, raised, but the risk of breaking my legs was somewhat less frightening than the perspective of being burned alive.

I announced as much to him, grabbed onto the sloped roof and hung out the window. And as soon as I unclenched my fingers, the ground quickly and sharply struck the soles of my shoes. Building walls, a fence and a wisp of sky were spinning before my eyes. I was sprawled out on the gravel, but immediately grabbed my pistol.

There was no one there.

"Jump!" I then shouted at my brother-in-misfortune and ran up to the back door. From behind it, I could hear muted screams for help.

Isaac climbed out the window, hung off the roof and fell downward with a thump. I kicked the door in with all my might, but didn't find success. I pulled it as hard as I could toward me, but again without result.

"Viscount, the keys!"

Levinson threw me a keyring. I caught it in the air, found the right key and unlocked the door. Together with the wisps of acrid smoke, Aaron Malk, who had been scratching away at the other side, burst in. I had to push him aside, clearing the way.

"Take care of him!" I shouted to the banker, then took several heavy sighs, ventilating my lungs. But before I had stepped into the burning building, the hiss of the backpack flamethrower came back and covered up the cries of the people calling for help. My face buried in my arm, I slipped around the corner, and noticed the silver reflections of a sewn-on aluminum foil coat through the sheet of flame that enshrouded the vestibule.

The arsonist was already rushing for the exit, but I still pulled my Roth-Steyr and sent a couple bullets out after him. They struck one of the gas tanks on his back, and the man was swallowed up in a large burst of flame. Me though, the air blast threw into the air and simply tossed outside...

I AWOKE FROM A SCATHING SLAP. The banker and his assistant had dragged me away from the burning bank, leaned me up against a fence and brought me to my senses with the only means available to them at the time.

My head was ringing very badly.

"Oh devil..." I muttered, massaging my temples with my palms.

"Are you doing alright?" Levinson leaned in over me.

I mumbled back a "yes," and the banker ordered:

"Aaron, gather our employees."

Malk ran off for help and I stood up, limped over to my fallen Roth-Steyr and placed the pistol into its holster. After that, I wiped the soot from my glasses, turned to the banker and sat next to him. The fire had reached the roof. Some of the tiles were already falling in, and though the fire-fighters arrived not long after, dragging their fire hose behind themselves, they weren't so much trying to put out the flames as they were trying to stop them from reaching neighboring buildings. It was a blessing that it wasn't a windy day.

"They will pay for this," Levinson said suddenly. "No matter who did it, they will pay..."

With a trembling hand, I took a tin of sugar drops from my pocket, tossed a mint candy into my mouth and noted pointedly:

"The key word here is 'who.'"

"What do you mean, Leopold?" The banker grew surprised.

I shrugged my shoulders, collecting my thoughts, then admitted honestly:

"I am not at all sure that the detectives will pick up the trail."

"Why not?" He grew surprised.

"Did you see the weapons those criminals had?" I snorted, beginning to enumerate them: "Flamethrower, Gatling gun, hand-held mortar! And also an armored car! There are army divisions that aren't equipped that well!"

Isaac Levinson measured me up with his careful gaze and clarified:

"You don't think they'll be found?"

"I know my colleagues," I chuckled. "You did hear about the tunnels being dug under your bank, right? Was anyone arrested after that? No? There you have it, then."

The banker took out a rumpled kerchief and began wiping down his soot-schmutzed face.

"And you?" he asked carefully a bit later. "You, Mr. Orso. Could you find them?"

"Perhaps," I answered just as cautiously.

"Then, do it!" Levinson demanded. He spent some time in silence and added: "Find them and kill them. Money is no object."

In reply to his offer, I just shook my head:

"Isaac, we work in an era of division of labor. I am prepared to take up the search for the robbers. You will have to deal with the rest on your own."

He nodded several times, thinking over my words and asked:

"Would five hundred francs do as an advance?"

"That would be more than enough," I answered, not trying to mess around with the price. "More than..."

A HALF-HOUR LATER, I was standing on the edge of Euler bridge rubbing my chin in thought and looking into the troubled waters of the Yarden. The advance was searing my conscious with a hot poker. I was in possession of five brand-new hundred-franc notes that any decent person would return to the banker without the slightest delay.

I had always supposed myself a person of the highest order of decency, which is why I was now standing in deep contemplation at the very edge of the bridge, stroking my chin and looking down. I didn't even have to lean over the railing. It had been pulled off by the armored car in its attempts to evade pursuit. It was pulled off, fell down and sunk to the bottom like a stone. According to eyewitness reports, no one had gotten out of the car either.

How could I possibly earn a check from this?

While I stood there, gazing unthinkingly at the river, a police carriage rolled up to the fence. Next to the driver, there was a red-mustached yellow-eyed detective sitting on the driver box with sergeant detective patches on his uniform.

I supposed that it was the inspector arriving, but just then the doors of the carriage flung open and the head of the CID stepped out, Maurice LeBrun in the flesh. What was more, he was accompanied by Bastian Moran!

Wearing a cloak with a white neck-scarf tied on carelessly, he wasn't very reminiscent of a police inspector, but his artificial serenity still inspired fear somewhat more than the rage-reddened bull-dog face of LeBrun.

Devil! – and so I fainted.

Devil! Devil! Devil!

Without this, I was already in Department Three's field of view for my potential involvement in the death of Robert White, who had been torn to pieces in the Judean Quarter, and now I was spotted at a second attempt to rob the Witstein Banking House! Senior Inspector Moran would be quite unlikely to consider this a simple coincidence. And if he tried to get a search warrant for my estate, I would be done for. The glass jar with the heart of a *fallen one* inside would be reason enough to accuse me of anti-scientific activities.

Devil, what made me drag that thing home!

I felt waves of panic rolling over me, but forced myself to calm down. Even with an order to search my family estate, it wouldn't be that easy. Not every *illustrious* person has the wherewithal to go inside a cursed mansion. And for normal people, even setting one foot on my property was a death sentence. The Diabolic Plague was no joke.

And I calmed down. But my tranquility didn't last long.

"What the devil is this man doing at the crime scene? He shouldn't be here!" The head of the CID shouted out on his way to the sentry constable.

He just cluelessly batted his eyes; then LeBrun turned around and flew directly at me with the single-minded determination of a torpedo.

I decided that he would probably grab me, persona-non-grata that I was, by my chest and throw me from the bridge, but I didn't move away from the gap in the fence. Instead, I got out the letter of attorney signed by Isaac Levinson.

"Mr. LeBrun!" I extended it to my boss. "In this investigation, I will be representing the injured party, the Witstein Banking House."

"What the devil?" LeBrun bellowed, ripping the paper from me and immersing himself in reading. "This is ridiculous!" he gasped a few seconds later. "Constable, how'd your head get so swelled up?!"

"In that I have been suspended," I reminded him, "there is no conflict of interest."

The head of Criminal Investigations measured me up with an unkind gaze and turned to Bastian Moran, who was smoking in total calm near the self-propelled carriage. He took one last drag of his cigarette and, with a flick, sent the butt into the troubled waters of the Yarden.

"Maurice, he has every right to be here," the senior inspector warned his fuming colleague.

"I don't like it!" the head of the CID declared in annoyance, returning the letter of attorney and demanding: "Constable, get out of here immediately!"

"Maurice!" Bastian Moran tried to persuade him. "We don't need complications with Judean society, now do we?"

The last thing I wanted was to be caught between hammer and anvil, so I hurried to disarm the situation.

"Excuse me, but there is no longer any need for my presence," I assured the upper leadership and gradually moved away from the gap in the fence.

"Is that so?" Senior Inspector Moran suddenly smiled. "And what is your verdict, detective constable?"

I shrugged my shoulders, but still gave voice to the obvious scenario in my mind:

"The robbers lost control of their vehicle when trying to evade police pursuit, went through the fence on the bridge and fell into the water."

"That sounds about right," Moran smiled. "Shall we pack it in then?"

"Not yet," I replied, gathering the bravery to oppose my senior in title. "We still have to find their accomplices and where they got the arms from. Other than that, we must recover the armored car and make an inventory of everything that was stolen. The bank manager insists that I be present for that, as well."

"Go!" Maurice LeBrun waved it off. "We will inform the bank of the precise time the armored car will be raised!"

"Thank you," I nodded and turned my gaze to Bastian Moran. "Is that all, senior inspector?"

"I suppose, constable, that you should first answer the investigator's questions," he said, shaking his head. "Based on your appearance, it seems you were present for the robbery, right?"

I tossed my gaze over my hopelessly soiled suit and smiled, showing that I had appreciated the inspector's joke.

"The bank manager and I were out for

negotiations with my Uncle, the Count Kósice, but by the time of the attack, we had already returned to town and were in the bank."

Senior Inspector Moran took out a pack of Chesterfields, slid a cigarette from it, then waved his hands at a red-mustached detective sergeant:

"Interrogate the constable!"

"Behind the police line!" LeBrun added, turning to his colleague and reproaching him: "Bastian, your genius idea of leaving an ambush party at the bank has deprived us of three excellent men!"

"Maurice!" the Department Three official smiled softly. "The idea, as you can see, completely and totally justified itself. Where we dropped the ball was in the execution. What would it have cost us to have stationed two armored cars there?"

"And who was it harping on about secrecy?"

I wasn't able to hear the senior inspector's answer, but I had enough to understand everything.

Bastian Moran had foreseen the bank robbery.

Curses! This story smelled worse than I originally imagined!

6

I RETURNED HOME long after midnight. The investigator had managed, in the most natural fashion, to drink up all my blood, no question of vampires! And though he brought me to the Newton-Markt in a service carriage, I'd had to find my own way back home. In other words, I went on foot.

I walked up onto the porch of my manor, limping, yet having little idea of how tired my legs were. As soon as I opened the front door, I was caught by the unusual aroma of cooking. I remembered the dinner I had been promised and winced in shame, but still went into the dining hall, lit by only a pair of candelabras, their candles burned down a fair amount. The table in the middle of the room was set for two, and Elizabeth-Maria was sitting at the head.

The girl gave me a salute with a glass of red wine and asked me pointedly:

"You know something, Leopold? I'm starting to get the impression that you're avoiding me."

"And what if I am?" I frowned, still standing

in the doorway. "What of it?"

"That would be very impolite," Elizabeth-Maria reproached me, and suddenly raised her voice as if she had the right to give orders here. "Theodor!" she called.

The butler walked into the hall through the second door, set down a dish and removed its top so gracefully that it looked like he had done nothing but set tables his whole life.

"I'll go get myself in order," I told the girl.

"Leopold!" she objected. "Dinner is getting cold!"

"Do you seriously think I can sit at the dinner table looking like this?"

"Leopold!"

There was a metallic ring in the succubus's voice, telling me that it was easier to try her cooking than explain why I didn't want to. Nevertheless, was I a man of my word, or not? To start, I went off to wash up and change clothes, then returned to the table, placed my napkin in my lap and started poking around in the incomprehensible victuals with my fork. I stabbed cautiously into a piece of meat, sent it down my throat and suddenly discovered that its subtle, picante flavor was actually quite nice.

"I never would have thought the cooking was so nice in the underworld," I generously complimented, chewing a second piece.

"Oh, Leopold!" Elizabeth-Maria rolled her eyes. "You have no idea of the lofty heights achieved by our culinary arts, especially considering the poor selection of products!"

Even if the girl was seriously counting on driving away my appetite, she didn't manage. I washed the spicy meat down with a gulp of water and set about shoveling down my dinner even more forcefully than before.

"Aren't you hungry?" I asked the succubus, who hadn't eaten a single morsel, instead just drinking wine.

"I got full while cooking," she answered.

"So this is all for me?"

"Just for you, my dear Leopold," Elizabeth-Maria confirmed. "That must flatter you. Not many get the chance to enjoy the work of chefs such as myself."

I nodded.

"We've never had much luck with cooks," I smiled, pushing away my half-emptied plate. "Our second to last one had to be fired over his penchant for alcohol. And the last one simply disappeared with all our silver tableware."

"Is that so?" the girl laughed uncontrollably and turned to the butler who'd just poured her more wine: "Theodor, how could this be? I'd have thought you'd have pecked that villain to death."

My servant didn't answer right away. He

held a pause, collecting his thoughts and started from afar:

"My ancestors have served the Kósice family for many generations. I have never had another master, and I could not even imagine that someone might not appreciate the stroke of luck it is to work here."

Elizabeth-Maria thoughtfully raised her red eyebrow:

"You're telling me that even death couldn't waver your loyalty?"

"Oh, mademoiselle!" the butler allowed himself a patronizing smile. "A dead man finds it quite simple to remain loyal. Worldly temptations and trials are no longer an impediment."

"Surprising permanence," the girl shook her head and turned her attention to me. "Leopold, don't you like it? You're not eating very much."

"I'm not hungry," I answered and asked: "What is it, by the way? I can't figure it out."

"It's heart," Elizabeth-Maria told me with a sweet smile. "In redcurrant sauce. And the main course will be chicken liver roasted with red pepper, tomato, basil and parsley."

"Organ meat," I screwed up my face, though I wasn't actually given to particular squeamishness. Life had taught me not to be.

"Dear, you yourself accused me of spending too much!" the girl reminded me. "Organ meat is cheap and nutritious!"

"The spices were probably more expensive than the meat!"

"Meat without spices is like steak without blood," Elizabeth-Maria shook her head and, to make sure nothing remained unsaid, thought it necessary to explain herself. "It's just not palatable!" she announced, getting up from the table and going into the guest room.

Theodor gathered the plates and asked:

"Would you like the main course now, or dessert?"

"Dessert," I decided. "And serve it in my bedroom. And also, light the boiler. I'd like to take a bath."

"As you say, Viscount."

The butler brought the dirty dishes to the kitchen, while I followed after Elizabeth-Maria. I took one step into the guest room and froze like I was entombed. I suddenly found myself face-to-face with a sharp saber taken down from the wall.

"Defend!" the girl said, but immediately retreated and turned away, spinning the blade in a tried-and-true motion. I heard the buzzing of a strip of air being split open by the finely-honed steel.

"Drop it," I asked her.

Elizabeth-Maria glanced at me with an unhidden smirk, but still returned the saber to its place above the fireplace.

"Do you not fence?" she asked.

"No."

"And why's that?"

"If you let your opponent get to within slashing distance, you've wasted the last moments of your life for nothing. That's what my father always said."

"And you agree with him?"

I nodded:

"Without reservation."

"Your good judgment is one in a million."

"It's in my blood," I shrugged my shoulders, thanking the girl once again for the wonderful dinner. I went up to my bedroom where Theodor was already bringing a saucer of tea and a little basket of biscuits.

But I wasn't able to drink my tea in peace: as soon as I had taken off my neckerchief, Elizabeth-Maria slipped into the door.

"You smell of death," she stated, thoughtfully twirling a red lock of hair around her finger.

"It's smoke," I corrected the girl. "I smell of smoke."

"No," she laughed uncontrollably, "it's

death."

"Please, leave me!"

"Leo," Elizabeth-Maria sighed, taking a seat on the bed, "I would do so gladly, but you're the one holding me up here, not the other way around."

"Balderdash!" I waved it off. "You could go to hell right now for all I care!"

"Your words are nothing but empty trembling in the air. What is important is your true desires. After all, it was no accident that you were so eager for the chance to have your very own succubus! In fact, you do not want to let me go. You thirst for something else entirely. So go and reap the fruits of your labor," Elizabeth-Maria led her hand over her thigh, "maybe one day you'll have enough of me..."

Desire rolled up in a hot wave, but I didn't move from my place. Even the thought of doing so didn't strike me. From under the mask of the wonderful girl created by my imagination, out stepped an unmistakably demonic countenance with eyes that burned with the fires of hell and a mouth overcrowded with tiny sharp teeth.

If I listened closely, I could hear her sharp claws scratching against the silk fabric of her dress. If I inhaled through my nose, it smelled of sulfur.

"Come now, Leo! Come to me!" The girl

struck an even more tempting pose and licked her upper lip with her split-end tongue. "After all, this is what you want! Your shyness prevented you from admitting your love, but you have no reason whatsoever to be shy around me. You are my lord and sovereign! You can do whatever you desire to me! After all, isn't that what you wanted?"

"No," I answered quietly, pouring myself some tea and taking a biscuit from the little basket. I took a bite, held it for a bit, enjoying the flavor and poured myself some of the hot bitter beverage. "I realize perfectly that a large part of you is in my own head. And the rest is a slimy, cold beast who I would never share a bed with, even under pain of death."

Elizabeth-Maria leaned her head on her hand and looked at me with unhidden interest. The crimson shadows in her eyes began to disperse slightly.

"So my attention doesn't flatter you at all?" the girl asked.

I pointed to the door.

The succubus laughed gruffly and got up onto the bed.

"Sooner or later, I will have your soul," she told me.

"Why won't you just leave me in peace?"

"I'm afraid, little boy, that will not be

possible." Elizabeth-Maria pretended that she was going to strike me on the cheek, but she retreated before finishing the motion. "We are bound by an arrangement and your soul is like a battered dingy: it is rocking on the waves, stopping my descent to the depths."

"Excellent metaphor," I remarked, praising the succubus's imagery.

"But, do you know, Leo, that there are so many holes in your soul that it will soon sink to the bottom and drag me down with it? To the very bottom and even further: directly to the underworld."

The girl turned away and strode off for the exit with such blistering speed that I was barely able to call back to her:

"And why are you so certain that I will sink to the bottom?"

"You smell of death," Elizabeth-Maria answered simply and went out the door.

I took another cookie and, mug in hand, walked over to the window and spent some time looking at the night-enshrouded city without a thought in my head. Nearer the downtown, the darkness didn't look quite as impenetrable. There you could see the glow of street lights warming the air. And on the top of every tall tower there were flashing signal lights. Then, very, very high up, you could just barely make out a dull orange flickering lost in the stars. That was the lights of a freight dirigible.

I smell of death?

Balderdash! It's just smoke.

Smoke and nothing more. But still, it couldn't hurt to wash up.

So I headed for the bathroom.

First, I locked the door behind me, then set my chronometer, wallet and both pistols on the shelf. I walked up to the huge copper tub, which stood in the middle of the room on wrought-iron claw-feet.

A weariness came over me from an unknown source. I leaned against the cold metal and suddenly realized that I was burning up all over. The Diabolic Plague, which hadn't been bothering me all day, had returned and I had the feeling that I was running down the fire-filled corridor once again. Only now, there wasn't a water-soaked curtain around me. In fact, the flame was inside.

Pustules on my body lit up with a crimson glow; I turned on the cold water faucet and stuck my arms under the frozen stream, but that didn't bring me any particular relief.

My heart was beating nervously and unevenly. I could taste blood in my mouth.

Then I lied down in the empty bathtub like a vampire climbing into a coffin, and the cold copper quenched the fire burning inside me with an unexpected speed. It grew chilly; I gave a little shiver and opened the second faucet, its pipe leading to a bulbous tank under which the little flame of a gas burner was trembling. I adjusted both streams, popped in the wooden stopper and relaxed, enjoying the silence and calm. I no longer felt either cold or hot. Gradually, I was overcome with calm and drowsy relaxation...

I was forced awake by a blast of cold air.

"Hey! I locked the door!" I said with reproach, not turning my head.

"Didn't anyone ever tell you how dangerous it is to fall asleep in a bath?" Elizabeth-Maria wondered with a quiet giggling. "You might fall asleep and not wake up again. Not ever."

"Eventually, we all fall asleep and don't wake up. Life is full of surprises."

"... said Judas Iscariot, as he took the thirty pieces of silver," the succubus added on to my utterance, continuing with a smirk: "'But it must be said that it has a very predictable end,' he added while throwing a noose around his neck."

"Is that so?" I snorted.

"That's what they say," the girl sounded off carelessly, placing her thin little fingers on the back and top of my head, messing up my hair, pressing, and massaging my skin. "Just think,

Leo, how easy it would be for me to apply a small modicum of effort and hold you under the water for a minute or two..."

"Drop it!"

"You're not afraid of that at all?"

"Drowning in my own bathtub is not one of my biggest fears, no."

"Oh, tell me what they are," Elizabeth-Maria purred softly into my ear. "I want to know you better so badly..."

"Be gone," I demanded.

"Sooner or later, I'll unravel all your secrets."

"You're wasting your time."

"Then just tell me." The girl went away from the bath and stood opposite the mirror, admiring the reflection of her own naked body. "Start with how you became a murderer, Leo."

"I'm not a murderer."

Elizabeth-Maria let my answer pass right by her ears.

"How many souls do you have on your conscious, huh?" she asked. "How many lives have you taken, Leo?"

"If you want to talk about my conscience, it's clean. Yes, I've had to kill, but it was only ever in self-defense."

"Is that so?" the girl laughed uncontrollably, totally sincerely this time, with her whole heart. "Do you really believe that? You killed a man today. Was that also self-defense?"

I went silent. I wanted to answer that it was, but I remembered shooting him in the back, so I just said nothing. The robber with the flamethrower had already left; he was guilty of many deaths, but to be honest, he was not a threat to my life at the time I killed him.

I simply wanted to get revenge for my fear and pain. I wanted to kill him, so I did. I took the role of high judge on myself.

And I didn't want to admit that. So I didn't.

But just after I opened my eyes, the succubus splashed me in the face with a handful of water.

"If you don't plan on talking with me, would you be so kind as to get out of the tub?" she demanded. "Taking a bath together is too fraught with potential loss of control for you, and you're so delicate and vulnerable. Or do you think you can risk it?"

I cursed wordlessly, got out of the bath and rubbed around my thighs with a towel. Making a show of not looking at the girl's naked body, I scooped up my things from the shelf and sloshed my wet feet out of the room.

"How did a young boy become a murderer, Leo?" came her next question, this time at my back.

And I stayed silent again.

I closed the door behind myself, carefully leaving it slightly ajar and headed off to sleep.

7

ALL NIGHT, SOMEONE was scratching at the blinds trying to break in.

All night, someone was messing around in my cabinet, moving my things around and cursing.

All night, a dead chef washed bloodied silver tableware.

All night, Theodor colored in a photograph of his twin brother with colored pencils.

All night, the naked Elizabeth-Maria danced circles with the saber and a huge kitchen knife.

But all in all, it was nothing out of the ordinary. I was just having nightmares.

All night, straight through.

IN THE END, I WOKE UP feeling beaten down, with a headache and a brokenness in my whole body.

Expending a certain amount of effort, I peeled my eye open. I extricated my hands from under the comforter and took a breath with relief.

The bumps were asleep. My skin, after being singed by the blood of the *fallen one*, had returned to its normal color, and my palms no longer felt like they were on fire.

Now that is excellent!

To be honest, after such a sleepless night, it wouldn't have surprised me at all to find myself covered in the glowing pustules of the Diabolic Plague from head to toe.

The only thing that worried me was my leg. I hurt it in my jump from the second story. A painful broken feeling had now taken up residence. But it would never be a problem: I had the habit of recuperating from any ailment like a stray dog. I hadn't even gotten a cold since I was a child.

After going into the bathroom, I got dressed, flung open the scratched-up blinds and looked from the hilltop onto the city, enshrouded in a layer of hazy smog even at this early hour. The sun had just begun to rise over the horizon and was coloring the gray smoke every shade of red, from the pale pink of rosé wine to the deep crimson of arterial blood.

Blood again? What in the world was that about?!

I swore to myself and went down to the first floor. I'd had no appetite since morning, so I went directly to the garden where the dead trees were stretching their denuded branches up to the sky. For a long time, the only thing remaining of the grass was dust. Just shrubs remained, shaking their dried-out flowers, black and fragile. The presence of the curse could be felt here even more unmistakably than in the manor, and I felt prickly little ants crawling up my spine.

But I didn't go back into my house. Instead, I walked a confused little path to a field containing a bare rock slab. I spent some time standing there in silence, then walked around the prickly bushes and stopped at the second gravestone. I stood next to it.

After that, I returned to the manor, took a seat on the upper step and nodded thankfully at Theodor, who had brought me out a saucer of tea and a little dish of marzipan candies.

"Thank you."

"Think nothing of it, Viscount."

I picked up yesterday's paper from the porch, shook it off, smoothed it out and took a look at the top headline.

"Engineer Disappears Mysteriously!" the headline shouted. My interest caught by the flamboyant delivery, I looked at the article over, but was not able to figure out exactly why the disappearance of a certain Rudolf Diesel from a locked train car had caused so much commotion.

After turning the page, I studied the

unfortunate story on the "event" in the Judean Quarter, but didn't glean anything new from it. Then, for interest's sake I read the article about the conductor's suicide and found another reason to be convinced that the psyche of all these art people was quite unstable. One falls into depression from losing a class ring of no use to anyone, and another offs himself over losing something as banal as a conductor's baton.

I wish I had their problems.

I took a look at a photograph from the conductor's funeral and suddenly saw the familiar oval of a pale face in it. Then I reread the article, ineffably more carefully this time. It seemed the coroner had discovered that the conductor did not have any close relatives, and that his colleagues had all gone off to tour in continental Europe. Then, with a modicum of sympathy, I asked my butler to take the saucer, mug and candies back to the kitchen. A nasty suspicion visited my mind. And I would have to check it at once.

But before heading for the city, I went up to the bedroom and clipped my Roth-Steyr holster to my belt.

A Cerberus is good, but next time, three rounds might not be enough.

SLIGHTLY LIMPING ON MY injured leg, I went down

the hill, turned into a stationary stall and acquired a notepad and a couple of slate pencils. After that, I headed for the sewing parlor. The tailor surprised me immensely after agreeing to sell a suit for half price. And yes, it was just as unbearably fashionable and dashing as my last one! I immediately changed into it, while I asked for the stinking char of my old clothes to be sent to the cleaners.

I went outside feeling like a new man.

I stood a bit on the porch. Not seeing any admiring gazes from passers-by and, slightly vexed at that, I went off to the city library. But when I happened upon a banner reading "Knives from around the world," I couldn't resist and took a look inside. And it wasn't at all about the advance burning a hole in my pocket. It was just that my old knife had been left in the ruins of the collapsing chapel, and there was no reason to bear this slight inconvenience, given that I now had the ability buy a new one.

Alright, alright! The advance was burning a hole in my pocket. Are you happy?

The knife shop turned out to be empty. I mean, there were more than enough bladed instruments and various other objects, but there were no customers, so the salesman immediately swooped down on me.

"What is it that you desire?" he asked, not

so much brown-nosing as being overly polite, letting me know imperceptibly that he could recognize my expertise. After a barely noticeably pause, he confidentially informed me: "We just got a new shipment. Nepalese kukri are back, as well as authentic African machetes"

"Not interested," I shook my head. "I need a medium-sized pocket knife."

"Clasp, or switchblade?" the seller clarified, looking at my fashionable attire and twirling his mustache pensively. "Or perhaps something more elegant? Mother-of-pear handles are quite in fashion right now."

I took a look at the glass case with collector's models, exotic numbers from foreign craftsmen and expensive ornamental pieces and clarified my needs:

"I need a functional folding knife with a titanium blade."

"Is that so?" the seller took up the challenge and pointed me into the neighboring room. "This way, please."

The small room was laden with racks and racks of all different kinds of implements of death and destruction. And implements they were; many were lavishly decorated, but all of them were very reliable and functional. No ornate shapes, no mother-of-pear handles.

Cutlasses, daggers and strong hunting

blades.

The seller led me to a glass case with a few dozen pocketknives and, as if apologizing for the lack of selection, said:

"It's all here."

I didn't hesitate long and immediately pointed at a knife that looked exactly like the one I had lost. The lock held in the simple gray blade firmly. The blade then gave way smoothly to a thin, ravenous edge. Its comfortable handle was decorated with two bars on each side made of ivory and polished red wood.

"How much?"

"One hundred francs," not batting an eye, the seller asked for the same amount I'd just spent on the suit.

But I didn't hesitate; the knife was worth every centime he was asking.

It was titanium and reliable. What's more, it was even beautiful. A combination that was impossible to resist.

With a heavy sigh, I parted with another one-hundred-franc bank note and walked out of the shop. Right on the porch, I took out the knife and a pencil, sharpening it to give my new tool a spin. I didn't have to cut through any paper. It had already become clear that the blade was as sharp as could be.

Well, what now? Limp on, I guess...

THE HUGE BUILDING of the Main New Babylon Library with marble sculptures on its gables, was only slightly smaller than the Newton-Markt, but it didn't impose on its surroundings in the same way. It didn't look so gloomy and oppressive. All around the small shady square before it, the streams of water coming from its fountain burst into the sky, sparkling in the sun. Meanwhile, the many benches under the trees were occupied by students from Imperial University. Those who couldn't find a spot in the shade were sitting with their books and abstracts directly on the marble steps of the portico.

Getting inside was no problem. I simply flashed my badge to the on-duty guard and asked where I could find their file on the *Atlantic Telegraph.*

The good-looking old man looked me over skeptically from head to toe and pointed at one of the corridors leading away from the foyer.

"Over there," he waved his drooping hand.

I took a step in the direction he was indicating and soon found myself in a spacious reading room. Its silence was only broken by the shuffling of paper and the creaking of iron quills. The students were preparing for their inexorably approaching exams and, differently from normal, were not playing their usual stupid games, so the matrons, who were slowly ambling between the tables had nothing better to do than meet the new visitor and ask about the purpose of my visit. In two words, I explained my problem and soon found myself leafing through newspapers, paying particular attention to the obituaries section, and the part dedicated to ups and downs in the lives of New Babylon's upper crust.

The newspapers were tacked to a board. The table they were on was in the darkest corner of the library, and I was burning myself out trying to find just any confirmation of my theory in their yellowed pages. The board did nothing to stop the resourceful students from cutting out bits of paper for hand-rolled cigarettes, and quite often, the most promising places were gaping with holes, but all the same, after flipping back a few months' worth of pages, I hit upon news of a similar event. Also, in the January edition, I found another mention of a no-less-strange death.

Were they actually strange, though?

I mean, would a normal person be surprised if a dancer fell into depression and suddenly stepped out the window, or a singer who abused alcohol took a bath, but instead of bringing a wash bucket and soap, brought a bottle of aspirin and a sharp razor?

Not at all! And even I could only shrug my

shoulders on the occasion of reading of such an event in the paper. Such things happened to creative people all the time, but I personally would not like to read such a story on Albert Brandt, no matter how angry I'd gotten at him in our last encounter.

But the poet, judging from what I could see here, was devilishly close to blasting a bullet into his own temple or jumping from a bridge. After all, every one of the art people who had left us before their time had lost some little trinket that had once been dear to their heart, not long before dying. In the words of their friends and relatives, the very thing that pushed these artists over the edge every time was losing such a precious object.

And though the tiniest amount of critical analysis caused my version of events to come apart at the seams, I did not dismiss the suspicions or write them all off as coincidences. A few hours later, I left the library with my notepad filled with names and addresses of people to interview.

BUT FIRST I HEADED for the Rome Bridge. It had once been built to connect the old city with the Embassy Quarter and, as a result, this shallow tributary of the Yarden had a stone slab put up over it. As time went by, the bridge became a favorite spot for artists, caricaturists and street musicians.

It was a surprising place, where life abounded. A place where it was never quiet day or night.

I didn't like it.

I was annoyed by the beggars, gypsies, fortune-tellers and charlatans that had occupied the area, trading in counterfeit relics of the Renaissance era and colored water, sold by them as the blood of *the fallen*. I felt a nervous shudder, looking at the muddy stream bursting out of one stone tube and, fifty meters later, disappearing without a trace into another. And I also couldn't bear remembering the month when this bridge had served as the roof over my head.

I even would have liked not to have come here today, but I simply had no choice.

A TALL, EXHAUSTED-LOOKING old man, was sitting in his usual place, beneath the statue of Michelangelo. Before him was an easel. In a box, there were a dozen very sharp pencils waiting to be used. None of the locals seemed bothered by the fact that artist's eye sockets were empty.

When I sat on the folding chair for clients, I stretched out my leg with relief. It had started hurting quite badly after the long walk. The artist, though, immediately reached for his pencil.

"It's been a long time, Leo," he said with unmistakable reproach sounding through in his voice.

The artist was missing his eyes, but wasn't at all blind. The *illustrious* gentleman's talent allowed him to see better than any sighted person, and beyond that, gave him the ability to look into another person's mind and transfer the images he saw there onto paper. Dreams or nightmares – it made no difference.

"Charles!" I smiled cordially in reply. "If your friends stop coming around, that must mean they are doing well!"

The artist frowned skeptically and rubbed his sunken cheeks.

"Am I correct in understanding this to mean that you have run into some troubles?" He wondered reasonably.

"I need your help," I admitted. "Could you draw a portrait for me?"

"Am I to understand that it will be free of charge?"

"The Viscount Cruce always pays his debts."

"You'll pay me back after you rob the bank?" snorted Charles Malacarre. "That's what you used to say, right?"

"Everything flows. Everything changes.

Now, I catch people who rob banks."

"I hope you are aware that the pay for that is somewhat lower," the artist smiled with one corner of his lips, and turned to the easel with his pencil in hand. "Concentrate, Leo."

I clenched my eyelids shut and tried to restore to memory the face I had seen flash by. Just then, his slate pencil started scraping on the paper.

The *Illustrious* Charles saw others' dreams. Charles the illustrator put them to paper. A magnificent combination of talents.

"Quiet down, Leo!" the artist asked, wiping the sweat that had appeared on his forehead with his kerchief. "Not so fast! The only time it helps to rush is when you're catching fleas."

I nodded and tried to relax. Charles had never refused working with me due to my overly active imagination. I had even taken it on myself to learn the basics of drawing, but I didn't find any success in it. I was wretchedly bad at drawing. Just hopeless.

"Curses!" the artist suddenly exclaimed, ripping a sheet from the easel on which the pencil lines had started coming together, not into the oval of a face but into incomprehensible shadows. "Leo, don't get distracted!"

I let out a fateful sigh and stared up, but that didn't help and the next sheet of paper was spoiled just like the first.

"Leo!" The illustrator set a dulled pencil aside in annoyance and grabbed for another. "Do you even know what you want from me?"

"I do, just a second!" I turned the paper over and stared at a grainy photograph from the conductor's funeral. To be more accurate, at a figure with a washed-out pale face in that photograph. "Is that better?"

Charles didn't answer and set about making a portrait in a fast, confident motion. He took a full five minutes, then tossed a lock of hair from his forehead and said:

"That was everything I could drag out of you. You're surprisingly not put together today, Leo."

"I wouldn't say that," I objected, looking at the pencil sketch. "It's just surprising..."

"Does this look like the guy?" the illustrator grew surprised.

"It does," I reassured him. "But the eyes..."

There were no eyes. Instead there were very densely shaded black dots.

And it was even a bit frightening.

"That's what was in your head," Charles reminded me.

I stood up from the little chair, grabbed the paper from the easel and, carefully folding it into a tube, asked:

"How are things going?"

"I can't complain," the artist answered, taking out a pen-knife with a worn-down blade and re-sharpening the now dulled pencils. "You wouldn't believe how many people wish to see their own dreams and amorous fantasies put to paper."

"Are you serious?" I actually had been planning on asking Charles to draw a portrait of Elizabeth-Maria, the daughter of the inspector general, naturally. But after those words, I decided against such a request.

"Some simply want to share their phobias," the artist announced poignantly. "Do you understand what I'm talking about?"

"I do."

People often feel they cannot handle their own fears. They eat away at the soul and burst out. Simpletons hope for help, but instead fall into the hands of cynical rapscallions, for whom others' phobias are bread and butter. The kind of people who, if they catch a whiff of weakness, will not stop until they suck a person dry.

I personally tried to stay a bit further from others' fears. It didn't always work, though.

"Thank you for the help," I clapped the artist on the shoulders.

"Don't be a stranger," Charles threw out, not stopping his pencil sharpening.

"Of course."

Having tucked the rolled-up portrait under my armpit, I walked off the bridge and almost immediately ran into a bearded old man turning a trdelnik over a fire. I couldn't resist, so I bought a couple of the spiral rings of sweet hot dough, coated in powdered sugar and cinnamon then returned to the statue of Michelangelo and handed one to the blind illustrator.

"Still crazy about sweets, huh?" the artist chuckled, accepting the treat.

"I suppose," I replied and headed to interrogate potential witnesses.

A POLICEMAN'S BADGE is a universal skeleton key; this simple document was can open practically any door. And at the same time, a policeman's badge is a frightening scarecrow to the wicked, completely beating the memory out of people, as well as their desire to talk.

If you want to find out something useful from a witness, either scare them half to death or ask them the right questions.

And asking precisely the right questions was also something that must be done in the proper manner. It was dumb to ask a person if they ever met a particular individual at the home of a now dead acquaintance. If it happened a few months ago, either they would say they've never met the person, or their description would be limited to a couple of cookie-cutter sentences.

Having a portrait of your suspect, though, was a different story. People were often somewhat more observant than even they realized. Many find that, after meeting a person just once, they can recognize them several decades later, and the vast majority have a fairly good memory of people they find attractive.

The face in my portrait was attractive. What was more, it was frankly beautiful, even despite having black holes for eyes but, all the same, none of my potential witnesses was able to remember the person it belonged to. And only when I had totally run out of hope that I would turn up anything, the concierge in the building where the dancer who jumped out a window had once lived suddenly gave a weak-sighted squint, staring at the pencil sketch, nodding very frequently.

"I remember this whelp!" He announced and hurriedly took a bulbous flask from his pocket. His hand shivering, he raised it to his lips and started sucking it down so greedily that his huge Adam's apple was jumping up and down. "I dream about those eyes," He whined after wiping his lips with the cuff of his uniform. "The horror!"

"These eyes?" I asked, confused after looking at the hatched eye sockets in the portrait.

"The very same!" The concierge confirmed and again started sucking away at the flask, which based on the smell, contained absinthe. "Cursed shadows!"

Lovers of the "green fairy" were nowhere near always in a good state of mind, and quite often confused hallucinations brought on by the drink with reality, but I believed this old man.

Shadows and eyes. Eyes and shadows.

I also remembered seeing something like that.

So, having decided not to waste any more time on nothing, I set off for the *Charming Bacchante*.

8

ALBERT BRANDT HAD SETTLED into a state of the greatest despondency. He finished all the wine, and now, with a pensive look was waving a glass of calvados, which had left oily traces down the wall of his glass.

"Are you drinking?" I asked, simply to start the conversation.

"I am," the poet answered curtly.

"Your inspiration isn't back?"

"Not a gram of it. I feel full of mediocrity. I cannot write, and am not in the mood to read. I don't want to see anyone. Even you, Leo. Forgive me."

"You've gotta get the hell out of here!" I demanded, pulling the curtain aside. "Go out, blow off the cobwebs. I'll keep looking for your ring."

"And where do you suggest I go?" the poet asked in surprise, lying about with his legs on the couch.

"Wherever you normally go."

"Leo! I cannot bring Kira to a bordello!"

"And you shouldn't. I'm sure you've tormented her dreadfully with your... affection. Let her catch her breath."

Albert shook his head.

"She gets mad if I go on a walk and don't ask her."

"Go out the back door," I suggested and began lighting the gas fixtures, as it had already grown dark outside. "I'll deal with Kira."

"That sounded... like a double meaning. Don't you think?"

"Albert, you're not helping! Do you want me to look for your ring or not?" I flared up, rolling a dense Persian rug to the wall. "Look at yourself in the mirror. You look mangy, old friend. You need to get out of the house!"

The poet looked obediently at his reflection, thoughtfully rubbed his mangled pinkie finger and sighed.

"No, I don't want to. I don't want to do anything. Call Kira in, would you?"

"Don't you think you're becoming a bit too attached?"

"It's love!"

"You're right, it's love, not a marriage! She needs to take a break from you, and you simply need to take a break."

"I'm not tired."

"Drop the act!" I grew angry. "Go suffer and complain about your life in some shitty old tavern! You'll have a bigger audience!"

"I don't want to see anyone, Leo, listen to me! My inspiration has left me, and who am I without inspiration? Just more typical mediocrity!"

I took the bottle and tipped it over threateningly, preparing to pour the calvados onto the floor.

"You won't be drinking here."

The poet looked at me with disapproval.

"You asked me to find the class ring yourself," I reminded him. "Just let me help you, Albert."

"I cannot leave Kira."

"Just stop it! If you want, I could tell her

that you went out to look for the class ring in all the pawn shops. After all, Kira knows how important it is to you."

"She does..."

"So, you see! You won't even have to lie. I'll do it for you. Or you could decide not to count on me and keep suffering in loneliness."

"You've convinced me!" Albert gave in. Without changing his old shirt, he donned his jacket, and grabbed his cane and top hat. But as soon as he went out the door, he looked back. "Tell Kira about the ring! Tell her I'll be back soon!" he said. "Will you?"

"I'll tell her your hemorrhoids are acting up," I snorted.

"That would be at your own risk! I couldn't even put two words together today, but when I sober up..."

"Scram!"

"Nice little suit, by the way," Albert suddenly noted and slunk out into the corridor.

I immediately set the rug aside, looked at my watch and stood in the doorway, leaning my shoulder against the jamb. I tossed a sugar-coated drop into my mouth, waited the five minutes I guessed it would take, then went down to the first floor.

The musicians, their clothes wrinkled, had just taken their seats. The stage was vacant, and the cabaret room had yet to fill up with people who'd come to party, so it was not difficult to find Kira. She was smoking by an open window.

"I'm coming, I'm coming!" the girl smiled when I appeared and pushed her cigarette out in the bottom of a porcelain dish. "Albert sent you, didn't he?"

"No," I shook my head. "Albert asked me not to tell you... and I wasn't going to, but I'm worried about him. Really worried."

"What has happened to him?" Kira grew alarmed.

"You see, he was struck with the idea that he knows where his ring is hidden and set off to get it. He didn't want to upset you, and even made me give my word that I wouldn't say anything, but I'm not feeling right about it for some reason..."

"To get the ring?" Kira was taken aback. "It was just lying around somewhere?!"

"I don't even know what fly bit him," I shrugged my shoulders, lost. "He let slip some mention of his connection with the bauble. I'm not sure it's just the drinking; he didn't seem like himself today!"

"You shouldn't have let him out," the girl grew gloomy. "You should have called me right away!

All I can do now is gesture helplessly."

"Am I my brother's keeper?" I quoted a book as old as it was forbidden, but Kira didn't pay my seditious turn of phrase any mind.

"You shouldn't have let him go," she repeated and bit her lip.

I turned to the stage where the presentation was supposed to be starting very soon and asked:

"I hope you don't need to reserve a table in advance?"

"What?" the girl shuddered. "No, you don't," she reassured me and hurried to disappear down the service corridor.

Without following her, I sat calmly at the nearest table and glanced at my time-piece. I waited for one minute more to give a break to my constantly hurting leg, and limped outside, where the darkness of evening was already growing denser. I did not stay long near the tables before the entry into the cabaret. I quickly walked past them and stood at the corner.

Soon, a figure enshrouded in a dark cloak appeared from the back door of the amusement facility and I secretly went after it.

On the narrow little streets, it was impossible to get through the revelers walking about in search of fun. Meanwhile, the kerosene lamps over the doors of the drinking establishments and the lamps behind the store windows practically did nothing to chase off the darkness, so I didn't have to try too hard to sneak. It was enough to simply move at the general rhythm of the street, keep my distance at a few dozen meters back and avoid well-lit places as much as possible. The only thing stopping me were the touts. Their job was to pick out carefree passers-by from the human stream and drag them into their den of sin.

But at least at first, the pursuit was reminiscent of a carefree night out. Further on, when the lively corners were behind us, I had to prowl, trying hard not to give myself away in the silence of the darkness-enshrouded skid row. The local inhabitants here had the custom of going to sleep with the coming of darkness, and only sometimes did you hear the noise of a late-night squabble or see a cloud of tobacco smoke rising up from a courtyard.

The neighborhood was changing gradually. The houses were becoming less and less well cared-for. The quality blinds were replaced with crisscrossing boards nailed onto window frames. The figure in the cloak was weaving confidently through the narrow alleys. It didn't stop even once in hesitation or turn back. All the same, I was in no rush to close the distance between us, even if that meant I was at risk of lagging behind and letting the gray dot melt into the impenetrable darkness.

I considered the risk justified. Just then, though, a rat jumped out from under my legs with an enraged squeak and I had to take shelter in a concealed pigeon-hole. When I decided to look back out a few seconds later, the street was already empty; I ran out to the intersection, but there was no one there.

Curses!

My hand involuntarily reached for my pistol, but it didn't seem like an ambush. I had the sense that bad luck had waylaid me at the very end of my journey. Which meant...

I looked at the neighboring buildings and excluded out of hand the ones on the other side of the street, blackening the sky with their empty window frames and the holes in their leaky roofs. The nearest manors here were a bit better cared-for; I decided to check them first of all.

After noticing a broken board in a fence, I grabbed the one next to it, I put all my weight into it, and broke the rotten piece of wood with ease. A dull crack dissipated in the darkness of the alley. The only one who would have been able to hear it was a guard dog, but I didn't hear any barks or chains. Just a lone cricket chirping not far away mixed with the far-off clanking of a steam tram's wheels on the rails.

I easily slipped into the hole I created and

got behind the fence without even dirtying my jacket. With the board still in my hands, I walked up to the corner of the building, looked at the small, cluttered courtyard and carefully walked over to a window with broken blinds. I stood on my tip-toes and took a look inside, but the abandoned apartment was dominated by an impenetrable gloom.

Abandoned? It was indeed!

It's hard to miss the fact that a residence has been left by its inhabitants. It even starts to smell different. And here too, it was very easy to smell either some kind of damp or simply the after-smell of the despair that had once filled the home.

That's how it was here. No people. Even the omnipresent stray dogs didn't look into this building. One thing was for sure, too – not even a terrible head cold could save you from the stench that accompanied it.

A dud.

Without going inside, I went back out the fence and walked up to the next building. I tried to get near it from one side, but almost immediately hit upon a locked gate. I walked to the other corner and also found no success there. The stone fence merged into the wall of the neighboring manor, a fairly classy building.

A wildly successful artisan must have once

lived here. But when the area started going into decline, and the trash on the streets piled up to the point it was hard to navigate, the whole family tree must have had to be moved to another neighborhood. Or maybe not. Maybe they latched onto this old place and stayed here until they realized that they themselves were no longer the same as they once were.

Squalor is not some infectious disease that strikes suddenly; squalor starts in the human heart.

Returning to the gate, I got down on my haunches and stuck my pinkie finger into the key-hole and turned it a bit. I pulled it out and, without particular surprise, noted an oil stain on the clean leather of my glove. Then I leaned a piece of board against the stone fence, slammed the toe of my shoe into it and lifted myself sharply upward. The piece of wood creaked, but it held out. Sometimes, it was good to be a lightweight! From there, I was able to climb onto the fence. I didn't stay up top for long, carefully jumping down into the courtyard. From there, I limped to the back door of the dilapidated manor, hissing from the pain in my leg.

The door was locked, but glass windows could hardly be considered a serious barrier to a criminal, who wants to get inside. And they weren't a barrier to me either; I carefully pressed one of the glass panes out, stuck my hand inside and undid the latch. Then I got my Roth–Steyr out of its holster, placed a round in the chamber and stepped quietly in the door.

A whiff of damp immediately hit my face, but here the damp was mixed with the light smoke of a candle and the stench of chronic illness.

Stepping quietly on the dried-out floorboards, I walked into the kitchen and peeked down the corridor. At the far end, I saw the flickering light of a candle flame reflected on the wall. Trying not to make a sound, I headed for the illuminated doorframe and suddenly caught a measured creaking sound.

Skreep-skreep. A moment of silence and again: skreep-skreep.

I stood for a moment, listening to the ringing silence, but still couldn't figure out what could be making the sound. What came to mind was the swinging of a pendulum, but I was able to say for sure that the sound was not the ticking of a clock.

No, it definitely was not ticking.

God knows why, but my back suddenly went damp with cold sweat and I got the desire to carry my legs out of here as quickly as possible. I overcame the momentary weakness, went further and looked into the spacious guest room. On the table there, I saw the uneven flickering flame of a candle.

The source of the incomprehensible scratching was embarrassingly banal. Some sickly man had thrown himself back into a rocking chair and was rocking away with abandon, not paying attention to anything around. His long thin black shadow was clinging to the wall, stretching out under the ceiling and spread-eagled on the wallpaper; the man was rocking in the chair, but the shadow was motionless.

The hair on the back of my head stood on end in horror. I definitely didn't want to play the hero, intending to slink back outside but, just then, the shadow turned its head and looked at me.

Curse me! That creature saw me!

After that, the shadow stretched out blisteringly fast into the person, and he got up from the rocking chair with an unnaturally viscous motion. I didn't even have time to blink before the person was next to me, holding me by the front of my shirt. He jerked me sharply toward himself like a professional wrestler giving a hip throw. The rocking chair saved me. Its creaky lumber softened the blow, which made slamming into the wall much less painful; I do not know by what miracle, but I didn't even drop my Roth-Steyr and, when the inhabitant of this abandoned manor threw himself at me again, trying to get me by the neck, I met him with a pistol whip. The kilogram of iron hit him in the skull and the frail man was simply knocked off his feet. Now, I was standing over him, so I took a second swing, this time with the butt into his forehead. With a woody clap, the back of the man's head struck the floor. My opponent went limp all at once, like when a mechanical toy breaks.

Bracing my palm on his sunken chest, I drew back the pistol for another strike, but before I could swing it, the shadow crawled back out of the immobilized man's eyes and mouth. It doddered up around me, pulled me with invisible chains and crushed down on me with a wave of exorbitant weariness.

Practically losing my consciousness from the otherworldly impact, I stretched out to grab a pillow that had flown off the rocking chair and used it to cover the strange man's face. After that, I poked the barrel of my Roth-Steyr into the pillow and pulled the trigger.

I heard a weak clap, and smelled the residue of gunpowder. The shell went rolling around the floor-boards. The shadow disappeared without a trace. The man shook. His arms and legs jerked in mortal agony, then he went limp.

Done.

With a morbid groan, I stood to my feet and turned my head, driving away the fog that was overcoming it. And though the pillow may have dulled the sound enough so that neighbors and random passers-by wouldn't have heard the weak clap as a pistol shot, any other inhabitants of this manor were probably not fooled by the trick; I had to hurry.

I clipped on my glasses, which had fallen off when I fell over, pressed my back up against the wall and checked my Roth-Steyr. The pistol was in perfect shape. The immobile titanium slide provided considerable protection from supernatural attacks. Thanks to that, at least I knew that, no matter what kind of shadow beasts were nearby, they wouldn't be able to damage my weapon.

The ringing in my ears started to slightly abate, and I peeled myself from the wall, walking over to the entryway, it's door boarded up from the inside. I didn't go up to the second floor. Instead, I looked under the stairs in search of a way down to the basement.

There I found a small door that was not locked; its opening menaced with an impenetrable blackness, and I had no doubt whatsoever that the thing I was looking for would be waiting for me down there.

Curses!

I hate basements! I just hate them!

I do not suffer from claustrophobia. Being in rooms without doors or windows doesn't make me particularly uncomfortable. I can walk calmly in the Metro, catacombs, and city sewer system, but basements...

Basements made me overflow with a completely irrational horror. I do not even know why. And how do you fight that which you cannot even begin to understand?

Just ignore it?

Good luck...

My pistol in front of me, I went down the steep stairs with a heavy heart, descending into the darkness. Contrary to my expectations, the air in the basement was dry and warm, and it smelled strongly of unfamiliar incense. And the murk, too, was not at all as hopeless as I had been imagining: the more I went down the rickety steps, the more I saw an uneven illumination coming from up ahead. And, after the semi-dark corridor led me to a room with fabric-draped walls, there was not a trace remaining of the former dim.

Everywhere I looked – on the short little tables, shelves, nightstands, and even on the soil floor – there were candles. The uneven oscillation of their orange flames dispersed the shadows and chased them off into the corners of the room.

The candles were burning everywhere, except in the darkness-immersed partition in the corner farthest from the entrance. And that was no coincidence. There were two crimson candle wicks there giving off little wisps of smoke, either intentionally blown out or accidentally extinguished.

I readjusted my grip on the pistol and switched off the safety. But as soon as I moved, the fabric on the partition burst, ripping into wisps of shadow rushing directly toward me! My Roth-Steyr gave a sharp jerk. The heavy pistol bullet caught the blistering shade, and a stripped-bare woman's body collapsed onto the floor. It rolled a bit, knocked over a few candles, then froze completely motionless among puddles of hardened wax.

Curses!

I moved back, pressed my back against the wall, and only then noticed something resembling an altar at the far wall. It was a vanity with a three-part mirror, and it was covered with a mound of baubles, all of them covered with old wax deposits, as if there had been candles burning in the same place over them for many long months.

My gaze was turned from the motionless body for just a moment, but that was plenty of time for the shot-through girl to turn from her side onto her stomach, pull her arms and legs under herself and start hacking up blood. Her face was pointed at the floor, obscured by long locks of thick black hair, but there could be no doubt that her dark eyes were now greedily drinking in my every move.

"Don't even think about it, Kira," I warned.

"Kira?" Her muffled laughter rang out in reply. The girl shook her head hard, throwing her hair in all directions. After that, she smoothed it back out in one graceful motion and asked: "Do you really think that's my name?"

"I just wanted to warn you not to do anything without thinking it through first," I announced in reply with all the calm I could muster, given the situation at hand.

Between Kira's upturned breasts there was a gaping bullet hole. From it, blood was oozing out onto her stomach, thighs and legs, but the girl didn't seem overly worried by the fatal wound.

She was smiling. She was smiling at me!

And also the shadow. The very same shadow that had been controlling the frail person in the rocking chair. The shadow was spinning like a top inside Kira, bursting out of her occasionally in blades of transparent flame, spinning with gray whirlpools in bottomless eyes that already looked less than alive.

Such eyes simply could not belong to a person, and that frightened me. The only thing saving me from nervous shaking was the heft of the gun in my hands, but to be perfectly honest, I was shaking at the knees more and more anyway.

I was afraid. And that beast knew it.

"Look who's talking about doing things without first thinking them through." Kira laughed uncontrollably and suddenly placed two fingers into her shot-through chest. A moment later, the girl pulled her hand from the wound, unclenched it and revealed a warped bullet. "Just a bit of lead and copper..." she said, surprised. "Did you really think that *this* could stop me?"

Her wound healed over; I gulped fitfully and told her:

"That was the plan, yes." Then I added: "To be perfectly honest, I wasn't planning on taking this to the point of shooting..."

"Smart boy," Kira purred, throwing the bullet over her back in a care-free motion. "You outsmarted me. Who'd have thought! You sniffed me out and wrapped me around your finger. What even made you suspect me?"

"A newspaper. You were in one of the pictures from the conductor's funeral," I said and demanded: "Release Albert! Release him, and we can go our separate ways in peace."

"Release him?" the girl asked in surprise. "Do you think I'm holding him? Do you not think it's rather his covetousness of my body?"

"Let him go and return the class ring," a nervous trembling started coming over me, but it was too late to retreat. "You will not take his soul."

"What makes you think I want his soul?" Kira frowned and whispered: "I need his *talent*! *Talent*, fear and despair! The last burst of emotion before stepping over the line. The dying heartbeat..." She stopped for a moment, then said in a normal, slightly bored voice: "But the most important thing, of course, is his *talent*. And I will take it and keep it safe and sound."

"Return the class ring, beast!"

"His weakness is unforgivable," Kira said as if she hadn't heard me. "A creator does not have the right to be weak. No sentimental stupidities, and no relics or little souvenirs. A true master lives in the present. He burns brightly and never goes out. He is ideal. He is worthy of his muse. All my... attachments..." the girl screwed up her face in disdain, "were to a person carrying a flaw inside. Every one like an apple with a worm. None of them achieved the ideal and none of them could ever achieve it."

"There is no ideal," I reminded her.

"Yes, there is!" Kira exclaimed with unexpected sharpness, even taking a step toward me. "And I will find it! It doesn't matter how long it takes. One day, we will be together!"

Shadows were dancing in the girl's eyes. They were luring me in and trying to get into my head, but I just gripped my pistol tighter.

"You aren't ideal either," the girl noted with what sounded like a bit of pity. "You also have a flaw inside. Why do you never remove your glasses? Are you ashamed of your eyes? Or is that your fetish?"

Kira extended her hand demandingly; I could only chuckle and move the loop of my glasses to the very end of my nose.

"Ah- ha!" the girl whispered, taking a step back involuntarily. "You're *illustrious*!"

"You've finally figured it out."

"Your *talent* is stronger than Albert's..."

"Back," I ordered, and the girl moved away. "Another step toward me and I'll shoot."

"Oh, come off it," Kira shrugged her shoulders. "Your *talent* will be mine, whether you want it or not. Do not be afraid, it will all be over quick..."

I pulled down on the trigger, but it gave way too easily and no shot rang out.

"I'm so weary of these new-fangled

toys!" the girl laughed uncontrollably. "Loops, levers... Nothing new since the time of Archimedes. Breaking them is nothing but pleasure, my dear *illustrious* gentleman..."

My attempt to rack the slide didn't lead to anything good, either. Quite the opposite, in fact. Inside the titanium housing, something began to rattle as if the trigger mechanism had suddenly dissolved into pieces and turned into a useless collection of junk.

"Copper and lead are nothing to me," Kira started smiling. "Not steel, nor even cold iron can help. I will kill you, *illustrious* sir. I will kill you and drink your *talent* down, no matter what it is. If you do not resist, I will do it the nice way. You'll enjoy it even..."

A wave of horror rolled over me; I threw my jammed-up Roth-Steyr at her and pulled the three-barreled Cerberus from out of my jacket's side pocket.

"Another little toy?" Kira snorted disdainfully. "Boys are so predictable..."

I didn't answer, instead simply pulling back on the trigger in silence. A shot clapped out. It started smelling intensely of pyroxyline and ozone.

Kira stared at the hole in her chest in incomprehension. The shadow inside her started twirling in a true hurricane of transparent fire and – clap! clap! – the pistol in my hand gave another two jolts.

Crimson blood started pumping out of the bullet holes. Kira stopped mid-stride and collapsed onto the floor, trying to get up, but it was to no effect.

"What is that?" burst out of her together with the blood gurgling out of her mouth.

"Sublime electricity and a full-aluminum jacket," I told her, changing out the spent magazine for a new one.

Infernal creatures and malefics could boast all they wanted of their ancient powers, but they were in no position to compete with progress; mages would never catch up to science.

You made yourself invincible to copper, steel and lead? Great! But what about the aluminum jackets of modern bullets? You taught yourself to put out the spark of a struck capsule and destroy a trigger mechanism? Excellent! But what do you think of these electrically-ignited powder rounds?

You cannot stop science. Science sweeps away everything in its path.

After reloading my Cerberus, I aimed it back at the girl, but I didn't have to shoot: the shadow inside Kira had already been extinguished and was blowing away like dust in the wind. The all-encompassing presence evaporated, and together with it went whatever was stopping this girl from dying. She went limp and just lied there, her face buried lifelessly in a pool of blood on the floor.

Not letting her out of my sight, I picked up my Roth-Steyr and moved back to the vanity. I found Albert's student ring there. It hadn't yet been covered by the streams of wax, so it wasn't hard. I then ran for the exit.

My fear didn't go anywhere. It was simply unbearable to be in this basement.

I found Albert Brandt in the *Venetian Doge*, a luxurious bordello with an obvious pretense of elegance and respectability. The poet was accompanied by three happy girls and a couple of society dandies of that type of over-aged playboy, who can never seem to burn through their inheritance, even though they spend entire days and nights in a row trying to do just that.

My friend was entertaining his audience with a recitation of his poems; the audience was paying him a strange amount of attention given where they were.

Blow me down! Only Albert could entertain the visitors of a bordello and its whores with a love ballad!

"Leopold! My savior!" The poet turned to me. "You are a genius! You see the very essence of things! I'm feeling a second wind!"

Leaving his drinking companions behind, Brandt walked over to the bar and tossed back the rest of the wine in his glass. He wiped his lips carelessly with his neckerchief and said with unhidden pride:

"I'm back!" and immediately added: "Some wine!"

An obliging drink slinger appeared next to us immediately. He filled Albert's glass and looked at me with anticipation. I waved him off, but the poet was already unstoppable. He demanded:

"Some lemonade for my friend!" Thus also providing unceasing attention to my person from all the respectable and not-so-respectable public in the establishment.

But it was good lemonade. I emptied the glass, allowed it to be filled again and asked the poet quietly:

"Where can we talk one-on-one?"

Albert led me to an alcove that was separated from the main room, plopped down on a pillow-covered couch and took a sip from his wine glass. I sat down next to him and drank my lemonade. The cold drink filled my body with a disarming freshness, chasing off my agitation.

"Leo?" Albert shuddered, quite surprised at the drawn-out pause. "You wanted to talk?"

"Yes. Take this," I said, handing the poet

his class ring.

"Holy Mother of God!" Albert grew joyful. "You found it? Where'd it end up? Under the vanity?"

"Doesn't matter."

Albert tried to put the class ring on his crooked pinkie, but didn't find too much success in that. He then tried it on his other hand, but that didn't work either, so he pulled a silver watch out of his vest pocket, attached the ill-fated ring to its chain and instantly lost all interest in it.

"I am indebted to you, Leo!" The poet assured me, in any case.

"You could say that," I confirmed and sighed. "By the way, about Kira..."

"Kira?" Albert shuddered. "How do you like her? Great body, no? And so passionate! You don't want to get to know her a bit better? You won't regret it, believe me!"

I just shook my head, not telling him that I had already grown more acquainted with Kira than Albert ever had.

What for? The value of the lost class ring was equivalent to that of the love that suddenly flared up in his heart. Her charms were set alight, but after the death of his "muse," the poet had become himself again: a thrifty, cynical, ladies' man, immeasurably talented and no less scatterbrained.

"So, what happened with Kira?" Albert asked.

"She doesn't want to embarrass you," I told the poet. "She wants to give you time to come back to your senses."

With unhidden doubt, the poet looked at me, but the drinking had lowered his critical thinking abilities, and Albert just waved his hand.

"A devilishly perfect coincidence!" He laughed uncontrollably after a brief period of consideration. "To be perfectly honest, Leopold, her company was beginning to bear down on me."

"And mine?" I asked.

"Never!"

"Then I need a tenner from you."

Just then, Albert looked at me with unhidden doubt.

"You, I remember, borrowed money from me recently, right?" He squinted, stroking his sand-colored beard.

"This is on top of that," I announced matter-of-factly, taking the bank note and sticking it in my wallet. After that, I gave the poet a notepad and a pencil. "Be so kind," I asked my acquaintance, "write something for me..."

"You want an autograph? Are you serious?"

"Write: 'I, Albert Brandt, do charge Leopold

Orso with finding my lost property, namely a ring from a Munich University student fraternity and, in accordance with the law on private investigative activity, I accept all responsibility...'"

At that point, the poet faltered, but I reassured him:

"Albert, these are normal formalities, nothing more," I said, hardly stretching the truth at all, simply forgetting to mention the two fresh corpses.

But that could never be considered deception, right?

PART THREE

REYNARD

Fears and Fears

1

T HE BEST DEFENSE is to attack. It wasn't me who thought that up, but it bears repeating. Although, if you really get it all the way, there is no real "best defense."

Simply avoid the attention of law enforcement, and you will have no need for expensive lawyers, false alibis and money to buy non-compliant witnesses. But if you're already being followed, the last thing you should be doing is putting your hope in chance and letting the situation run its course. Attack, or you won't even have time to blink before you wake up behind bars.

I knew better than anyone how hard it was to stay outside the field of view of the supposedly clumsy mechanisms of justice. That was why, after my conversation with Albert Brandt, I didn't go home to heal my spent nerves with tea and a biscuit, I headed directly for the Newton-Markt. And I went there with a crime report form already filled out. I gave the thin stack of paper to the constable on duty, took a seat at the rough stall farthest from a lowlife handcuffed to the railing and prepared for a long wait.

I wasn't worried in the slightest.

If I'd had to zap some normal robbers, even if they were constant recidivists on the most-wanted list, I would have been beset with issues.

My suffering would have been flowing like from a cornucopia. Murder is murder; the crown does not approve of its subjects depriving others of their lives. But infernal creatures on the other hand, came under a special article. Citizens did not merely have the right, but were, in fact, required to take all necessary measures to kill them. And, though the phrase "all necessary measures" was usually taken to mean an immediate call to the police, vigilante hunts for the spawn of the underworld were by no means forbidden.

The important thing was not to make a mistake. Stuff a succubus with aluminum or titanium and you're good, but if you shoot a random street person, you're going to end up behind bars. The laws of the Empire were wise and just.

The investigators on duty tonight brought me back to their desk-bound colleague with understanding, and even treated me to a mug of coffee. After getting a clear story from me, they sent out a team of constables to the scene and left me to rest on the very same bench in the vestibule. And I was unreservedly thankful to them for that. In the lockup chambers, the conditions were nowhere near as comfortable, which was to say nothing of their fairly specific aroma.

THE ON-DUTY CONSTABLE elbowed me awake just before morning.

"A self-propelled carriage is waiting for you by the garage," he said as soon as I'd cracked my eyes open. "You should hurry, detective constable."

"Yeah, yeah," I yawned and went to the back door, where there was a police armored car waiting at the gates. It had an ungainly appearance, reminiscent of an iron box on wheels. Next to its flung-wide doors, a driver was smoking in a leather pea-coat, service cap and police-issue trousers.

"Detective constable Orso?" He stuttered at my appearance.

"The very same."

"Senior Inspector LeBrun would like to see you," the freckled boy then told me. He tossed his butt under his foot and unceremoniously put it out with a turn of his high boot. "Are you ready to go?"

"Yes."

"Then let's go!" The driver took the wheel, opened the passenger door from inside, and pulled down on his leather cuffs. He left his goggles to wobble on his chest. After all, we had the wind glass to keep us the fast-moving air out, even with our armored top thrown back.

I went inside and the boy cranked the start

lever for the powder engine. A muffled clap rang out and the seat under me started shaking. With a jerk, the armored car started moving, but stopped immediately. The driver had to do the whole lever procedure over again.

"Come on!" the boy grimaced. "Alright you damned old Nobel, don't fail me now!"

Just then the engine started giving measured sneezes, devouring the granules of compressed TNT. And, as the products of the Nobel Powder Engine Company enjoyed an uncanny infamy for their fickle mechanisms among those in the know, I tensed up nervously and warned him:

"There's no need to rush it..."

"Come off it! It just seized up!" The driver waved it off and gave the steering-wheel a hard turn, aiming the self-propelled vehicle at the carriageway. "And no horses!"

"Horses don't blow up," I reminded him.

"Yeah, but they do bite and kick!" the boy objected. "It's totally safe!"

"Tell that to Santos-Dumont."

But I couldn't bring the boy to reason.

"That's experimental stuff!" He retorted glibly. "I know a thing or two. I've worked on these engines. It's just kicking back."

At first, our motion was accompanied by noticeable kicks, but as we increased our speed, the ride grew more smooth and even. The armored car turned onto a bustling street and the driver became less talkative; the carts and coaches there were in no rush to let us through. There were also pedestrians everywhere, blocking the carriageway. Even the lazily-moving steam tram had to honk, stubbornly demanding to be let out. The engine started kicking much more frequently. The seat under me started shaking again, but soon the armored car passed the jam and began confidently picking up speed once again.

Ten minutes later, the self-propelled carriage was stopped at the intersection outside the manor; I flung open the carriage door and walked up to the police administrators, who had already managed to arrive at the crime scene.

Bastian Moran was smoking near the wide-open gate. Maurice LeBrun was trying to explain something to him in annoyance, but Moran suddenly got distracted and roared out to me:

"Constable! What do you think you're doing? You were dismissed from service, yet you went and got yourself into a firefight! Two people are dead! Do you want to end up behind bars?"

In his snazzy checkered suit, he looked like a business man on his way out for a morning stroll. But his heavy face with its powerful jaw and cold eyes helped me recognize him and not have too patronizing an opinion of his displeasure.

I listened to the reproach in silence, then said with as much respect as possible:

"Mr. LeBrun, I was conducting an investigation for a private client, but I am prepared to accept any punishment..." I handed him Albert Brandt's work order.

"For a private client?" the head of Criminal Investigation Department frowned, grabbing the sheet of paper from me. He placed a monocle in his right eye, ran his gaze over the uneven hand-written text and frowned disdainfully: "A student's ring? You were being paid to look for a student's ring, and it ended in a double murder?"

"The situation is not as straightforward as it looks at first glance," I objected. "The deaths were in self-defense!"

LeBrun frowned indignantly and handed the note to Bastian Moran; he read the work order with unhidden skepticism and shook his head.

"What was the purpose of your putting on this whole presentation, constable? No one saw you here. You could have simply left and not told a thing to anyone."

"It's my duty!" I answered, slightly overdoing the panache.

"Duty?"

"My duty as a policeman."

"Ah, that's right!" Bastian Moran smiled, not able to hold back a smile: "Or maybe you just left something here that would point back to you."

I went silent, then the senior inspector threw away his cigarette butt on the road and carelessly readjusted the white muffler he had wrapped over his short coat, preparing for a look around the crime scene.

"Let's begin, constable!" He commanded, pointing to the gate.

I walked past the sentries at the entrance and walked into the house first, copying my path from the day before. In the room with the rocking chair, it turned out to be so crowded with investigators that I couldn't get through; they were conducting an investigation and scrupulously composing descriptions of the things they found in the manor. The shell that rolled away to the baseboard had been circled in chalk. The deceased was lying on the floor, covered with a sheet.

The only people I could see were from Department Three. It was unclear why the head of the Criminal Investigations Department had come here.

"Don't stand in the doorway, constable!" Maurice LeBrun hurried me along. "Tell me what occurred here!"

"Just a minute!" Bastian Moran exclaimed, asking for the sheet to be pulled back from the dead man. "Why did you shoot him through a pillow?" He asked in surprise when one of the investigators had pulled it back. "What was your reason?"

"I was wearing a new suit. I didn't want to get blood on it," I admitted.

"Original," snorted Senior Inspector Moran. He then demanded: "Take it off."

The investigator carefully pulled the pitted and charred pillow from the dead man's face and I shuddered involuntarily. Maurice LeBrun, though, couldn't hold back from some strong language.

"What the devil, constable?" He objected. "There's no way this guy's been dead less than a year!"

Overnight, the corpse had somehow turned into a real mummy; strips of skin were pulled tight over his exposed skull. His eyes were deeply sunken in, and his sparse teeth were yellowing under the thin strips of his gray lips.

"Not just a year, much longer," Bastian Moran decided. "That was the servant. The living dead."

"Have you had the misfortune of coming up against such things before?" The head of the

Criminal Investigation Department asked in confusion.

"I have," confirmed the senior inspector. "Maurice, I believe that there is no need for your continued presence here. We have it under control."

"Drop it, Bastian!" LeBrun answered unexpectedly sharply. "I will not make a claim on this investigation, but I must be informed on what occurred. At the end of the day, a subordinate of mine is mixed up in this!"

Senior Inspector Moran could only shrug his shoulders.

"As you say, Maurice," he smiled and turned to me. "Tell me, constable."

"The shadow..." I began, but Bastian Moran interrupted me just then.

"From the very beginning!" He demanded.

I had to tell them in all detail about the lost class ring, my suspicions about the poet's girlfriend, following her, and our scrap in the guest room.

As surprising as it may seem, they didn't interrupt me even once.

"You're sure you saw a shadow?" Bastian Moran asked when the report was over.

"As clear as I see you now," I affirmed.

Then the senior inspector allowed the deceased to be covered with the sheet again and ordered me to hand over my police-issue weapon. I pulled my Roth-Steyr from its holster. I could hear pieces of the trigger mechanism jostling around inside it. I extended it to an investigator.

Bastian Moran dismissed his subordinate and asked:

"What happened after that?"

"After that, I checked the basement."

"Show me."

I walked to the stairs and stopped short, not sure I had the resolve to go down the creaky steps in total darkness. Also, the thought of going into the basement still made my skin crawl. But then, one of the constables walked up with a weighty electric torch and I had no choice but to crawl into the hole.

The candles in the basement had long since burned out, and the yellowed puddles of wax were reflecting back in the light of the torch; the beam slid over the dirt floor and lit up the dead body, which looked disturbing and scary.

What was left couldn't be called a body as such; her dried out skin looked like it was stuck to the bone and skull, still topped off with a tuft of black hair. White fragments of her ribcage were poking out of her skin; they must have been damaged when the bullet hit them.

"You shot her with a Cerberus?" The senior inspector asked. "Our forensics team discovered three ten caliber bullets with aluminum jackets."

"It was a Cerberus, yes," I affirmed. "Shall I surrender it?"

"Why?" Maurice LeBrun frowned. "It doesn't have any rifling."

"My first shot was from the Roth-Steyr," I reminded him, "but she just laughed it off and pulled the bullet from the wound. It must be around here somewhere."

"Invulnerability to copper," Bastian Moran thoughtfully hung on his words and suddenly turned around: "What do you see here, constable? What kind of place is this?"

I took a look around.

"What do I see?" I repeated, looking at the molten-wax-coated vanity. "I see hunting trophies. Many trophies. She had been collecting them for many years."

"Quite the imagination you've got there," Maurice LeBrun grumbled and asked: "Bastian, what kind of creature is that?"

The senior inspector stayed silent, so I answered:

"She considered herself a muse."

"A real muse?" The head of the CID was taken aback. "Was she Greek?"

"That's right."

"She was a nasty little vixen," LeBrun gave a shiver.

But then Bastian Moran did nothing to rush to conclusions. I suppose he knew perfectly well that malefics could die the same as any normal person. They would never be able to remove a bullet from their own shot-through chest, daring you to your face, as she had.

"What attracted her to these people?" Senior Inspector Moran asked, trying to lift the conductor's baton from the edge of the table, but finding it encased in the wax. "What did they all have in common, constable? What do you think?"

"They were all talented," I supposed, going silent, then adding: "And also *illustrious*..."

Bastian Moran looked at me and his lips distorted into an incomprehensible smirk.

"*Illustrious*!" He stated acridly. "Alright then. I should have been expecting something like that. The curse of the blood of *the fallen* is the scourge of our time!"

"Forgive me, Bastian, what did you say?" Maurice LeBrun was astounded.

I was no less dumbfounded at the head of the CID; such utterances were easily stretching into treasonous territory. It was doubly surprising to hear it from the mouth of someone who's duty it was to eradicate sedition.

The senior inspector, it seemed, didn't notice our surprise, though.

"The blood of *the fallen* is foreign to people," he declared instructively. "It's like pouring acid into the mechanisms of a clock. How many *illustrious* have died from the Diabolic Plague? How many permanently disabled, or made infertile? Even her Imperial Highness was only able to have one grandchild!"

"Less successors meant less squabbling for the throne," LeBrun objected, his neckerchief soaking through with sweat.

"That is true," Bastian Moran agreed, "but blood is not water. Her Imperial Highness has a heart disease. And even though doctors have made great strides in recent years with organ transplanting, any transplant still requires a suitable donor. Not just an *illustrious*, but a close relative. Otherwise, her body would reject the tissue."

"Reject? You're talking about organ transplants, now?!" The head of the CID was taken aback. "Unthinkable! Giving up the throne to the heir under the knife of these skinflints! Just imagine! How can you cut a living heart out of a person? How can you even think of it?!"

"Science must constantly push forward," Bastian Moran shrugged his shoulders and added oil to the fire. "The human body is not just some gift from the heavens, after all. It's just a tool."

LeBrun wiped his reddened cheeks with his kerchief and said with gusto:

"You know, Bastian, I never took you for a dyed-in-the-wool reductionist!"

The senior inspector noticed a careless smile sliding over my lips, and suddenly demanded explanations:

"Constable, what has got you going? Do you know the meaning of the word 'reductionist?'"

"I do, senior inspector," I answered respectfully. "But you are more likely a provocateur than a reductionist."

The head of the CID couldn't hold back an outraged snort, but Moran didn't air his grievances to me, instead clapping his colleague on the shoulder.

"I apologize, Maurice, but it's not for nothing that they say that habit is second nature. I got carried away. Don't take it personally."

"I wasn't even thinking of it," LeBrun answered and headed for the stairs. "Bastian, I hope we aren't already finished here?" he turned around half way.

"Will that be all, constable?" The senior inspector asked.

"I have nothing more to say to you," I answered and went after the head of the CID.

"Well, then, let's leave it at that."

We came up from the basement, and there already I reminded him:

"Isaac Levinson is still waiting on materials from the bank robbery."

"The robbers' armored vehicle is scheduled to be raised at four," LeBrun informed me. He then made a begrudging promise: "I'll make sure copies of the forms are provided for him by that time."

"If you would be so kind," I nodded and turned to Bastian Moran.

"You are free to go, constable," he released me.

After leaving the house, we went out the manor gate and the half-dark of the early morning was quickly blown out by a blinding magnesium flash. While everyone was trying to get rid of the silver light still in their eyes, the newspaperman scooped up a huge camera in his arms and moved to a new place. His assistant poured some more incendiary powder into the tray and rushed to get behind him.

"You are, in fact, very prudent, detective constable Orso," Bastian Moran stated. He had greatly appreciated my thought to inform not only the police administration but also the editors of the *Atlantic Telegraph* of the events. He started smoking and added pointedly: "But, to your detriment, you are also remarkably vain..."

I let that remark go in one ear and out the other.

Perhaps I really was the tiniest bit vain. Who among us is without sin?

2

I CERTAINLY WAS NOT, but I had been very naive. I could no longer count on a return voyage in a self-propelled carriage, so after bowing out, I limped down the alley with a hopeless sigh in search of a free cabby. But it was in vain; alas, the streets were empty.

The leg I'd injured in the jump was in unbearable pain and the way up to Calvary started to seem like quite the feat indeed, equivalent to the dreaded curse of Sisyphus. So, with all my desire to get into bed as quickly as possible, I headed for the Greek Quarter. And though the *Charming Bacchante* was still locked at this early hour, I battered on the door until the night guard came down to see what the noise was and let me in. The spirit of a warm crowd, cigarette smoke, harsh fragrances and the smell of booze was still lingering in the room.

Lurching, I went up to the second floor and knocked on the poet's apartment, risking finding a drunken orgy there, but no, inspiration had descended on Albert. Leaning over a wine-covered table, he was muttering something to himself over and over again as if delirious and hurriedly transposing the rhymes that were overflowing from his mind onto the writing paper. A great many drafts were towering on the edge of the table, lying about on the floor and filling the trash bin.

The poet didn't even turn when I flung open the door, and I didn't distract him either. I would hardly have been able to anyway without resorting to shooting my pistol into the ceiling. I removed my jacket in silence, hung it on the handle of one of the desk drawer handles and sat down on the ottoman.

Sleep!

WHEN I AWOKE, it was almost midday. The itch of inspiration had already left Albert by that time. He was sprawled out in a chair next to a flung-open window, mending his health with soda water and apple juice.

"Sorry, Leo," the poet turned when he heard the creaking of the springs, "I do not remember your arrival." He yanked on the chain of his pocket watch, which was still weighed down by his heavy student's ring and asked: "Where did you end up digging up my old ring, then?"

"Nowhere," I waved it off and, remembering the fact that the poet had already moved all the furniture to find it, decided not to lie about some deep crack in his floor. "Someone sold it to a pawn shop. One of my colleagues recognized the ring's description."

"What rapscallions!" Albert admired the expertise of the robbers I had just invented. "They'd cut the soles out of your shoes while you walk!"

"Only if you don't do it first as a bet," I joked and, wanting to end the dicey topic fast, asked: "I think it's high time we go out and get some refreshments, don't you?"

The poet noticeably went green.

"I don't think so," he shook his head. "Curses! Where did Kira go off to? She made the best sharbat I've ever had!"

I got up from the ottoman, took my jacket from the desk drawer handle and couldn't hold back a quip:

"I suppose sharbat wasn't the only thing she did well."

Albert frowned in annoyance:

"This is nothing to laugh about. Her sharbat was simply one of a kind."

"I enjoyed it, yes. Come out, I'll be waiting for you on the street."

"Don't you have to go to work?" The poet grew surprised.

"Not today," I shook my head.

Actually, I should have gone to see Isaac Levinson first thing this morning and bring him up to speed, but I decided to put off my visit to the Banking House until evening when the preliminary results of the investigation would already be in hand.

Downstairs, I ordered a coffee, a scramble and some toast. I took one of the tables in front of the stage and put my injured leg in a more comfortable position. Looking at the canal, its muddy waters being crossed from time to time by heavily weighed-down boats, I ate breakfast in no particular hurry, then started drinking my coffee with a biscuit.

Albert Brandt only deigned to come down an hour later. He looked at the overcast sky with a dissatisfied grimace, adjusted his hat and announced:

"I normally am not in the habit of making appearances at such an early hour."

With a smirk, I nodded:

"I guess you're right. It's only one P.M..."

"What's on your mind?" The poet asked, taking a seat opposite me.

"I do not know," I shrugged my shoulders. "I just need to kill some time somehow. I have a meeting scheduled at four. What could we get up to?"

Albert frowned:

"Where can you take a guy who doesn't drink? The museum?"

"Maybe we should go to the hippodrome?" I suggested, much to my own surprise.

The poet just shook his head.

"Leo, if you are of such limited means that you have to rely on Fortuna for bread, I could lend you a bit of money to tide you over until your next payday."

"Drop it, Albert!" I waved it off. "You know I cannot bear gambling."

"And you also don't like big crowds of people," my friend reminded me. "So what is making you want to go to the hippodrome?"

"I don't know," I confessed. "But there's just no fresh air in the city. At least there, you get cleaner air blowing in off the ocean."

Because of the lack of wind over the building roofs, today, the factory smoke was gathering into fully-fledged clouds. The sheet of dark clouds stretched out over the sky and the sun just barely shone through it as a colorless, white dot.

The poet wiped his sand-colored beard in thought and relented.

"Have it your way! Let's go!" And when I

took out my wallet, he waved it off chivalrously: "Forget it, my treat."

Without arguing, I got up from the table and winced at the pain in my leg.

"Curses!" I exclaimed, leaning on the edge of the table. "Albert, we'll have to find someone to drive us."

"What are you talking about?"

"I hurt my leg jumping from a second-story window. They had very high ceilings!"

Albert whistled in surprise:

"How'd you end up doing that?"

I sat down on the chair and reminded him:

"What about the carriage?"

The poet whistled, calling a street boy over. He handed him a small coin and told him to go find a free cabby.

"So then, what happened?" he repeated the question when the errand boy had run away.

In two words, I told him about the bank robbery and the poet shook his head in unfeigned surprise:

"Well, holy shit! I spent all day working yesterday and didn't even read a newspaper!"

He set about inquiring all the details from me, then we took our seats in the carriage that pulled up to the venue and I commanded:

"To the races!"

WITH ITS UNASSAILABLE appearance, the hippodrome was reminiscent of a coastal fort. The massive construction had been erected on a cape that jutted out into the ocean. On the other side of the harbor, it had a partner in a lighthouse tower, which was of a similarly colossal scale.

A strange place for an amphitheater, don't you think?

What can you say, it was part of the inscrutable plans of *the fallen.*

The structure hadn't always been a hippodrome. At one time, the sand of the arena had run red with the blood of gladiators. Horse races only started to be organized when the municipal authorities of the time got bored of the spectacle of people, animals and infernal chimeras killing one another. After that, the amphitheater was supposed to be rebuilt into a fortress, but that never got off the ground; they never found an enemy capable of threatening the capital of the all-powerful Second Empire.

When the carriage stopped on the square in front of the hippodrome, I stepped out onto the reddish granite paving stones and threw back my head, surveying the gloomy building, its gray severity broken up only by a great many flags and colorful streamers.

Stone towers, arches, passages, raised

walls – the amphitheater was not a fortress, but it also was not inferior to ancient defensives structures in any way. And it was hard to say how its fate would have turned out if the development of artillery hadn't made building such fortified constructions an utterly pointless endeavor.

Another special feature of the hippodrome was that it lacked a name. A peculiar joke of *the fallen* – erect a grandiose structure that surpasses the famous colosseum of Rome in every way, but leave it nameless.

Albert settled accounts with the cabby and headed for the ticket offices. I hurried behind him, hissing through my teeth at the pain in my sprained leg.

"A friend of mine has a stall with all kinds of curiosities," the poet then said, "I bet we could find a cane there."

A lanky young man in a fashionable suit with an old cane would be a spectacle you could call comical without any exaggeration, so I shook my head categorically.

"It's not worth it!"

"As you say," Albert did not insist and pointed at the dirigible hovering over the arena. "Shall we take a place at the very top?"

"I appreciate your sense of humor," I grumbled in reply, "but it's beginning to tire me today."

"You can't seriously tell me you can't scrape together a measly fifteen franks for a ticket, right?"

"I am quite serious!"

The poet laughed uncontrollably.

"Let's go, Leopold! Let's go! We'll try to catch luck by the tail!"

I was in no way preparing to place the last of my advance on the races and followed after my friend, thinking in confusion on where in the hell I had gotten the idea to visit this betting parlor. The wind from the ocean was, of course, nice, but it was hardly likely that anyone other than me would come here just to get fresh air.

And there were more than enough spectators at the races. In one long file, they stretched out into one of the gates. Through another, they formed a jumbled mass – disenchanted, emotional and hoarse from screaming – they poured in and spread out through the area. The causeway on the other side was strewn with little tickets from bum bets.

And, naturally, there were nimble boys scurrying about throughout the crowd as well. No, not young pickpockets, but little vendors, selling anything and everything: newspapers, beer, sandwiches, gossip...

"Monstrous crime!" one of them chirped,

shaking a fresh release of the *Atlantic Telegraph.* "Horrible murder!"

I shuddered, expecting to hear about the muse, but the boy took in a full chest of air and sputtered out at the speed of a machine gun:

"Procrustes has returned! Mangled corpse! Body parts ripped out! Get your papers here! Procrustes has returned!"

What?! Procrustes had returned?! The paper boys were fanning the flames of a sensation again, raking up the affairs of days long past.

Albert Brandt immediately slipped the boy a ten-centime coin and set about looking over the top headline with interest.

"There it is!" He just whistled. "Stunning!"

Not able to hold back, I followed the poet's example and also bought a newspaper, but opened it straight to the police blotter page. Squeezed out by the unexpected gruesome murder, the story about the deaths in the art world was way in the back, and it didn't show my picture, or even mention my name.

I remembered Bastian Moran's remark on my excessive vanity, nervously crumpled up the paper and threw it into a waste-paper basket in annoyance. It didn't land in the basket, but I didn't go pick it up either.

To hell with it! Let it get lost for all I care!

"Well, shall we go?" I gave a jerk to Albert, who was distracted by the paper.

"Wait!" he waved. "Procrustes has returned! Can you imagine?"

"You put too much faith in paper boys!"

"Puddles of blood! Body parts ripped out!" Albert wouldn't even think of toning it down. "Do you know, Leo, you were too little, but I used to follow the news on Procrustes with great interest. This has all the hallmarks of his work!"

Procrustes was the name the newsmen had given to a murderer, who used to tear his victims apart with his bare hands. Any new crime by him was sure to cause a huge echo in society, and newspapers had been releasing flashy headlines like that for many years now: "Monstrous Slaughter!" or "Procrustes gives Police the Runaround!"

The murders happened every six months or even a bit more often, but the investigators didn't even get a millimeter closer to figuring out who it was in all that time. Then, Procrustes simply disappeared.

Died.

"Forget it, Albert!" I cut my friend off. "He died a long time ago. How many years has it been since you've heard anything about him, six? Seven? It's been too long!"

The poet could only wave it off.

"Werewolves never stop! He is not capable of overcoming his animal nature!" he announced matter-of-factly. "A long break? And why not? Procrustes might have been out of town. But now, he's back!"

"He also might have died," I noted reasonably, "and the paper boys are trying to squeeze blood from a stone. I'd bet on that one."

"How do you like my poem *Inhabitant of the Night*?" Albert seemed not to have heard me. "If Procrustes really has returned, that would be quite the hot topic."

"You'll make a laughing stock of yourself," I warned and extended a crumpled fiver under the ticket window. "Two tickets, if you would," then turned to the poet and advised him: "Better throw that foolishness out of your mind..."

Albert answered with a glance full of skepticism and carefully rolled his newspaper up into a tube.

"You haven't convinced me."

"You'll be sorry."

"Don't fight it, old buddy. It's a gold mine!"

Bickering, we walked under the raised arch and, there Albert ran straight off to place bets. I decided against throwing my money to the wind and, feigning carelessness, leaned on my elbows against the stone stairway banister, waiting for my friend. Actually, though, I was simply giving my weary legs a rest.

Then suddenly, a shiver ran up my spine as if a draft had managed to go straight up my jacket. It was a stiff breeze and thorny like a thistle bush.

I turned around without delay, shifted the loop of my glasses down to the very tip of my nose and looked at the people walking past above my darkened lenses. I didn't notice anything suspicious and was already preparing to put my glasses back in place when I suddenly caught a strange shadow coming off one of the viewers' shoulders with the corner of my eye. It would sometimes dissolve into an indistinct mirage, and sometimes take on a certain share of definition, but my gaze could never catch it no matter what I did.

I immediately rushed off after the unfamiliar man and, without the slightest doubt, would have caught him, if I hadn't twisted the foot on my sprained leg. But then, as I groaned in pain and restored my balance, the strange gentleman had already fled from my sight, and I felt Albert grabbing me.

"Leo!" he grew surprised. "Where are you going?"

"Nowhere now," I winced, having realized that I couldn't remember the uncanny stranger's face, or even clothing.

Anyway, what would I have said to him? "Hey! You've got a shadow on your shoulder!?"

Nonsense!

"Let's go!" The poet hurried me on. "The race is starting!"

In one of his hands, he was squeezing a pile of little bet tickets, and in the other there was a rented pair of theater binoculars. Seeing that, it became clear that Albert was firm in his intention to spend this time as best he could; not even a trace remained of his earlier skepticism.

We walked through into the hippodrome and went up the stairs, which had been worn down for centuries, until we reached the second deck. There were plenty of viewers up here too, but the huge size of the amphitheater meant that it was still not hard to find a free seat; the ancients built in style, you could not take that away from them.

A huge field spread out before us; in the middle, there was green grass. Around it, there stretched the oval of a racetrack. At the same time, you could have a half dozen other athletic competitions here. It wasn't for nothing that Baron de Coubertin had insisted on holding the Third Olympic Games precisely in New Babylon.

The pandemonium that reigned over it now was fairly extreme...

The sky, as before, was blanketed with a

gray sheet of clouds, so Albert waved off a parasol offered to him by an old man, sat on the stone bench and took out his flask. He removed the stopper, and the subtle aroma of calvados drifted up to my nose.

I took the yellowed ivory binoculars from the poet and craned my neck, looking at the dirigible hovering over the arena. Despite the gusts of wind, it was staying in one place as if it had been glued there; the whole hippodrome must have been as easy to see from there as the palm of your hand.

"The horses run on the ground, not in the sky," Albert reminded me, taking another gulp.

"I am aware," I grumbled and handed over the VIP theater glasses.

Elizabeth-Maria von Nalz was sitting there, hand-in-hand with the nephew of the Minister of Justice, a doughy young man in a suit worth six times what mine was. My heart began to groan as if it had been pierced with a rusty needle.

"The horses don't run in the skyboxes for the mucky-mucks either," the poet chuckled, following my gaze.

I tore myself from the binoculars, looking expressively at my friend and asked:

"Did you bet a lot of money?"

"What does it matter to you?" Albert flared up, hurt to the quick by my insinuation. "I mean,

I'll make it all back right now just from Admiral. He'll definitely come in first!"

"So, he's the reliable favorite? Who gave you the tip?"

The poet just snorted pointedly, took the binoculars and set about following the horses as they burst from their stalls. With an unbelievable speed, the main group carried past us; then I elbowed the poet in the side and wondered:

"Well, what?"

"Admiral is in the next race," Albert told me, not pulling away from the oculars.

"Oh, that garbage!" I waved it off and shook my head: "How can you trust unintelligent beasts and their riders with your money? The only thing those riders are good for is their low weight."

"Remind me, Leo, who was it that dragged me down here?"

"Hey, I'm just trying to move the conversation along."

"Ah, then!" The poet took the call, then parried without the slightest hesitation: "Dice or roulette is a much more chance-based game. There are always perennial favorites at the races. They look at the horse, and look at the jockey. They study the stats and figure out what the condition of the horse and rider is at race time. How they get along, how they work against the competition. It's a whole science, my friend. A whole science!"

I chuckled.

"But the guy who handles it all is some creep who wouldn't be ashamed of taking a couple tenners from you and another dozen simpletons for a supposedly sure bet."

"A fiver. It was just a fiver," Albert corrected me. "And the bet really is a sure thing. Admiral will come in first."

"You're throwing your money away. You'll realize that soon enough."

"Wanna bet?" The poet suggested.

"It would be base on my part to profit from your loss," I refused. "Look, they're already taking out the horses."

Albert looked into the binoculars again, then handed them to me.

"Just look at that beaut! He's simply fated to win!"

I glanced and involuntarily found myself appreciating my friend's confidence. Admiral was impressive. Bundles of muscles pumped away beneath the graceful animal's shiny coat. Its movements were smooth and confident.

"I say!" The poet took the binoculars and purred out an incomprehensible song to himself. After that, he jabbed me in the side and nodded at the arena. "Really, just look!"

"Yes, I'm looking, I'm looking," I mumbled

without particular enthusiasm.

Start! The horses burst from their places, and Admiral immediately tore out in front. He sped along like the wind and, after the second turn, was ahead of his nearest competitor by more than two full body-lengths.

"Come on!" Albert shouted out when the racers sped past us. "Hit it! Faster!"

And soon added another couple words that were totally and completely inappropriate.

And it really was something!

The stallion in second, with white speckles on his forehead, suddenly started speeding up and began to reduce the distance between himself and the favorite. The jockey in a black helmet and red vest was glued to his back.

"Run, devil beat you!" The poet yelped out. "Run!"

But by then, the distance had gone down to half a body-length. Then the horses got up nostril to nostril. As they came around another turn, Albert glued himself to the binoculars again.

"Giddy up, you old screw!" he muttered angrily under his breath, occasionally punctuating his appeals with words that would make even a longshoreman scratch the back of his head in embarrassment.

But then, the poet jumped to his feet, swung his arm up and released the bet tickets into the air. I, though, gave him an encouraging clap on the shoulder.

"Throwing your money away?"

"Argentum!" Albert moaned. "Leo, did you see that? Argentum went around Admiral like he was standing still!"

I didn't want to pour salt into my friend's internal wounds, so I simply took his binoculars. I looked at the VIP box and was simply taken aback for a moment when it seemed that I met eyes with Elizabeth-Maria. I quickly lowered the binoculars and calmed my floundering breathing.

Elizabeth-Maria must have been looking somewhere in front of me. Not at me. She had long forgotten about the existence of the ungainly detective constable. Had long since cast him from her mind. The inspector general was right. I was no match for her.

But, all the same, I could trade a few words with her by chance. I might even be able to find a reason for it, but the sensationalist newspapermen were pecking away at the supposed return of Procrustes and had pushed the story about the murderous muse off into the police blotter section.

Curses!

My mood was instantly spoiled. I glanced at my time-piece and asked:

"Albert, are you going somewhere?"

"Huh? No! There's three more races!" My gambling friend called back, shuffling through his remaining bet tickets.

"I've gotta go. See you later."

"Until next time!" The poet waved it off and took some nips of his calvados flask, but immediately came to his senses: "Leo! Come by tomorrow! Without fail! Do you hear me?"

"I hear you," I answered and set about carefully descending the slippery steps to the lower level. My leg hadn't started hurting any less, and just one careless step threatened ending in a fall that would be just as funny to watch as it would be painful.

But I made it. I didn't even lose my balance once.

And afterward, already coming out onto the square in front of the hippodrome, I suddenly felt that something was wrong and turned around in bewilderment. I was taken aback in surprise to find myself face to face with Elizabeth-Maria.

My Elizabeth-Maria, the succubus!

I was overcome with indignation, but I didn't make a scene.

"What the devil are you doing here?" I simply whispered quietly when the girl had caught up to me and taken me by the hand.

"You didn't come home last night," Elizabeth-Maria reminded me, "and I started to get worried."

"How did you find me?"

"You and I are connected, don't forget that."

"Well, don't do this again!" I ordered.

"Leopold," the girl squinted unhappily. "That all depends on you and you alone." And, after making an abrupt transition back to being sweet and caring, she cooed out: "Shall we go home, dear?"

I shook my head:

"I have business."

"May I come with you?"

"No," I cut her off, and grudgingly explained my decision: "Your presence would be improper."

"More corpses?"

"Not mine," I answered, slightly bending the truth.

"You still smell of death, Leo," Elizabeth-Maria lowered her voice. "Of death and fear."

"That's enough!"

But it wasn't so easy to brush the succubus off.

"Is it true that I stick out like a sore thumb?" she smiled. "You know, dear, I was actually mistaken on your account. I supposed that there was some ailing shame preventing you from opening up about your feelings to that *illustrious* bean pole. But no, you simply are not capable of it. You are deathly afraid of being rejected! You have so many fears..."

"Have you all come to an understanding or something?!" I couldn't resist, but immediately got myself together and called a cabby. "Take the lady home!" I ordered him, sitting Elizabeth-Maria in the carriage and handing him a crumpled fiver. "We'll talk later."

"As you say, dear," she answered coldly.

I ignored her unhappy tone and headed off to find a free carriage. It was time to go to the raising of the armored car...

3

I HAD ARRIVED EARLY to the Euler bridge. I had bought some candied nuts from a hawker and was now loafing about on the embankment nibbling on them and looking into the cloudy water of the river.

The sky was not visible this evening. Quite the opposite, in fact. The city was enveloped in a gray fog, so the first sign I saw of the tug was puffs of black exhaust coming from its smokestack. Only a few minutes later did its rusted body with low, creeping walls come into view.

Assuming it was precisely this washtub

that had been designated for the raising of the armored car, I headed for the hole in the bridge wall that had been strung in front of with a strong rope and little red flags to make it safe.

I didn't walk up close to the opening, instead walking up to the railing a few steps from it. No, fear of heights was not one of my many phobias, but falling down from a sudden gust of wind wouldn't have been fun at all, regardless of my mental condition. From such heights, there was no difference at all between falling on water and falling on concrete.

And, as I'd supposed, the tug was anchored directly opposite the hole in the railing, and soon a diver came out on its deck dressed in a rubber suit with a hard round helmet; a sickly sailor deftly attached a flexible tube to him and, turning the wheel of a compressor, started pumping down air. The diver stuck his thumb upward, grabbed onto the cable of the steam hauler on the aft of the tug and slowly descended down into the water.

I looked around, not understanding why the investigators were late, but only then noticed Maurice LeBrun and Bastian Moran standing on a stone loading dock off the square. They had already gone down to the river and were observing the tug team with measured interest. Not far away, there was a police coach and four constables stopping the newspapermen and gawkers from getting close.

I supposed the armored car would be set in that very spot after being raised, so I hurried to find a place to stand near the police leadership. But the same detective sergeant I'd seen earlier, red-mustached and yellow-eyed, saw me approaching and tore himself from his paper. He waved me toward him. When I got closer, he dismounted and extended a few sheets of paper to me, filled with even lines of printed letters, blurred and dull from the carbon-copy paper they were transferred with.

"A copy for the Witstein Banking House," the investigator said and demanded: "Sign here."

I placed a flourish and pointed at the loading dock.

"May I..."

"Yes, you can go through," the detective sergeant allowed, and leaned back over his tablet, filling out the header of the armored-car investigation from in advance.

After rolling the papers up into a tube, I walked down to the loading dock and stood a bit away from the top brass. I couldn't hear what they were conversing about. Senior inspector Moran immediately turned toward me and melted into a malignant smile:

"Viscount! I can see an unasked question

in your eyes!"

The disappearance of the word "constable" from my usual address cut me to the core, but I didn't make it known and only shrugged my shoulders carelessly.

"I'm surprised to see people from Department Three here, yes," I confirmed, trying on the role of representative of the Banking House. Also, at the same time, I was resigning myself to the fact that my forthcoming reinstatement to my former post was now something impossibly ephemeral. If not to say quite improbable.

"And why's that?" The senior inspector asked in surprise.

"There are no infernal creatures or spies mixed up in the robbery. It all seems rather straightforward."

"Straightforward?" Maurice LeBrun flared up. "You think you know enough about this to say that?!"

Bastian Moran clapped the head of the CID on the shoulder and nodded.

"I cannot disagree with Mr. LeBrun on this issue," he said didactically, looking me in the eyes, "there isn't one centime of straightforwardness in this matter. Viscount! Even in these difficult times, robbing a bank with flamethrowers and handheld mortars is a bit unorthodox. Or do you not think so?"

The inspector general's steadfast gaze pressed into me and knocked me off guard, but my dark glasses helped me keep my presence of mind. I repeated calmly.

"I still think it's quite straightforward," I repeated again, pointing to the tug with my tube of forms. The tug's fore was raised up over the water, but the aft was clearly dragging down. "Or it will be in a quarter hour."

"Oh, to be young again," Senior Inspector Moran shook his head, took out a pack of Chesterfields, lit a cigarette and smiled. "I wish I had your confidence."

"You can say that again!" Maurice LeBrun agreed with him and dug through his pockets, but instead of a cigarette, took out a tin of sugar drops.

I also decided to enjoy a candy.

"It is extremely beneficial for me to take part in the uncovering of this mysterious conspiracy," I announced, popping a mint sugar drop into my mouth, "but the aspiration to fame that you saw in me doesn't prevent me from telling the difference between what I want and what is real."

"Perhaps, perhaps," Bastian Moran nodded.

But the head of the CID wondered logically:

"Are you telling me the Judeans spent up everything they had on your considerable advance?"

"Come now, senior inspector!" I laughed with all ease I could muster. "The advance was just a formality. Just a pretense for me to figure out the situation firsthand."

"I thought it was straightforward," Inspector Moran immediately reminded me of my recent affirmation.

"It will be as soon as the armored car is raised," I turned back and looked at the tug that had begun slightly drifting from the center of the river to one side. Behind it, stretched out the white surf. From time to time, you could see the roof of the armored self-propelled carriage peeking out between the waves.

Bastian Moran followed my gaze and shrugged his shoulders:

"Let's wait and see."

Maurice LeBrun snorted then in a totally undefined way.

I even started getting the sense that certain progress must have been made since our last meeting, but I decided to hold back from too much inquiry.

Everything would become clear on its own soon.

The tug at that time was approaching the

loading dock, and puffs of acrid black smoke were rolling over us. The rusty tub began to tip slightly backward. The steam crane gave a heart-rending creak, winding in the underwater cable. The aft finally sat properly, but before a short wave crashed over the side, the armored car revealed itself. Cloudy streams of water were pouring out of all openings in the self-propelled carriage, then the wheels, steeped in the river muck and sea weed, touched down on the unloading dock, and the sailor that jumped ashore set about hauling in the cable.

I imagined what it must have been like to fly off the bridge in that iron casket, then slowly sink to the bottom without any hope of rescue, and involuntarily felt a nervous shudder.

The robbers must have died when the vehicle hit the water.

When the sailor had unclipped the cable, a constable came out in a waterproof jumpsuit and high rubber boots. Using a crowbar as a lever, he applied his weight and the jammed door suddenly flung open in one abrupt burst. Cloudy water gushed out underfoot, and I hurriedly jumped back, not wanting to get my shoes soaked.

But I was still able to notice the fact that the cabin was empty.

There were no drowned people inside, neither in the driver's seat, nor the passenger's;

there was just some incomprehensible iron box flickering in the light with fresh rust and a set of metallic rails attaching it to the steering wheel.

But where were the people? Where were the people?!

"Back door!" Bastian Moran ordered.

The constable broke the lock in a few confident strikes, then stuck the flattened end of the crowbar between some folds and easily broke them, but the armored car's back seat was also empty.

No bodies, and no stolen valuables were to be found inside.

"What the devil?" I couldn't hold back from the surprised exclamation, walking straight through the puddle that formed and looking inside. "Where'd they go?"

"As you can see, Viscount, not everything is so unambiguous here," Senior Inspector Moran noted instructively.

Maurice LeBrun squeezed out a sour smile and kept his distance from the armored car.

"Bastian, it turned out that you were completely right. And you hold all the cards," he grumbled. He then called the detective sergeant over and ordered: "Make a note in the report!"

"Sir, yes sir," he sounded off in a military manner.

But I just stood there flapping my eyelids,

having a weak understanding of what they were talking about.

Moran perceived the head of the CID's declaration as a matter of course and pointed to the iron box for the constable in the water-proof overalls.

"That box! Pull it out!" He demanded.

The police man tried to carry out the order, but it turned out to have been battened down very tight.

"Break it out!" The senior inspector allowed. "The main thing is not to damage the box... more than necessary."

Then the constable pulled it off the rails without particular ceremoniousness and hauled the box out of the cabin. He placed it directly on the earth and stood up straight in anticipation of further orders.

"Open it!" Bastian Moran ordered. He then looked at Maurice LeBrun and melted into a satisfied smile.

The wave of good fortune that came over him could be physically felt in the literal sense.

"Now here is the riddle to end all riddles! A person going missing from a room locked from the inside is child's play compared to this!"

For the first time in a long time, I was in complete and total agreement with my senior colleague.

If there weren't any people in the armored car, who had been driving it? It couldn't be that some unknown craftsman had put the route into that incomprehensible iron box as a mechanic puts the melody in a music box, right?

How could you possibly consider all the nuances? Absurd!

It should be said, though, that it would become clear soon enough...

The constable tore the lid off the metallic box, but what was waiting for us inside was a total disappointment: the box was filled with the remaining scraps of a twisted mechanism.

"Before the fall, witnesses heard a clap that resembled an explosion," the detective sergeant reminded us.

Bastian Moran nodded thoughtfully, then began staring at me.

"Viscount!" he smiled. "In that none of your client's property was found in the armored car, I suppose that your further presence here is unnecessary. I'm sorry, but this is still a confidential investigation."

I hesitated, then Maurice LeBrun waved his hand at the constables standing in the distance.

"There's no point," I smiled. "As a matter of fact, I should be going now anyway. I must update my employer on the case."

And I took a step up the stairs, not wanting

to end up thrown out of the police cordon before the eyes of the random gawkers and colleagues. Or were they already former colleagues?

Be that as it may, on the embankment there were city-dwellers crowding up. I didn't hang around though, and headed for the nearest cafe, intending to have a bite to eat and gather my thoughts before telling Isaac Levinson about the complications with his case.

THE NEAREST PLACE TO GET a bite was the *Golden Lilly*, a small coffee shop with an open terrace overlooking the Yarden Embankment. In the sky, there were black clouds gathering, but if there was bad weather or rain, I would be protected by the canvas overhang, so I chose a seat with a view of the river and lounged about in a chair with soft padding and waited for a waiter. The drafts didn't scare me.

When they brought the menu, I ordered a couple of croissants and a pot of black Ceylon tea and looked at a triple-decker steamship floating up the river. The colossus went quickly upstream and, for a moment, it seemed that it was I who was traveling on the water, and not the passengers of the *Samuel Morse* at all.

It should be said that I wasn't occupied with that thought for long; I turned away from the window and began studying the documents from the detective sergeant. At first, I didn't notice anything interesting, but soon, I reached the list of valuables stolen from the bank, and then I could barely hold back from slapping myself on the forehead and swearing out loud.

I understood! I understood why Bastian Moran was acting so improperly!

The list was empty; a single line was all it contained. The robbers hadn't taken anything; not one safe had been broken into.

And a rational question arose: had something gone wrong during the robbery, or had the criminals simply been following a pre-arranged plan?

I finished my hot tea and came to the conclusion that I didn't remember seeing any panic. Each of the robbers had completed their assigned task: the bomber had destroyed the wall and placed the thermite charge on the vault; the flamethrower had gotten into the bank and cleared out the building methodically, while the soldier with the hand-held mortar and the machine gunner had chased off the police men and provided the armored car with an unimpeded escape. It was a fully real tactical operation.

The criminals also knew about the ambush – the barber shop had been shot up before anyone of the police officers that were embedded there had revealed themselves. There was no way this could have happened without traitors in the Newton-Markt.

If the bomber didn't make a mistake with the explosive charge, and the gunners had taken the risk of a direct confrontation with the police not in order to rob – the safes were not opened, after all! – the only logical explanation left for what had happened was that the criminals had been ordered to destroy something in the bank vault. Probably, it was some documents, in that the papers had all burned up while the jewelry, gold coins and bullion, even though it had melted, was not truly destroyed by the fire.

So then, it was papers. Did that sense? Sure.

And with that, I came to a dead end. I had no idea what the robbers were really after. The only unsolved clue that remained was, as before, the armored car.

How had they been able to lead their pursuers by the finger? Even if you accept the unbelievable fact that their self-propelled carriage was being driven by a mysterious mechanism, no genius on earth would be able to place the proper order of actions on the narrow streets of the old city inside it.

At the very least, there must have been a driver behind the wheel while it was in the Judean Quarter. But then, at what stage did the box appear? The box was screwed tightly shut. It was no more than five minutes of work, but the police never let the armored car out of their sight for such an extended amount of time.

And, at the end of the day, where had the Gatling gun gone? Senior Inspector Moran had let that fact slip from view. After all, it must have weighed quite a bit. It was attached to the vehicle, and so taking it all the way off would have taken no less than a quarter hour.

They couldn't have sunk a fake to throw the pursuit off their trail, right?

I called over the boy who was clearing off the tables, gave him five francs and sent him to a book stall to buy the most detailed map of the city he could find. After that, I started underlining places in the protocol of where and when the armored car was seen by witnesses, thinking on the motive for the crime as I did so.

What for? What extreme circumstance could drive people to such a dangerous outing? There was no lost love for cop killers. They were bated like rabid dogs! What was at stake here?

When the boy I'd sent out for a map returned, I was so elated that I let him keep all the change. I immediately regretted it, but it was too late. I unfolded the huge paper sheet on the table and set about marking the supposed route of the armored car, including key places and times it had been seen. The investigators in charge of the preliminary investigation had done a huge amount of work here, and even had the energy to add information about each witness's watch, but they hadn't considered it necessary to actually draw out the route on a map. And that wasn't too surprising. At that time, the self-propelled carriage was already resting on the bottom of the Yarden.

The waiters were shooting sidelong looks at their strange visitor and whispering amongst themselves, but they didn't have the resolve to come over and say anything. I, though, didn't pay the gossips any mind. Once again, I was grasping at straws trying to make things add up.

The armored car sped away from the police coach at the exit point from the Judean Quarter. From there, it had been spotted by a sentry on Mendeleev Avenue, and the self-propelled carriage had almost hit a traffic controller at the intersection with Galileo Street. From there, the robbers had disappeared again, then a few minutes later, appeared on Euler Bridge.

The problem came down to the fact that it would have actually been impossible for them to reach the bridge in those few minutes!

It couldn't have been a mistake either – the first thing that is pounded into every constable's ear after being hired is to make sure you get a time with every report. One person may make a mistake, or even two, but if three or four agreed, it must have been right.

So that means there really were two armored cars, then?

I sucked on that thought from all sides. I outlined the block where the robbers got away from the pursuit a second time, payed for my tea and headed off to find a free cab, feeling like a clever fellow once again.

I went to the office of a realtor, who had been recommended to me a few months earlier by my fiduciary. The gold-lettered business card had been hanging around pointlessly in my wallet that whole time, but now it was coming in handy.

In the office, I carelessly threw it to a clerk wearing an old-fashioned frock coat with elbow patches sewn over his sleeves:

"Viscount Cruce..." and was suddenly led into his senior partner's office.

A flashy name and fashionable outfit were a majestic thing! And it didn't matter that the *illustrious* aristocrat was bankrupt with a mountain of unpaid bills.

"Viscount!" A gentleman of commanding stature wearing a suit stood up from behind the desk. His suit was so ideally tailored to his figure, which had already begun to slightly deteriorate, that my estimation of my fiduciary fell sharply.

If he had recommended a person who spent that kind of money on tailors, that must have meant that he had no respect for his employer's money.

"Would you like some wine? Brandy?" The man offered. "Or, if you'd like, a cigar?"

"I'd prefer to get straight to business!" I refused decisively and spread out the map I'd riddled with marks on the desk. "I'm interested in renting a property on this block. A spacious hangar or a warehouse with a straight driveway."

"Allow me to think..." the realtor faltered.

No such luck!

"I haven't got time for that!" I cut him off. "My business partner will be arriving from Rome tomorrow, and his idiot of a secretary took the pains to inform me of that fact via telegram just one hour ago. This affair will not bear delay!"

"So, you're sure you want this neighborhood specifically?"

Yes, devil take me! I need precisely that neighborhood, and no other!

"It is a business, the details of which I am not at liberty to disclose. I need to rent a warehouse there and only there. Another thing: I am prepared to buy out any current renters or pay for a sublet if someone is willing."

The realtor glanced at the map with unhidden doubt, thought briefly and jabbed his finger into the western part of the space I'd outlined.

"There are coalhouses here. I suggest we start there."

Curses! I could have guessed myself! From late autumn until the beginning of spring, the warehouses were bursting with coal for heating private residences, offices and shops, but when it warmed up, demand for fuel fell and some of the warehouses were left empty until the next season. It was easier not to touch them at all than to clean them all the way up and try to find renters who would get out by the end of September.

I couldn't resist snapping my fingers, as it just played to the image I was creating of an eccentric aristocrat full of ignorance in matters of business.

"Coalhouses, but of course! Let's go there at once!"

The realtor sighed fatefully, not burning with the desire to get his fashionable suit all ruined in the coal dust.

"Unfortunately, I have a meeting scheduled that I cannot cancel. I'll send my assistant with you," he easily navigated his way out of the complex situation. "I assure you, my man is very well-informed."

"Great!" I lit up. "Let's go!"

And so we went.

THE COALHOUSES TURNED OUT to be a ghastly hole. On one side, there were barracks that ran up against them with broken windows and doors, already scheduled for demolition. On the other, there was an overgrown weed-filled wasteland, the fence to a boiler-house and the back of a dye shop. With that, the next building over was overflowing with noise from the lively street.

An ideal place. No one would see, hear or know a thing.

You'd never think of a better one, but the guard at the gate must have seen the armored car. I wonder how they got around that? Had they slipped him 25 francs, or was he working on the inside?

As it turned out, it was neither. The robbers simply hadn't worried about his "tall tales."

When I walked through the open doors and looked at the guard box, I immediately decided that the bored-looking gentleman sitting there was too attractive to be a simple guardsman. But all the same, I clarified:

"My good sir, could you please tell me how to get in touch with the manager here?"

The well fed man of thirty years sighed and answered with poorly hidden annoyance:

"You're looking at him!"

"Is that so?" I couldn't hold back my surprise. "Things are going so badly that you're subbing for the night guard?"

"Things are going amazingly as long as my renters don't start treating the night guard to rum!" the manager furrowed his brow. "Some people! Do they even think? They rent a warehouse, and get the guard drunk! Nonsense!"

"That truly is nonsense," I agreed. "And what, he goes nuts when he drinks?"

"He's been drinking for three days straight," the man confirmed, then grew suspicious: "And what do you want?"

"We wanted to rent the warehouse," the realtor's assistant slipped into the conversation.

"Business is picking up!" the manager threw up his hands. "It used to be months I couldn't find renters, but you're the second ones to come this week!"

I didn't hesitate for an instant and gave a rage-filled tirade off the cuff:

"Curses! It was no accident that the telegram came late! They're trying to throw me overboard!"

The manager's mouth gaped in surprise:

"What are you talking about?"

"My associates and I agreed to rent..." I cut off the story half-way and sharply asked: "Who signed the agreement? Galliamo? A swarthy with a mustache like a circus performer?"

"Not at all," the manager muttered, thrown off by my unexpected charge. "A gray old man came, who introduced himself as Martin Guichard."

"That rapscallion had a dummy rent it out! Did he leave an address? Did he pay by check?"

"No, cash."

"Is he here now?"

I took a step onto the property, and the manager immediately jumped out of the guard booth:

"Just what is going on here?!"

"Is he here now?" I repeated my question.

"No!" The manager shouted out savagely. "He got the guard drunk, the low-life, and hasn't shown himself for two days now! But what is it to you?"

"He's totally disappeared?" I drooped, not exaggerating one bit.

The robbers had left without leaving an address. I might as well be looking for wind in a field!

"We should probably go," the realtor's assistant started fussing.

I cast my gaze on the gloomy constructions and the coal-dusted earth, shifted my gaze to the glossy face of the manager and leaned into him in confidence:

"Tell me, would you mind if I took a little peek at their warehouse? You have my word that I won't touch a thing. I won't even go inside. It is very important to me. Very important. Curses! I would even buy out their rent! But, if you're busy... If you cannot leave the gates..."

On my honor, I do not enjoy convincing people this way. Sure, I don't actually like people very much, but what I've learned in life is to play on others' weaknesses and fears. The manager was not in the mood to sit in the dark booth, and our visit here looked to him like a free show, sent down by fate itself. Refusing himself the simple pleasure of just having a bit of fun was something this simpleton just wasn't capable of.

"I can show you, it's no matter!" He waved his hand and asked the realtor's assistant: "Could you look after the gate while we're inside?"

We walked up to the warehouse. Immediately behind it, there began a coal-covered square under the open sky. The manager set about undoing the heavy padlock.

"They actually haven't brought anything yet," he muttered, turning the key. "If there were some property, then maybe I shouldn't, but why not show him an empty warehouse? It's just a warehouse..."

I noticed the track of a rubber tire imprinted in the coal dust and, just in case, stuck my hand in my pocket and grabbed my Cerberus, but the room was, in fact, absolutely empty.

My companion turned on his electric torch and shined it on the far wall.

"Will this do?" He turned to me. "You can store so many goods in the summer! We don't clean the others, but just look how this one's been mopped up!"

And they really had cleaned the warehouse to a "T;" I stepped across the threshold, removed my glasses and shook my head in feigned delight.

"How spacious!"

"And you know what?" The manager waved his hand excitedly. "Come by on Friday! If those scoundrels still haven't shown up, I'll give the warehouse to you."

"Deal!" I melted into a smile and squeezed his outstretched hand.

I had no doubt that I would have to come back here again. The beam of the torch showed a few round casings on the floor, and that fact convinced me of my theory once and for all. The robbers had waited out the police search in this very place.

The hitch came in the fact that, while I could conduct an independent investigation, I could not hide evidence. Then again, if I got a real private investigator's license...

I walked outside and pointed the manager to a cart approaching the gates.

"That's for you!"

"What a bad break!" he flapped his chubby arms and ran up to the guard box. "Come by on Friday!" he shouted from a run.

"Without fail," I promised and walked up to the cart.

"Well, how'd it go?" the realtor's assistant overtook me.

"It's already rented out for the next month," I sighed and repeated the exclamation that had stuck in my ear: "That's what you call a bad break..."

I GOT RID OF MY COMPANION easily. I simply dropped him off in front of the office, and ordered the cabby to take me to the Judean Quarter.

Isaac Levinson lived on a quiet street where three-story manors nestled up to one another like a pack of stray dogs huddled together for warmth in the dead of winter. All the roofs were touching at the edges. Some buildings even had shared walls, which created the sensation that they were some sort of fortress wall hiding the inner lives of Judean society from outsiders. I was let in to see the banker without any delay. It was enough to simply introduce myself.

It should be said, though, that I did not get by without some nuance. To get from the second floor to the third, I had to use a different set of stairs. The door to his office, as I managed to note, had steel corners, while the windows where outfitted with grates. What was more, there was nothing of value in the room: a table with a decanter and telephone, a clock with three faces, a pair of armchairs for visitors, a bin overflowing with telegraph ribbon as well as a cabinet stuffed with folders. The only place you could have even hidden a safe would have been in the wall behind a portrait of her Imperial Highness...

"Leopold, I'm glad to see you in good health!" Isaac Levinson smiled at my arrival and even stood up from the desk, but I could sense a certain restraint in him. I suppose he wasn't able to decide on what basis to demand I return my advance.

Counting out hundred-franc notes for me, I saw the man had entered a true state of mental turmoil: the robbery, the fire, the deaths; the kind of stuff that would get anyone out of their rut. But, when the emotions subsided and he was made aware that nothing had been stolen, an idea had probably taken root in the banker's head: "Just why should I pay someone for work that the police do for free?"

Revenge? Come off it! Revenge is something ephemeral, but five hundred francs is five hundred francs.

I even grew a bit ashamed. That said, I wasn't feeling ashamed enough to return his money; if a long line of noble ancestors gives you anything, it is a healthy cynicism.

Mr. Levinson's indecisiveness was not rooted in any fundamental decency, but in the simple fact that he was intending to earn a healthy sum by buying out my debts; that was all. Otherwise, he probably would have met me with the demand to see receipts for the fifty francs I'd received with the obligation to return it in a very short time period and with a completely extortionate interest rate.

I wouldn't have been surprised at all, by the way, if such a document was already sitting in the desk drawer.

That was precisely why I went straight on the attack.

"Bad news, Mr. Levinson! Bad news!"

The declaration did not bemuse the banker, but instead of the sentence he had prepared, he involuntarily asked:

"What happened?"

"The armored car was empty!" I announced. "The robbers were not inside it when it sank!"

"Are you sure?!"

"I watched them pull it up from the bottom myself! There was no one inside the self-propelled carriage. You'll get the report tomorrow."

Isaac Levinson fell back in his seat with a thump, finished his water and sighed heavily:

"This gets more and more complicated with every passing hour."

"Yes, this is not what you'd call pleasant news," I nodded, taking a seat in the arm chair and tossing one leg over the other. When his calm began returning, I shared the next portion of bad news: "My colleagues don't even think it was an attempted robbery!"

Isaac Levinson gave a nervous start and asked:

"And what do you think, Leopold?"

"I don't think it smells like a robbery either," I declared dogmatically, not sharing my theory that the malefactors may have been trying to destroy certain documents. Instead of that, I asked: "Mr. Levinson, can you think of anyone who might want you dead?"

The story was painfully obvious, but the higher a person climbs up the social ladder, the more important he considers himself in his personal model of the world.

"That is impossible," Isaac Levinson decisively cut me off, but then I saw that the seed of doubt had hit fertile ground, so I didn't add anything.

Silence reigned in the office for a minute, then the banker added:

"That's not how we do things!" And immediately hit me with a barrage of questions: "How is the investigation coming along? Has there been any headway? What scenarios are the police exploring?"

And though perhaps the thought of the five hundred francs he'd lost for nothing hadn't completely left him, it was certainly now on the back burner, driven back by a new, somewhat more significant problem. Another time when I simply hated my *talent*...

"The police are just twiddling their thumbs," I declared with no innuendo. "They haven't even found the place where the criminals left the armored car."

"And you? Have you found it?"

"I have," I confirmed. "And I'm going to the Newton-Markt right now to inform the higher-ups."

"Oh, please do," Isaac Levinson nodded favorably.

"And how is the debt buy-out coming along?" I then asked.

"I offered five centimes on the franc, but no one agreed to sell for less than thirty," he smiled, feeling in his element once again. "Don't worry. That's just because Count Kósice has yet to make the announcement of your untimely end at the age of five. Mark my words – soon, ten centimes will seem like a generous offer."

"I trust you in this matter."

"But there is one subtlety," the banker unexpectedly skipped ahead. "I control your finances, but I am not monitoring the process of your coming into your inheritance. That could lead to unnecessary complications."

I remembered the expensive suit the realtor was wearing, the same realtor my own fiduciary had sent me to, and suggested with a clean conscious:

"Prepare the documents. I'll sign everything at our next meeting."

"Alright, excellent" the banker relaxed. "Keep up the investigation and keep me up to date on the situation. And now, you'll have to excuse me. I have to make a few business calls."

"At this late hour?" I asked in surprise, casting my gaze at the wall clock.

It was showing nine-fifty-three.

"The Transatlantic Cable is simply a wonder," he laughed. "In New York right now, the work day is in full swing."

"Then I wouldn't dare keep you any longer,"

I got up from the chair and headed for the exit.

A taciturn servant led me to the entrance door, and I set off for the Newton-Markt.

4

IS MONEY ITSELF EVIL? Or is money the root of all evil?

It's a contentious issue. But I know one thing for sure: if I hadn't been such a cheapskate my whole life, I would have ended up in a lot less trouble. Or, at the very least, I could have put a lot of it off for an indefinite amount of time. But then, after writing my report to the head of the CID, I was feeling too stingy to hire a cabby, so I went home on a steam tram. It climbed unhurriedly up the winding slope to Calvary; the place this all started.

To be honest, though, I always preferred ascending the hill on foot. As you walked a meandering path and looked at the city, you could feel the air get fresher with every step. The smells normally suppressed by the char of the city start to peek through – the aromas of wet leaves, freshly cut grass, and spring flowers.

Every time I walked it, I got the impression that I was ascending from the kingdom of the dead, leaving not a stinking cloud of smog, but the subterranean kingdom of Hades itself. And bit by bit, the heavy burdens of grief and concern began to weigh down on me less and less.

Like returning to childhood.

But not this time.

THERE WAS A CHINESE man waiting for me at the bridge.

It was Mr. Chan's helper, propped up on a pillar jutting out of the soil. He was cleaning his finger nails showily with a grimy dagger. In his frayed cap and slightly oversized jacket, he seemed like a scarecrow that had fled from the fields; I don't know how a bird would have reacted, but the sight of him scared me practically to the point of hiccups.

"Mr. Orso!" the enforcer smiled with tranquility and joy, like an innocent child. "Mr. Chan is quite upset with you!"

"What for this time?" I clarified and stopped a few feet from him. Getting right up close to a man with a dagger was not the most intelligent thing to do if you were not a werebeast or a succubus.

How could I not think of Elizabeth-Maria here? But she was far away...

The man chuckled and started enumerating reasons:

"Overdue debts. A Judean trying to buy your debts for almost nothing. Your own uncle refusing to acknowledge you. Your having lost your job. Your inability to pay Mr. Chan back."

I did not argue. It was dumb to argue with a simple messenger. I just asked:

"And what is he going to do about those things?"

The enforcer laughed uncontrollably and stood up from the pillar.

"Your debt is not so great in Mr. Chan's terms, but if you let one go, what's to stop others?"

"What does Mr. Chan want?" I frowned, removing my dark glasses with my left hand.

"Your ear, white-eyes." He repeated the epithet another time, not hiding his mockery.

The chance to torture an *illustrious* gentleman unpunished put him in a state of ecstasy.

"That is very ill-advised."

"No one messes with Mr. Chan."

"And no one is messing with Mr. Chan. He will receive all his money to the last centime."

The man nodded.

"He will. But first he will receive your ear."

"It isn't very smart to do something like that to a policeman," I said weightily, looking him from top to bottom. The enforcer was two heads shorter than me, but he was fast and crafty as a ferret at that.

"You can't hide behind your Pharaoh's badge any longer, white-eyes," the thin cutthroat laughed uncontrollably and took a step toward me. "Don't squirm. This will all be over soon..."

Soon? I took a deep breath and waited for the attack of anger rolling over me to settle down, then demanded in a totally calm voice:

"Stay where you are."

"And what if I don't?" The man snorted, but suddenly froze mid-stride. All I had to do was show him the Cerberus in my hand. "Let's not complicate things," he whispered.

"Let's not," I agreed.

"Are you going to kill me?"

I didn't answer, but not long after, I heard a rustling in the bushes behind my back and warned him:

"If you don't call off your goons, you'll get a bullet in the gut. It'll rot for a week, maybe two. Peritonitis, ever heard of it?"

I wasn't totally sure that the threat would work, but my *talent* came through for me once again, and the man waved his hand nervously; the rustling in the bushes went silent.

"You'll pay for this, white-eyes!" The cutthroat promised, trembling rabidly.

He wasn't afraid to die. He was afraid to be

strapped to a hospital bed. But would there even be a hospital bed? More likely, it would be some dirty mattress in an opium den. It just took one misstep, one show of weakness, and people would stand in line to feast their eyes on your torment.

He didn't want a fate like that for himself. And we both knew that now I would have to pay not only for the overdue debt, but also for this sudden fear attack I'd given him. I'd stuck my finger in an old wound, and earned myself a mortal enemy in the process.

"Drop it," I demanded.

The cutthroat threw his dagger into the grass.

"Now, walk away from the road."

The man obediently made way; there was a scornful smirk playing on his lips. He was firmly intending to get revenge, and was under the impression that he would have it very, very soon.

I walked around him, keeping my pistol trained, turning only when I'd reached the bridge and saying:

"Tell Mr. Chan..." then went silent, realizing that I couldn't change anything with words.

"Tell him what?"

"Nothing," I shook my head. "He'll figure it all out."

Then I kneecapped him with my Cerberus.

The cutthroat collapsed to the earth with a muffled shout. Two shadows leaped from the bushes and threw themselves on their injured leader. I quickly went back and continued moving away until the bridge was behind a corner, no longer visible. Then I turned around and darted home at full speed.

Sure, no one was actually following me, but I only felt safe in the dead garden. The curse gave off a slight burning sensation, which used to give me an eerie, uncomfortable shiver, but now made me breathe a sigh of relief.

Come visit some time! Come visit, if life is good!

I burst out in a soft chuckle and started walking toward the manor, giving off an alluring glow in the darkness through the windows of the guest room.

"Did you run here?" Elizabeth-Maria grew surprised when I entered the house short of breath.

"I didn't want to be late for dinner," I grumbled in reply.

"You aren't even nearly late, though," the girl laughed uncontrollably and commanded my butler: "Theodor, time has come to set the table."

I didn't try to blame a lack of appetite, but still clarified in any case:

"Organ meat again?"

"You think too low of me," Elizabeth-Maria smiled wickedly.

For dinner, she served beef stew with a vegetable ragout.

The meat was tough and over-peppered, but I still didn't criticize the girl's culinary talents. She was being unusually quiet today, and that was totally fine with me.

Dinner passed by with the silence of the grave.

Only when the plate was emptied did I throw myself back into my chair and ask in surprise:

"You decided to switch to white wine?"

Elizabeth-Maria took a look at her glass and shook her head in confusion:

"You know, Leopold? I was sure I'd bought three bottles of red, but two of them seem to have disappeared."

"Don't look at me, I don't drink. And Theodor doesn't abuse alcohol either."

"Curious," the girl stretched out the phrase in contemplation.

Without assigning particular significance to the fact, I headed to my bedroom. When I was in the corridor, I met with my butler, who was carrying a tray with a tea set.

"But what about dessert, Viscount?" Theodor grew surprised.

"Bring it up to me," I asked, myself turning into the bathroom. I removed my jacket, rolled up the sleeves of my shirt, and looked at my arms, burned by the blood of the *fallen one*. The pustules of the Diabolic Plague were growing dim, and hadn't bothered me the whole day, but by evening, they started to itch unbearably once again. And, no matter how long I held them under cold water, it didn't get any better. Quite the opposite, actually – my head started spinning.

When I went into the bedroom, a platter with tea and a basket of cookies was sitting on the bedside table. I locked the door behind myself, checked the blinds and lay down in bed. I poured some tea in the glass, picked up a ragged little edition of *Alice's Adventures in Wonderland* and unexpectedly realized that I didn't have the strength to move my arms or legs.

My weariness set in with an overwhelming weight and, no matter how I tried to struggle against it and concentrate on my reading, my eyes started closing on their own. Taking yet another peck at the tea, I gave in and fell back limply on the pillow.

And an instant later, I was asleep.

I AWOKE WITH THE OVERBEARING sensation there was someone in the room with me.

And my feeling was right. Whoever it was, they were rustling papers, rifling through my drawers, and stirring up my closet.

Someone was looking for something. They looked and cursed mutely to themselves.

"Bugger! Bugger! Bugger!" muttered my anonymous guest, as he turned the room topsy-turvy.

Meanwhile, I simply lay on my bed with my eyes closed and waited for the vision borne of my fevered imagination to fade away.

A carriage horn rang out piercingly, further increasing my consternation.

I got up on one elbow, but the blinds were closed, and my bedroom was full of dense, impenetrable shadows. I couldn't even see a single sign of light: there was nothing coming under the crack in the door, and the crimson pustules on my upper body weren't even glowing.

The last thing actually made me happy, but...

But there was still someone in my room.

I struck a long match on the side of the box, lit a gas lamp and squinted, waiting for my eyes to grow accustomed to the light. But then, I couldn't hold back and cursed out:

"Curse me! Don't let it be you!"

In response, I heard a gurgling, as if the person had opened their throat and poured a few swallows of wine down it.

It should be said that my "as if" turned out to be very prescient, as that truly was what I was hearing.

On the window sill, there sat a white-haired leprechaun in a top hat so rumpled it looked like an accordion bellows. He had a green camisole flung open on his chest, and boots that were too small, making his thick toes stick out the tip with their unevenly chewed down nails. His broad leather belt with a copper clasp was holding a fairly large kitchen knife close to his body.

The red-eyed albino pipsqueak – and the height of my uninvited guest didn't even reach one meter – tore himself from the emptied bottle, retched and suddenly asked:

"Where'd you hide the good stuff, Leo? Rum, whiskey, vodka, brandy? You're a big boy now. Big boys don't drink sugar water!"

"Be gone!" I demanded, throwing myself back into the pillow and screwing up my eyes, chasing off the escaped memory.

My head was splitting as if it had been I that lapped up all the wine Elizabeth-Maria had bought, not the leprechaun, and now I was suffering from a terrible hangover.

"Kiss my ass!" The little man called back, having prudently jumped down from the window sill, making himself a much less easy target.

But I didn't start throwing pillows at him. Instead, I took a few deep sighs and tried to cast the crazy vision from my head. And I practically managed, but then came a knock at the door, accompanied by the voice of Elizabeth-Maria.

"Leo, open up!" she called. "They've come for you!"

Before I could stand to my feet and open the door, the leprechaun came out from under the table and was standing next to it. He slid the latch aside and took a nimble step back into a shadow. But when Elizabeth-Maria entered the bedroom, he slapped her below the back as hard as he could, and leaped nimbly into the corridor to the sound of a piercing woman's scream.

"Bugger! What an ass!" His rollicking laughter echoed down the hall.

"What was that?!" A rabid Elizabeth-Maria shouted at me.

"What'd it look like?"

"Like a handsy gray-haired leprechaun!"

I just sighed and set about pulling up my pants.

"Leo!" The girl raised her voice. "What was that?"

"A nightmare," I answered, buttoning up my shirt.

"Since when do your nightmares spank

me?" Elizabeth Maria frowned, but immediately smiled: "Leo, is that your secret desire?"

"More like your secret fear."

"Balderdash! I would let you spank me as much as you like!"

"Not that," I shook my head peevishly. "You're afraid of losing control. Think about that at your leisure. And lock the wine cabinets. We've got an infestation on our hands."

Elizabeth-Maria measured me up with her gaze, but said nothing, just flinging open the window, trying to get the lingering smell of alcohol out of the room.

"Why did you have to go to work at such an early hour?" The girl asked, looking out at the street.

And in fact: The crimson ball of sun had just barely started coming up and was at the very edge of the horizon, peeking out through a layer of clouds. It was five or six o'clock, no later.

I looked at my time-piece, and I was right.

"No good deed goes unpunished," I muttered, having no doubt that the call was connected with the robber's hide-out I'd discovered yesterday.

Either the investigators had managed to get the trail of the robbers and needed to clarify some data, or Senior Inspector Moran had decided to give me a tongue lashing for taking action on my own. I couldn't possibly imagine that the police leadership was burning with desire to thank me.

"I say!" Elizabeth-Maria readjusted my poorly tied-on neckerchief, then smiled sweetly and warned: "Keep your fears to yourself, Leo. Otherwise, I'll tear their arms off!"

"You'll have to catch him first," I snorted, replacing a spent shell in the magazine of my Cerberus with a new round, and placing the pistol in my jacket's side pocket.

After that, I pulled out the lower drawer of my bureau, and took my towel-wrapped Roth-Steyr from it. This one was my property though, not police-issue. I hesitated for a moment as to whether to bring it or not, but remembered the Chinese men who might be following me and decided another barrel couldn't hurt.

But basically, the earlier I called on Mr. Chan to assure the old skinflint that I would soon return my debts to him, the better it was for me. At the same time, I remembered that some nebulous factor in the formulation of our loan contract should stop him from insisting unilaterally that I immediately pay back the whole debt, so I just had to be patient.

I figured we'd come to an agreement somehow. If I'd learned one thing in life, it was how to find a common language with loan sharks.

I GRABBED MY DERBY HAT in the entryway, and walked out under the very, very cloudy sky. I snapped my dark glasses to my nose in a habitual motion, I opened the gate, walked outside and froze like I'd been buried. There were three automatic Madsen-Biarnoff carbines pointed right at me.

"Hands on your head!" A red-mustached detective sergeant commanded. It was the same man who had handed me the investigation report forms. "On your knees!"

Sometimes you have to carry out orders without delay or any unnecessary questions. Just do what they say, then try to figure out what's going on.

And now was just such a time. With the fingers of the three constables trembling on their triggers, there was no point in talking about rights or demanding explanations; one of them might just have a nerve snap.

So I got down on my knees and put my palms on the back of my head.

Slowly and in silence.

The detective sergeant walked up behind me, dexterously spun one of my arms behind my back, then the other, clipped me into a pair of handcuffs, then started rooting through my pockets.

"What is happening?" I stopped short, but

the investigator just hissed in reply, deftly pulling my Roth-Steyr from its holster.

It was scary; the constables were far too on edge. I could simply feel their nerves tingling, as if their hands were itching to open fire at the first sign of disobedience.

And that scared me. It scared me with how wrong-headed it was.

What bad luck must have befallen me that they were now looking on me as an enemy?

Some foolishness...

At that moment, the leprechaun came out of the self-propelled carriage. Stroking his neck, he turned away to the back wheel of the armored car and started pissing on it in a business-like manner, calmly and without the slightest hint of hurry. But when the nearest constable looked over, the imp had already hidden in the bushes. The only thing left was a yellow puddle pooled on the ground.

"Dogs..." the police-man frowned uncertainly.

The detective sergeant meanwhile deprived me of my knife, my Cerberus, my lighter, my wallet and my watch. He then took a step back and commanded:

"Get up," and immediately warned: "Slowly!"

I jerked forward, stood to my feet and took

a look around:

"Would you mind explaining this?"

"No such luck!" The detective sergeant simply shoved me toward the armored car. I had to crawl into the cabin with barred windows; the armored door was instantly clapped shut, and the lock clicked.

Curses! What the hell happened?

THEY TOOK ME STRAIGHT to the Newton-Markt, but didn't let me out of the car at the front door, or even in the normal garage. I didn't get out until we reached the room for arrestees. And it would have been fine if I'd just been let out there, but no, with rifles pointed at me, they cuffed my legs together.

Usually, this was done only to especially dangerous recidivists and malefics, so my back immediately soaked through with sweat. It turned out to be surprisingly easy to deal with the panic, though.

No one had even tried to detain Elizabeth-Maria, which meant that they simply didn't know about the succubus, and no matter what they were going to accuse me of, associating with infernal creatures would not be part of it. That meant this wasn't about the death of Inspector White...

So I calmed myself down, clanking together

the shackles that forced me to walk in very short steps like a Chinese concubine before the eternal Emperor. I was led through the Newton-Markt by three investigators with police-issue revolvers drawn and the detective sergeant walking in front. We shuffled past a few empty intersections and incomprehensible corridors, but when we stopped in front of the familiar door of Department Three, I wasn't surprised in the least.

The fact that they didn't release me from my shackles even in the interrogation room was an unpleasant surprise, though. What was more, my legs were also attached to a set of rings interred in the wall, and my handcuffs were attached to a set of iron loops on the table.

I didn't ask the reason for such extreme safety measures.

I already knew it would be useless.

I had no desire to look at the bare, windowless walls anyway, so I threw myself into the high back of the chair and lowered my eyelids. The headache that had been bothering me since I woke up started taking a slight step back, but just as sleep started knocking, the lock on the door clacked open and Bastian Moran walked into the room.

If the senior inspector was in fact disappointed with my calm demeanor, he didn't show it. He threw a stuffed folder on the table, took a seat opposite me and started smoking.

I kept silent. He did too.

"Aren't you wondering why you were arrested, Mr. Orso?" Bastian Moran asked when he had finished his cigarette.

"When someone is *arrested*, they are told the reason immediately, senior inspector," I reminded him, suppressing an involuntary shiver, "so technically this is not an arrest, but a kidnapping. Just for the record."

Senior Inspector Moran, beyond all shadow of a doubt, caught the treacherous quaver in my voice and smiled.

"Leopold," he said softly, "take a look at these reports for me. Now you tell me why you're here."

"I have no idea," I shrugged my shoulders as much as the handcuffs allowed.

"You have no hunches?"

I was simply overflowing with hunches, but I just shook my head:

"No."

"You don't seem too surprised."

"A sudden arrest is usual business for people who find themselves in the field of view of Department Three."

Bastian Moran raised a high brow in unhidden surprise.

"Are you accusing me of bias?" He wondered, and an incomprehensible half-smile started playing on his thin lips.

I didn't yield to the provocation and answered, not making it personal:

"Your colleagues have earned a reputation as impatient people, inclined to rushed conclusions and even more rushed actions. But, for my part, I can't imagine why..."

The senior inspector nodded, taking my words into account and opened the folder lying before him.

"Some of my colleagues are not, in fact, very patient. But I am," he announced, tearing himself from the papers and immediately changing the topic: "I suppose that you are aware of the balance retention principle? If someone is balancing on one leg, he just needs a light push to fall over and hit the ground. But a person standing firmly on both legs cannot be overturned so easily. However, that same man, if riding a steam-tram, would have to hold a handle to avoid falling over at a stop, whether on two legs or one. And he's likely to do it with two hands."

In utter confusion, I took the senior inspector's reasoning into account, but couldn't figure out for the life of me what he was driving at.

"I never accuse people of crimes based on just a single piece of tangential evidence. I wait until I have enough to bring the matter to court. Viscount, I can connect you with a crime, and I will."

"Try," I answered simply.

"The first connection is that you told Inspector White about the planned robbery of the Witstein Banking House," Bastian Moran announced. "What was more, you had business at that bank."

I didn't confirm or deny that, only demanding:

"Keep going!"

"You led the inspector into the basement of the barbershop where he was found murdered a few days later."

"I wasn't there," I considered it necessary to remind him of my earlier affirmations.

"I doubt that very much," Bastian Moran threw out sharply and set on the table a photograph of Jimmy, burned by the attack of the Diabolic Plague. "What do you think was the cause of the constable's death?"

"I have no idea," I declared without delay. "Some kind of dark wizardry?"

"The Diabolic Plague. To be more accurate, it was one of the rare curses that causes this disease."

"And how does that connect me with the inspector's death, exactly?" I couldn't hold back from asking, immediately recognizing my error, but it was too late.

He had me in his trap.

"Really? *You're* asking *me* how?" The senior inspector guffawed with a satisfied look. "Could you remind me what happened in your manor sixteen years ago? What was the reason for the death of your mother and all your servants?"

"The Diabolic Plague," I said, practically grinding my teeth in vexation.

Dolt!

"And there's another connection!"

"That doesn't prove anything!"

Bastian Moran measured me up with a haughty gaze, then took out a pack of Chesterfields and removed a cigarette.

"But I don't need any proof," he declared, lighting his cigarette. "I know you are guilty. And I've known so all along."

"That smells like bias."

"Nothing of the sort." The senior inspector tapped his ash and set a few time-yellowed photo cards in front of me. "I suppose, Viscount, that you are familiar with these pictures."

The word "Viscount" sounded out so politely, that it couldn't have been anything but subtle mockery. I didn't pay any mind to his poisonous intonation, though.

I took a look at the photos.

And they were, in fact, very familiar to me. They showed people who had died of the Diabolic Plague. It was our servants, who had just enough strength to make it out the gate and die on the street. Their bodies, baked from the inside, their twisted limbs, the dirt of the autumn street.

It happened sixteen years ago, but the past wouldn't let me go and dragged me down.

"I see that you are familiar," Bastian Moran nodded. "I assume you have also studied the investigation report, yes?"

There was no reason to deny the obvious. They only let you check out old files from the archive with a signature, so I simply nodded.

The senior inspector smiled and took a thin stack of sewn-together papers from his sacred folder. It was the very report that I had earlier signed off on with no hesitation.

"Be so kind, Viscount," Bastian Moran asked me, "and open to the last page."

I somehow pulled the report to myself and opened it to the place he pointed, then the senior inspector hinted:

"Note the signatures."

I looked at the very bottom of the page, then cast my eyes back up at Bastian.

"Detective Sergeant S. Moran," read one of

the lines that I had earlier not paid any mind.

"Everything is accurate," Bastian Moran confirmed. "I took part in the investigation myself."

"Investigation?" I snorted and threw the report back to him. "You call that an investigation? You didn't try very hard to find the murderer!"

The senior inspector shrugged his shoulders indifferently and extinguished his butt on the burn-covered table top.

"The reason for Department Three's interest was something slightly different," he told me.

"And what was it?"

"We were preparing to arrest your father for associating with Christians," Bastian Moran told me calmly. "Boris Orso was also suspected of involvement in the murder of Count and Countess Kósice."

"Complete nonsense!" I snapped.

"Oh, I assure you, Mr. Orso," the man shook his head. "We had more than enough evidence on the first point. And considering his strained relationship with his wife's parents, and the way they were murdered, I personally had no doubts on the second either."

"Empty words!"

"A bomb was thrown into the carriage of

your grandfather and grandmother," the senior inspector reminded me. "That's got anarchist written all over it."

"There's no motive."

"Your father was experiencing financial difficulties, in that a large portion of his personal funds were being sent to support illegal Christian cults. And, believe me, we collected more than enough evidence for that. It was simply in another file. The file on Boris Orso."

Clanking my chains, I threw myself back into the uncomfortable chair and asked, wanting to steer the conversation away from the dangerous topic:

"What does everyone have against Christians? They fought on the Emperor's side, but after the overthrow of *the fallen*, they suffered even harsher persecutions than before!"

"Christianity is a destructive cult," Bastian Moran answered calmly. "They are dangerous. Mysticism and conspiracies never led to good things, and they were the Christians' bread and butter for many centuries. They invented themselves a god..."

"They invented?" I groaned. "And what about *the fallen*? What about the infernal creatures? Hell exists. We have a plethora of evidence for that, and if that is so..."

"Hell, heaven, the soul..." the senior

inspector waved his hand contemptuously. "Obscurantism for the illiterate! They thought up a fairy tale and clamber after supposedly immortal souls, as if grasping at straws. It's all because of their fear of death. Did you, Viscount, not know that?"

"Are you saying *the fallen* weren't real?"

"No, but who's to say they really came down from the heavens?"

"Where else could they have come from?"

"From Venus or Mars. From Jupiter, or the far side of the Moon. From other star systems. They could be from anywhere! Forget about mysticism and sacred mysteries and put some faith in science!"

"You're still a reductionist..."

"And what of it?"

"It doesn't matter," I waved it off and asked: "My arrest was caused by my father's support for Christians?"

"Naturally, it was not!" the senior inspector smiled gently. "I just explained why you came into my field of vision. In order to refute your suspicion of my bias."

"You have yet to accomplish that," I noted.

"Is that so?" Bastian Moran asked in surprise. "Your father was suspected of involvement in the murder of a Count and Countess..."

"He was never formally charged!" I interrupted him.

"You're right," he didn't argue. "But only because everyone thought Boris Orso dead from the Diabolic Plague. Unfortunately, because of the quarantine, the investigators were unable to check the manor, but from eyewitness accounts, your father was home that evening. As, it should be said, were you and your mother. Now, you must understand the reason for my surprise when I found someone with the surname Orso among Inspector White's subordinates. Detective Constable Leopold Orso, just think! Ten years you're missing without a trace, then you suddenly jump out like a devil from a box, register your father's death certificate and start living in a home that is still under quarantine!"

"I had immunity."

"Nonsense!" Bastian Moran waved it off. "I'll tell you what really happened! Your father found out about his imminent arrest and took to running, forcing everyone to think he was dead! He used the Diabolic Plague as a cover! He was the only killer in that house."

"Not at all," I shook my head. "He never would have done such a thing to mother. He wouldn't have let her die..."

But my denying the senior inspector's conclusions based on my own didn't deter him at all.

"Your mother was gravely ill," Bastian Moran declared. "Bringing her with would have been unintelligent. I suppose that Boris simply wanted to keep her from unnecessary suffering."

"Unnecessary suffering?" I grew angry. "Have you ever seen someone die of the Diabolic Plague?!"

"Have you?" The senior inspector asked. "Have you, Leopold?"

"I have," I confirmed. "I was at home that night. I saw our servants die. My father saved me. The curse wasn't cast by him. We were all at home."

Probably, Senior Inspector Moran was counting on his provocative questions getting me to tell him some facts about Jimmy's death, so he smiled sourly and carried on.

"So, did your father love your mother? Or was she just a source of funds?"

My eyes grew cloudy with a red film. I wanted unbearably badly to jump over the table and beat all the soul from this impudent man, but I managed to fight back the anger that had seethed up in me, and started taking measured breaths, calming myself down.

I was helped by the clear understanding that this was the very reaction they were expecting from me. Of course, the shackles on my arms and legs did a fairly good job of making me more judicious. It would have been harder without that.

I winced and looked at the senior inspector with unhidden skepticism.

"So then, you have," I started to lay out the result of his interrogation, "my connection with the bank, the murdered police, and the crime scene. But what about motive?"

Bastian Moran shrugged light-heartedly.

"Inheritance, perhaps?" he guessed. He then suddenly declared: "But, enough of that! Leopold Orso, you're under arrest for the murder of Isaac Levinson, his family members and servants."

It felt like a kick to the solar plexus.

"What did you say?" I couldn't believe my own ears.

"Yesterday, you broke into the manor where the victim lived and killed everyone inside. I am not sure if it happened on the grounds of some hostility between the two of you, or if the whole cause was a financial dispute, but the fact remains. You killed them! The women, the children..."

"That's enough!" I snapped and, clanking my chains, slammed my palms on the table. "What nonsense are you bringing out now?"

"This is not nonsense," the senior inspector looked at me with unhidden contempt. "It has been established in writing that you visited the residence of the banker last evening at six twenty-four P.M. No other people entered or left the house after that. When their cook returned at dawn, she found bodies. That is irrefutable evidence of your guilt!"

"What a crock!" I mumbled, trying to process what I'd heard.

At six twenty-four P.M. No one entered or left the house after.

Twenty-four... No one entered or left...

At dawn...

And suddenly my mind was cracking: such accuracy couldn't have been obtained by typical evidence, but if they had been following me, they would have arrested me yesterday right after I shot the Chinese cutthroat.

"You were staking out Levinson's home?" I asked, and stared expectantly at the senior inspector.

He nodded.

"After such an eyebrow-raising attempted bank robbery, it seemed like a fairly good idea to me," he confirmed.

"And the stake-out established the time I entered the house, when I left it, and the fact that no one but me came in or left?"

"That's right!"

"And at what time did I leave the manor?" I clarified.

Bastian Moran flipped through the papers in the folder that was lying on the table and said:

"You spent twenty-eight minutes in the home," then he smiled understandingly and noted: "You had plenty of time to kill them."

But I waved it off in annoyance.

"The Department Three report states that I left the home of the deceased at six fifty-two P.M.?"

The senior inspector looked at me with unhidden suspicion, but all the same affirmed:

"That is true. I do not understand why that makes you so happy!"

"It doesn't matter," I melted into a careless smile. "Bring on the charges. This conversation is boring me."

I smiled carelessly. I was still frozen in horror on the inside, though. If Isaac Levinson hadn't managed to call his business partners in the New World yesterday, the only thing that could save me from the gallows now was a miracle.

"Is that so?" The senior inspector squinted. "May I ask why you are so confident the trial will end in your favor?"

"It is the middle of the night in New York

right now," I answered simply. "Everything will become clear by midday."

"In New York?"

"Mr. Levinson had vast business interests."

"You mean to say..."

I nodded and confirmed.

"When Isaac and I parted ways, he was intending to make a call to the New World. The operator must have registered the time the conversations began and the time they ended, and whoever the banker was talking to will surely say that they spoke to Mr. Levinson precisely."

Bastian Moran stood from the table in silence, took all the documents back into the folder and left the room.

I laughed uncontrollably at his back, stretched out my legs and threw myself back into the chair.

I had plenty of time to wait...

THE SENIOR INSPECTOR returned some time later.

He took a seat opposite me, looked me over in contemplation, then stated with unhidden exasperation:

"You could have left the manor and sneaked back in through the roof."

I asked with a showy lethargy:

"Did they find signs of a break-in? And what was stopping you from looking over the crime scene earlier?"

"You could have easily provided an alibi," Bastian Moran continued as if he hadn't heard me.

"Anyone could have done that!" I objected, beginning to boil over a bit again. "Anyone could have broken in!"

"You are connected with the murdered party and the crime scene. We'll find a motive. Don't you doubt it. But for now, what remains is to prove that you had the ability to commit the crime. To start with, that will be enough."

The senior inspector stood up from the table, flung open the door and let a thin gentleman in a white doctor's robe into the room. The medic, with the exhausted look of a nonstop drunk on his face, placed a galvanized iron box on the table and threw back the lid. He then took out a scalpel and a test tube one-third filled with an oily suspension.

"May I begin?" He clarified.

"Yes, please," Bastian Moran gave his permission.

"Now, in order to avoid misunderstandings, could you restrain the patient's head?"

The senior inspector walked around behind me and, his palm on my forehead, held my head against the high back of the chair.

"What are you doing?" I objected. "Stop

this!"

The imperturbable medic wet a piece of cotton with rubbing alcohol, grabbed me by the pointer finger, and carefully disinfected a pustule with it.

"Calm down, we just need a few drops of blood."

"What for?" I roared, but I still didn't pull my arm away.

The scalpel looked devilishly sharp, and I had no desire whatsoever to end up with a severed tendon or a finger cut through to the bone.

The incision was entirely painless; the medic placed the edge of the test tube against it, took a few drops of blood and placed a piece of cotton against the wound.

"Press down," he hinted, shaking up the contents of the tube. He hadn't told me to do it because of any particular sympathy he had for me, or any abstract concept of love for his fellow man, but simply because of his naturally inborn professionalism.

Bastian Moran released my head and wondered:

"Are you sure that was enough?"

"That was plenty," the medic attested.

After agitating the test tube intensely, it acquired a singular grayish-pink shade, then the liquid began to separate.

"Does the reaction take long?"

"No more than three minutes," the doctor answered, sticking his hand under his robe and taking out a pocket watch. "Maybe even less."

"What is going on, devil take you?" I objected, but didn't receive an answer.

I was ignored, simple as that.

The medic was watching the test tube intently, but Bastian Moran took a seat at the table, lit a cigarette, then clarified:

"And how accurate is the test?"

"The test is completely accurate," the medic answered. "Either yes or no."

"Are you sure?"

"Absolutely. Successfully diagnosing the active stage of this hereditary disease is possible in one hundred cases in one hundred!"

But the senior inspector didn't find his assurance convincing.

"The active stage?" He frowned. "What do you mean by active stage, doctor? I wasn't warned about that!"

"The active stage is one month from the day of the last transformation," the medic told him, continuing to study the test tube, this time against the light.

"What the devil?!" I snapped, pounding my hands on the table with all my might. "What is going on? Explain this!"

The medic looked at the senior inspector; Moran stretched out, released a stream of smoke at the ceiling and chuckled unhappily:

"In Levinson's house, we found signs of a werebeast, which would give the murderer a fairly good chance of avoiding the noose." Bastian Moran stretched out again and turned back to the medic: "Doctor, what happens to someone with this, as you put it, hereditary disease, if a lawyer in court is capable of proving their insanity at the time the crime was committed?"

"Electro-shock therapy combined with drug therapy usually has fairly good results, but I would insist on a lobotomy, which guarantees full recovery in one hundred percent of cases. And, naturally, forced sterilization."

"You see, Leopold, if you come clean right now, you could save your life. Just say you did it in your sleep. Perhaps the court will take that into account."

"They would have to," the doctor confirmed.

"To hell with your advice!" I cursed out. "I didn't kill anyone! I am not a werebeast!"

But the seed of doubt had hit fertile soil, and that shook me up.

Say you did it in your sleep...

Could I really be sure this wasn't just another nightmare? Could the tension of the last days have had an effect and pushed my sick imagination in that direction? Had my restless *talent* turned me into a beast?

Nonsense! Maybe the reagent would show a reaction, but that still wouldn't make me a murderer!

The liquids in the tube continued separating; the blood was pooling in a thin layer at the very top.

"Well, how'd it go?" I couldn't resist asking. "What do you say?"

The medic didn't even glance at me. He took the watch from his vest pocket again, pulled back the lid, snorted and set the test tube on the table.

"Nothing," he informed the senior inspector.

"Are you sure?" Bastian Moran jumped.

"Look for yourself," the medic pointed at the test tube. "No reaction to argentous reagent. None at all."

"So, this proves that the suspect is not a werebeast?"

"This proves that he has not undergone any transformations in the last thirty days," the medic clarified his verdict.

I chuckled.

"Well? Are you satisfied? What more evidence do you need?" I then shook my shackles defiantly and demanded: "Let me out of here! This instant!"

"Everything in good time!" Bastian Moran frowned and left the cell together with the doctor.

He didn't remove my shackles, though.

The bastard! The arrogant, egotistical bastard!

BASTIAN MORAN NEVER returned to the chamber. Instead of him, sometime later, two constables and the already familiar detective sergeant entered. One of the privates unlocked my handcuffs, and the other undid my legs; then I stood from the hard chair, rubbed my raw wrists and accepted a paper bag of my belongings.

"Sign here," the detective sergeant put the register in front of me, dipped his iron quill in a portable inkwell with a copper lid and pointed at where I was to place my signature. After that, he put one more piece of paper on the table.

"Non-disclosure agreement," he told me, but I had already seen it.

I signed it.

"And you must appear at interrogations as a witness."

I placed yet another signature and frowned.

"I hope this is all?"

"It is," the investigator nodded and

extended me a sealed envelope. "Take this."

"What is it?" I grew surprised.

"A notice," the red-mustached detective answered vaguely, then ordered the constables: "Take Mr. Orso to the exit."

With the bag in one hand and the envelope in the other, I went out into the corridor and, accompanied by my vigilant escorts, left Department Three. In a steam lift, we went down to the basement where I was led to one of the many service entries and pushed out the door.

Enjoying the air of freedom, I came down from the porch, then noticed that Newtonstraat smelled of smoke and char and I was instantly struck with a short, nervous cough. The weather hadn't changed a bit in comparison with the previous day. The sky was covered by low clouds as before, and smog was still reigning unchallenged in the city, creeping in a gray film between the buildings and over the ground.

"It'd be nice if it just rained already!" I thought and walked around the police headquarters, but my body felt like not my own. It led me to the side on my exit from the alley. Then I sat down at the nearest bench and carefully touched the tips of my fingers to my head. An aching pain had picked up in the right side. A slight pressure caused sharp waves of pain as if I was touching raw nerves, but the unpleasant sensations soon went on the decline, returning my clarity of thought.

What luck. I was clearly very lucky today.

I mean, the death of Isaac Levinson and everyone else living in his house had turned out badly, but Senior Inspector Moran had made a great mistake when he decided to close this high-profile case with a daring cavalry charge. I could understand him, too. Important people demand results, which is where the temptation to push me against the wall with his supposedly irrefutable evidence came from. But it didn't work.

I opened the bag, distributed my wallet, knife, and lighter between my pants pockets, then checked my weapons. The Roth-Steyr I placed back in the holster, and I slipped my Cerberus in the side pocket of my jacket. I stomped the dirt off my knees, which were still soiled from kneeling and only then opened the envelope I had been handed at my release.

Inside, I found a letter stating that I was being fired from my job as a police constable.

I folded it carefully, stuck it in my inside pocket and started walking the familiar route back to Ohm Square, through which the nearest steam tram line passed. From there, I went directly to the magistrate; I arrived, as it were, as they were opening, walked around the office, spoke with the clerks, filled out a couple declarations and, an hour and a half later, came back out with a fresh private investigator's license in hand.

No, it wasn't that I was hoping for clients to line up around the corner for a failed detective constable, it was all much simpler – I already had a client in mind.

So I went directly to the Judean Quarter.

5

THE JUDEAN QUARTER was all abuzz. The narrow little streets were dark with the attire of Orthodox Judeans. People were ceaselessly walking from one business to another, discussing actively and always hurrying onward. The Orthodox Judeans were, naturally, not the only people doing business there. There were plenty of normal citizens as well. Uniformed constables also flickered by at every intersection.

It should be said that the situation wasn't nearly as hot as I was expecting. No matter how strange it seemed, the paperboys had their role to play in all this, too. People were reading fresh news and getting into screaming matches, but it didn't cause thunder and lightning like at the

Newton-Markt and the magistrate. Almost no one looked on the murder of the banker as an attack on their society as a whole. At every corner, you could hear one and the same thing: "Procrustes has returned!"

They were all harping on about Procrustes, and that fact gave the metropolitan police the chance to find the real murderer before the situation got out of control; this time, everyone was playing right into the paperboys' hands as they tried squeezing yet another sensation from a stone.

THE QUIET LITTLE STREET the banker lived on was the only calm place in the whole Judean Quarter. The police had simply taken over the whole block, capping it off with an armed division at each of the two intersections. Nearby, no matter how unexpected it may seem, there were some strong boys strolling about in normal clothes, dirty and big-nosed. All that was needed was to express excessive curiosity to a local inhabitant or shout out some curse toward these guardians of public order, and they would immediately get involved, explain something quietly to the brawlers and the situation would come to its conclusion.

For some time, I considered the events, then went directly to the police cordon. When a constable came out to greet me, I slowed my pace and took Isaac Levinson's letter on the investigation of the bank robbery.

"No entry," the policeman warned. In the event of possible complications, he had a helmet on his head, and a baton hanging under his arm on his belt.

"I work for the Witstein Banking House," I told him and extended an order signed by the recently deceased banker.

The constable sized me up with his cautious gaze. Perhaps he even recognized me, but he still read through the document.

"That's above my paygrade. Wait here," he said after a bit of hesitation and went away to discuss it with one of the local self-defense squad.

The policeman took my note with him and left me standing in the middle of the street asking myself if I was being an idiot for not having gotten my visit here agreed on in advance with the higher-ups at the Banking House. Perhaps I should have gone through Aaron Malk, the deceased's assistant.

But, it all worked out.

A balding, Roman-nosed Judean of compact build approached me after five minutes. Without leaving the police cordon, he motioned for me to come toward him, and I took a decisive step across the intersection. The constables didn't make any obstacles this time, and my escorts and I hurried to the house of the deceased Mr. Levinson.

Everywhere around, there were horse-drawn carriages and vans; in addition to the investigators, forensics experts, police photographers, coroners' assistants, lawyers and all other kinds of strange people had come to the crime scene.

And he led me to a carriage. He flung open the door and took a step back, inviting me to go inside; I stood up on the running board and waited a moment, looking over the elderly gentleman in a black morning suit and striped pants. Then I sat down on the seat opposite him.

The doors immediately closed, separating us from the hustle and bustle outside, and the unfamiliar Judean addressed me:

"Viscount Cruce, I presume?"

"Just Leopold is fine," I answered, carelessly tossing one leg over the other.

"Abraham Witstein," the man introduced himself and smoothed out my retainer on his knee. "Vice-President of the Banking House for continental Europe."

"Do you do business on both sides of the Atlantic?"

"And also in both Indias, the African

colonies, and the Celestial Kingdom," the banker added. "Correct me, Leopold, if I'm wrong, but are you not the main suspect in poor Isaac's murder?"

"Oh, no," I smiled calmly in reply. "Just a witness. After I left, Mr. Levinson managed to have a talk with some partners in the New World."

"Great to hear," Abraham Witstein nodded, mechanically rubbing a huge green gem – perhaps an emerald – in the clasp of his tie. "And what brought you here, could you tell me?"

"As you see," I pointed at the document in the man's hand, "Mr. Levinson and I were, in a way, business partners. I was hired to investigate the attack on the bank. He, in his turn, expressed the desire to do business with me, buying out my debts and helping me come into my inheritance. As a result of this deplorable incident, my losses will come to, at the very least, thirty thousand francs."

"Quite the imposing sum," the banker noted with no hint of mockery, "but the deceased signed a contract with you in the name of the whole company, so I don't see any reason for us not to continue our relationship."

"In full measure?"

"Viscount," Witstein frowned, and I heard annoyance in his voice for the first time, "Let me tell you something directly: I don't see why we should pay for police work beyond what I already give in taxes."

With a calm demeanor, I took out my fresh private investigator's license and extended it to him.

"First, at present, I represent myself and only myself. Second, if you've got someone motivated by results, you'll have someone working more intelligently."

The banker studied the document, then looked intently at me and reminded:

"Isaac gave you an advance of five hundred francs. That money was from the bank, not his personal funds. May I inquire as to how you earned it?"

I closed my eyes for a moment, gathering my thoughts, then informed the man of my activity. Abraham Witstein heard out my report and asked:

"And what next? Your appearance here cannot have been an accident, right?"

"I would like to take a look at the crime scene."

"You are investigating the bank robbery, not Isaac's murder."

"Don't mock me!" I snorted and waved my hand internally. "These crimes are connected to one another! They must be! First there was an attempted bank robbery, but they didn't steal anything, and now the manager of said bank has been murdered! Those are all links in the same chain!"

"They say it's Procrustes, but Procrustes might as well be a natural disaster. He is uncontrollable."

"Let me inside, and I'll be able to tell you if it was Procrustes or not." I looked at his indifferent countenance, which did not contain even a hint of concern and added: "I'll tell you only as a representative of my employer, you can use this information however you think necessary."

"And what do you care?" The banker wondered. "Beyond my desire to make a name for myself with the huge amount of publicity, you mean?"

"I must be aware of all the factors."

"You must?"

"That's right." I raised my hand and showed my wrist, dappled with scabbed-over abrasions. "It takes you out of yourself, if you must know, when you are handcuffed and accused of a murder you didn't commit."

"So, revenge and vanity, but not a sense of justice?"

"You also forgot to add greed."

"What do you think you'll see in there?"

"Well, I don't suppose it will be anything pleasant."

"Don't say a word to the papers!" The banker then declared. "You must not talk about what you see in there with anyone but me. Not even the police."

"My license allows for that," I confirmed.

"I haven't hired you yet, Viscount," Abraham Witstein shook his head. "Perhaps I'll hire you depending on how your investigation of the house goes. But perhaps I won't. Just hold your tongue. Agreed?"

"Alright. So, do you see fit to allow me into the house?"

"Go on!" The banker gave me his permission, stepping out of the carriage after me, saying something brief in a language I couldn't recognize.

The big-nosed giant peeled himself from the wall and pointed at the entrance door, but the vigilant constable bluntly refused to allow us in the house and ordered us to wait on the porch. What to expect, he did not say.

A few minutes later, an investigator came up in a uniform, heard out the man escorting me and with an unhappy air, began giving us instructions.

"Do not touch anything. Do not step in the blood," he began enumerating on his fingers, "do not distract people with questions. Do not faint," he then put up his pinkie and added: "But the most important thing is not to puke."

"I'll manage," I answered, but as soon as I crossed the threshold immediately grew happy that I hadn't had time for breakfast, otherwise I might have broken a rule.

It smelled in the house. Even at the door in, I could sense the stink of decay, coagulated blood and all the other aromas that accompanied death. In my time, I had once been in a real slaughterhouse, but it actually smelled worse here.

There was no one in the entry, but there were smears of blood on the floor circled in chalk. Stepping over them, we walked down the corridor, and there came upon the first body. A strong boy, based on his appearance, it was one of the night guards. He was sitting with his back propped up against a wall next to a wide-open door. The deceased's head was hanging to the side like you see in people with a broken lumbar.

There were bloody footsteps coming from the room. The imprints of bare feet could be made out clearly on the beige-painted boards. The investigator allowed us to look inside. In the dark cell with one window, there were another two corpses. One of them had an arm torn out, and had his face terribly mangled by a set of claws; the second's larynx had been ripped out by a powerful bite from the killer. On the walls, which were sporting a blue and gold wallpaper, there were dried blood marks everywhere.

There were two coroner's assistants handling the corpses. They were used to this kind of thing. The police photographer, though, was green in the face, leaning out an open window taking frequent gulps of fresh air.

"There was no one else on the first floor," the investigator said and led me up.

On the way, I saw that the distance between the bloody footprints on the floor was slightly more than the length of my own pace. I got down on my haunches and, using the widely-set fingers of my right hand, measured the size of the foot. After that, following after my guide, I walked up to the second floor and took a rest on the railing, giving a rest to my banged-up leg.

In one of the rooms, there came the momentary flash of a magnesium spark. I heard the clacking of heels and another photographer jumped past us.

"Running for the bucket," the investigator told us, himself not looking so great.

"Is that where it happened?" I asked, preparing in advance for a ghastly spectacle.

"No, this is the governess's room."

I took a look into the room. There was a

naked body lying on a blood-soaked bed. I hurriedly stepped back from the door. The wounds left by the powerful jaws were simply horrifying. The head was hanging by a small strip of skin; the room wasn't particularly messy, though.

"What happened to the flesh missing from the bite holes?" I asked the investigator.

"We haven't found any," he said and warned: "It gets worse from here."

"Are they all in the same room?" I supposed.

"Indeed. Do you need a quick break first?"

"No."

And we went into Isaac Levinson's office, but, to be honest, I wasn't able to really look at anything. I just inhaled the thick stink, cast my gaze on the corpses piled one on top of the other, and jumped back like a bullet.

"No barfing!" The investigator reminded me strictly.

In a few endlessly long moments, I calmed my breathing, then asked:

"Are they all there?"

"The whole family. But only the banker was tortured. There are bruises on his wrists from being tied. The ropes were removed later."

The severe atmosphere was affecting the investigator, otherwise he wouldn't have shared such details.

"Is that all?" I clarified, walking away to the stairs.

"The bathroom is also full of blood, but there are no signs of struggle there."

"Outside!"

We walked down to the first floor. I practically ran to the entryway and leaned over a bucket placed in the corner, already half full of vomit. When all my bile had finished coming out, I wiped my lips with my kerchief and, entirely calm, walked back to the Banking House Vice-President's carriage. I got inside and immediately took out my tin of sugar drops, trying to get rid of the vile taste in my mouth; Abraham Witstein suddenly extended his hand:

"May I?"

"Be my guest!" I gave my permission.

"I certainly hope they're kosher," The banker quipped, then nervously laughed at his own joke. He placed a sugar drop in his mouth, wiped his fingers with a fine linen cloth and asked: "Your thoughts?"

"It wasn't Procrustes," I answered confidently.

"And what makes you say that?"

"Procrustes never bit anyone. He used to just beat and tear. Ask about it in the newspaper archives. Send a request to the Newton-Markt."

"If it wasn't him, then who was it?"

"It was someone who wanted something directly from Isaac Levinson. Someone fast, smart and cold-blooded. Most likely a werebeast. He came in through the roof. He got undressed first, and only then dealt with the guards. Other than the governess, he drove all residents of this home into Mr. Levinson's office and killed them before his very eyes. Then, he tortured Mr. Levinson. Before it ended, he sated his hunger, washed up and went out the way he came in – through the roof."

"Sated his hunger?"

"He ate a bit of the governess. By that time, he had almost returned to human appearance. The bites there are of obviously smaller size than the jaw marks on the guard's neck."

"Did the killer get what he was after?" the banker asked unexpectedly.

"I doubt it," I shook my head. "Levinson was tortured to death, so they must not have gotten anything useful."

"Perhaps the murderer is just a sadist."

The man's guess hit on something. I unexpectedly remembered another group of people who simply enjoyed torture, murder and eating human flesh. They would become animals and move so blisteringly fast, that a normal person wouldn't even manage to scream before a set of sharp fangs were stuck in their neck. And after that, they wouldn't be able to scream, because they would be choking on blood.

The Werefoxes, a group of Chinese whelps.

Could Mr. Chan have paid the Foxes for the murder of the Judean who had just crossed his path?

The offer Levinson was making, five centimes on the franc for my debt cannot have made the moneylender very happy. He did send his cutthroat for my ear, after all. But then I, incidentally, sent him crawling back with his knee cap shot through...

There were many ways to make a person angry; you could curse them with your last words, spit in their face or take the easy way and just pop your foot up between their legs. But all that was mere child's play when compared to messing with this old skinflint's money.

The Werefoxes, my stars...

"Leopold!" Abraham Witstein cut off my thinking, his set of portable writing implements at the ready. "You may continue investigating the bank robbery." He made a small note under the old order, then breathed on a stamp and placed it over his signature. "As for Isaac's murder, I cannot hire you for that case. It has taken on too much resonance."

"Will you be announcing a reward?"

The banker frowned peevishly and admitted:

"If I don't, my partners simply will not understand."

"How much?"

"One thousand for reliable evidence on the murder. Five thousand for the murderer."

"Alive?"

"By all means," the banker confirmed. "Otherwise, we'd go bankrupt from the hearses bringing in fresh bodies just dug up from the graveyard."

I nodded. And he was right. Five thousand francs was quite a significant sum. Passers-by would be standing in line for it.

"But, between you and me," Mr. Witstein told me in confidence, "if you have significant evidence of identity, we could pay you for the body. It would be three times more than just for evidence," and immediately corrected himself: "We are not ordering you to murder him! But we also don't want to be seen as limiting your right to self-defense, and would look on you with understanding if you did have to kill the beast. But only if it is truly necessary!"

I nodded. Catching a werebeast alive was a suicidal mission, doomed to fail from the start.

"If any issues arise, look for me in the *Benjamin Franklin*," the banker warned.

I got out of the carriage, headed for the nearest steam tram stop and the bitter scent of smog seemed like the aroma of heavenly ambrosia itself; it covered up the vile aftertaste in my mouth better than any sugar drop.

THE FIRST THING I WENT to do was have a talk with Ramon Miro. It was lunch time, so it wasn't so hard to find the constable. It was actually enough to simply have a peek in to *Archimedes' Screw*.

It should be said that I did not actually go into the bar myself. I instead sent a young boy who'd been spinning circles on the street with a stack of fresh newspapers under his arm in after my friend. For obvious reasons, I didn't want to show my face to my other former colleagues.

Ramon came out of the bar five minutes later. On seeking me, he screwed his face up into a look of disgust and walked silently past me down the sidewalk. I followed after and started walking next to him.

"Are you going far?" I asked, matching his pace.

"I'm going to drink!" The constable grumbled.

"Is your shift already over or something?" I grew surprised.

Ramon Miro was going out to drink in his

uniform. What was more, instead of his normal peaked cap, he had a helmet on his head. His belt was weighed down by a baton, and there were hand cuffs swinging next to it.

"I don't give a damn!" the brawny man waved it off.

"What do you mean?" I asked in surprise.

"I've been let go!" the constable chuckled bitterly, turning down an imperceptible alley. "They gave me a kick in the ass! Tomorrow is my last shift. I'll be getting my severance pay, and then I'll be free as the wind!"

"They fired you?" I couldn't believe my own ears. "But why?"

"Look at who's asking!" Ramon snorted. "Because of that funny business with you and the inspector. That's why!"

"There was no funny business."

"We should have told them about the tunnels under the bank right away."

"We had an order from the inspector," I reminded him.

"Excellent! But now the inspector is dead, I'm out of work and, they say, you are too."

"Right you are."

"Right you are!" the constable aped me. "But I, meanwhile, have a family to feed!"

He stopped before a dilapidated drinking establishment, but before he was able to fling the door open, I grabbed his hand.

"Ramon! When was it that you managed to get married?"

"I'll never get married if I don't find a new job!" my friend grumbled. "Do you know hard it was for me to get this one? No one wanted to hire a half-blood like me!"

I could have joked that it would be even harder for a half-blood to get married, but decided not to go asking for trouble and pushed the constable into the bar.

"Go in already!" And when Ramon had received his mug of light-colored beer and was standing at a dirty, scratched-up table in the corner, I noted pointedly: "So, it's work you're looking for?"

"Are you suggesting we rob a bank?"

"No," I shook my head. "And I'm not even suggesting we go looking for the robbers."

"What are you suggesting then?"

"I know about a job opening for a night guard at a coalhouse."

The constable looked at me with unhidden doubt, but nodded all the same:

"First shift would work."

I dictated him the address and advised:

"Go there in your uniform. The manager is looking for a reliable man."

"I'll take a look," Ramon decided, finishing

his beer, atop which was hovering a moist foam. He then squinted and continued: "Somehow, I don't think that's why you came looking for me, though."

"What do you know about Werefoxes?" I asked, my mind made up not to waste time on long and cautious inquiries.

I didn't know my way around the Chinese Quarter that well, so attempting to inquire among the locals, when considering recent events, could end in my disappearing without a trace down some dark alleyway. Mr. Chan had a certain weight among the bandits who lived there.

Ramon Miro looked at me with interest, then shook his head.

"Tell me!" He demanded. "Tell me everything from the very beginning or stop interrupting my drinking and get out of here!"

I turned to a clouded window under the ceiling, gathered my thoughts and chuckled.

"I mean, there's nothing in particular to say, Ramon. I just want to know where I could find these scumbags."

The Werefoxes were a legend of the Chinese Quarter; its very own scary story.

When yet another disfigured body turned up in the gutter, or another stubborn man who got on the wrong side of the local triads disappeared without a trace, or when some sad sack got his ears and fingers taken off, but wouldn't talk about who did it, everyone knew the Foxes were behind it. And, like any legend, the Foxes were impossible to catch. That said, they never stuck their necks out too far either, working only inside the Chinese Quarter.

And that was precisely what Ramon countered with when he heard my story about the murder of Isaac Levinson.

"They're writing about Procrustes in all the newspapers," he added.

"It's not Procrustes!" I grew angry. "Did you even hear me? Procrustes never ate his victims!"

"But the Werefoxes have never left the Chinese Quarter," the constable parried. "They know damn well what would happen to them if they drew the ire of Department Three."

"Everyone's only been talking about Procrustes for the last couple of days. The Foxes could have figured the crime would be ascribed to him!"

"Leo!" Ramon sighed. "Admit it, you just want to pin the murder on your moneylender, in order not to have to pay back your debts."

I decided not to repudiate that potential motive. My hands were practically scratching from my desire to be rid of Mr. Chan once and for all.

"How much do you owe him?" Ramon

suddenly asked.

"With interest?" I started thinking. "Around ten thousand francs."

"Holy hell!" the constable exploded. "I could see murdering for that kind of money."

"So, you see."

"I meant I could see you committing murder, not him," Miro corrected me. "You're up to your ears in this stuff, old friend, but you do have a motive. I, though, am not going to even go near him!"

In my friend's words there was a clear hint, so I took out my wallet and placed the last hundred-franc bill from my advance on the table.

"I need information."

Ramon covered my money with his palm and asked:

"Information and that's it?"

I hesitated. Digging around in the Chinese Quarter alone was extremely dangerous. No *talent* could stop you from getting stabbed in the back, after all. Ramon would be extremely helpful in that situation, and also he had the right connections.

"The reward for information on the murderer of Levinson is one thousand francs," I stated slowly. "For the murderer, dead, with evidence of guilt, they'll pay three thousand. And alive, they'll pay five."

"Five thousand is pretty good money," Ramon squinted.

"Five thousand split two ways."

"No way!" the constable cut me off. "If you can get the moneylender, you'll also be writing off ten thousand in debt, but the risk for both of us is the same! If you want my help, you'll have to play fair!"

I spent some time thinking over his words, then rolled out a counter offer:

"Three thousand for you, the rest for me. Will that work?"

"Hands in," the constable agreed weakly, understanding how difficult it was to catch a werebeast alive.

I was reminded of another of my father's sayings: "Don't split up the pelt of a bear you haven't caught yet," but I decided not to bring it up. Even without that, Ramon knew perfectly well how slim the chance of success was in our little adventure. Just a little horse bet had made him take the risk and support my dangerous theory.

When the constable left his empty mug behind, I warned him:

"We'll need a lupara."

Ramon's face puckered, as if he had just pounded a glass of lemon juice. He demanded:

"Get me fifty franks."

"What do you need that for?" I frowned. "The sergeant in the arsenal has enough tenners! You haven't even been fired yet!"

"But what about bullets?" Ramon reminded me. "Judge for yourself, a ten caliber bullet with a silver jacket won't be cheap. And I'm not planning on hunting for Procrustes with my ass hanging out!"

"Forget about Procrustes!"

"The Werefoxes are a normal gang," the constable assured me. "The Foxes, the Ninjas, the Thuggees – they're all just simple murderers, in no way connected to the underworld. They have an ominous reputation, sure, but that's all they have. The end of the nineteenth century is on the horizon, devil take me! Leo, the time of magic is behind us!"

"Just last week, we were hunting a succubus," I reminded him.

"Did I say anything about infernal creatures?" Ramon shrugged his wide shoulders. "There's still plenty of that trash in our world, but there haven't been any mysterious magical orders for some time! People are simply not able to keep secrets, as you well know. A gang of werebeasts isn't even taken seriously enough to be the subject of jokes. Do you think Department Three doesn't have any informants in the Chinese Quarter? These damn Foxes are just muddying up the situation and scaring illiterate blockheads with mysticism..."

I did not share my friend's skepticism, but I also did not neglect taking advantage of it.

"Why do you need silver bullets then?"

Ramon laughed uncontrollably.

"Leo! I know you too well. You say we're going after bandits now, but in five minutes, we'll be on the hunt for Procrustes. And no matter who says it, werebeasts are no fairy tale..."

"... they are just victims of a hereditary disorder," I finished my friend's sentence.

"With a severe allergy to silver," Ramon continued.

"You're a Mechanist!"

"I'm a realist," the constable shot back.

"But Mr. Realist here doesn't want to pay for bullets with the hundred I gave him?"

"Leo, your petty-bourgeois small-mindedness is going to be the death of me! You're an aristocrat, a member of the ancient House Kósice!"

"One hundred francs is one hundred francs."

"One hundred francs is four constables standing next to you while you ask questions," Ramon declared. "Leo, what's going on with you? Are you seriously planning on climbing into that cesspool with no cover?"

"I figured dealing with that was your business," I snorted, counting out five tenners.

"Count it. I'll do it." My friend took my money and headed for the exit. "I'll see you at eight at the Newton-Markt Metro station," he warned me before slamming the door behind himself.

"Agreed," I nodded and only then realized that my friend had not deigned to pay for his beer.

And I'm the small-minded petty-bourgeois?!

6

I PASSED THE REST OF THE DAY as if in a fog.

I returned home, ate lunch, and when an attack of the Diabolic Plague came over me yet again, I laid down to rest. As a result, I woke up at sundown, my throat dry and my head heavy.

There was a small trail of blood coming out of my right nostril. I walked into the bathroom and asked Theodor to bring me some ice. I wiped off the dried blood, shaved, which I hadn't managed to do yet today, and started getting ready for my outing.

I did not put on my new suit, as my old one had been sent back from the cleaner's.

Remembering where I'd be going, I decided on boots over shoes, then I looked out the window and decided to throw a light canvas pea-coat on over everything.

Little black clouds were starting to gather in the sky.

Slightly limping on my injured leg, I went down to the first floor, took my derby hat from the rack and turned to Elizabeth-Maria, who had come out to see what all the fuss was about.

"When should I expect you for dinner, dear?" the girl cooed.

"I have no idea," I admitted. "I might not be back until morning."

"Leo, if there's one thing you're not, it's a homebody."

I didn't answer and went outside. The low sky was hanging right over my head. Twilight had already started creeping in from the East. The wind was tossing the black branches of dead trees all about and whistling down chimneys. Foul weather was approaching.

I could feel it.

Very soon, sharp gusts and torrential rain would rip the white flowers from the blooming apple trees and smear them in the mud. But it would also wash the dust and fresh soot from the buildings. In this city, there is no bad and good, disgusting and horrible, or black and white. It's all just half-tones and shades of gray, gradual transitions between the ugly and the acceptable.

The border is inside us. Only we can decide in a given situation whether a certain shade of gray is black or white. But one thing is unshakable. Evil. That which cannot be considered good, no matter your viewpoint, and no matter the benefit it brings. The murder of the banker's family was just such an event, and I was just itching with the desire to find the guilty party in this monstrous act.

With just one thought in mind, namely that this monstrous act must have been orchestrated by Mr. Chan, it itched twice as bad and my right eyelid started to twitch.

Righteous indignation and greed were truly a hellish combination.

AS WE'D AGREED, RAMON MIRO was waiting for me in front of the Newton-Markt Metro station. When I limped up to him, it was already rather dark outside, and everywhere around was glowing with electric light. In the Chinese Quarter, we wouldn't be able to count on such great illumination, but fortunately, Ramon had more foresight than me. On the marble rim of the fountain, next to his four-barreled lupara, there was a powerful square torch, similar to the one Inspector White had brought with to the tunnels.

"Did you find anything out?" I asked, walking up to my partner.

"Yessir," he affirmed.

He was wearing an unmarked police-issue rubberized cloak to the search for the werebeasts and, if it weren't for the weapon, in his rumpled cap and worn-down boots, he could easily have passed for a recent retiree, vaguely poor and dangerous. Where we were going, there were more than enough people like that. More than enough opium smoking veterans.

It would have been much harder for me, despite my shabby clothing, to get lost in the crowd – my height gave me away. When you're two meters tall, you look like a bean pole walking in a crowd of short people.

"What did you find out?" I clarified when we were down on the platform waiting for the train.

"It's not as bad as it seemed," Ramon cocked an eye with a look that seemed to imply the three thousand was already in his pocket.

"But what specifically?" I clarified, starting to boil over a bit.

"The Foxes really were werebeasts."

"Were?" I grew unpleasantly surprised. "What do you mean 'were?'"

"Just what I said," the constable snorted. "They used to work for the triads, but as long as they didn't poke their noses out of the Chinese Quarter, our guys wouldn't touch them."

I nodded. The Metropolitan Police didn't care much for maintaining law and order in the Chinese Quarter; the triads kept it instead. But, in order to stop the newcomers from spreading their influence to other streets, immigrants from the Celestial Kingdom were allowed to settle outside the historical borders of the neighborhood only with the permission of the Ministry of Foreign Affairs; Chinese people who had taken oaths of loyalty to the Second Empire only needed the magistrate's permission. And even that rule wasn't followed very strictly.

"What changed?" I hurried my partner, who had gotten distracted by his lupara getting tangled in his belt.

"That comes later!" he waved it off.

A long honk rolled out, and a steam train enveloped in wisps of smoke burst forth from the tunnel. Its brakes screeched. Pushing the city-dwellers aside, we got into the third-class car and took a spot in the corner after unceremoniously squeezing a couple of worker-types out.

"Do you remember the riots after the battles in the Third Opium War? It was a big issue five years ago."

"I do."

The unexpected alliance of the Celestial

Kingdom and Japan allowed the united forces of the Eastern governments to hold a number of close battles with the Russian Army, reinforced by colonial corps from the French and English.

"The riots were infamous," Ramon chuckled unhappily. "You weren't working yet, but I got to stand on the line. I've seen quite enough of that now. I still walk a different route every time I'm near those places."

"Closer to business," I demanded, clenching the handrail. The car was reeling from side to side, and I even started to fear that it was slightly going off the rails. But no, the steam train gradually slowed down, rolled out to the station and stopped.

The constable pushed the crowd of guys next to us out of the way, and continued his story:

"The Chinese were trying to make inroads beyond their Quarter, and the Foxes made a few appearances."

"And that was the straw that broke the camel's back for Department Three?" I guessed.

"That's exactly right." Ramon affirmed. "The triads had to give up the criminals. After the disorder was suppressed, the police simply twisted their arms. They say you shouldn't talk about that story with locals. They all pretend nothing happened."

"So am I to understand that they were all caught?"

"I do know of one fortunate individual," the constable told me, "who missed all the fun on the continent."

"And?"

"When he came back, he started taking under-aged street boys. The kind their own mother would cut up for a couple francs. None of them actually have the disorder, but the vermin can still overwhelm with numbers and force. So, as I said before, the Foxes are just a normal gang now."

"All the easier, then," I chuckled and asked: "Did you get the bullets? At least one werefox in the gang is real."

Ramon tapped on the fore-stock of his lupara.

"I got some great bullets: lead with a silver jacket. Just what the doctor ordered."

Then the train began slowing its pace once again, and the constable started for the door.

"Let's get out here," he called me to follow.

When the car stopped to the sound of a steam hiss, we got out onto the platform and walked up to the street. The Metro station was in the middle of the Chinese Quarter, and life all around was bubbling over.

Everywhere we looked, there were Chinese

lanterns glowing, and fires lit in the windows of restaurants and gambling houses. Barefoot rickshaw drivers were dragging their carts around, local inhabitants were scurrying every which way, going about their incomprehensible business. Freaks who'd come here for fun were having a look around.

On the outside, it was all very seemly, but I knew that as soon as I got off the central street, all this grandeur would vanish as if by magic. With every step, I saw more opium smokers and dens, and at every intersection, there were more and more pimps trying to hawk underage prostitutes.

"Who are we waiting for?" I asked Ramon, who had stopped at the edge of the road and was spinning his head all around in confusion.

A beggar came up to us with a mug for donations, but the constable told off the panhandler with such abandon that he blew away like the wind.

"Are you angry?" I grew surprised, in that Ramon was normally known for his tough nature.

"I cannot stand the poor," the constable shrugged his shoulders. "My mother always said that they bring bad luck."

"Are you afraid of them?" I squinted.

"A cousin of mine got hit by a train, and he lost half an arm. And also, Novak from squad two, after getting stabbed with a knife, his fist dried up," Ramon remembered, going silent and staring at me with suspicion. "Your doing, no? Just try using it on me, I'll make you toe the line."

"Who, I'm asking, are we waiting for?" I chuckled, making a nick for the future just in case.

I had never noticed such weakness in my friend.

"My contacts," Ramon explained and dragged me after him to a noodle spot. A paper dragon parade set to the sound of drums snaked between us and the door. "There they are!"

And though the metropolitan police did ignore some of the lawlessness inside the Chinese Quarter, white gentlemen on the main streets didn't have to worry about being robbed, stabbed or even having mud slung at them. The presence of policemen reminded the triads that they must remain prudent. Although, that only did work on the main streets, and there were closed-off alleys where no one was watching over what happened.

When we got closer, the door of the noodle shop flung open, and four constables came out onto the veranda. One of them was a local. The Chinese man was holding a semi-automatic Madsen-Biarnoff rifle on his shoulder. The others' belts were weighed down with revolvers and batons.

Ramon stuck a one-hundred-franc bill imperceptibly into the hand of the oldest one and asked:

"Do you have the address?"

The gray-mustached constable with a wrinkled face didn't answer for some time, instead just staring.

"*Illustrious*?" He winced, chewing on his weathered lower lip and warning: "Don't take your glasses off. They don't like your kind here."

"No problem."

"Franz!" Ramon patted the gray-mustached man on the back. "So, did you get the address or not?"

"The Reynard is in the *Jade Staff*. It isn't far."

"Is that a bordello?" I supposed, based on the name.

"It is," the constable confirmed, buttoning up his uniform to the top. "We'll keep watch on the street. You go inside. Will that do?"

The gray-mustached man had clearly been counting on shaking another couple hundred from us for the help, but Ramon left him disappointed.

"It will!" he threw out, unbuttoning his cloak and freeing himself from his holster belt with its four hundred fifty-five caliber automatic

Webley-Fosbery revolver. The device weighed more than a kilogram and yet was not known for particular reliability. That said, it was more accurate than a normal revolver in field conditions.

The constable spit under his feet with vexation and shrugged his shoulders.

"Then follow me!" He called and walked off down the sidewalk.

We hurried after him and the police came behind us.

We went down the main street, and the crowds didn't thin out one bit. The local inhabitants, in their traditional Chinese garb, were trying to lure some of the many gawkers to come into their restaurants, jewelry shops and gambling establishments, but most of them were interested in other kinds of entertainment. Many of the passers-by could barely stay on their feet. Such people could be identified either from the bleary gaze and pale skin of an opium smoker, or the reddened face of an absolute drunk. There were almost no women to be seen.

Soon, the constable turned down a side alley, and it was as if we found ourselves in another world. The shadows grew thicker, mud started champing under our feet, and we had to hold our breath from the unbearable stench; along with the perfume of sewage thrown out of windows, there was acrid smoke hovering over the earth and the smell of food being cooked. Everywhere around us, there were blinds and doors being slammed shut. We had to walk down the narrow passages between the scuzzy building walls where you couldn't get through without bumping shoulders with a few people. I could hear the rumbling of drums and popping of crackers not far away, but the sounds seemed muted somehow. They quickly got lost in the winding streets.

New Babylon was a city in which there was no black and white, but in the Chinese Quarter, it was devilishly hard to find anything positive.

I couldn't stand it here, and tried to avoid coming whenever possible.

"People shouldn't live like this," I muttered, stepping over yet another body just lying in the middle of the road. Based on the intense smell of opium, the man was a smoker who had just finished smoking right here not long ago.

"You think we should send them back to the Celestial Kingdom?" Ramon snorted after hearing my words.

"Forget about it," I waved it off.

My headache slightly receded. The bad presentiments were forgotten, and I started steeling up some nerve. On the central street, it was possible that some shopkeeper working for

Mr. Chan would recognize me, but not here, not in this labyrinth of confused little streets, where darkness reigned unchallenged.

The gray-mustached constable walked our path intently. It wasn't likely that we would come across anyone on it, so when we came up to a crooked little house with incomprehensible symbols on a banner, no one said a word as not to give the crooks advance warning of the police raid, allowing them to flee at full speed, or barricade the windows and doors.

Quiet and calm.

"The back door is on you," the senior officer commanded two of his subordinates to stand behind the bordello.

"We just watch?" He clarified.

"Just watch," the constable stated forcefully. "You have two minutes." And, when they disappeared into the darkness of the night, he took out his onion-shaped pocket watch and turned to us. "Inside is the old Reynard and two guys from the gang. Do not turn your back to them."

"Where is the Reynard?" I asked, drawing my Roth-Steyr.

"In a room on the second floor. I'm not sure which one exactly. There are girls sitting at the entrance. After that is the smoking room and the stairs," the gray-mustached constable explained, then asked: "I beg of you, please try not to shoot."

"Alright," I promised and, pulling back the bolt on my pistol, delivered a round into the chamber.

"It's time!" The constable then commanded.

We walked up to the entrance to the *Jade Staff*; I shoved the door open, and Ramon was first to jump into the room, which was lit with colorful torches, and filled with half-naked girls, their waifish bodies covered only with semi-transparent mantles. The girls gave a piercing shriek, and a short boy recoiled from the billiard table and threw himself at us with a billiard cue in hand. Ramon knocked him off his feet with a strike from his gun stock; something gave a vile crack, and the bandit spread out motionless on the floor.

I stepped over him, grabbed a billiard ball and threw it with all my might at a man who was running away from us. It hit him on the back of the head, and he collapsed, slid on the painted boards and froze, the top of his head slammed into the wall.

"Great left-handed throw," Ramon commended me and looked cautiously into the smoking room. "Clear!" He told us after looking into the wisps of sweetish smoke that filled the air there.

Grabbing another billiard ball from the

table just in case, I joined my partner and prodded him down the stairs that led to the second floor. But, just a moment later, a certain detail forced me to slow my pace and call out to Ramon:

"Stop!"

The toxin-filled air was making my head spin and I don't even know what exactly put me on my guard: the light breeze, the cracked-open kitchen door or the white-haired leprechaun loafing about on a bench with one leg over the other swinging his toe-less boot.

It was probably the totality of it.

But, when the small man pulled away from his pipe, exhaled a thick stream of smoke and nodded at the cracked-open door, I cast my doubts aside and flew in the direction he was pointing.

"Be gone," I ordered as I ran.

"Leo, where are you going?!" Ramon was taken aback.

I noticed a ripped out wall hanger as if someone had been running to get out of this place before being grabbed by the gills, and turned to my friend:

"They warned him! Those bastards warned the Reynard!"

Ramon cursed out quietly and extended me the torch.

"We should have paid them more," he declared. "Your loss."

"Get fucked!" I cursed, taking the torch in my left hand and commanding: "Come on! Move it!"

My squat partner, his lupara at the ready, walked into the kitchen. I stole along behind him, immediately stepping to the side to light up the room.

There was no one, just ovens, boilers and pans. There was no one, sure, but the door leading outside was flung wide.

We made no rush. It was one thing trying to catch a werebeast unawares, but another thing entirely to track such a creature if it's expecting you.

"Cover me!" Ramon gasped quietly, gathering his spirit. "Let's earn me my three thousand!"

Right after my friend, I went out into the bordello's courtyard, which was lent a white color by the undergarments hanging from clotheslines there. I immediately caught an aftershock of aged fear. It spread out on my tongue like a sour flavor. It was a very harsh sensation, like the smell of old piss.

The Reynard wasn't planning to run. The Reynard was afraid, but was preparing to give resistance to the outsiders.

Loneliness and fear had filled the werefox, having long grown accustomed to being able to rely on his pack. The instinctive fear of a stronger predator was impressed in his very nature. And that was precisely what forced the lone Fox to throw himself at the competition with abandon, showing everyone – and most of all himself! – that he was the scariest creature in this forest.

"Don't leave my side!" I warned my partner, hurriedly scanning from one dark corner to the next with my torch. "No matter what happens, don't leave my side. Not even one step!"

No hope whatsoever remained for the other constables to help us; they wouldn't be coming into the courtyard. The best we could hope for was for them to sound the alarm near the main entrance.

Ramon stepped out in front. He cast a bedsheet to the side and immediately spun around, set on edge by an incomprehensible rustling behind him; he handled his lupara so deftly that it seemed weightless. I walked next to him as if glued there, trying to guess where to expect the attack from. There were horrifying shadows growing up on the white sheets like the screens of a cinema; my heart was beating rabidly. My imagination was playing on my nerves, giving life to the fears gathered in my mind.

We didn't even notice when the hunters became the hunted.

Bit by bit, the fog thickened and it seemed we were wandering around the middle of the hippodrome, not at all in the internal courtyard of a bordello that could be spit across easily both lengthwise and across.

"Let's go back!" Ramon decided when an unpleasant snicker billowed out next to us.

And we started back toward the door. From time to time, the drumming thump of rapid footsteps rang out nearby and strange shadows played on the bed sheets. My hulking partner had simply begun ripping down the laundry and throwing it underfoot, but we still were not able to get to the kitchen, or even the exit from the courtyard, for that matter.

Curse this fog!

My knees shook. Fear rolled over me in waves. Hundreds of needles stuck into my soul, sapping my strength. The Reynard could come out from behind any of these sheets, jump on my back, bite my neck...

Suddenly, a quiet rustling sounded out and the width of the nearest sheet was split down by a long slash. Ramon lunged toward it, but whoever it was started laughing uncontrollably in a villainous tone, already in a different place.

"Don't leave my side!" I whispered out,

pulling my friend back.

We were standing back-to-back, listening to the sound of the night in panic. The sound of quick scampering, the rustling of fabric ripping, noisy breathing. And then, there was movement at the very edge of my vision. The kind you catch for just a second from the corner of your eye, but you turn, and no one is there.

The beam of my torch was moving from side to side, but I still couldn't manage to shine it on the beast running circles around us. The Reynard was playing with us. The Reynard was having fun.

But us? We had to accept the rules of the game as he set them. My fear began to somewhat subside. I came to the understanding that Ramon's lupara and my torch would allow us to bring the werefox's advantage down to zero. Just let him come to us...

And then, with a noisy crack, the torch burnt out. I tried to bring it back to life, but no matter how I slammed on the button, nothing happened. It just started smelling more and more of burnt wire.

"Do not run," Ramon whispered. "The most important thing is not to run..."

Movement in the dark, rustling on the verge of audibility, movement in the air.

The beast was near. The beast was tired of

playing.

He wanted blood.

And then, I let the fear sweep through my head, completely fill my consciousness and reanimate any phobias that were lying dormant there.

I was afraid of animals. But I was even more afraid of becoming like him. I was afraid of letting out all the evil that was hidden in the depths of my soul.

Empty fantasies? Oh no. I had plenty of reason to be afraid...

I took a deep breath, closed my eyes and gave a hoarse laugh.

"You like games?" I rasped quietly in another's voice, full of smoke and drink. A moment of silence took hold. The Reynard felt the presence of another predator and froze, not knowing what to do about it.

My dried lips stretching unpleasantly over my teeth, I took Ramon by the hand, not letting him step back and I continued:

"I like games too!" The hoarse voice tore itself from me with a noisy gasp, but that didn't hamper its effect. "Shall we play?" I suggested to the Reynard. "Let's play hide and seek! I love to seek. I love it so much..."

Laughter ripped itself from my ribcage painfully and I finally melted into my fears; they flowed over my body in a fit, settled in, spun around and tried to break me.

I held out, though I had to lean on Ramon a bit.

"We could play, or we could talk. It's up to you!" I rasped again in another's voice. "But believe you me: you aren't likely to win my game. And, it's the kind of game you can't lose more than once..." The rasping laughter scratched my throat like a harsh nail file.

I don't know how long I would have been able to balance here on the very borderline, keeping creeping nightmares at bay and at the same time holding them by a leash, but then the fog and shadows began spinning and weaved together into a short Chinese person. He was mobile and flexible, like the mercury or melted gold his yellow pupil-less eyes were filled with.

Curses! I guess Reynard was a deceptive nickname. The Reynard was a woman!

Just then, a pint-sized woman stepped out of the darkness with a boyish figure, slender if not to say plain. And I didn't even want to think about what she was doing in a bordello.

The sides of her thin nose trembling, the Reynard flung open her mouth, revealing a set of crooked teeth, and took a whiff, trying to make sense of what she was feeling. She saw a weak person, but her animal instincts, which the beast had become accustomed to trusting incomparably more, were telling her that a stronger predator had joined the game.

The last few years, the Reynard had lived with a dread that another animal might invade her territory one day, and I didn't hesitate to take advantage of that. My fingers dug into her fear, and I joined it with my own phobias to get the upper hand. My *talent* had not led me astray...

Letting go of Ramon's hand, I took a step toward the Reynard. With my left hand, I grabbed her by her thin jaw, pulling her toward me in a decisive motion.

"Was it you who gutted the Judean?" I rasped, looming over the woman.

The Reynard shook her head cluelessly, not feeling up to answering. The fear inside her had balled itself up into a steel trap, and the werefox wasn't even thinking about triggering it with the sharp claws that crowned her fingers.

"It wasn't you..." I realized and threw her aside. "Be gone!" I ordered her, and the Reynard immediately dissolved in the shadows.

The fog began breaking slightly. Ten meters from us, we began to see the yellow fires of the bordello's windows once again.

"Leo, when did you become a master ventriloquist?" Ramon took a step toward me, cautiously turning his head from side to side. He couldn't believe that the danger had gone.

"I am full of talents," I answered, forcing my fears back into the murky abyss of my own subconscious.

For the second time in only a day, I had had too much, but instead of the sour taste of vomit, my mouth was filled with the aftertaste of a terrible hangover. My arms and legs were trembling. I almost fell over. I was feeling bad and in pain. I couldn't let go of the feeling that I was no different from the Reynard. That there was an animal hiding inside me as well.

Nonsense! It's just fear. An idiotic fear that shouldn't ever be let out.

I straightened up and placed my pistol in the holster. My glasses, for some reason, had ended up in the breast pocket of my jacket. I returned them to their place, then picked up the burnt-out torch from the ground, and popped two mint sugar drops into my mouth at once.

"Leo, are you alright?" Ramon asked, not having the patience to remain here any longer.

"Completely," I replied, wincing in pain. "Let's go!"

WE LEFT THE COURTYARD through the back gate. We let the constables go, not telling them anything had gone wrong, and hurried to the Metro station; Ramon assured me that he would find the way back no problem.

And I didn't argue. Weariness had set in with a heavy weight. My head was splitting in pain once again.

"There's something I'm not understanding, Leo," he stated when we were already on the platform waiting for a train. "Why did you let her go? Why let her get away?"

"She wasn't our suspect, Ramon," I winced and my head started spinning from side to side to the quiet cracking of my spinal cord. "She wasn't in the Judean Quarter, and that's that."

"Where did you get that idea? You said you were sure that your moneylender must have poisoned the werebeast against the banker!"

"That was my bias talking."

"But how can you be sure?"

I looked at my friend, took a heavy sigh and lowered myself to explanation.

"The height and jaw shape don't match up to our victims."

"Explain."

"The murderer from the banker's house was tall, maybe even taller than me. The distance between the footprints on the floor was a bit longer than my gait."

"But what if he was running?"

"No, the footprints weren't smeared. Foot size was from twenty-nine to thirty centimeters, and that means, using the de Parville index, that the murderer's height is...

... at least two meters, maybe more. As long as he doesn't have dwarfism.

And don't forget his gait, either."

"Of course," Ramon nodded. "What else?"

"Bite shape," I explained. "The jaw is too wide in animal form. Our perp was able to rip the throat out of one of the guards."

"But the Chinese werebeast was smaller, so the bite would have been narrow," my partner sighed and cursed out in vexation: "Devil! I can kiss that money goodbye!"

I chuckled and clapped him on the shoulder:

"Don't worry about it. We've got an agreement."

Ramon snorted and asked acridly:

"So, you want to go hunt for Procrustes after all?"

"Procrustes died a long time ago. We tracked down one werebeast, and we can track down another."

"Is that so?" Ramon grinned. "And just how will we do that, I ask you? What do you know about him other than the fact that he is tall?"

"Other than the fact that he is tall?" I thought about it, remembering what I'd seen in the Judean's manor and began enumerating: "He is thin. His feet barely made a mark. He has a high instep. His left foot was a bit longer than the right and wider, I bet he's a lefty. And he must not be from here. Such beasts cannot stop themselves from killing, so it wouldn't have just started now."

"Look at you, Sherlock Holmes!" he laughed uncontrollably. "What do you think, do I make a good Doctor Watson?"

"You make a good enough likeness to earn three thousand and the gratitude of the Witstein Banking House."

"You can keep the gratitude to yourself," Ramon cut me off. "I'll take the money. I inquired about the pay for a night guard at the coalhouses. It's not so good."

"When's your first day?"

"Day after tomorrow."

"I'll find you," I promised.

"Please do."

Just then, the train rolled up to the platform. We went into the wagon and left the Chinese Quarter to the drumming of its steel wheels.

I was hoping that I'd never have to come back here again. Never ever.

PART FOUR

PROCRUSTES

Instinctive Reflexes and Accelerated
Regeneration

1

ANXIETY IS TOXIC.

Too highbrow? Alright, fear is poison.

On its own, fear can be fleeting, but its aftereffects can last for many years. For the first few minutes, though, it can really make people shiver.

And now it was making me shiver.

I should have gone to bed earlier. That always helped. But I was dominated by the thought that I would be lounging around all night in an empty house, and hearing a scratch at the blinds caused an attack of nervous trembling.

I did not want that. Any other day, sure, but today it was unacceptable.

So I went out to stay at Albert Brandt's.

IN THE *CHARMING BACCHANTE*, there was smoke up to my shoulders. The warmed-up audience was smoking, drinking wine and devouring the scantily clad dancers with their eyes. Even I spent some time standing in the doorway, watching the stage until I caught myself on the thought that I was being a creep. But her legs were as slender as Elizabeth-Maria von Nalz's...

I squirmed.

Then, I got through to the bar and asked the owner, pointing at the ceiling:

"At home?"

"At home," she replied and added

proudly: "He's been working all day!"

And Albert actually was working. When I got up to the second floor and glanced in the door, he was leaning over the table and putting something to paper with a quill in the uneven light of a kerosene lamp. But when I came in, he immediately looked away, crumpled the manuscript and threw it in the top drawer of his desk.

"Inspiration's struck?" I asked, undoing my mud-caked boots.

"Better!" the poet laughed wholeheartedly, satisfied with his life. He took the class ring sitting in front of him, and attached it to the chain of his pocket watch. "I've met *her*!"

The declaration didn't surprise me in the least; Albert had always been thrall to a healthy, affectionate nature.

I set my dirty boots behind the door, placed the billiard ball I'd forgotten to take out of the pocket of my canvas pea-coat on the shelf and, finally, sighed wearily:

"Who is she?"

"True love! The meaning of my whole life! A fire that warms me and lights up my bleak existence in bright colors."

My pea-coat removed, I poured myself a glass of water and noted in passing that the poet was drinking just soda water today, so I drained the glass and chuckled in an outpouring of my emotions:

"Yet another comely lass?"

My friend was already over Kira, though. There was no reason to stick my foot in this delicate matter another time. All these art people had unstable enough psyches as it was.

"Comely?" The poet groaned. "Leopold, if you keep talking like that, I'll have to challenge you to a duel!"

"Woah! So, it's yet another fair lady, then?"

"There's no 'yet another.' She's the only lady for me! Irreplaceable! I've been waiting my whole life for her. Her and only her. She has a beauty that stops your heart in a sweet languor. The entrancing sounds of her voice make you pray that you will meet again..."

The symptoms were very familiar, so I took a seat on the ottoman and, with a condescending smile, asked:

"And how do you call this new lady of your heart?"

"She didn't introduce herself," Albert fell into a gloomy state, as if he had remembered a very unpleasant fact. "Can you imagine it, Leo? She didn't even tell me her name! She said only that she was bound not by a wedding ring but by some other, higher calling."

"Well, did you set up a date?" I clarified,

knowing the answer in advance.

"Well, sure," the poet confirmed calmly and leaned his elbows on the table: "And how are things with you?"

"You won't believe it."

"So that good, then?"

"Actually, it's that bad." I laid back on the ottoman and reminded him: "You told me you knew a guy who could get a cane?"

"You're still limping? Alright, we can pay him a visit tomorrow morning, if you've got time."

"I do," I replied and, in my turn, asked: "The barkeep told me you've been working all day. What are you working on?"

"I'm working?" Albert drew out the words pensively, stroking his straight-parted wig. "Oh, yeah! Poetry is hard work, especially when all your thoughts are occupied with the image of..."

"Your mystery girl," I sighed. "But aren't you writing odes for her then?"

"As I said before," Albert frowned, "I'm working on the poem *Inhabitant of the Night*!"

I squirmed.

"The one about Procrustes?"

The poet nodded.

"Right now, he's all the city can talk about. The craze hasn't passed me by either. We creative people are sway to the mood of the masses, after all..."

"And you took a run at turning it into a whole poem?"

"Well, sure," Albert laughed. "It's all conjecture, devil beat me, but I need to pay the bills somehow, as you well understand."

"You're selling your talent."

The poet's eyes lit up with an unnatural light, and he laughed hoarsely:

"I'll sell my whole soul one piece at a time. The people like it! They always call for an encore! At midnight, I'm performing for a most respectable audience..."

I frowned involuntarily.

All of Albert's performances without exception ended with one and the same: debauchery and fisticuffs. The poet had the *talent* to charm people with the sounds of his voice, but when his inborn *talent* for performance combined with his finely honed gift as a poet, it caused people to fall into ecstasy, and not only his exalted ladies, but hoar-headed gentlemen as well. The *Illustrious* Mr. Brandt's recitals were always accompanied by a true hullabaloo, but the owner of the *Charming Bacchante* invited Albert back to perform again and again, because it got her establishment in the society pages of most local papers almost every time.

It seemed that I wouldn't be able to get a good night's sleep tonight.

Albert rolled an empty bottle under the couch, trying to hit the place where he'd heard a mouse rustling around, and suggested:

"Will you come down to watch me?"

Normally, I would have watched the poet with pleasure, but today I wanted to refuse.

"I'm afraid, a poem about Procrustes is not going to sit well with me tonight..."

"Drop it!" Albert cut me off, not accepting my refusal. "Don't be such a narrow-minded moralist! Come watch my reading..."

I could have just stood up and gone down stairs, as I had often subjected myself to love poems for the sake of Albert's amusement, but now the weariness was pressing down on me with a fully tangible weight, and I waved my hand against my desire.

"Go on!" I allowed and, threw back my head and stared at the ceiling.

Albert cleared his throat and recited expressively:

"Inhabitant of the night,
Mindful of the light,
I cannot figure,
Whose body you now wear,
But find you I will, killer,
And I'll give you there,
Bullets of silver,
Thirteen sounds fair..."

Strange intonations came through in the poet's voice. They cut into my soul and re-awoke old memories, so I couldn't hold back from a short chuckle.

"What?" Albert shuddered, his concentration gone in an instant. "What are you whinnying about?"

"Who's whinnying?"

"You're whinnying like a mare, Leopold!" My friend flared up, reacting very squeamishly to my opinion of his paltry rhymes. "Could you explain what exactly you found so funny?"

The poet reminded me of an angry school teacher, telling off a bad student, but I didn't use that analogy and bring him to white-hot rage, I just waved my hand ambiguously:

"It just gave me dirty associations. What was it... 'The human form, a fiery forge...'?"

"Blake?!" Albert exclaimed. "You're saying it reminds you of William Blake?"

"I'm just saying the association came to mind..."

"Association!" Albert drew out the word, puckered up and turned away. "That was just the introduction," he grumbled back some time later.

"Don't get mad," I begged him in a conciliatory manner.

The poet turned away, preparing to break

out in a hateful rant, but just then bottles started clanking in the liquor cabinet.

"Damned rats!" Albert growled out in a fit of anger, grabbing a dueling saber from an elephant-foot umbrella holder.

I got up on an elbow expecting free entertainment, but there weren't any rats in the liquor cabinet. The rustling was now coming from the clothes cabinet.

The poet swore prodigiously, cursing the whole species in one go, opening the door and recoiling quickly when, out from under his legs jumped an albino leprechaun in a green frock coat, an accordion-ed top hat and boots with the tips cut off.

A moment later, the small man was next to the liquor cabinet, grabbing the nearest bottle and, with the deftness of a marmoset, he flew up onto the mezzanine. There, he yanked out the cork with his teeth, took a sniff and melted into an entranced smile:

"Absinthe!" He stuck it down his throat, and gasped loudly: "Bugger, that's good stuff!" And looked at me with unhidden superiority: "This is ambrosia, Leo! The nectar of the gods!"

A sharp pain shot through my skull. I pressed my palms to my temples dolefully and closed my eyes tight in the hope that the apparition would go away on its own, but it was in vain.

"Leopold," Albert said with a quivering voice, "my absinthe!"

"Pig!" The leprechaun stuck out his long pale tongue, took out a tobacco pouch and started rolling a cigarette. "You vile, odious pig!" he muttered, spitting out the bits of tobacco that came into his mouth.

The poet fell down on the couch in depression and turned to me:

"I'm raving, aren't I? Leo, don't just sit there, say something!"

The leprechaun called back instead of me.

"Have you got a light?" He bellowed, chewing on the rollie in the corner of his mouth.

"Get out of here!" I demanded.

I didn't have to ask twice; in a blink of the eye, the albino was down from the mezzanine and jumping out the door.

"So you saw him too? I'm not crazy," Albert noted judiciously and, clinking the neck of a bottle on the edge of his glass, poured himself some wine. "What was that, Leo?"

I sighed.

"Sometimes, children have imaginary friends that no one can see but them," I said, looking at a crack in the white paint on the ceiling. "That is nothing to be afraid of. It's normal. You run into problems, though, when other people also start to see your imaginary friends."

The poet choked on his wine and stared at me with a large degree of amazement.

"That ugly mug is your imaginary friend?!"

"Childhood friend," I told him. "I hadn't seen him since I was five. I have no idea why he's back now. It must be related to my chronic stress."

Chronic stress and an aggravated case of the Diabolic Plague.

"Was he always so... indulgent?" Albert asked, dabbing his wine-drenched shirt.

"Not really. We used to just play chess," I smiled at the half-forgotten memories. "Or go up on the roof and look at the city. We used to make bark boats and play with them in the fountain. We would run in the garden, and play hide and go seek. I didn't often win..."

"Aw hell," the poet gasped. "But why a leprechaun?"

"I have no idea," I confessed. "Perhaps it's got to do with my Irish roots. One of my grandmas was from there. She used to read me fairytales at night."

"And what's wrong with his shoes?"

"Sandals used to hurt my feet. And don't ask about the top hat. I don't know where he got that thing from."

At that moment, the music below went quiet; Albert finished his wine and started getting the papers scattered over his table together in one pile.

"You're full of surprises, my friend," he shook his head.

"Says the guy who's trying to woo a mystery girl?" I couldn't resist joking back.

The poet waved his hand, carelessly tied his bright neckerchief and got his morning coat from the cabinet.

"As far as I understand, I shouldn't count on your presence, then?" Standing before a mirror, he shot me a sidelong glance.

"No!" I let out.

"I just don't understand how you can be so mundane..." Albert snorted and set off to read his poems.

But I remained there on the ottoman. I lied there and looked at the ceiling, wracking my brains over where to search for the banker's murderer before the police did. The investigators from Department Three wouldn't get distracted by the mythical return of Procrustes. They would study the evidence and begin very soon – if they hadn't begun already! – to look for a left handed out-of-towner who was tall and thin. And, unlike me, the police had enough force and capability to blow through all the hotels and tenements a werebeast from out of town might lay its head in.

All I could do now was stay ahead of the investigation – figure out exactly what the murderer took from the banker and how it was connected with the bank robbery.

With only that thought in mind, I fell asleep.

I WOKE UP LATE, my neck stiff from the uncomfortable position.

I sat up on the ottoman and noted with surprise that Albert had already managed to leave the house. Then I walked past it to the window, pulled back the curtain and nodded, having received confirmation of my guess. It would rain soon. The sky was saturated with gray clouds. It seemed like it was late at night outside.

Albert couldn't bear direct sunlight, but felt truly alive and alert in weather like this. The back of my head was aching though.

I stood before the mirror, and looked cantankerously at my haggard physiognomy and decided with a significant degree of relief that the crimson tinge in my eyes was starting to turn back to its former colorless shade. I clipped my dark glasses onto my nose, buttoned up my jacket and, pea-coat in hand, looked out the door for my boots.

My boots had been cleaned and polished.

When I went down to the first floor, I caught the heavy smell of old booze. Even the flung-wide windows were no help. My injured leg giving out, I limped to the door, but the tables of the street cafe hadn't been set yet, so I had to send a boy playing around nearby to the nearest coffee shop and go back to the bar.

"Where did Albert get off to?" I asked the owner's nephew who was wiping down the bar. "Has yet another suitor stolen him away?"

"I don't know," the young boy with curly black hair shook his head, "but before he left, he sent out for a bouquet of roses."

"Prodigal spender," I chuckled and asked him to pour me some coffee.

The boy ran up, I took an apple strudel from him and went up into the poet's apartment. I did not want to spend any more time than I had to in the aroma of old perfume, booze and sweat that reigned there.

ALBERT BRAND RETURNED after I'd already finished breakfast, and was speculating on where to start the investigation. The poet looked very unhappy, and I couldn't hold back from paraphrasing a Russian classic:

"Now you've become another's wife, eh?"

"And I'll be true to him for life," Albert

caught my reference, but immediately winked: "No, Leo, it's not all so bad. What's more, my show last night was a phenomenal success! I would even call it breathtaking!"

"They'll forget about Procrustes soon," I assured the poet.

"Nonsense!"

"He's dead, Albert!"

"Where did you get that idea? They write about him in all the papers!"

I could have tried to convince the poet, or joked that even Houdini couldn't get out of the grave without moving the slab, but I stayed silent and just frowned:

"It's all just ballyhoo." and immediately stopped myself. "Hold on! When did it all start again? It wasn't with the banker at all, was it? There were other stories!"

"There was another murder, yes," said the poet. "Do you remember the day we were walking to the hippodrome?"

That's right!

I snapped my fingers and walked over to a bedside table, with a towering pile of newspapers on it.

"Did you throw that issue away?" I asked, leafing through the yellowed pages.

"No, I didn't. Look, it's there somewhere."

Soon, I actually did find the paper I needed

and immersed myself in reading.

The murder from two nights ago in the area of the Emperor's Park had caught the attention of the newspapermen for its animalistic cruelty: a strong thirty-year-old man had his limbs and throat ripped out. Expert opinion was that even the strongest man on earth wouldn't have been able to cause such mutilation as the dead man suffered.

On the grainy photograph, I could see the wall of a house, its grayed whitewash streaked with blood. There was a very large amount of blood. And no one had heard or seen a thing.

The poet walked up and looked over my shoulder.

"What scheme are you hatching now?"

"I'll start by taking a look at the crime scene. Albert, can we go get the cane?"

The poet did not refuse me the help.

"It isn't far from here. I'll take you there and get to work." The poet tried on a straw boater hat and added acridly: "I need to finish the poem about Procrustes before you stomp this legend into the ground."

I sighed heavily:

"Believe me, Albert. You wouldn't want to meet this legend if it came in a bad mood."

"Procrustes in a bad mood?" The poet laughed, adjusting his neckerchief before the mirror. "Leopold, your sense of humor gets darker every day!"

I waved it off and went out the door without waiting for my friend. I went down to the first floor, stood under the awning and immediately noted a free self-propelled carriage with a thin Chinese driver in a pair of foppish white gloves. Next to him, leaning on an expensive cane, there stood a withered old man in a military-cut field jacket.

Curses! Mr. Chan had decided to have a personal conversation with his listless debtor!

A nervous trembling came over me, but I immediately got myself together and calmly walked up to the moneylender. He got into the back seat of the self-propelled carriage and issued an order to the driver:

"Leave us!"

When his servant was outside, I closed the door and leaned my elbows against it in silence. I wasn't going to be the one to start this conversation.

"Mr. Orso," the moneylender then said, and pursed his lips. "Mr. Orso! Look at me! I'm talking to you!"

With a quiet, slightly whistling voice, I would normally put my debtors into a state of horrified fear. Normally – but not today.

"New Babylon is a surprising city," I

drawled out slowly, continuing to look at the calm surface of the canal, "the wonderful and the horrible are so closely intertwined here that it can be hard to tell them apart. And there are no angles or sharp edges, either. It it's all just shades and blurred half-tones. A solid gray."

"Have you lost your mind?" Mr. Chan grew surprised. "I didn't say you could speak!"

"Gray," I nodded, agreeing with my own thoughts, "just a solid gray. Above it is a small layer of white, too small to be visible. Below, everything is identically black. There is a bit more of the good, but the evil is more active. It throws itself in your eyes more forcefully."

"Stop it!"

I removed my glasses and looked at the moneylender.

"Mr. Chan! When you sent your cutthroat out with an order to remove my ear, you went so far under that you can no longer be considered part of that gray. You are evil. And no matter what I do to you, I will have a clean conscience."

"What impudence!" The old man grinned.

But he looked away before I did. His smooth pampered face fractured like a porcelain tea cup, and gave way to innumerable wrinkles.

Mr. Chan had left the Celestial Kingdom fleeing the rage of the immortal Emperor. He was flattered to have an *illustrious* gentleman among his debtors. He liked raising my interest rates and setting all kinds of new and interesting conditions, but at the base of his predilection lie normal fear.

Fears poison you. I already said that, right?

I smiled and went on:

"Now, there's nothing stopping me from saying out loud that I think it was you, Mr. Chan, who poisoned the werebeast against my partner Isaac Levinson."

"That's a lie!" the old man quickly retorted.

I chuckled.

"I suppose you will be able to convince the Judeans of that, but imagine how many boots you'll have to lick!"

Mr. Chan did imagine it, and false blood ran down his face.

"Don't joke around with me, boy!"

"One thing you should never do is send cutthroats out after me."

"Pay your debt!"

"I'll pay it when the time comes."

"The time has come!"

"Mr. Chan," I said with all possible respect, "look at the documents we signed. There are no dates mentioned in them. I will pay the debt as soon as I get control over the fund, and no sooner. That was the condition of our deal."

"My reputation is suffering..."

"We can talk about compensation when I come into my inheritance," I cut him off. "Incidentally, would you like to become my fiduciary? My last one, unfortunately, met a sudden end..."

"We can talk about that later," the moneylender stated threateningly.

He was a strong man, and did not allow emotion to rule him. That said, sober calculation had told him not to chase a rat into the corner.

Rats trapped in corners are too dangerous.

I never forgot that, so I smiled amicably, gave a shallow bow and stepped back from the self-propelled carriage, not waiting for him to order me out of there.

My knees were shaking and giving out, but all the same, when I got near Albert Brandt, still under the awning, I was no longer showing the discomfort that had overtaken me.

"Shall we go?" was the only thing I said to the poet.

"Who is that?" Albert pointed to the self-propelled carriage, driving away from the cabaret to the measured claps of its powder engine.

"A business partner."

"You could have asked him for a ride."

"I don't want to trouble an old man," I laughed in reply.

Albert snorted pointedly and we went on

our way.

On foot.

And it wasn't at all an act of small-minded revenge on the poet's part. It was just that his acquaintance's shop was very near the Emperor's Academy and it was faster to walk the confusing little streets of the Greek Quarter directly than tracking down a cabby and rolling down the overcrowded avenues and back streets.

"Alexander Dyak gets on excellently with reductionists," Albert told me, adjusting the carnation in the buttonhole of his morning coat. "He is also an unrecognized inventor. He's always messing around with all kinds of tools and tinkering with transformers. Students drag him ancient baubles, teachers visit to fill out their own collections of rare objects. You wouldn't believe it, Leo, the different kinds of people who gather there! Every other time you look, you see people laying out huge sums of money! They come in for a new electric jar, but leave with a little porcelain statue, all cracking and ancient. Weird people!"

"Collectors," I shrugged my shoulders.

"And students are like magpies. They'll take anything back to their nest that meets the eye. One of them this year has figured out how to nick manhole covers. A rare year for graduates, they say!"

I laughed and asked:

"So, tell me about your friend? What area is he active in?"

"I have no idea," Albert answered frivolously. "He's got a whole laboratory in his basement, but as you know, I don't understand science very well."

We crossed a stone bridge over a narrow canal into the historic part of the city and started walking directly for the square. There were benches all around the glade with students nesting in them like worried little sparrows. Those who couldn't find seats were sitting on the marble edges of the fountains, and some were just lounging about on the grass.

The whole neighborhood was filled with cute little two- and three-story homes with a never-ending array of bookshops, cheap snack bars, laundromats and little shops selling school supplies. If there ever were open seats on the outdoor verandas of the cafes, you almost never saw them. The owners didn't make particularly great profit from the many visitors, though. Most of them ordered just tea or coffee, and as for food, made due with the fruit of knowledge. The most profitable local businesses traded in nocturnal alcohol sales and renting out the upper floors and attics of nearby homes.

At first glance, this whole area was ruled by

cleanliness and order, but as soon as you turned down a back alley or walked down a narrow little street from one tavern to another you would get a face-full of the smell of freedom and libertinism. Freedom smelled of piss. Libertinism had its own aroma always marked by strains of vomit; after flying out of their parents' coop, most students had achieved the wisdom to avoid excessive consumption of cheap beer not long after the beginning of their studies.

We didn't stay on the seedy little streets long, soon emerging onto Leonardo da Vinci-Platz. On the spacious square, there were noticeably more people, and the severity of the business-like frock coats of the die-hard reductionists there was fairly diluted with the frivolous and colorful attire of creatives; beyond the department of natural sciences, the Emperor's Academy had a school of high arts inside it as well.

Someone was playing the violin. Another person was dancing right in the middle of the street. Artists were lined up with their easels, getting the details right in their drawings of the slender spires of the academy, which gave off an unbearable shine both on sunny days and in the distinguished yellow of today's overcast skies. It should be said that some of the young people weren't doing architectural studies, they were fashionistas just sauntering by. They looked like kerosene lamps come to life in their straw hats, angular jackets and wide dresses with expanded waists.

My canvas pea-coat clearly lost out in elegance to Albert's morning coat and, even though my boots were shining with a fresh coat of polish, they still could not compare with the poet's finely lacquered shoes, so I hurried my pace involuntarily.

Near the memorial to Leonardo da Vinci, there were a few people fencing with wooden foils. Next to them, students in theater course were rehearsing. Hawkers with trays and bulbous coffee pots were carrying pastries. Boys with fliers were running around in all directions.

One of them noticed Albert's foppish appearance, slipped him a theater program and ran further, yelling in a hoarse voice:

"Last showing of *Moon Circus*. It's the finale of a big tour! Don't miss it! Tight-rope walkers and a bearded lady! The strongest man in the world! Acrobats and tamed lions! Maestro Marlini is a virtuoso of scientific hypnosis! Don't miss it!"

The poet snorted and stuck the flier into his pocket.

"You need to get out sometimes," he said in reply to my inquisitive gaze.

After leaving the square, we turned down

the next little street and almost immediately found ourselves before the store *Mechanisms and Rarities.*

"This is it!" Albert pointed.

It was strange inside. No, that's not quite right. I had been in some truly strange places, and in comparison with those, this shop looked like the height of normalcy; even the stuffed crocodile hanging from the ceiling and the sparking electrodes couldn't make it that strange. My surprise was brought on by the way this place combined the contradictory.

On one side, the cases were filled with the latest electric jars, measuring instruments and writing implements. The other side of glass cases were filled with stamps, books, rare coins, porcelain statues, clocks and other antiquarian junk, of interest only to true connoisseurs.

But there was one thing that didn't fit the category of "mechanisms," or "rarities:" directly over the counter, there was a canvas with a panorama of some defensive structures near a river under a cloudy autumn sky that sprinkled the gray sea with fine droplets of drizzle. The picture was illuminated with two electric bulbs; their light gave the image a strange depth.

I was so distracted by the canvas that I didn't even notice the owner of the shop right away. He was a thin gentleman of sixty years in a frock coat with an antiquated cut. His hair, combed back, underlined his high forehead with its deeply receding hairline. His mustache and sparse beard had a touch of gray.

Albert exchanged a handshake with the shop owner, then introduced me:

"Leopold, my good friend."

Alexander Dyak greeted me cordially, then came out from behind the counter and threw back his head to look at the picture that had captured the attention of his new acquaintance.

"That is Kronstadt," he explained. "It is in the area of Petrograd, the capital of the Russian provinces."

I nodded and said, much to my own surprise:

"My grandfather is from Russia."

"Oh!" The shop owner grew animated. "And what was your father's name?"

"My father was named Boris."

"Leopold Borisovich! Nice to meet you!"

I smiled at the name I was unaccustomed to hearing and asked:

"You're making me blush. Now, I'll feel impolite not using your patronymic."

"Think nothing of it!" Alexander Dyak guffawed. "I left Russia fifteen years ago. If someone were to use my patronymic now, *that* would feel really strange!"

We laughed; the poet ran his hand over the glass and said with pride:

"Leo, whatever you need: a screwdriver or a powder engine, you can find it all in our man's warehouse. And anything you can't find, he can get for a good price!"

"Well, I don't need a powder engine right now!"

"Then what do you need?" Mr. Dyak clarified in a business-like manner.

"A cane," Albert Brandt answered, bowing over the glass case of gold guineas. "Leopold hurt his leg, and he needs a cane."

"In that case, you'd better go to a doctor," the store owner suggested.

"Drop it, Alexander! Young people heal better than a junkyard cat!"

"How many junkyard cats have you seen in your life?"

The poet laughed uncontrollably.

"In my hungry years..."

"Stop it, Albert," I brought my friend to reason. "Whether you see it or not, Mr. Dyak, I will soon need to do a lot of walking, and without a cane, I won't be able to get by..."

"And in that my friend is a bit strapped for cash," Albert Brandt added without circumlocution. "We decided to go to you. I remember that you were telling me about an invention..."

"What do you mean invention..." Mr. Dyak frowned. "I just put a couple mechanisms together. Why do you listen to the ravings of old men? Much less what *I* said?"

After such a rebuke, I would have been dragging anyone else to the exit, but now I was just standing and moving my gaze from one man to the other as they argued. If Albert had beaten anything into his own head, it would be impossible to tell him otherwise, but the old man was a tough nut to crack, too.

"It'll just be a few days!" the poet continued to insist.

The electric lights burning under the ceiling flickered; Alexander Dyak nervously shuddered and cursed out:

"Damn these current fluctuations!"

"Alexander!" The poet tapped severely on the edge of the counter with his finger. "Don't get distracted! We can talk about the current fluctuations next time. What about the cane?"

"You could convince the dead to walk, Albert!" the shop owner complained and crawled under the counter. "Here, look at this," he demonstrated us a cane with a rubber cap that grew slightly thicker in the lower third as if two knees joined there.

The poet immediately grabbed it and

handed it to me.

"Try it out!"

"Albert!" The old man boiled over and again got distracted by the frequently flickering light bulbs. "I'll have to check the cable..." he muttered to himself in agitation.

"You can check it..."

"Right now!" Mr. Dyak cut him off. "The last thing I need now is a fire!"

"Leo," the poet commanded me. "Try it out!"

I took a few steps, leaning on the cane as I did, and it gave under my weight just slightly every time. It definitely wasn't the rubber cap giving either, it was more likely a powerful spring inside.

"On the end of the handle, there's a cap," the owner of the shop told me. "Under it is a torch, check it."

The miniature bulb was unusually bright, but the small refractor behind it made the beam disperse fairly quickly, so it didn't go very far.

"The generator and electric jar are in here!" Albert grew giddy like a school boy. "Can you imagine? Isn't it lovely? No need to keep changing the battery! Just take it and use it! How congenial!"

"Very convenient," I agreed.

Alexander Dyak looked at us as if looking at two small children and shook his head.

"Be careful with puddles, though," he warned, taking the cane. "The high capacity electric jar discharging all at once would be very strong. I categorically recommend against submersing it in water by more than a third." He drummed his finger on the thickened part and returned the cane to me. "Can I count on your good sense, Leopold Borisovich?"

"Most assuredly," I told the inventor.

"No need to worry about rain, though. Drops and splashes shouldn't pose a risk."

"You didn't tell me about that!" Albert reproached the store owner.

"Well, I still haven't gone mad enough to entrust this cane to you!" Alexander Dyak waved it off. "Although I am no longer totally sure of the soundness of my own judgment..."

"How much do we owe you for the rental?" I then asked.

"Just get it back to me safe and sound," the old man replied. "I'm awfully interested in how reliable and tough the joint mechanism will be. I don't walk that much anymore, and there's no other way of evaluating wear and tear."

"Can I keep it until the end of the week?"

"Yes. And now, you'll have to forgive me, I need to deal with that wire!"

The light bulbs under the ceiling were now flickering incessantly. I didn't distract the man, thanking him again and making back for the entrance. Albert held back for a moment and asked:

"Nothing for me?"

"I would have written!" The old man pushed the poet out the door and hung a sign reading: "Closed."

Based on his agitated appearance, the problem wasn't the electrical wire at all, just another invention.

"A man of the world!" Albert assured me, sighed and added: "Just very easily distracted."

"How did you meet him?" I asked and leaned with all my might on the cane to test it out; it gave a slight spring, but that was all. "I don't take him for a lover of poetry."

"Stamps," the poet answered simply.

"Stamps?"

"Postage stamps," Albert confirmed. "Students from all over the world study here. Their friends and relatives send them letters. If only you knew what kind of rarities come through this place!"

"I had no idea you were a philatelist."

"Me? No," my friend assured me. "But I have friends of friends with a certain interest in it. It's all quite complicated..."

Things were rarely simple with the poet, so I didn't interrogate him too much on the matter. I walked along, getting used to the cane and wondered:

"Why'd you drag me down here? Was it not for the cane, then?"

Brandt shrugged his shoulders.

"Alexander gets lonely," he stated. "No family, no friends. He emigrated from god-knows-where in Russia, but never really got close to anyone. He's always messing around with his inventions, but he never makes them public. That takes its toll, believe it or not. He's starting to give out."

"So you thought you'd give him some entertainment?"

"I'd like to keep buying stamps from him for many years," Albert laughed and took out his pocket watch. "And now, I beg your forgiveness, but I have a date."

"The mystery girl?"

"That's right." The poet sighed dreamily and warned: "If you were planning to spend a night in the city, you'll have to find alternative accommodations. I'm afraid I won't be able to host you tonight."

"Are you afraid, or do you hope?"

"Leo, you see to the root of the problem, as always!" Albert laughed uncontrollably, clapped me on the shoulder and walked off to the main building of the Emperor's Academy. He was whistling away some tune, which I could still hear.

I shook my head and went off in the opposite direction.

I had business to attend to.

2

WHILE I WALKED to the nearest steam-tram stop, I finally got used to the cane. Slightly springing at first, it gradually took weight on itself and gave more resistance until the spring was compressed all the way down, and it became stiff. No more free motion, just up and down, up and down.

What did embarrass me a bit, though, was that the generator gave off a faint buzzing noise. But, here on the lively streets it dissolved into the urban soundscape and didn't bring any attention to me from passers-by.

I WASN'T ABLE TO FIND Ramon at home, so I looked into a small snack shop nearby, where the constable had the custom of having lunch before going to work. And that was exactly where I found him. I walked in the spacious room with hams hanging from the rafters, took a seat next to him and asked:

"How's it going?"

Ramon stopped digging in his paella with his fork and sized me up with a gloomy gaze.

"Saturday!" he sighed. "My last day of work!"

"As for your last day," I took out the *Atlantic Telegraph* from the eleventh and slid it over to my friend, "I recommend you spend it wisely."

The constable began reading the headline; I ordered a sweet pastry and a cup of coffee.

I should have ordered something more substantial, but having a hearty lunch usually put me right to sleep.

"And what," Ramon snorted in confusion, looking at the data on the horrible murder, "now you're planning on hunting for Procrustes?"

"Forget about Procrustes!"

"Leo, I'll never understand you! What do you want from me, tell me directly!"

I could barely suppress a heavy sigh.

"Ramon! What is the chance that two different werebeasts appear in the city at the same time with identical habits?"

"It doesn't say anything about a werebeast here," the constable objected. "Also, the murder happened three days after the new moon, and werebeasts are usually not feeling so hot at such times."

"Normal werebeasts, yes," I corrected my friend.

The constable pushed his unfinished paella away, picked up his glass of sangria and threw himself back into his chair.

"Normal werebeasts?" He didn't understand. "What do you mean?"

"Miscreants who transform at the full moon," I explained. "Even in New Babylon, they are no rarity."

"Every new moon, there are extra patrols in the Emperor's Park," Ramon confirmed. "Though a lot of the people they catch on such nights are mere lunatics."

They brought me my pastry, I took a bite, chewed it, poured my coffee and nodded.

"At the new moon, normal werebeasts do not attack people, which is why the newspapermen remembered Procrustes."

"But if it isn't Procrustes," the constable frowned skeptically, "and not a 'normal werebeast,' as you put it, then who is it?"

"A werebeast who can control his animal nature at any time, regardless of the phase of the moon," I answered.

"Is that possible?"

"Naturally."

Ramon rubbed his chin thoughtfully.

"Let's say you're right..."

"I am right; there's no 'let's say' about it!" I cut him off. "The wounds from the first corpse are completely the same as those from our murderer."

"You didn't see the first corpse."

"There's enough written here."

The constable had grown tired of arguing with me. He looked at his watch and asked me a question point-blank:

"Even if you're right, what does that give us?"

"We can track the murderer."

Ramon laughed uncontrollably.

"A tall thin lefty, perhaps an out-of-towner? In New Babylon? Leo, that's still the same as trying to find a coin by turning over rocks on the sea shore! We'll have to interview millions of people!"

"Not at all," I objected calmly. "Tell me, what do you see in this picture?"

The constable took the paper, looked at it for some time, then suggested:

"A back alley?" But immediately corrected himself: "Blood?"

"That's right!" I confirmed. "The murderer couldn't have avoided getting covered in it from head to toe. You can't seriously suppose he walked down the street like that, right?"

"It was late at night," Ramon mumbled,

"there wouldn't have been anywhere open to buy new clothes. But the park was right next to it. He could have cleaned his clothes there."

"In dirty water with no soap?" I dropped a hint of doubt, thought over his supposition and nodded. "Yes, he could have. But I doubt he had enough restraint for that."

"Do you think he was afraid of being caught?"

"Wouldn't you have been in his place? An ugly murder, bloody footprints leading to the park. Slinking through the bushes would be the logical move, right? The werebeast couldn't have known exactly when the body would be discovered. He was in a rush."

"I'll allow it. But can you imagine how many people they'll have to interview? And actually, re-interview! Do you think we'll be able to find anyone who the investigators haven't already gotten to?"

"The investigators simply didn't know who to look for or what to ask," I declared.

Ramon finished his wine and chuckled:

"But you do?"

"Hunger and pain," I said and repeated: "Hunger and pain."

"Hunger?" the constable squinted, remembering my tale about the slaughter in Levinson's house. "The bite marks on the governess?"

"That's right. Staying at the crime scene was very dangerous, but he murderer didn't only wash the blood off himself, which is logical, but also had a bite to eat. He was overcome with hunger. Something in his nature was tormenting him.

Werebeasts do not often experience a particular desire for human meat, unless they're reminiscing. They simply want to eat and are not very picky about what."

"I believe you," Ramon sighed. "So, what you're saying is that he must have disrobed prior to the Levinson murder, cleaned himself off afterward, then gotten redressed? Are you saying his experience in the park taught him to do that?"

"That would fit my theory, yes."

"Alright, and the pain?"

"Turning into an animal and back is always painful. At full moon, the pain is weaker. With a new moon, the pain is simply unimaginable. If the werebeast is not carrying a dose of morphine with him, which I very much doubt, there is only one way to reduce his sensitivity: drinking."

"How do you know that?"

"I just do."

"You think we should search the drunks and booze-hounds?" The constable stood from the table and took the bag containing his uniform from the floor.

I got up after him, paid and grabbed the newspaper.

"Ramon, listen!" I stated, chasing my friend into the doorway. "We just need to go on a little pub crawl near the crime scene. The investigators can hardly have spent much time searching the snack shops, because any normal murderer would rush to get as far from the crime scene as possible."

"Alright," the constable gave in, "we'll go and ask. What a bugger it is to pound the pavement until the dead of night, though."

"Just make sure you get an agreement on the lupara."

"Without fail," Ramon promised. "I wouldn't come near that creature without my lupara. I'll need a tenner from you, though."

We agreed to meet at six in the evening at the entrance to the Emperor's Park nearest the crime scene, and Ramon Miro went off to work. I accompanied him with a thoughtful gaze and checked the contents of my wallet.

If we couldn't catch the murderer very soon, we'd have to start begging.

Or robbing banks.

It should be said that I was now feeling significantly more open to that idea...

I DIDN'T JUST IDLE ABOUT waiting for evening, though. To start, I circled the crime scene a few times at different radiuses, then I noted the exits from the park and asked some local boys the address of all taverns, bars, coffee shops and snack shops in the area that were open late. I also inquired about hotels and tenements.

My beat started at the nearest drinking establishments, and as expected, I didn't figure out anything interesting. No one could recall a tall, limping lefty, though every other person did bring up the recent murder, the intrusive newspapermen and the policemen who'd flooded the area.

When I was a child, my father would often say that a wolf is fed by his legs; I remembered that saying more than once while working as a constable, but today I felt it in my bones.

Now, a private detective, there's someone who really gets fed by his legs.

Walk, walk and walk some more.

And also, ask questions.

"Hello! Have you seen a tall thin man in dirty or wet clothing in the last few days? He might have been drinking a lot, and ordering food with it. He would have been dining alone. Why am I asking? I am a private investigator, here's my license. He's a troublemaker who had a disagreement with a client of mine and ended up beating him up. Right in the park, can you imagine? You don't remember him? Are you sure? He is a lefty, maybe that'll jog your memory? Friday, he smelled strongly of liquor. No, he wasn't here? Do you have any idea where such people might be found? Just a moment, I'll write it down."

And I hit the street once again. And the streets were simply seething. In the morning, still no one knew a thing, and in the second half of the day, the new papers came out, and on every corner, all I heard was the same: "Extra! Extra! Procrustes' next vile deed! Slaughter in the Judean Quarter! Dozens killed! Bodies ripped to pieces!"

I winced in pain and walked from one pub to the next. Without a cane, my injured leg would have long ago given out once and for all. After these few hours wandering the sett-paved alleys, I wanted just one thing: to sit somewhere and gather my strength.

But there was no time left for such a thing; I had to go meet Ramon now.

When I got to the agreed-upon place, the constable was sitting on a bench, lupara over his knees, watching the people leave the park. Twilight was growing denser, and the street traders were gradually starting to pack in their goods.

I bought a glass of carbonated water with syrup and wet my dried-out throat, then took a seat next to my partner and took a breath of relief. My legs were still shaking.

"I'm burned out. I haven't got any strength left," I complained to Ramon, handing him the map. "You can see here the streets I've already covered."

The constable evaluated the work I'd done and asked:

"Not a shred of information?"

"Not a one," I confirmed.

"I talked with our guys there," Ramon stated thoughtfully. "They say no one felt pity for the murder victim. He was the total package: morphine dealer, street mugger, and a he liked to stab people. How he ended up in that neighborhood, no one knows."

"What else did they say?"

"That they released bloodhounds to track him down, but it was the day after the crime. The dogs could only track him to the ponds."

"What ponds?" I wondered, finding the place on the map and nodding. "Ah, I see."

"They found the place there where the killer washed the blood off his clothes. They were also able to make a cast of a boot imprint. You were right, based on the size of his shoe and his gait length, the killer is very tall. But the most interesting part wasn't that: the shoe print is characteristic of tennis shoes, a huge fashion craze in the New World right now."

"Is that so?" I thought and told my friend the story I'd been feeding the pub owners and waiters.

Ramon frowned.

"That won't work."

"Why not?"

"No one will give up a client to an investigator if he paid his bill and left a tip. At the very least, they won't strain their memory. Inspector White always said: if you want to find something out, make people want to help you."

"Easy for you to say!"

"The killer is very tall, so are you. Maybe you're relatives?"

I squirmed.

"Don't joke about that!"

"So, you're relatives," Ramon Miro continued pushing his story. "Your Uncle came from the New World and disappeared. Or better yet, not your uncle, your cousin. That sounds more likely."

I nodded.

"That could work," I decided, having thought over the proposition from all sides. "My cousin suffers from a predilection for alcohol, and a mutual acquaintance of ours saw him a few days ago in the Emperor's Park, where he was flopping off overpasses into the water for public amusement."

The constable stood from the bench and tossed his lupara up onto his shoulder.

"I suggest we start from the gates nearest the ponds," he suggested.

I had no objections to that, so we went on our way.

DO YOU THINK LUCK came with us? Hell no! Looking for a person in New Babylon was like looking for a needle in a haystack with no matches, sieves or magnets. All the police of the metropolis should have had plenty of time to track down this already-known criminal; that was to say nothing about us two amateurs, without even a sketch of the suspect!

A tall, thin lefty. A dirty, hard-drinking glutton. New World.

That was all we had at the beginning. And it was also all we had now.

"Why don't we just say screw it to the whole thing, eh?" Ramon Miro frowned dolefully after four hours of unproductive wandering around the fleshpot district.

"Can you really afford to say 'screw it' to three thousand francs?" I snorted, though I was on the verge of giving up myself given how tired my legs were.

"We'll search this block and *basta*!" the constable decided. "I still need to hand in my uniform. It's my last day of work, or have you forgotten?"

I hadn't had particular hope of finding the werebeast today from the very beginning, but the chance of finding our man on Saturday night was as high as it would ever be, so I corrected my friend:

"This block and the next. There's still two hours until midnight."

"To hell with you," Ramon relented and pointed at the banner of a place called the *Danube Rose*. "Shall we go in?"

I walked the three stairs down, flung open the door and took a step into the garden-level room, bathed in the dull glow of kerosene lamps. I smelled the appetizing aroma of unfamiliar cookery. My stomach immediately gave a groan, and my mouth started watering.

As if to indicate the excellent quality of the cuisine, there were no seats in the snack shop whatsoever. There were black-haired middle-aged men sitting at all the tables. They were eating dinner unhurriedly, drinking and discussing away in some guttural language or another.

Magyars or Romanians?

I tried to stop the server boy, but he just turned his head and ran away, bending under the weight of the plates piled on his tray. I walked up to the bar. A chef looked out of the kitchen and threw up his hands in embarrassment; he couldn't understand me. Or he was pretending he couldn't.

In places like this, they didn't talk to police, private investigators, or any other strangers. In places like this, they didn't like outsiders sticking their nose into the business of their little society. And it didn't matter if that society was made up of Magyars, Chinese, Italians or Russians.

It wasn't fear, not at all. It was just the way things were.

I turned to Ramon, and declared for all to hear:

"How much longer are we going to look for him? It's already dark outside! That drunk is bringing shame on his family!"

"You shouldn't talk about your cousin like that," the constable reproached me habitually.

"He's your cousin, too!" I threw out my next reply without delay.

"He's just my mother's sister's husband's nephew!"

"Doesn't matter!" I waved it off. "If we don't find him, we're as good as dead! I wish he'd have stayed in New York! Why'd he have to come here?

Who invited him?!"

People are curious. People are often interested in things that have absolutely nothing to do with them.

The hubbub quieted down somewhat, and an elderly gentleman of respectable appearance came out to us. He had a magnificent gray head of hair and his mustache was the same.

"Are you looking for someone, my young guests?" He inquired with an obvious accent. The sound of the voices finally went silent, and everyone started staring at us, waiting for an answer.

"Our cousin!" I sighed. "He came here from the New World and went on a bender! And we have yet to find him!"

"He didn't happen to have come in here a day or two ago?" Ramon joined the conversation. "We've heard tell that he fell into a pond at some point. And he is not ashamed of looking people in the eyes!"

"Fell into a pond, you say?" The aged Magyar thought it over and shook his head. "No, I don't remember any wet people coming through."

I didn't hide my disappointment and drooped my shoulders with no exaggeration. But I still made one more shot at it:

"Please sir, try to remember. My cousin is tall, even taller than me! You'd have to remember him."

The visitors began making noise again, and, I suppose, someone told something to the old man, because an interested look started flashing up in his eyes:

"And what does he look like?"

Ramon and I exchanged confused glances.

"He's tall and thin," I told the man all the notes I had and threw up my hands. "Curses! I've barely seen the man for fifteen years! He didn't send a single photo in all that time!"

The Magyars conferenced on something, and the elderly man declared:

"A tall, thin man did come around. But we do not know where he went."

" It gets harder with every passing hour!" Ramon sighed bitterly, demonstrating an outstanding acting talent. "So where should we look now?"

"You're asking me?" I objected. "As far as I'm concerned, let him go to every tavern in the outskirts of New Babylon!" Then I asked the gray-mustached man: "Did he at least look alright? He wasn't caked in mud from head to toe like we've been told?"

"He removed his jacket. It was hot. He was standing confidently on his feet. He didn't seem drunk," the gray-haired Magyar assured us. Then, he exchanged a few phrases with the chef and server boy, and perked up his ears. "No, he wasn't drunk."

"Was he at least eating?" Ramon sighed. "Or just drinking?"

The elderly gentleman asked the chef again and told me:

"He ate, and quite well at that. He ordered goulash and half a suckling pig."

"And to drink?" I continued.

"A bottle of slivovitz," the Magyar confirmed.

"For him, that stuff is like water to a fish," I waved my hand, feverishly trying to come up with something else to pull out of him before my questioning aroused suspicion. "You said he had a jacket? What color?"

"Dark. Black, probably."

"I see. And did he say where he was going next?"

"No, but he took a link of salami. A big one! And another two bottles of slivovitz. He wanted to treat his friends."

I nodded and clarified as a follow-up:

"Do you remember what direction he went in?"

The graying Magyar just shook his head.

Having thanked him for the help, we left the snack shop, and I opened the map under the nearest street light.

"Do you suppose he went to a rented apartment?" Ramon asked, watching me draw in the murderer's potential route from the nearest gates of the Emperor's Park to the *Danube Rose*.

"Or to a hotel. If you suppose that the werebeast wasn't just on this street coincidentally, it makes sense to search the area. He could have had breakfast or lunch in the area as well."

"I'd bet that the murderer was sleeping nearby," Ramon decided. "Judge for yourself, would the type of guy to take a link of salami for the road also not rent a corner room nearby?"

My friend's words sounded reasonable, and I looked in contemplation at the banner of the Magyar diner, illuminated by a street light. Around that bright spot, there was a darkness growing denser; very occasionally, little beams of light would escape from between blinds or curtains that hadn't been closed fully. It was as if the area had died out.

"Well, where could he have gone?" I muttered. "It was late at night, not so different from right now."

"Let's take a look around, then," my partner suggested.

We walked up to the next intersection and immediately froze in place, having seen a banner with the laconic inscription "Hotel," illuminated by a pair of gas burners.

"You think this is it?" Ramon poked me in the side.

"Check your lupara," I warned him, unbuttoning the clasp on my pistol holster just in case. The Cerberus, then, I moved from my right coat pocket to my left.

The constable took out his gun, and we headed into the hotel, looking carefully from side to side. And though there were no bushes or dark hiding spots on this narrow little street, my heart started beating very, very unevenly, and the taste of bile welled up in my mouth. I got scared.

It should be said that I didn't give vent to my fears, though, instead just walking up onto the porch and knocking at the door. No one answered. Then, hoping that our visit at an unreasonable hour wouldn't attract the attention of a dangerous guest, I knocked another time, and the eye slit opened up.

"Hello sir, what can I do for you?" the sleepy porter yawned.

"Do you have any vacancies? For the night?"

Somewhere closer to the center of town, my appearance may have been considered improper, but everything was much simpler here.

The hotel employee flung open the door hospitably, letting his late-arriving guests enter the lobby.

"We have plenty of rooms!" he said.

I took a step over the threshold, and Ramon jumped in behind me.

"Police!" The constable hissed out frighteningly, pressing the night porter to the wall. "Not a sound! Got it?"

The well-mannered little shrimp with pomaded hair nodded in silence. Unannounced police raids of hotels in the outskirts were usual occurrences; he must have grown accustomed to them by now.

I checked the vestibule quickly, taking a look into the room where they set tables for guests in the morning on my way and returned to the porter.

"We're looking for a possible guest of yours, he's tall and thin. A few days ago, he would have brought in a link of salami. Have you seen him?" I asked, not lowering my gaze from the stairs to the second story.

"But, stay quiet!" Ramon didn't forget to warn him.

The puny little man nodded, but somehow very falteringly.

"Room twenty-two," he whispered, "but he isn't there now."

"What do you mean?" I was struck. "Has he checked out?"

"He usually goes somewhere at night, and returns after midnight," the hotel employee explained. "He has his own key to the front door."

"What name is he registered under?"

"Smith. Jack Smith."

"Give me the key to his room," Ramon Miro then demanded. "Now!"

"But I can't!" The night porter objected. "That's against the rules!"

"Procrustes, ever heard of him?" The constable got up close to him.

And just then, it reached the little man so abruptly that he almost wet himself.

"Is it him?" the porter rasped out, taking our word at face value.

"It is," I replied, taking out the badge I'd still completely forgotten to hand in. Total coincidence, naturally. "What does this say?"

The porter turned the badge to the light.

"Detective constable Leopold Orso," he said aloud. "Criminal Investigation Department."

I took the badge back and commanded him:

"Keys, now!"

We walked up to the desk. There, the hotel employee took the key to room twenty-two from a hook on the wall and gave it to us.

"How many rooms?" Ramon didn't forget to clarify.

"One. It has a shared bathroom at the end of the hall."

"Sit here and don't move a muscle," the constable ordered; in response, we heard the creaking of a decanter on the edge of a cut-glass cup.

I walked through the vestibule, remembering the position of the entrances and exits just in case, then turned back and asked:

"Do you have an attic?"

The night porter took a few greedy gulps, left an empty glass and said:

"It's all boarded up."

Ramon came up next to me and whispered out quietly:

"Alright, so what should we do? Leaving just one of us is a nonstarter."

"Let's check the room, then you come back."

"Sounds good," the constable nodded and warned the porter: "No funny business. Got it?"

"Yes!" he gave a choking squeak. The fact that one of the guests was a legendary murderer had knocked him completely off his feet.

Ramon and I went up to the second floor; there I put my dark glasses in my breast pocket, took the cap from my cane's handle and switched on the torch.

"You first," I warned my partner, taking out

my Cerberus.

"Got it," the constable nodded, taking position in front of the door labeled number "twenty-two."

I stuck the cane under my armpit and turned the key carefully in the lock.

The mechanism was well oiled. It didn't even squeak. Just one turn and done.

Ramon tore into the room aggressively. I jumped in behind and gave the room a pass with my torch. Cabinet, bed, table by the window. There was nowhere to hide, but my partner didn't agree.

"Cabinet," Ramon gasped hoarsely, taking the lopsided colossus in his sights.

I threw open the doors. There was nothing hiding there among the jackets and pants hanging from hangers. Then the constable pointed at the bed.

"Over there!"

Under the bed, we found only a traveling suitcase; I returned the bedspread to its place, stuck my Cerberus in my pocket and commanded my partner:

"Run back down!"

Ramon hurried to the porter, while I pulled on my gloves and set about searching. The lack of order and other procedural subtleties were the least of my worries now.

No one judges the victor.

I didn't light the gas lamps, simply continuing to light my way with the torch in the handle of my cane, trying not to point it too many times at the curtained windows. The trash can was filled with sausage wrappers. Next to the wall, there were a few empty slivovitz bottles. I decided not to touch them, instead pulling the frayed suitcase from under the bed, and quickly checking its contents. Beyond a used ticket for a dirigible from New York to New Babylon, there was nothing interesting inside. Underwear, tooth powder, a razor, other little things.

Then I went to the cabinet and patted down the clothes; I found the very same level of success.

All the jackets and pants were brand new. They had been made to order from expensive black fabric. All of them were the same, like peas in a pod. And they all had their tags ripped out.

One jacket wasn't enough.

Very prudent. Blood on black doesn't catch the eye, and no one is surprised to see someone wear the same jacket as the day before.

I checked the table drawers and even pulled the mattress off the bed. Then I got up on a chair and pointed my light at the top of the cabinet. The only thing there was dust. Standing on my tip toes, I stretched out to the wooden ventilation grate. I could just barely touch it, but it sprang out readily into my hand.

So there's his hiding spot!

It should be said that calling this a hiding spot was rather overstating it. It was just a secret place to hide valuable things from criminally-inclined housekeepers. Nothing more.

I pulled a metal box from the ventilation and, in that I didn't have time to open the lock with a bent paper clip, I broke it by jamming my knife under the latch.

On top, there was a glass syringe, a strap and a little bottle with a morphine solution. It immediately became clear that the first murder hadn't at all been random. Either the werebeast had disagreed with the victim on price, or the deceased had simply decided to rob this out of town drug addict. Probably the second. The wad of colonial dollars, wrapped in a rubber band, caused an envious respect in me.

I stuck the money in my coat pocket, picked up a swollen envelope and removed two passports from it. The first was issued to someone named Gerhard Lanka, a resident of the colonial state of New York, forty-two years from birth; the owner of the second was a forty-year old Jonathan Barlow from Melbourne, Zuid-India. Tellingly, there was no entry stamp in either of them.

That meant there must have been a third one somewhere.

I set the passports aside, made sure there was nothing left in the box, and left the room, not making too much effort to hide the mess I'd made in searching it. I got to the stairway and took a seat on the top step, giving my tired legs a rest.

"Well, how'd it go?" Ramon Miro asked, setting down his lupara.

"It's him," I confirmed, having completely forgotten about the porter.

And he, on hearing these words, practically had a fit; he was just bent over the table transfixed.

The constable frowned peevishly, went up the stairs and held out his hand.

"You shouldn't sit in such a visible place," he grumbled, helping me to my feet.

And then, without a single sound, the entry door swung open.

We might not have even noticed it if the scared-half-dead night porter hadn't squeaked out:

"Procrustes!"

Ramon let me down and spun in place, drawing his lupara. Barely able to stand on the narrow steps of the steep stairway, he braced the buttstock of the weighty gun on his shoulder and roared at a sickly looking gentleman of forty, who had just made a step over the threshold:

"Don't move, police!"

In the same moment, the hotel guest made an imperceptible jump from his place and burst through the vestibule. His ungainly lanky figure simply dissolved into a blur, but Ramon was already holding the murderer in his sights, so he immediately pushed down on the trigger.

A shot thundered out and the man performed an unbelievably acrobatic somersault, dodging the bullet. He touched a foot on the windowsill and jumped aside in a single motion. And it looked just as dashing when Ramon missed a second time: the silver-coated lead slug broke through a window and flew outside.

The unhittable murderer darted for the stairway. The constable fired at him again, and the fiery tongue of a dual spark licked the outstretched head and shoulders of the werebeast, but the bullet still didn't hit him; it just smelled of burned hair.

The strong oaken banisters saved us. The killer dug into them at a run, and only for that reason failed to reach the recoiling constable. Ramon slammed into me. We went head over heels from the stairwell onto the second floor. We immediately slammed the door to the stairway behind us and even secured it shut with our handcuffs just to make sure.

"In the room!" The constable snapped, walking backward through the corridor with his gun at the ready; three of the lupara's four barrels were giving off a gray gunpowder smoke.

I threw myself at his heels, and slammed into it from outside like a battering ram. A scary cracking rang out. By some miracle, the door held out and didn't come off the hinges.

"Unlock the door!" Ramon hurried me on. "Step to!"

The beast's next, stronger strike broke through the door and the constable slowed his pace, trying to catch the monster in his sights as it crawled into the corridor.

And it really was a monster now, a true werewolf! The former man's face had turned into a snout with a ghastly set of jaws. Its shoulders had become wider, and its lean torso was now crisscrossed with muscle fibers. Its clothes were now just pitiable shreds hanging off a body that had sprouted a coarse wiry hair.

The werewolf gradually came down the corridor; Ramon continued to walk backward not shooting, afraid to waste his last bullet. He made me some time, while I, arms shaking, stuck the key in the keyhole. Or tried, anyway. They key just wouldn't go in.

I was afraid.

Curses! I was pulsating all over in horror!

But I gave it one more try and turned. That time, the handle gave smoothly, and inside I saw the face of the leprechaun, who slammed the door right in my face with a deafening thunder clap.

At that very moment, the werewolf made a fierce jump, going on the attack; Ramon hurriedly pushed down on the trigger, and though he almost hit his target, he missed again!

The werewolf contorted his body in a totally unbelievable way, making use of all his inertia. He ran over to the wall and changed from a run to a jump at the constable. But he had already stepped aside, and the late strike simply gave him extra momentum. Ramon then rolled down the corridor, leaving me and the werewolf one-on-one.

Fear? All the fear here was in *my* head. This beast didn't know fear.

He only knew that he wanted to eat. Eat and kill, but first eat.

Hunger drove him on better than any fear, and when he jumped at me, I didn't try to find salvation in my *illustrious talent*, I simply flung open the hotel-room door, which opened outward! The werewolf slammed into the unexpected obstacle like a cannonball and his sharp claws dug through the paneling, but a moment later, he struck it with all his considerable weight, and the door was simply reduced to dust. The beast gave a kick to the jamb and yelped, breaking out of the door, as I rushed away. I immediately flew toward my partner, who was picking himself up off the floor. I again knocked him off his feet, and myself collapsed next to him.

Curses!

When the werewolf had chucked the broken paneling aside, I got onto my back and held my cane in front of me in a vain attempt to delay the rabid beast, at least for a bit.

I didn't have much hope for that, but then a shot thundered out.

The Webley-Fosbery revolver in Ramon's hand spit fire, at once deafening me and blinding my right eye; the werewolf caught the bullet in its wide chest and stumbled. A moment later, the terrifying wound covered itself over as if the seventy grams of lead and copper had dissolved right into the monster, but the constable didn't stop pulling the trigger of his automatic revolver until he had emptied the whole cylinder.

Six four-hundred-fifty-caliber bullets was no laughing matter. Six four-hundred-fifty-caliber bullets would buy us a few valuable seconds.

That was enough time for me to get up from the floor, place my cane against the wall in the corner, and put all my might into the joint with its lower third. The wood snapped. The crushable metal creaked, and the mechanism broke in two. I then met the werewolf with a poker made of splintery wood. I simply held the cane fragment in front of me and stuck it in his grinning maw.

The monster wouldn't have been able to get away now, and didn't even try. His terrifying teeth simply grabbed the cane and bit through it with ease, simultaneously breaking through the electric battery inside.

A blinding shock issued forth sparks! The werewolf was thrown back and hit the wall. After that, leaving deep scratches in the whitewash, he crawled on all fours and froze, shaking his head in confusion. From his open mouth, there was a mixture of spit and blood pouring out. The electric current hadn't fried his innards, but it had disoriented him and knocked him off course.

I cursed, took out my Roth-Steyr and opened fire.

Clap! Clap! Clap! Streaks of blood flew out after the bullet strikes. When the pistol's magazine was empty, Ramon had already broken down his Webley-Fosbery and changed out the spent rounds for another clip of new ones.

The copper and lead had done no harm to the animal. The wounds, like before, healed over immediately, but the werewolf, who still couldn't come to his senses after the electric shock, started crawling toward the exit, nimbly pounding his paws on the floor. Shooting as he walked, the constable ran out to chase him, but the monster just slouched his shoulders, taking bullet after bullet with his wide back. It just rolled down the stairway. One moment more, and the werewolf was already outside.

"Devil!" Ramon cursed out, running up to the entrance door. "He got away!"

"To hell with him!" I wheezed out, going down after him. "Porter! Ramon, where did that wimp get off to?"

Pushing back the latch, he walked up to the table and frowned:

"He's here. Don't scream."

I had actually already managed to notice the blackened puddle of blood in the corner.

"Is he dead?" I asked Ramon.

"He's dead," my partner confirmed, reloading his revolver with trembling hands. "We messed up, Leo," he gasped. "We messed up bad!"

And I couldn't argue with that.

The murderer got away, the porter was dead, and the hotel guests were now starting to look out of their rooms, terrified by the shooting. Soon, all the local watch would be hurrying here.

"I wonder if there's a back door?" I chuckled, when the piercing trill of a police whistle came in from the street.

"Leo, this is no time for jokes," Ramon frowned. "We aren't going out the back door, alright?"

I gave a good-natured curse and took a seat on the lowest step, not wanting to dispute my overly principled comrade on running from the scene of a crime. Considering the clues we'd left behind, a dumber idea never could have come to mind.

But I still couldn't resist a jab:

"Just say it. You're afraid to go outside."

"I am," Ramon confirmed. "It's almost like you didn't see the way that bastard was able to dodge silver! I was shooting from point-blank! If you want to keep investigating this, it'll have to be without me! Three thousand is a lot of money, but it definitely isn't enough to get my head sewn back on."

"Wimp!" I laughed uncontrollably, though my head was spinning in a vortex. "You'd better think about what you're going to say to your colleagues."

Ramon snorted:

"You lie your own way out of this! You asked me for help. You didn't want to get into the details. That's all I know."

"Sounds good," I nodded, in that my Private Investigator's License and the note from the Witstein Banking House left me with quite a bit of room to maneuver.

But I wasn't going to lie. In fact, I was intending to lay everything out with no reservations.

Honesty was the best line of defense in these matters.

Or at least almost the best...

I took out a lighter and lit the corner of my police identification badge. I watched it get swallowed up by the little flame and warned my friend:

"The porter volunteered to show us the suspect's room. We went in, and it was very messy..."

And then there came a sloppy bang on the door.

"Open up, it's the police!" they wailed from outside.

"There's still time to run out the back door," I joked again, then sighed and waved my hand. "Alright, unlock it..."

3

THEY RELEASED US the next morning.

First me, then Ramon a half hour later. I waited for my friend on a bench in the internal courtyard of the Newton-Markt and, together with him, went outside. There, we exchanged glances and, without a word, hobbled into *Archimedes' Screw*. We walked in silence; we no longer had the strength for conversation.

We had been forced to talk all night.

First we were interrogated by the detectives who showed up at the crime scene, then the interrogation was continued by two persnickety detective sergeants, and it all ended with a very unpleasant talk with head of the CID Maurice LeBrun.

My having a private investigator's license and a note from the Witstein Banking House drove my former colleagues fairly frantic, but I'm sure that the only reason I got out without being accused of a crime is because no one wanted to puff up another scandal. The murder of Isaac Levinson and his entire family had been far too high-profile.

So they let us go, taking yet another non-disclosure agreement on our way out the door.

No matter! I wasn't planning on sharing the details with newspapermen in any case. It wasn't the right time for that...

BY VIRTUE OF THE EARLY HOUR, *Archimedes' Screw* was half empty, but we still got seats in the farthest corner.

"We made a real mess of things, didn't we?" Ramon sighed. After that, the barkeep brought out a glass of white wine and a soda water for him, as well as a pitcher of lemonade for me, took a few small coins and left us in peace.

"You can say that again."

"I definitely would have been fired," the former constable drew out his words with a smirk, "if they hadn't managed to fire me already."

"See how well it turned out," I smiled, filling my glass with lemonade.

Ramon looked sourly in reply.

"Do you know what the pay is like for a night guard at the coalhouse?" He asked.

"Oh yeah, speaking of money!" I took the wad of colonial dollars from my right boot and started counting them, flexing the corners of the bank notes.

"What is that?!" Ramon was alarmed.

I threatened him with a finger, finished counting and split the pile into two equal ones. I extended one to my friend.

"What is that?" He repeated his question, not touching the money.

"Think of it as an advance. Eighty dollars," I answered, placing the now fairly thinned-out stack in the inner pocket of my jacket.

"With the exchange rate where it's at now, that's four hundred francs, right?" Ramon stared at me, still not having grown out of his policeman's habits. "Leo, did you really conceal eight hundred francs?"

"I didn't conceal it," I objected, adjusting my glasses, "I appropriated it for our investigation."

"Prove it."

"Does the werewolf know about the money? He does. Say his informer in the Newton-Markt gives him a description of the objects collected from his room, but sees that the one hundred sixty dollars is missing. He'll probably want to get it back. After that, he'll come straight for us!"

"Then why'd you give half to me?"

"If I can't deal with him, I'll send him to you for the remainder. I believe in you, Ramon."

He was staring at a model of an Archimedes' Screw hanging directly over the table, and spent some time thinking over my words. Then he put the money in his pocket and demanded:

"And now, explain to me what gives us the right to spend this money on our own needs."

"It's quite simple," I laughed. "Do you want to give money to a criminal, even unwillingly? The more you manage to spend, the less goes back to the werewolf! Or are you counting on taking him down one-on-one?"

Ramon didn't place much faith in my

hypothetical example, but still he frowned in annoyance:

"Bite your tongue!" Then he threw himself back in his chair and told me: "While they kept us waiting at the Newton-Markt, I managed to trade a few words with a constable I used to know; everyone involved was ordered in very strict terms to keep their mouths shut. They warned them that, if the story were to leak to the papers, the inspector general himself would lead the investigation to find the person responsible."

I squirmed. I certainly didn't want to attract the attention of that ghoulish old man.

But I didn't mention it. I poured out the rest of the lemonade into my glass and said:

"You should have stuck him with the electricity right away!"

"You're right. Who's arguing? Now you won't even be able to get close to him with a stun baton. A trick like that can only work once," Ramon noted reasonably, getting up from the table. "Forget about the werewolf. Let Department Three track him down."

"Where are you going?"

"To sleep! Tonight, I'll have to be ready for my new job." He bowed to me and advised: "Leo, work on the bank robbery. If you need help, get in touch. But don't say another word about the werewolf. I'm not suicidal."

And he took a step toward the exit.

I shrugged my shoulders and left right after him.

The weather was spoiled. The former gray film stretched out over the sky had turned into shaggy clouds, dark and hostile. A wind had picked up also. The abrupt bursts were shaking the trees and howling in chimneys. Wisps of smoke would puff up out of them and be dispersed in an instant.

I stood there for a bit, gathering my thoughts, then I caught a cabby and told him to take me to Leonardo da Vinci-Platz. From there, I started walking in the direction of the shop *Mechanisms and Rarities*, preparing in advance for an unpleasant conversation with the inventor, but Alexander Dyak, to my great surprise, was not angry I'd broken the cane. He simply waved his hand:

"What else could I possibly have been expecting? I was young once, too, you know! Breaking and losing things at your age, Leopold Borisovich, is business as usual. Don't worry about it."

I became a very slight amount self-conscious, and gave him some money.

"Oh, come off it!" The shop owner waved me away and rubbed his thin beard. "It wasn't much of a loss for me. When you make everything yourself, you only have to pay for the parts."

I chuckled and continued counting out bank notes.

"I still do need a cane, though."

"Buy a normal one!" Alexander Dyak objected. "I'm not interested in money. I'm interested in scientific investigation!"

"I've conducted more than enough experiments, no doubt about it," I noted calmly and set the twenty dollars on the counter. "And I can say with complete confidence that the discharge of your electric jar was not strong enough to fully paralyze a werewolf, but it was enough to disorient him and make his limbs twitch. The weak point in its construction was the point where the shocks were attached, but that only became a problem when I used it improperly. Until... uhhh... the break, I managed to walk twenty kilometers with everything working like a Swiss timepiece."

The inventor shook his head, but did eventually accept my money. After stuffing it in his robe pocket, he came out from behind the counter and locked the entrance to his shop.

"Leopold Borisovich, please come with me," he called, heading into the back room.

I went after him and gave an admiring whistle, looking at his workshop, which was outfitted with all the most recent technology. One wall was lined with machine tools and workbenches, while the other was taken up by a drawing of a Pullman train car and a huge blackboard covered with chalk splotches. There were boxes towering everywhere I looked. In the corner, I came upon a generator and the chemistry vessel cabinet. On the desk, beyond a microscope and chemistry set, there stood two huge gas burners.

Alexander Dyak pointed at the wooden stool, dabbed his iron quill into the inkwell and leaned over the thick amber book.

"Start from the very beginning," he demanded. "Make a special note of symptoms of the shock and the times they were noted."

I set about unbuttoning my pea-coat and asked him:

"Are you interested in the effect of electricity on otherworldly beings?"

The inventor looked strictly at me, but softened up and lowered himself to explain:

"In the list of my many interests, that is one, yes. It should be said that I am not sure if werewolves technically belong to the category of otherworldly beings, though."

"Victims of a hereditary disorder?" I chuckled and, with relief, took a seat on the stool.

"That is a fact confirmed by science," the

store owner nodded importantly. "And now, Leopold Borisovich, I beg you to gather your thoughts. Every detail is important."

I gave forth a fateful sigh. Another interrogation! I then set about describing how the werewolf reacted to the electric shock, his convulsions, loss of orientation, and delayed reaction time.

Alexander Dyak bowed his ear down to me, asking me to explain from time to time, how long a certain phase had lasted, every time causing certain complications. The struggle had settled in my memory in torn-up fragments. And it lasted no longer than a few minutes from beginning to end anyway.

"So then, you'll be needing another cane?" The inventor asked when he had sucked me dry, pushed away the book and clapped shut the copper cover of the inkwell.

"That would be nice. If it isn't too much trouble."

The store owner nodded thoughtfully and suddenly suggested:

"For ease of use, I could equip it with two removable electrode spikes. It won't take much time."

All I could do was laugh.

"I do not think I'll be going out for another hand-to-hand fight with that beast any time soon."

Now it was the inventor's turn to laugh.

"Trust my experience, Leopold Borisovich. Life is unpredictable! If I'd have known that I'd be leaving technical school..." with those words he cut himself off and waved his arm in annoyance. Then he uncovered one of the boxes and got out a cane, which looked somewhat more plain than the first. "You'll have to wait a bit."

"As you say," I relented in that it wouldn't have been too smart to be stubborn right now. If a person wants to help you, you shouldn't give them a slap on the wrist, right?

Alexander Dyak squeezed the cane in a vice, deftly removed its rubber cap and undid some screws with an adjustable wrench.

"I expect a more detailed report from you next time," he warned. "I hope this ingenious improvement will turn out useful..."

"What really would have been useful is silver bullets that hit their target," I sighed. "My comrade was shooting practically from point-blank, and missed four times. I've never seen anyone move so fast before."

"He didn't hit even once?" the inventor asked, continuing to work on the cane.

"Not with the silver bullets, no. He filled the beast with around twenty regular ones, but the wounds healed themselves over."

Alexander Dyak wiped the sweat from his forehead and told me:

"I suppose it's to do with his instinctive reflexes."

"What, excuse me?" I didn't understand.

"Are you familiar with the work of Ivan Petrovich Pavlov? He spent quite some time on this topic."

"The Nobel laureate?" I remembered the vaguely familiar name and admitted: "To my great shame, I cannot claim to have read much on him."

"Alright, then I'll try to explain." The inventor removed the generator and electric jar from the cane and set about digging in his cabinets in search of a part. "The body possesses its own memory and set of reactions to external stimulus. As your hand would unconsciously move away from a fire, so did the werewolf move away from the silver: reflexively. These creatures are already much faster than a person, but in such cases they can react without even the slightest delay. This is not just my theory, either. Mr. Pavlov has proved it in practice."

"Did he perform experiments on werebeasts?"

"In Russia, they have a much simpler view of such things," Alexander Dyak confirmed. "And also, it doesn't matter how the silver is delivered.

Some kind of supernatural or, if you will, intuitive sense kicks in. The werebeast simply knows, and its body reacts on its own."

"Nonsense!" I dismissed. "Werebeasts are not such a rarity. From time to time, they do get shot. And with silver bullets, at that."

"Unfortunately, their disease is not only transmitted genetically. People who are exposed to it often find themselves infected as adults."

"And?"

"The instinctive reflexes are only passed down genetically," Alexander Dyak told me. "The people you're talking about, if I can put it this way, lesser werebeasts, do not have them."

The store owner attached the generator to a steel plate. To it, he screwed an electric jar and started messing around with the metal cables.

"I am quite curious to know, Leopold Borisovich," he smiled, "how the electric shock affected its reflexes."

"Is there no other scientific way to injure a werebeast at a distance?" I wondered.

"I'm afraid that I cannot help you with that," the inventor shook his head. "Poisons don't work on werebeasts. Aluminum doesn't do any particular harm. Their bodies just heal over. Any wounds from metal, wood, stone or bone are covered within a few seconds."

"One second!" I furrowed my brow. "It

didn't even expel the bullets back out! I had the impression that the bullets were simply dissolving in its body!"

"Dissolving?" Alexander Dyak grew surprised. "The metabolism of this creature is simply unbelievable!" He jumped to his feet and set about pacing from one corner to another, thinking something over in agitation. "But in that case... if it disperses throughout the body in a moment... x-rays..." he muttered to himself. "Radon... ulcers... Curie..."

I sat in silence, afraid to distract the inventor. He returned to his workbench, began putting the cane together again and warned me:

"Don't distract me, I'm thinking. Read a newspaper for now."

I had little interest in newspapers, and even less interest in those that were more than a week old, but I did not want to contradict the store owner. I took an armful of old issues and leafed through them, marveling at the strange selection. On top, there was an issue of *The Atlantic Telegraph* with the loud headline "Engineer Disappears Without a Trace," after that came some issues of the *Stock-Market Bulletin*, one with a quote circled in red pencil for a company that had some kind of connection with coal mining.

"Surprising!" Alexander Dyak laughed

uncontrollably. "Science can perform real miracles, you know. For some reason, though, we always seem to be pounding in nails with a microscope. Leopold Borisovich, you do know what a microscope is, right? Right now, we are using a microscope to pound in average, every-day nails." The shop owner got into a bad frame of mind. In his voice, I could hear unhidden bitterness.

"If my request is not accepted..." I was the one to start speaking, but the inventor just waved his hand.

"Drop it!" he sighed. "This isn't your problem, and not even mine. We've just all been put in such a position that we have to spend all our energy on totally useless projects. Science is standing in place, and, no matter how shameful it is to admit it, certain people are perfectly fine with that. What's more, they apply significant force to keep it that way for the foreseeable future."

"I'm afraid I don't totally understand you," I muttered in confusion, tossing the papers aside.

"Rudolf Diesel. Does that name ring any bells?" Alexander Dyak then asked.

"An engineer and inventor," I remembered the recent article. "He disappeared from a steamer cabin on its way from Lisbon to New Babylon. The police suspect suicide. But I couldn't figure out what exactly he was intending to reveal to the court of public opinion."

"There wasn't a word in the papers about his inventions," the store owner assured me. "But now, these paper-pushers are actually trying to present him as a charlatan."

"But you don't agree with that?"

"Diesel was trying to make an engine that could work with liquid fuel. For example, kerosene," the inventor told me, screwing off the handle and replacing it with a rubber-coated one. "There won't be a torch this time," he warned.

"Doesn't matter. So, what did you say about the new engine?"

A kerosene-powered engine? It sounded unusual.

"It was a real alternative to steam power. But first, Diesel's ideas were rejected in Petrograd, then hack writers ridiculed him in Paris, and now he has simply disappeared together with all his inventions. Very convenient, don't you think?"

"You suspect murder?" I clarified, not knowing how to think about the shop owner's discoveries.

"I am not a detective, nor a criminal reporter, so I won't judge," Alexander Dyak shrugged his shoulders and leaned on the cane. "I only know that his engine would have seriously reduced coal consumption in the distant future. People have been killed for less."

I nodded.

In the New World, the production of self-propelled carriages using compact steam engines was in full swing. No one there was even thinking about liquid fuel, considering that Nobel's powder engines had not become widely popular due to their low reliability and the limits on the sale of granulated TNT, which it used as fuel.

"And still..." I muttered thoughtfully, "you can't stop progress. Laziness and greed are indefatigable. I am sure that Mr. Diesel's inventions will come out in some way or another soon."

The inventor walked around the room and extended me the cane.

"I doubt it," he shook his head, wiping off his grease-caked palms. "You, Leopold Borisovich, have no idea how far greed can take a person. Diesel is not the first by any means. Lenoir and Otto also managed to publish their works, but as soon as Kostovich suggested changing to kerosene, his workshop burned down. He was the first victim, I suppose."

"But not the only one?"

"The deaths of Daimler and Maybach always seemed suspicious to me, as well. Diesel kept his inventions a secret for a long time, but..." The inventor waved his hand, vexed, and changed the topic: "What are we doing talking and talking on the same topic? How do you like the cane?"

"It's no worse than the first one," I decided after a few steps, but when we came out into the main part of the store, I asked: "Anyway, why do you think Diesel's works aren't simply going to be published under someone else's name? Is it somehow connected with the rise in coal company stocks?"

Alexander Dyak laughed.

"You are a very quick-witted young man," he stated, standing behind the counter. "Would you like to know why? I'll tell you. It's all about business. When, after the Franco-Prussian conflict, Alsace-Lorraine and the Ruhr came under direct control of the Emperor, many courtiers lined their own pockets quite handsomely. Because the Ruhr is coal, and coal is money. And if there's not enough money, you can take a loan on your future income and spend it, for example on the Donets coal basin. Then, keep taking loans and start buying up coal basins in Siberia. You could make a manufacturing empire, and you'd still have decades to pay off the loans. What is the value of human life on the backdrop of that?"

"Not much?" I squinted.

"Absolutely nothing!" The shop owner laughed and took the cane from me. "First, you need to turn the latch," he cracked the thicker lower third, "then you just flex it."

As the cane came in two, a pair of steel spikes protruded from its upper half. Alexander Dyak pressed the button to turn it on, and between the electrodes, there flashed a curving bolt of electricity.

"Not the simplest construction," the inventor sighed, "but it stops water from getting inside, and mud from filling up the mechanisms. Come by tomorrow. I'll think over the riddle you posed. I do have one idea, but it needs specific chemical agents."

"I'd be so very grateful!" I laid out the cane, unlocked the entrance door and waved goodbye to the inventor. "See you tomorrow!"

I went outside and headed off in search of a free cabby.

Thinking about a global conspiracy of coal magnates left me briefly worried. I had enough problems on my own.

DO YOU THINK I WENT to sleep?

I would have done so with pleasure, but the life of a private investigator is not at all as free-wheeling as you'd think from reading pulp mysteries. At the very least, I had to make a report to my employers from time to time.

So I headed for the hotel *Benjamin Franklin.*

The sky had finally grown dark by that time. A fine mist started gradually coming down, and, as often happens before bad weather really sets in, abrupt gusts of wind started chasing dust devils down the streets.

Inclement weather was on the approach. I could feel it clearly, but I didn't understand how close it really was.

THE HOTEL *BENJAMIN FRANKLIN* was in an ancient manor, gloomy and strong, made of dark stone with thin loop-hole windows on the first floors and open terraces on the upper ones. Its facade came out onto Emperor Clement Square, which was so elongated that it was more reminiscent of a wide avenue. This was exactly where the most expensive shops and hotels in New Babylon were located. The price of a cup of coffee in a restaurant around here had long been the subject of satirical jokes and newspaper caricatures.

The whole way there I spent thinking about how to frame the conversation with Abraham Witstein. I wanted to present my investigation from the best possible angle, but all the smart thoughts instantly flew out of my head when Bastian Moran came into view. The senior inspector was drinking coffee at the bar on the first floor, and couldn't hold back a vexed grimace when he saw me come in.

Our dislike was mutual.

I hurried to the porter, introduced myself and – what a miracle! – it turned out that Mr. Witstein had actually put me on his guest list. Just to make sure, the clerk made a call, heard out the instructions and pointed at the elevator.

"Fifth floor. Someone will be waiting for you outside the elevator."

On my way into the elevator, I told the operator the purpose of my visit; he closed the doors, turned the lever all the way to the right, and we gradually, practically free of any jumpiness, went up to the highest level.

And when I got there, there really was someone waiting for me. A Judean of compact build – the very same, slightly bald and big-nosed man from before – let me in and accompanied me to the hall of the "Emperor's Suite," where Abraham Witstein was reading newspapers. Everywhere around, there were original paintings hanging from famous greats. One of the walls was occupied by the famous diptych "Storm on the Estate of the Splendid Raphael," and "Emperor Clement topples a *Fallen One*." The gilding on the furniture used more gold than the crown of her Majesty itself.

"Would you like some coffee? How about a cigar?" The banker offered. "Maybe, some whiskey?"

"No, thank you," I refused, taking a seat in the chair at the coffee table.

The luxurious hotel interior had an oppressive effect on me. This was no place for a man in a canvas pea-coat.

"I am impressed, Mr. Orso," Witstein said, not allowing me to get to business. "You are quite the promising young man."

"Excuse me?" I didn't understand.

The banker laughed uncontrollably, finished his coffee and shook his head:

"You've been working for me for less than a day, and you're already twisting my arms, demanding that I put you on a short leash."

I remembered seeing Bastian Moran downstairs and licked my dried-out lips.

"Is that so?"

"Indeed, Mr. Orso. It is indeed!"

"Could you tell me the details?"

"You won't get any details," Abraham Witstein cut me off, suddenly having become composed and serious. "I would like to take a look at the investigation agreement, if you would be so kind."

The big-nosed man turned around and stretched out his hand.

I didn't protest, or demand an explanation. I simply handed over the document, threw myself back in the chair and tossed one leg over the other.

"So, am I to understand that this is not over?" I asked, having popped a raspberry sugar drop in my mouth.

"You are very shrewd," the banker sighed, "but you must learn to follow the rules of the game. I didn't give you permission to investigate the death of poor Isaac but, when asked what you were doing, you pointed the finger at me, putting me in a devilishly awkward position in the process. I will not allow that to happen again."

I thought over what I'd heard and clarified:

"Am I understanding correctly that you now want me to act in an unofficial capacity?"

"I was given a very clear recommendation not to interfere in police business, and do my job," Abraham Witstein stated, looking out the window in despondency. "But the fact that the bank robbers are still unpunished is also unacceptable. I have nothing more to say to you."

"Unacceptable," I repeated, trying the word on for size. It sounded very promising, approximately like a last chance for redemption for a death-sentenced criminal, his neck already in the noose. It sounded like I could stay in the game, but if I caused even the slightest inconvenience now, I would be cast adrift once and for all.

Nevertheless, I couldn't resist asking:

"Mr. Witstein, have you already announced the reward for the head of the murderer of Levinson and his household?"

The banker looked at me like I was a madman.

"My dear Leopold," he stated deceptively softly. "I would be most obliged if you could cast the idea of finding the murderer from your head once and for all."

"Already gone," I answered, barely bending the truth.

Hunting the werewolf no longer entered into my plans. After all, inborn reflexes are a terrifying thing! But the matter of the reward was not just idle curiosity, so I repeated:

"So, have you announced it or not?"

"I have," the banker answered and put up his newspaper.

Not wanting to further impose on my employer with my company, I went down to the first floor and once again caught the unkind gaze of Bastian Moran. I walked over the senior inspector's table and asked his permission to sit opposite him.

"What are you so angry about, Mr. Moran?" I asked, staring at the policeman point-blank. "You got what you wanted, isn't that right?"

The senior inspector placed a miniature tea cup of white porcelain on a similarly snow-white little saucer, adjusted the scarf around his neck and raised an eyebrow.

"And what, in your opinion, did I get, Viscount?"

"Mr. Witstein no longer needs my services. As far as I understand, this is your doing?"

Bastian Moran smiled, and I was categorically opposed to whatever was hidden behind it.

People only smile like that when they hear a piece of news that is both pleasant and unexpected.

The senior inspector didn't know a thing! But, what the devil happened then?! Who had knocked me out of the saddle, if not him?

"I had no idea, Viscount," Bastian Moran shook his head, "that you and I were companions in misfortune."

"What do you mean?"

"The inspector general ordered a special commission set up to investigate the bank robbery and the murder of Levinson. He supposes that these crimes are more closely related than it seems at first glance."

"Have you been removed from the investigation?" I couldn't hold back my surprise.

"I have," confirmed the senior inspector. "Because of your arrest, which many thought a bit... hasty." He finished his coffee and suddenly asked: "You want some advice?"

I got up from the table and guessed:

"Keep my distance from this whole thing?"

Bastian Moran nodded.

"And will *you* be doing that?" I reproached him. "If you were taken off that case, what are you doing here?"

"Me? I'm drinking coffee." The policeman answered.

Sophistry had never impressed me, so I went silent and headed for the exit. At one of the money changers' I exchanged my colonial dollars for francs, placed the thick wad of bank notes in my wallet, and started walking toward the nearest Metro station.

My head was very, very heavy. Thoughts were swarming in it like an upset hive of bees, but I no longer had the strength to figure out the charade. What I wanted to do was lie in bed and sleep a few days in a row. What was more, I didn't even have any idea where to start with investigating the bank robbery.

The only thing that came to mind was to interrogate the guard who had been fired from the coalhouses for being drunk on the job.

I decided to pay a visit to Ramon Miro closer to nightfall, to ask the address of his predecessor, but night fell quicker than I was expecting. In one moment, an impenetrable blackness came over me, followed by a sprinkling of little stars.

To put it more simply, someone threw a canvas bag over my head, then cold cocked me with all their might in the back of the head.

Darkness and stars. And so I went out...

4

I SUPPOSE, AFTER THAT, THEY dragged me somewhere and turned my pockets inside out.

But I didn't feel it. I didn't feel anything. I was trying to swim out of the dark abyss of unconsciousness, but I was not able.

I woke up feeling cold and in pain. My nose was itching from the dust, so I sneezed. In my head, though, it felt like a dynamite bomb had gone off.

I moaned and tried to feel the injured back of my head, but wasn't able to move my arms or legs. Then, I somehow peeled my eyelids back and immediately realized that the person at fault for my deplorable condition was no mere street robber, coming after my thick stack of bank notes.

Stripped down to my skivvies, I was sitting in the middle of a wooden-box-laden warehouse, and my ankles and wrists were tied very, very tightly with aged, dry leather belts to the back and legs of a massive chair with a high back. Another belt was pulling at my chest.

Outside, it was raining, causing a measured tapping on the roof. Somewhere behind me, I heard an incessant joyful dripping. Under my legs, a whole puddle had formed.

I was not in a hospital.

Despite my headache, I could tell that clear as day.

Even if the hit to my head had caused temporary lack of common sense, and I had been brought to an asylum, that wouldn't explain the strange boxes all around, the dust on the floor, the cracked plaster or the tightly boarded-up windows with rust-colored marks where the nails had once been pounded into the darkened boards.

And also, where were the nurses? Where were the doctors? Devil beat me!

I remembered Isaac Levinson's fate and

began feverishly squirming with my arms and legs, trying to get free. But it was in vain. The leather belts, even though time had dried them out, were fastened down tight. I tried to rock back and forth, or tip myself over, but that was also a failure. The chair was too massive. Its legs had been screwed into a fairly large wooden board for additional strength.

In exhaustion, I threw back my head and saw drops of water falling one after the other from the ceiling. It seemed that they would land right on my face, but every time they hit the floor somewhere behind me.

I didn't want to die.

So I began to pray. I simply spoke out the only prayer I knew to myself. The very prayer Our Savior left us before he ascended.

And yes, I prayed! What else remained for a person in my position?

"Maybe, it wasn't a good idea to take the werewolf's money," a thought popped up in my mind a bit too late. "Maybe Ramon and I made him a bit angrier than we'd imagined. He's not likely to be satisfied with a simple apology now."

And just then, the door creaked behind me.

I didn't turn my head, just grit my teeth and waited for a quick resolution, but instead of the werewolf, there appeared three awkward figures in white cloaks and face masks with slits for eyes, which were glowing from the inside.

They're *illustrious*! I had been kidnapped by a group of *illustrious* gentlemen!

"Where is the box, Viscount?" suddenly asked the kidnapper standing in the middle.

I moved my jaw, stretching my numb lips out into a smile a number of times, then clarified:

"Are you sure you don't have me confused with someone else?"

The figure to the left gave a start, intending to slap me in the face, but froze awkwardly midway as if the abrupt movement had cause him pain. The ringleader took his sidekick by the elbow and calmly explained his question:

"We are talking about an aluminum box with a thunder rune engraved on the top."

"How should I know anything about that?"

"It once belonged to your grandmother, the Countess Kósice. It was deposited in the Witstein Banking House for safe keeping not long before her death," the *illustrious* gentleman told me with the same calm voice, deprived of all emotion.

I cleared my throat and couldn't resist a nervous quip.

"Aluminum melts at quite a low temperature," I told my kidnappers. "As far as I know, the box was destroyed in the bank robbery."

"Balderdash!" The figure to the right gasped

out abruptly. "You won't fool us with that forgery!"

"Forgery?" I asked in confusion, cluelessly batting my eyes.

The kidnapper in the middle sighed in pity and stated penetratingly:

"Viscount! It was very negligent on your part to make the duplicate box from aluminum copper alloy. Fifteen years ago, such alloys hadn't been invented yet." The *illustrious* gentleman stuck his arm in the slit in the sack and took out a few pieces of paper covered with printed text. "According to expert analysis of the ingot that remained from the box, it contained no less than four percent copper. That would make it an alloy that was patented just one year ago, and which remains a seven-seal secret. The Egyptians and Persians would pay through the nose for it, but it isn't for sale. Do you know why? Mainly because it is used to manufacture dirigible bodies! Duralumin, you've heard of it, I'm sure."

And the kidnapper on the left walked up to me again.

"Where is the real box, Viscount?" He demanded an answer.

"I have no idea what you're talking about."

The figure on the right coughed and, with the hoarse voice of an elderly smoker, began putting more nails in my coffin:

"You spoke with the manager. You learned of the box from his list of safe contents. In the safe, the remains of a forgery were found. Then, after yet another conversation with you, that same banker was found dead. In my opinion, that is more than enough to prove a guilty verdict!"

"Don't rush it!" The *illustrious* gentleman in the middle stopped him. "In respect to the memory of our dear friend Emile Rie, I give you one last chance to return the box of your own accord. Otherwise, we'll have to fall back on other... methods."

In respect to the memory of Emile Rie?!

I remained frozen with my jaw hanging open in surprise for some time.

Emile Rie was better known as the Grand Duke of Arabia and even better known as the brother of Emperor Clement, his constant chancellor. What games were they playing with me?!

But no, the games were over.

"Well, without a third degree interrogation, we won't get anywhere," the kidnapper on the right declared.

The kidnapper on the left nodded, agreeing with his partner.

"Hey, stop!" I grew alarmed. "I don't have any boxes! I didn't replace the box!"

"So, you see," the kidnapper on the right

sighed again and clapped his comrade on the shoulder, "he's not giving us any choice."

"I'm not watching!" The ringleader shrugged. "I'll see you in the club."

"I've also got a lot to do," the kidnapper on the right then muttered, working loose a pocket watch chain from under the bag, "and also, the inclement weather could leave us trapped here for some time."

"Go on then! I'll do it all myself," the henchman suggested. "Just first help me with the apparatus."

The kidnappers exchanged glances, and I was swept over by a panic attack.

"Stop this!" I shouted. "I don't know anything! The fact that I was in the bank was a mere coincidence! Levinson invited me, that was all!"

They simply didn't hear my admonishments, though. The ringleader approached me from the back and, no matter how I flailed my head, pressed it to the back of the chair, lashing it down with a belt. His assistants rolled up a cart with an incomprehensible looking machine and began attaching the wires that came from it to the bolts holding the chair together.

I cursed, calling thunder and lightning down on their heads, and assured them of my innocence.

"I don't have any box! I have never even seen it!" I whooped out, writhing in the chair, not so much even in a vain attempt to break free as it was in a desire to loosen the very tight belts. The one on the left was squeezing down tight, but the dried-out leather had totally lost any elasticity, making it sting as it cut into my fist.

"The earlier you tell us, the faster this will all be over," the ringleader advised me after that, clapping me on the shoulders and walking away.

Behind him went the others as well. Their footsteps clacked down the iron stairs, then voices began carrying up from below as if the kidnappers had gone down to the first floor. Soon, there came the creaking of rusty hinges and the door clapped open with a boom. A minute later, I started hearing the rattling of a powder engine, and when its sound gradually quieted down, my whole world was filled with nothing but the tapping of rain on a slate roof.

I spent that whole time thrashing like a psychotic. The left belt was yielding more and more, and it wasn't at all because of the kidnapper's lack of caution. It was just that the manacles, even when secured tight, were not made for wrists as lean as mine. My skinniness gave me a fairly good chance of escape, and I definitely would have gotten out of it, but there wasn't time. Heavy footsteps began sounding out from the stairwell once again.

One of the kidnappers had returned, and I was immediately left without the slightest illusion that I would manage to get out of this scrape alive, because he returned with his facemask removed.

With a sickly grunting, the *illustrious* gentleman pulled a white facemask over his head and threw the now-unnecessary mask onto a stack of boxes, then turned around and snorted crossly.

"You've understood everything perfectly," he confirmed, having made an evaluation of my wry countenance. "Perfectly."

"You're making a mistake!" I implored him.

"Nothing of the sort," the old man cut me off, his shoulder bandaged up and a hand on his sash as if a bullet fired upward had fallen in the crack between pieces of his armored cuirass. Despite his advanced age and recent wound, he was holding it together confidently and didn't seem either decrepit or ailing.

He scared me.

"I have no idea about any box!" I assured my kidnapper again.

"Doesn't matter!" The *illustrious* gentleman laughed hoarsely, then began rolling up his right sleeve and my eyes lit up from the black runic lightning bolt on his forearm; the tattoo looked old and discolored.

Chuckling to himself under his nose, the old man went over to get a coal bucket, and placed it near the incomprehensible apparatus. One of its components I did recognize though. It was a steam engine. Using a scoop, he filled the feed bin, poured in ignition fluid and lit a match on the side of a box. A smoky little flame popped up, and immediately caught on the igniter.

The *illustrious* gentleman stood up straight and began staring at me with his colorless eyes.

"You killed Gustav, and you will answer for it," he stated calmly.

"I didn't kill anyone!"

Or did I? If I did...

"I knew Gustav for more than half a century," the kidnapper continued, as if he hadn't heard me, "and you roasted him like a pig. Who could forgive such a thing in my place?"

"I didn't roast anyone!" I repeated.

The old man shook his head and took the papers the ringleader had left there, leafed through them and started reading extracts from my statements:

"Here, you reported, 'I shot the robber with the flamethrower, and he exploded.'"

"That was self-defense!"

"He was walking away from you!"

"He had just burned two dozen people!" I grew angry despite the bone-chilling horror. "He just walked in and burned those poor people up! What about that?!"

"I don't give a damn!" the kidnapper made a face. "I didn't know them. And also, they were Judeans."

"Are Judeans not people?"

"The guilt of the Judean people is so great," the old man answered calmly, starting the steam engine, "that they have simply lost the right to exist."

I was taken aback for a moment.

"Guilt?" I asked, starting to understand something. "Are they guilty because their ancestors crucified Our Savior?"

The old man just laughed in reply.

"I have little care for who they did or didn't crucify," he told me, coughing. "But it was precisely they who opened the door for *the fallen*, and that is an indisputable fact."

"Our Savior ascended from the cross into heaven," I objected. "Our Creator grew disappointed with us and stopped caring. *The fallen* are just a consequence of that..."

"That may be so," the kidnapper shrugged, wincing in pain and rubbing his collar bone. After that, he turned one of the levers and turned on the generator. "I see that you are well versed in this issue, but a blank crucifix on your back will not protect you from electricity."

"Stop!" I screamed. "You can't!"

"I can!" The old man answered calmly and lowered the breaker in an abrupt motion.

I shook from the harsh electric discharge and tears started welling up in my eyes, but all in all, the shock wasn't as painful as I thought.

The old man smiled and announced:

"This will all end as soon as you answer our questions. Then you can die easy and without any more torture."

"Get fucked!" I cursed, and spit out blood from my bit-through lip.

"It looks like we're just getting started, then!" The kidnapper assured me and turned the lever to one o'clock. "If you want to get tortured, that is your right. You'll tell me everything you know eventually, though. Everyone does."

"I don't know anything about any box!"

"Don't try to lie to me," the kidnapper cut me off and sent a charge down the wire again.

The trembling was now noticeably stronger, but when I got my breath back, I decided it would have been incomparably worse if I had unpaid debtors taking me to task.

It was as if the old man could read my thoughts.

"Do you think we're just trying to scare

you, and you just have to bear the pain?" With these words, the eyes of the *illustrious* gentleman not only went white, but began glowing. "Do you believe the memory of Emile will protect you?" The old man took a break to loosen his neckerchief, and suddenly broke into a scream: "Well I didn't give a damn about him, anyway! That waste of breath couldn't hold a candle to Clement! His pointless ambitions jeopardized all of us, and our whole operation! The brainless cretin!"

I wanted to ask what relationship the dead brother of a dead Emperor had with us, but the kidnapper lowered the breaker once again and I shook in convulsions from the electricity flowing through my body.

That punishment was more painful than the ones that came before it. I only came back to my senses after having a bucket of water dumped on my head.

The old man slapped my cheek and stood behind my back.

"Have you heard of the electric chair before?" he asked with an unpleasant smirk. "In the New World colonies, they use this wonderful invention to execute witches, malefics and all other such filth. It works faster and more reliably than burning at the stake. It's also cheaper."

I tried to squeeze a curse out of myself, but

my teeth were chattering too hard.

"We will not be rushing it like that, though," the ominous old man assured me and walked back over to the generator. "We will increase the power gradually so you can really feel what it's like to burn alive!"

And another shock!

I shook and shook for what seemed like an eternity. When I opened my eyes again, it smelled strongly of burnt hair.

"Electricity bakes you from the inside," the *illustrious* gentleman informed me, walking the narrow passage between the piles of wooden boxes to the nearest window. He first knocked out one board, then a second and a third, opening a path for fresh air to get into the room.

While he was distracted, I pulled on my left arm with all my might, but though the bucket of water had soaked my clothes and the leather belt, my arm was still strapped down tight, and I couldn't pull it out.

Come on! Just a bit more!

But I couldn't.

The kidnapper returned and lowered the breaker with no warning. The power regulator wasn't fully wound that time, but I still shook until I saw sparks in my eyes, and had spasms and hallucinations.

One of the hallucination got up on the box

behind the old man's back, pulled up his white face mask and, with a careless grimace, threw it on the floor. After that, the leprechaun took out his tobacco pouch and set about rolling a cigarette. My imaginary friend, borne of my *illustrious talent*, pain and loneliness, was not planning on helping me even though it only would have taken just one stab from his cooking knife...

"Bastard," I gasped and went limp in the chair.

The old man thought I was swearing at him and turned the power regulator up all the higher yet again.

"You're only making this worse for yourself," he told me. "Just tell me where the box is. Just tell me and it will all be over."

"No," I shook my head.

"It's your choice."

The electricity stabbed me this time with the fury of a hundred lightning bolts, but I didn't lose my consciousness. I would have liked to, but I just couldn't. The pain was stopping me. It was welling behind my eyes and piercing through my head every time I even tried to close my eyelids.

It started smelling of burning again, and when the old man finally turned off the power, I wasn't able to move my arms or legs. My body was simply numb.

"The power level is just gonna keep rising," my torturer told me calmly. "Your internal organs will start cooking very soon."

"Shove it up your ass," I wheezed out. "And shove it up your ass, too..."

The last words were aimed at the leprechaun. His hand-rolled cigarette stuffed into the corner of his wide frog-like mouth, he slipped the edge of his kitchen knife under the top of a box next to him, and tried to pry it open, but the nails were pounded in tight.

"They say electricity is sublime, but it can also be a punishment," the old man whispered. "Think of how it treated Gustav!" And, not turning the piercing gaze of his *illustrious* eyes from me, he stood up straight and slammed down the breaker.

My scream must have been heard at the other end of the city. My back twisted into an arch. My head started splitting at the point where the belts were stretching out over my forehead, then at the back of my head, which started feeling pressed into the chair back so hard that sparks were coming from my eyes.

Then, the old man stood up straight and broke the circuit.

"Why do you have to bear such pain?" He asked.

"I don't have the damn box, idiot!" I gasped

out hoarsely.

And another shock instantly ran through my body.

"I cannot bear lack of respect," the *illustrious* gentleman warned me. "Your heart will not hold out much longer, so you'd better start talking."

I just shook my head.

The leprechaun finally got the top off the box and pulled an ancient hand grenade from it. It was round, and had a cast-iron body. The discovery baffled the small albino man. He tossed it up at the ceiling a few times, then for some reason, began twisting in the wick.

The situation was growing less and less appealing to me with every passing moment. Though, it seemed, it couldn't get much worse...

The kidnapper had his own opinion of the gaze I was casting past him, so he tried a nicer tact:

"Perhaps, I'll even let you keep your life," he threw out a fishing line and sniffled in confusion, having caught the scent of strong tobacco smoke coming through the odor of burnt hair.

The leprechaun, meanwhile, took a few more deep, purposeful drags.

"Hellfire!" I exclaimed when the small man placed the crimson point of his ember on the fuse, left the grenade on the box and jumped down onto the floor.

Burning fuse, bomb, box. A pile of boxes.

Were they empty? Almost certainly not!

At the very least, the old man didn't think so. He burst out of his place with such a lighting-like furor that the only possible explanation for his swiftness was that it was his *illustrious talent*. In one moment, the old man hurdled over the boxes blocking his path and picked up the iron ball, but the flame from the wick had already disappeared inside the head; he couldn't put it out now.

The *illustrious* gentleman didn't falter thought, and cast the bomb powerfully through the window he'd recently pried the boards from. The explosion thundered out just then; a column of condensed air butted me painfully in the chest, overturning the chair I was sitting on. I slammed into the hard floorboards, yet again with the much-suffering back of my head...

I WOKE UP TO WATER dripping on my face. A thin little stream was falling from the ceiling; it was hitting me on the forehead and splashing into my eyes and mouth.

I was lying there and could not believe my luck. The shrapnel from the rifled cast-iron body had missed the boxes, and none of the additional bombs inside had gone off. The old man, meanwhile....

Actually, what happened to him? Where was that bastard?

And just then some slow footsteps sounded out.

Clip-clop. Clip-clop.

I was twitching feverishly trying to free my left arm, but I didn't have to bother. Just then, who should come out from behind the boxes but the disheveled leprechaun.

"Help!" I asked him.

The short albino moved his top hat back on his head, looked me over thoughtfully from top to bottom, then tossed his cigarette butt in the puddle next to my head, and left my field of view. A moment later, I heard a pair of toe-less boots clacking down the iron stairs.

"Bastard!" I shouted behind him, and gagged on the water falling down into my mouth from the ceiling.

I lay there gathering my strength, then caught another dribble in my mouth. Then, my head raised, I spit the water at the unyielding belt. Then I did it again and again.

If I did not manage to get out of here before the mean-spirited old man and his friends returned, it'd start all over again. And if he did wake up...

I didn't even want to think about what

might happen.

After I wet it, the belt became much more forgiving, and a few minutes of struggling later, I finally pulled my hand from its hellishly tight embrace.

It got easier from there. The other belts weren't screwed to the chair, just buttoned, so getting out of them was easy. I got out of the chair into the puddle, lied there, gathering my strength, then, quietly whispering curses through my clenched teeth, stood to my feet. And when my head was spinning a bit less, I looked at the explosion-twisted pile of wooden boxes.

The old man was propped up against a wall. The cast-iron body of the grenade, which had flown apart into several large fragments, had crushed his head and almost torn off one of his arms. The rest of the pieces had hit the wall and windows; everywhere around there were chips of whitewash and wood.

I was doubly fortunate – the old man had not only gotten a one-way ticket to the other side, but had also taken the brunt of the blow himself. If he hadn't, this really would have been hellfire for me, too. The box the leprechaun had opened was wall-to-wall packed with bombs.

There were enough combustibles in the room to launch us to the moon.

I cursed out loud and moved back onto the

stairs. With dread, I walked over the metal railing and looked around the room, which looked to be a small warehouse or a coach house. It was filled with boxes of weapons. Near the entrance gate, there was a police armored car that had been brought inside; I would bet my life it was the very same vehicle used in the attempt on the bank.

But it didn't matter now. I had to hurry down. Down!

I found my things piled up on a workbench under the stairs. In the heap of clothing, I found my holster and Roth-Steyr and, as I was, barefooted and wearing nothing but my undergarments, I rushed to the gate. Pistol in hand, I looked out at the street, but the rain was falling in a solid sheet and I couldn't even see the neighboring buildings. Basically, the courtyard was empty...

Locking the door, I threw open the back door of the armored car and got behind the six-barreled Gatling gun installed in the back. First, I adjusted the belt, then I checked the levels of the electric jars and gave the barrels a few idle spins.

Everything was working like clockwork. Or, to be more accurate, like a sewing machine.

The back of the armored car was pointing at the gates as if to defend the building. That gave me a very compelling argument in the event that the two ornery old men showed up and wanted to herd me back into their secret lair.

I just sat there for a few minutes, not feeling strong enough to move either my arms or legs, then I checked to make sure the iron lock bars on the gates were shut tightly. Only after that did I put on my shoes and clothes, going as gingerly as possible around my chafed wrists and ankles. I grabbed a short split-end crow bar from the workbench. Using it, I opened the first box I came across, and inside that, I found a set of semi-automatic Madsen-Biarnoff rifles wrapped in oil paper.

The neighboring box had ammunition. I gutted it and outfitted myself with a couple of magazines. I loaded one into my new souvenir and immediately chambered a round, then quietly laughed to myself under my nose.

Life was working out for the best.

I had a fully loaded semi-automatic carbine under my arm and a machine gun in the armored car. What else could you need for total happiness?

As it turned out, 'hand grenades' was the answer. Not those cast iron monsters with fuses, but more modern ones with wooden handles and chemical igniters. I threw two boxes of grenades into the car as well, and I pulled another box up an inclined board into the car after it. That one contained heavy granulated TNT for the motor, a hand-held Madsen machine gun in factory packaging and rounds for it. Then I stood next to a table looking at a backpack flamethrower considering whether I really needed the ghastly armament. In the end, I placed its tanks very carefully into the back of the vehicle, setting the hose atop them, the jet piece on top of that, and the mask with glass eye-holes at the very summit.

My interest was also piqued by a hand-held mortar fed by an over-the-shoulder pack. It's air-feed sent the charges down a flexible hose, allowing the weapon to shoot quickly. The compressed air tank also allowed the construction to have a total weight of less than twenty kilograms.

Should I saddle myself with such a weight? What for?

Though actually, why have any of this stuff?

Why even bring the weapons with me at all? How would I ever use them? Was I going to start a little war?

But, in the end, my good sense capitulated to my greed, and I continued to open boxes and gut cases. Soon, among the pile of pistols and carbines, I found a drum mortar I had already seen once before in action. With it, I took fifty rounds, then decided not to limit myself and picked up another couple of rifles and some extra ammunition.

Even if I didn't use it, I could sell it.

With that thought in mind, I pulled the Gatling-gun-belt packing machine into the car as well, making sure not to forget eight-millimeter rounds for my Roth-Steyr either. I looked over the shocks. They were sagging, but not as badly as I was expecting. I started considering which of the means of destruction near me would be best if I found myself in a grapple with the werewolf.

Unfortunately, there were no high-caliber rifles stored in the warehouse.

Eventually, I decided on a box of semi-automatic K63 Mausers. But on my way back to the armored car, I took note of a few boxes not covered with the same thick layer of dust as all the others. On their unpainted boards, I could clearly make out a faded logo. It was the very same lightning rune I'd seen earlier, all black and angular.

I opened the one nearest me and inside, I found a tube with a handle, trigger and a locking device in the middle; on one side, it had a folding sight. The other side ended in a trumpet bell. In the same place, there was a mask with thick leather and glass eye-pieces and an awkwardly tacked-on respirator. In the second box, two lengthened shells were adorned with iron blade-stabilizers. These rounds were reminiscent of miniaturized versions of the bombs thrown from dirigibles, but they also had something in them of the charges for field mortars.

A few years ago, in reports from the fronts of the Third Opium War, messages seeped out that a Russian inventor had come up with some kind of bomb launcher. Perhaps this was it.

But how did such a modern weapon end up here?

I skimmed a typed-up manual and thoughtfully prodded the launch-tube box with the tip of my boot. Then I got up and pulled it over to the armored car. I dragged it up the boards into the car, sending the box of rounds the same way. Finally, after a heavy sigh, I took a seat on the lowest step of the stairs.

When my head had started spinning less, I got up to my feet and returned to the second floor to find the body of the old man who had been torturing me; even though corpses tended to be the quiet type, they could sometimes be made to give up clues.

Trying not to step in blood, I bowed down over the dead body and rooted through his pockets, but I was not able to find a wallet or documents of any kind. Then, with my pocketknife, I snipped the tendons of his broken right arm and cut the shred of skin holding it on.

I then wrapped his amputated forearm in a piece of canvas, gathered the police protocols scattered around the room and went down into the courtyard.

I first took a look out the gate to make sure there still was no one nearby, then I raised the bar on the gates, flung them open and climbed into the cabin of the armored car.

I'd learned how to drive a self-propelled carriage in police training, but it had been a few years since I'd actually sat behind the wheel of one. I had to strain my memory a fair amount to remember the steps to start it in the right order.

First ignition, then it feeds the engine granulated TNT. Then reverse...

The armored car gave an unexpected, abrupt jerk. I was thrown forward onto the steering wheel. Only at the very last moment did I come to enough to avoid a collision with the gates. My breathing slowed down. I slightly pressed my boot sole down on the gas pedal, taking the self-propelled carriage out of the carriage house in several stages. It immediately became clear that I couldn't see a thing through the slits in the front armored sheet. I threw it back, but my view didn't get especially better. The windshield had torrential rain pouring down on it, anyway. Standing on the running board, I took a look around; everything I could see was clear, though I couldn't see far in the hazy gray rain.

They'd taken me out of the city! Come to think of it, though, that was actually for the best...

Leaving the engine in idle, I ran back to the warehouse, dragged a canister of kerosene out from under the workbench and left a trail of flammable liquid going into the depths of the building. There, I tipped the container on its side and hurried to the exit. The flames scratched at the doors, then rushed outside in a huge burst.

Sitting behind the wheel, I slammed my foot down too hard on the gas pedal, evidence of my lack of practice, and the armored car jumped forward abruptly, passed the gates and almost flew into a ditch. Losing traction in the deep mud, the self-propelled carriage jerked up back onto the road. As soon as it started gaining a little speed, a deafening explosion blasted out behind me! The warehouse roof lifted off. The first floor collapsed into burning wood and pieces of brick. A second explosion went off after that, and all that remained of the arsenal were smoking ruins.

"This way, it won't be easy for my kidnappers to tell if I was in there," I decided, then remembered the stolen armored car and grew upset at my own lack of foresight.

But was I really going to return to the city in such weather on foot?

I'd be lucky to get there in the carriage...

5

I DROVE THE ARMORED CAR into my carriage-house.

A plague-ridden estate is not a place you'd expect to be searched; curses do come with certain advantages, after all.

Once inside, I asked my butler to bring a canvas package down to the icehouse, and went into the guest room where I could hear a strange gnashing sound.

As it turned out, Elizabeth-Maria was sitting in an armchair sharpening the blade of the saber in measured movements. The succubus didn't even look up at me.

With my tight fingers, I unbuttoned my pea-coat and handed it to Theodor, who was back from the icehouse. I also handed him my wet derby cap.

"Light the water heater in the bathroom. I also need some burn cream," I warned my butler before he left.

"You spent another night away from home,"

Elizabeth-Maria stated in an accusatory tone, not stopping what she was doing for even a moment. Shing-shing, shing-shing.

"I did," I confirmed.

"And you missed lunch."

"I did."

"If I don't know where to look for you, I cannot help."

Help? The succubus wanted to help me?

I almost laughed out loud.

"Where's all this concern for my wellbeing coming from all of a sudden?" I asked, leaning on the doorframe. "Wouldn't my untimely end be great for you?"

The succubus raised her head, and for a moment, her pretty face gave way to a vision of a creature not of this world.

"Your death is not in my best interest," Elizabeth-Maria declared and, seeing my disbelief, clarified: "Right now."

"Your claws aren't deep enough in yet?"

"That's right," the girl confirmed. "Leo, your premature end would upset us both, so I ask you to keep me informed of your plans for the day."

"Without fail," I laughed and pointed to the living flowers in a vase. "You went to the city in this weather?"

"Food doesn't just come here on its own, you know."

"We could have managed."

"Not at all," Elizabeth-Maria assured me, "proper nutrition is the basis of good health." She set the whetstone aside and asked: "Will you tell me where you disappeared to all night?"

"The safest place on earth: the Newton-Markt."

"Problems with colleagues?"

"Nothing serious," I answered, leaning away from the doorframe. "What's wrong with the saber?"

Elizabeth-Maria snorted indignantly:

"Weapons need to be cared for, Leo! It was in a simply horrible state!"

I nodded, but still didn't consider her reason sufficient for the difficult task she was undertaking.

"What else?"

"Your leprechaun!" The girl roared out, her eyes burning with an evil flame. "He's darting around the house, poking his nose around, watching me in the bathroom, stealing wine! It's driving me crazy! I'm gonna catch him and cut him to pieces!"

With these words, the curtain against the far window swayed, and a quiet mumbling came together into a self-satisfied:

"Bugger!"

It should be said it could have just been a

cross-breeze combined with the ringing still in my ears.

"Are you sure regular steel will even kill him?" I asked after that.

"Regular steel?" Elizabeth-Maria laughed quietly. "Your grandfather worked fairly hard to nourish this saber with blood and death. Believe me, this thing could even put a demon to rest!"

"Great!" I nodded. "If you catch that buffoon, start with the legs. Cut his toes off so his feet will fit into his boots."

"Without fail," the girl promised. "But I cannot guarantee that I will be stopping there."

"Check behind the curtain," I then advised her, and walked out into the hallway.

Some things cannot be just let go, even for friends, be they imaginary or not.

A piercing shriek came from the guest room followed by the thundering boom of an armchair turning over; I just shook my head and, leaning heavily on the banister, went up to the third floor. In the bathroom, I stood before the mirror, looking thoughtlessly at the reflection of my peaked face, then I got out of my clothes and instantly realized that I didn't even have the strength to wash myself. I put some salve on the burns on my wrists and ankles, walked into my bedroom and fell asleep.

WHEN I AWOKE, IT WAS late evening. I spent a long time lying on the bed looking thoughtlessly at the ceiling, then I forced myself to get up and close the windows. My head felt like it was filled with cotton. There was a foul taste in my mouth of candied plums, but all in all, my general state didn't bring any unpleasant surprises.

I had taken a sunset nap, nothing more.

I took a sunset nap, got one in the head, and had a few electric shocks...

No matter!

I'm still alive – and that's OK. I know of at least one person who can't boast as much.

I headed off to the bathroom, quickly rinsed myself off and again applied some soothing balm to my burns. After that, I tied a towel around my thighs and shuffled off barefoot to the bedroom but there, Elizabeth-Maria was already playing housewife. On the bedside table, she had placed a tray with a covered dish, a teapot and a little basket of lemon cake cut into pieces.

"You need dinner," she declared in a tone that wouldn't bear objection. Then she looked intensely at me and made a face: "If you say those are stigmata, I think I'll be ill."

"Stupid joke," I frowned, sitting down on the bed.

"Well, you are carrying a cross on your

back..."

"That's enough!" I demanded, not wanting to discuss either my tattoos or the chafing on my wrists and ankles. I lifted the cover of the dish and looked in confusion at the incomprehensible dish made of roast vegetables and meat, chopped fine and mixed together. "What is that?"

"You're gonna like it," the girl smiled. "It's a traditional Indian dish..."

"I cannot bear foreign foods."

"You need to eat," Elizabeth-Maria declared, not hearing my objections.

What I wanted to do was call Theodor and order him to take the dinner away, but I suddenly realized that I was insanely hungry. So I just asked:

"Did you catch the leprechaun?"

The succubus turned around, shot me an unkind gaze, suspecting a trick, and stated promisingly:

"I will."

Just then I heard a satisfied: "Bugger." When she left the room, though, was unclear to me. I couldn't even see it. After I stuck a spoonful of the exotic delicacy into my mouth, it went down like molten lead.

It was very, very tasty.

I poured some tea and took a sip. The very hot water burned the roof of my mouth and tongue so much that there were tears welling up in my eyes. But still, my overall impression of the exotic delicacy was more positive than negative.

In the end, I ate it all, though at times it seemed I was swallowing pure fire.

After dinner, I took out the police report copies I'd taken from the robbers' den and began to read them, but I couldn't make out a single word. The letters were jumping around before my eyes, my eyelids stuck together, and after a few minutes of self-torment, I threw myself back on the pillow in exhaustion.

Sleep!

I fell asleep instantly and slept through the night like a murder victim.

I was dreaming of Elizabeth-Maria von Nalz. The daughter of the inspector general was smiling sweetly and pulling me in by the arm for a kiss, but every time I touched her soft skin with my lips, I felt an electric shock.

What in the world...?

WHEN I AWOKE, THE LEPRECHAUN was sitting on the window sill, his legs crossed, leafing through the police report, occasionally fumbling around to turn to the next page. He had a fresh bruise under his eye, and his lower lip was swollen. The extra flourishes gave the albino man's face a surprising completeness, making him seem somewhat more real than my normal fantasies.

"Oh-ho, you've stepped in it this time, laddy!" the pipsqueak looked at me mischievously as soon as I'd clapped my eyes open. "You stuck your nose where it didn't belong! You're done for!" And for credibility, he led his thumb across his throat in an imitated slicing motion, but as soon as I turned for my boot, he jumped straight to the floor, threw the report up at the ceiling and hopped out the door.

I got out of bed, gathered the sheets of paper that were all around the room and walked up to the window. Outside, the night had just barely begun to gray, and I could at least be glad that it had been the leprechaun that opened the blinds, and not some beast from outside.

With a heavy sigh, I took a seat on the window sill, put the report pages back in the right order, and suddenly remembered that the leprechaun and I had once managed to coexist quite peacefully.

Just me and my imaginary friend. And there had also been a chess board involved.

The leprechaun wasn't such a bastard then.

It should be said that, as soon as I began reading the police report, my nostalgic memories instantly faded.

The expert analysis of the safe deposit box

had been ordered by Senior Inspector Bastian Moran, and, plain as day, the request showed the number of the very safe deposit box rented by my grandmother, the Countess Kósice. I didn't find any analysis ordered on any of the other safe deposit boxes, either.

I threw the report on the bed and took my timepiece from the bedside table. It was showing six forty-five, but there was no sleep remaining even in one eye, so I decided to spend the morning wisely. I quickly got myself together, went out into the hallway, and as soon as I started down to the first floor, I was overtaken by the leprechaun riding the banister. In one moment, he slid down, jumped off nimbly onto the floor and darted off into the kitchen.

Theodor followed him with his imperturbable gaze, handed me my cloak and cane, then, as if a matter of course, remarked:

"I don't want to accuse anyone of anything, Viscount, but silverware has started disappearing again. And this time, we can be quite sure it was not a thieving chef!"

"Oh!" Elizabeth-Maria delighted, joining us. "The little freak wants to line his pockets, does he?" She looked into the kitchen, but the leprechaun's trail had already run cold.

"I am not accusing anyone of anything," my butler repeated.

"We'll figure it out, Theodor," I promised. "Has only silver tableware been disappearing?"

"Yes, only silver forks."

"There weren't so many of them left as it was," I shrugged my shoulders and headed for the exit, but was stopped by the succubus.

"Leopold!" The girl articulated expressively. "Can I count on your good sense?"

"Without a doubt."

"So, you'll be back home for lunch then?"

"I can promise dinner," I told her, going out into the drizzle dribbling down from the sky.

The weather hadn't especially changed overnight, though the downpour had been exchanged for continuous rain, and the wind wasn't shaking the tops of the trees quite as hard. It was cloudy. The city was enshrouded in a gray wetness, and the iron tower on top of the hill was just barely peeking out of the semi-transparent haze of droplets filling the air.

Albert Brandt must have been in quite good spirits.

I had already walked up to the gate when I remembered the package I'd left in the icehouse. I went back home and asked Theodor to go fetch it.

"But put it in a briefcase!" I warned my butler, leaving the house again. "I'll be in the carriage-house."

There, I hung my cloak and derby hat on a wall hanger, threw open the back door of the armored car and cursed aloud when I saw the back of the car still filled with boxes. They were making the armored car lean noticeably to the left.

I pulled out the nearest box, dragged it to the wall and stretched out my sore back with a moan. I decided not to push myself too hard, so I got out a couple boards, leaned them against the back of the car and started to unload. When my butler came in, the only boxes left in the car were the grenades and the long ones with the curious rounds and launch tube. I did not drag them out. My back was already breaking as it was.

"Viscount!" Theodor said, not showing any surprise upon seeing the armored vehicle. "Your briefcase!"

"Leave it there!" I ordered him, digging through the boxes against the wall for the Mauser K63's, and taking the topmost pistol. I set the detachable shoulder stock aside. I wouldn't be needing that. I unwrapped the pistol from its wax paper, thumbed back the hammer and pulled the trigger. It didn't need any extra cleaning, so I immediately loaded it, placing in one bullet after the other. I didn't limit myself to that, either, and loaded another two cartridges. I placed them in the side pockets of my leather briefcase. The pistol itself I had to put next to the frozen package.

And though I was armed to the teeth, I decided not to tempt fate yet another time and left my property through the back door. I went down the steep incline, jumping from stone to stone and ducking under wet branches, until I reached a ditch. Then, I jumped over its cloudy stream to get to the street.

If someone was waiting for me at the gates or the bridge, they were going to be bitterly disappointed.

AFTER GETTING DOWN THE HILL, I immediately headed to the coalhouses and managed to intercept Ramon Miro before he'd left from work.

"Let me treat you to a coffee," I offered when my friend, yawning, emerged from behind the gates of his new place of employment.

"So just like that, out of the goodness of your heart, you're just coming to treat me, huh?" He frowned in disbelief.

"Nothing of the sort," I laughed. "I need advice."

Ramon sighed heavily and waved his arm:

"Alright, let's go."

We walked down the streets. The water in the gutters was black from all the coal dust and soot. We walked into the first coffee shop we came across on Mendeleev Avenue.

I stuck to tea and toast; Ramon took a coffee and three sunny-side-up eggs.

"What's going on with you, Leo?" He asked after they'd brought our order.

"Nothing good," I frowned. "I managed to search the robbers' hideout, but they weren't there anymore."

"You didn't think to tell the police about it?" Ramon looked at me expressively, his eyes red from lack of sleep.

"The robbers will never go back there," I shook my head. "And also, I'm not sure who I can trust in the Newton-Markt."

Ramon Miro finished his coffee and admonished me:

"Tell me about it!"

In two words, I told him a razor-thin story about randomly finding a weapons cache, and another even more random fire but, fortunately, he wasn't at all interested in the inconsistencies and plot holes; he wiped his fingers on the napkin and extended a hand:

"Let me see it!"

The copy of the police report in hand, Ramon familiarized himself with the expert analysis, then quickly looked through the remaining papers and returned them to me.

"Someone in the Newton-Markt is up to

their eye-balls in this," he remarked, having reached the same conclusion as I did. "But I'm more interested in the aluminum box. Are you sure you don't know anything about it?"

"Nothing!" I assured my friend. "Swear on your mother's grave?"

"Let's not go nuts!" Ramon calmed me down, sent a bit of egg into his mouth, chewed it and asked: "Why make a duplicate of the box?"

"They needed to make a fake so good that no one would suspect it. I think that means it was someone in the bank. They didn't want to attract attention."

"They also had access to the safes, but only occasionally," Ramon Miro decided.

"Why?" I asked in surprise, refilling my emptied cup of tea.

My friend looked at me like a dumb intern.

"No one is interested in the box on its own, right?" He began from afar. "They want what's inside. So why wouldn't the thieving employee just take the box home, open it up and put it back? It only makes sense if the thief could get into the safe just one time. And it didn't matter if the boxes were a bit different, because the description only showed the material and the rune."

"Logical," I nodded, staring at the rain-covered window in contemplation.

Outside, there was a wind picking up. The small gray drops were now going more sideways than downward.

"Aluminum boxes with runes on the top don't get made every day," I articulated some time later. "What do you think, can we find the workshop?"

Ramon finished his coffee and threw up his hands:

"Foundry Town is a big place."

Foundry Town was the name of an expanded neighborhood on the factory outskirts where there were both lone craftsmen, and whole factories.

"Aluminum isn't the most popular material, either though" Ramon continued thinking it over. "It doesn't matter precisely which craftsman took the job, we just have to look for a person who was asking around for aluminum workers."

I looked at my friend with sincere respect.

"You've got it!"

"Yes, that reminds me! A few weeks ago, I read about an attempted robbery at Baron Dürer's factory in the newspaper. The robbers took a shipment of aluminum that was intended for the von Zeppelin factory."

"Is that so? Was the metal ever found?"

"I have no idea."

"You see, the fake box was made of a rare

alloy intended, as it were, for the building of dirigible bodies! That can hardly be a coincidence."

"I'd even say it's a safe bet!" Ramon Miro clapped his hand on the table. "A cousin of mine has a workshop in Foundry Town. I could have a talk with him, but what do I get out of it?"

"Half."

"Half of what?" my friend clarified.

"Half of the reward offered by the Banking House for solving the crime."

"Didn't you get an advance on that?"

I took out my wallet, counted out five tens and threw them on the table.

"Is that enough?"

"Quite," Ramon nodded, sticking the money in his pocket. "Could you describe the rune?"

"I'd better draw it," I suggested, throwing a broken thunder bolt onto my notepad and ripping out the page. "Here, take this."

"Where should we meet? Just know that I'm going to sleep now. I'll go to Foundry Town after lunch."

"Then look for me in the *Charming Bacchante*. Remember? We used to go there after our shift some times."

"I'll find it."

Ramon Miro clapped on his cap and walked out the door; I took the copies of the police reports and put them back in my briefcase, paid for the both of us and grudgingly pulled on my coat.

I was categorically opposed to going out into the drizzle, but often our sympathies and antipathies have absolutely no significance. If you've gotta do it, you've gotta do it. That very same impartial resolve is what had almost gotten me fried alive on the electric chair yesterday.

It was dismal outside. The sky was gray, the buildings were gray and the road was gray. It made little difference that the mud had a black coloration and I could see the little spots flickering by of the arrant fashionista's umbrellas. Respectable individuals used umbrellas of a strict black color only.

I didn't have an umbrella so, not wanting to get wet, I caught a cab. I splurged, but for that, ten minutes later I was already at the front door of *Mechanisms and Rarities*. And the shop, despite the early hour, was open. Its owner was standing bewildered with his head thrown back, looking at a flickering bulb hanging down from the ceiling.

"The current is unstable again," Alexander Dyak told me instead of a greeting.

"And a good morning to you, too, Alexander," I greeted him. "Have I come at a bad time?"

"Come now, Leopold Borisovich!" The shop owner threw up his hands. "It's a bad time for the rain, but you, as it were, I've been awaiting impatiently."

I perked up my ears:

"Have you thought something up?"

Alexander Dyak smiled cunningly.

"Everything has already been thought up. The problem is actually making it," he said and asked: "Did you bring any rounds?"

"Rounds?" I asked pensively, remembering the dimensions of the werewolf and nervously getting on edge. "Will ten caliber rounds do?"

"That's up to you, Leopold Borisovich!" Alexander Dyak assured me.

I nodded in confusion, in that I didn't just need rounds, but also a gun.

"I'll be back in a half an hour," I warned the shop owner and went back out into the rain.

Outside, a bit of drizzle got into my face. I stood there, trying to remember the location of the nearest gun store, and stepped off down the sidewalk, splashing water from the shallow puddles with my boots.

I didn't have to spend much time looking for a gun store. I found one just a block away. The shop, bearing the proud name *The Golden Bullet* could not boast an excess of customers in the inclement weather, so as soon as I went inside, a salesman appeared next to me.

"Are you looking for anything in particular?"

"Ten caliber," I named my demand, looking carefully at the hunting rifles hanging on the wall.

The young-looking salesman thought about it for a short time, then unlocked one of the cabinets and took out a one-barrel lever-action gun.

"Winchester eighteen sixty-eight," he said, extending it to me. "Five rounds in a tubular magazine, one in the chamber."

I turned the gun over in my hands, assessing the balance, and asked:

"How much?"

"One hundred sixty-four francs and fifty centimes," the salesman rapped off without a moment's delay. "You won't find it cheaper. We get them direct from the New World. And, you get ten rounds free when you buy!"

I was fine with that price; without trying to bargain, I dug out my wallet.

"I'll take it."

"Would you like a case?"

"No, thank you," I refused, counting out the money. I caught the salesman's surprised gaze and explained myself: "It's a gift."

"I see," he nodded and asked: "Will that be

all?"

"Have you got Cerberus rounds?"

"Ten millimeter? Yes."

"Have you got silver ones?"

The salesman walked away to the counter, leafed through a catalog and with unhidden disappointment told me:

"No, unfortunately we don't have any in stock. It isn't a very popular item, you see. But we could have them delivered by the second half of the day."

"Let's do that," I decided. "I'll leave the Winchester here until evening, and I'll come back for the lot all at once. How much do I owe you with three silver rounds?"

"One hundred seventy francs, thirty-five centimes," the salesman told me the total.

I paid, stuck a box of rounds in my briefcase and asked:

"Do you know much about pistols?"

"You selling or buying?"

"A business contact from the continent is offering a large shipment of Mauser Sixty-Threes, but I'm worried that he's been slipped some stolen army guns."

The salesman shrugged his shoulders indefinitely:

"That model has never been issued to a military unit anywhere in Imperial borders. You don't need to worry about that. But for a cut, we would be able to accompany the transaction."

I nodded, but didn't show him my Mauser; the salesman's answer had put my theory that the *illustrious* gentlemen had pilfered the guns from army warehouses in serious doubt.

In deep contemplation, I left the store and, under a drizzly rain, I hurried back to the shop *Mechanisms and Rarities*.

ALEXANDER DYAK, AS BEFORE, was sitting bored at the counter and looking angrily at the light bulbs flickering under the ceiling. On my return, he immediately came to life and instructed me:

"Hang the 'Closed' sign."

"I really am uncomfortable depriving you of your earnings..."

"Drop it!" laughed the inventor. "Who's gonna go shopping in this dog's weather? Also, the door has an electric bell!"

I couldn't dispute him on that count; I hung out the sign, locked the door and walked into the back room after him.

"Rounds, if you'd be so kind," the shop owner asked, taking a pair of calipers from a tool box.

I unpacked the cardboard box and extended a ten caliber rifle round to the inventor.

Alexander Dyak measured the diameter of

the brass cartridge case and advised me:

"I can make ten bullets. Will that be enough?"

"More than enough," I smiled. "What kind of bullets do you need?"

"Experimental ones," I answered the shop owner evasively. "Remove your cloak, Leopold Borisovich. That will take some time. And I will need your help."

I hung my cloak and derby cap on a hook near the entrance door and asked:

"What should I do?"

"Prepare the rounds. Don't touch the powder charge. Just change out the bullet."

"They're buck-shot."

"Doesn't matter," Alexander Dyak waved it off, lit a gas burner and set about loading a crucible above it with a dark-silver metal.

"Is that lead?" I grew surprised.

"Were you expecting something more exotic?" the inventor laughed. "You'll get your exotic! Leopold Borisovich, are you familiar with so-called radioactivity? It was discovered by the wife of a Mr. Curie."

I just shook my head.

The store owner lit a second burner, loaded aluminum into the crucible over it and started setting up molds, carefully re-checking their dimensions with the same set of calipers.

"The essence of it is that certain chemical elements, mostly metals, are capable of emitting particles..." Alexander Dyak glanced at me and waved an arm. "Not important! There are holes in the theory that stop us from doing anything useful with it."

"Alright, I'd still like to figure out what this has to do with anything," I stated, disemboweling yet another round.

His discussion of these exotic facts did precious little to inspire me. Silver could kill werebeasts. That was an indisputable fact. I didn't want to hear about any other kinds of metals.

But the inventor, meanwhile, opened another cabinet and removed an iron box containing pellets of a silvery-gray metal.

"This is uranium," he told me, grabbing one in his pincers. "A radioactive metal. It is not dangerous as long as you don't carry it on your person or take it internally. Radium has the same effect, but it is incomparably stronger; after working with it, Curie's wife's arms were covered with boils and sores."

"And how does that help us, exactly?"

"The effect of radiation on the body has been little studied, but some scientists suppose that it could cause serious injury to any living creature."

"How serious?"

"Potentially lethal," Alexander Dyak assured me. "And werebeasts should be more even more harmed than a normal creature. Their main peculiarity is an unbelievable regenerative ability, which sometimes requires them to incorporate foreign objects in their body, later excreting them as slag. The bullets are not expelled from the wounds, yet they heal over, isn't that right?"

"It is," I replied. "Are you sure that such a metal can cause serious enough damage?"

"Documented proof of my theory is exactly what this experiment is setting out to get," the inventor muttered, pouring molten lead over the pellet in the bullet mold.

I fundamentally disagreed with his method of experimentation.

"This is not an experiment, this is life."

"Many scientists have sacrificed their lives for the sake of science," Alexander Dyak stated calmly.

"And I would not like to share their fate."

The store owner smiled and, in a well-practiced motion, tapped a finished bullet out of the now-cool mold.

"Leopold Borisovich!" He shook his head. "I didn't promise you miracles. But from a scientific point of view, the chance that this experiment will have a positive outcome is extremely high. It's just impossible to say in advance how quickly the after-effects will become apparent. The metabolism of a werebeast is much faster than that of a human, so we should expect it to take five or ten minutes to kill. But shoot at the body. The bullets must remain in the body, is that clear?"

"It is," I nodded. "Sorry for my extravagance. It's just nerves."

"Nothing to worry about."

"In any case, I do not plan on totally forgoing silver bullets."

"A truly scientific approach," the inventor praised my foresight and suddenly asked: "Have you got a good timepiece?"

"Yes, and what of it?"

"Can I count on a detailed report, indicating the exact time and effects observed after shooting my bullet into a werebeast? The data would be simply invaluable to science."

"It's the least I can do," I nodded. "But I cannot guarantee that the werewolf and I will be meeting today, tomorrow, or any time in the foreseeable future."

"Let's hope for the best, then!" The inventor broke down laughing, setting ten of the new bullets in a row in front of him.

I squirmed.

Alexander Dyak cocked his eye and set about coating the lead bullets with molten aluminum.

"Lead is susceptible to the effect of defensive magic," he explained. "You gave the werewolf quite the thrashing. He may be better prepared next time. Aluminum is much more reliable in that regard."

"Yes, an aluminum jacket would not be inadvisable," I agreed without particular enthusiasm.

My one and only fight with the werewolf had beaten any desire to hunt for the creature from me. And to hell with the reward on his head...

I LEFT THE INVENTOR'S SHOP an hour and a half later with ten rounds and without any particular confidence that they would help me defeat the werewolf or even cause him any serious injuries. But still, fifty grams of lead, aluminum and uranium had the same stopping power as fifty grams of lead alone; a ten caliber shot would be able to knock anything off its feet, no exceptions. Not just a werewolf, even a legendary northern troll. I'd like to see one try me...

Outside, it was drizzling as before. Down the sidewalks, there were streams flowing, their dirty water gurgling happily down the gutters.

The city-dwellers had grown sick of waiting out the bad weather and were no longer lying low in their houses; rain umbrellas started popping up here and there. Cabbies had the leather and canvas tops of their carriages up, and their downcast little horses were clip-clopping down the causeway with an unhappy look, splashing water up from the puddles.

In a newspaper kiosk, I bought a fresh paper, then caught a free carriage and ordered it to take me to a part of the outskirts, which had been settled by immigrants from Eastern Europe. The cabby demanded payment in advance, and only after a one-franc deposit did he agree to drive to the neighborhood, which was steeped in a peculiar infamy. It had the reputation of not being the most relaxing place. Some even considered it totally lawless.

I hadn't been there for six years, but nothing in particular had changed in that time. It was the very same people, and the very same faces. Even though the buildings had become a bit dingier, and the number of broken windows had gone up.

No, it wasn't decay. It was just that none of the locals treated the neighborhood with respect. Some were just staying here briefly on their way to the New World. Some were intending to move to a more prestigious neighborhood eventually, or even earn some money to take back home. Some left, others came, but even those who were born in the neighborhood didn't consider it home, and nor did those who were fated to die here for that matter.

My father and I had spent a fair amount of time here, but what brought me back was certainly not sentimentality. I was interested in a door with no banner above it on the corner of Lomonosov and Siberia Streets.

The door was in the same place as always. It was just as dingy and sloppy as before, but now there was an advertising board screwed onto it depicting a sultry beauty and the words: "Smoke and lose weight!"

I pushed down on the handle, but it was locked! I looked around and walked across the street to a snack shop with a colorful red and orange bird on the facade.

Labeling the buildings here was not in the spirit of the neighborhood; either you knew your way around without placards and signs, or you were an outsider, and thus not welcome.

The snack-shop was called *The Phoenix*. I already knew it, but never felt much like myself on these little streets.

"He'll be in at one," an elderly waiter wearing a white apron told me. He was standing at the entrance door and looking outside through a rain-splashed window. And he was speaking, naturally, not about the chef in the kitchen.

I glanced at my timepiece and hung my derby-hat and cloak on a free hook on the rack. Then I took a seat at the window, which gave me a view of the whole intersection, and I thought about what to order.

"Tea and blini with honey," I said when the waiter arrived, much to my own surprise, "and potato vareniki. With salo and fried onions."

My father and I had come into *The Phoenix* once every month or two. First, we would knock on the unlabeled door across the intersection, then we would come here. And despite our chronic lack of funds, dad was never cheap and ordered all the sweets I ever asked for. Pastries with whipped cream, sweet pies, rooster-shaped lollypops, ice-cream...

While waiting for my order, I pulled a pile of papers from my briefcase and looked them all over quickly, paying special attention to the crime blotter. But no, there was no mention of our attempt to detain the werewolf, nor the explosion outside the city. Not in the *Atlantic Telegraph*, the *Capital Times* or the *Bulletin of the Empire,* which was to say nothing of the *Stock-Market Bulletin.*

Nothing. Silence.

Seemingly as one, all the newspapers' top headlines were dedicated to Nikola Tesla and

Thomas Edison's upcoming visit to New Babylon; the sharp-tongued newspapermen were declaring almost directly that the Sublime Electricity conference was fated to end in bloodshed. There was a bit less written about the fact that the heir to the throne was once again in the hospital for observation, but they couldn't sensationalize that story any further no matter how hard they tried. Everyone had learned of Crown Princess Anna's weak heart soon after her birth.

At that moment, the waiter placed a deep dish of vareniki on the table in front of me and a little saucer of sour cream.

"Shall I bring the rest now?" He inquired.

"Post haste," I nodded, and soon before me there was a Russian-style teapot, a dish of blini and a little pot of honey.

I closed my eyes, enjoyed the fragrant aromas of my childhood, gulped it all down, then, without any remorse whatsoever, stood to my feet, threw a rumpled fiver on the edge of the table and set about putting on my coat and hat.

The waiter didn't say a word. He remembered me from times gone by.

As I already said, these were the very same people and the very same faces; nothing ever changed here.

Without buttoning up my cloak, I crossed the street and, without knocking, the door swung open. Not long after that, a hunch-backed man in a gray rain slicker came through it. His head jumped, ducking under the low door jamb. He stood up straight and announced:

"I have a few questions."

The hunch-backed bootmaker looked me from bottom to top and smiled.

"Not nice ones, I suppose?" He supposed. "I heard you became a policeman, Leo."

"Everything flows, everything changes," I brushed it off and shrugged my shoulders. I then set my briefcase on the edge of the table and took my package out of it, which was just barely starting to thaw out.

The old craftsman turned the piece of canvas over, and raised his confused gaze to me.

"What is that, Leo?" He pushed away the *illustrious* gentleman's forearm, which had been torn out in the explosion.

"I need to know who made this tattoo," I said calmly, as if we were talking about shoe repair.

His trade as a bootmaker had never brought much money in this quarter, and Sergei Kravets made ends meet by doing tattoos for local criminals. Every time the police found a dead body covered with tattoos, they would go to the bootmaker, demanding that he tell them the name of the victim. He never told them a thing, but he would immediately lock up his shop and go off to tell the bad news to the victim's kin.

I knew perfectly well of his principles, but had no doubt whatsoever that I would get an answer in any case.

The craftsman threw himself back into his chair and looked at me with an incomprehensible expression. In his weak eyes, I could see reflections of the kerosene lamp.

"That wouldn't be right," he declared.

"It was you who said the questions would be unpleasant," I reminded him.

The craftsman shook his head.

"They say you're not a policeman anymore," he declared pointedly.

"Everything flows. Everything changes." I repeated.

"Leo, did you kill this man?"

I just shrugged my shoulders, neither giving a 'yes' nor a 'no.'

I simply didn't know the answer to the question.

Sergei Kravets came to his own conclusions on what that meant, lit another lamp and got out a powerful magnifying glass. He studied the tattooed rune and announced:

"This is very old work."

"How old?"

"Based on what I can see, the man lived

most of his life with it."

I nodded. That was most likely true. And in that this man was older than seventy, the man who had made it was long dead now.

"I will not tell you any names," Kravets continued as I expected. He then went silent and added: "You know something, Leo? This could actually have been done by anyone."

"What do you mean?"

"The symbol is flawless. There isn't a single smudge. If you want my opinion, this is not a tattoo in the traditional sense. It's a kind of brand. Someone arranged lots of needles together in a special stamp."

"I see," I sighed and clarified: "Anything else?"

"No," the craftsman shook his head.

I rolled the arm up in canvas and returned the package to the briefcase.

"There isn't anything else you want to ask?" Kravets stopped me.

The question hit a sore point. I turned slowly and leaned on the door frame.

"You don't know the answer!" I retorted to the craftsman. "He wouldn't have told you!"

"You're right," confirmed the old boot-maker.

"Then what are you talking about?"

My father had sent me to get my tattoos

here exclusively. He had never explained, and I still couldn't decide for myself if it was all just the raving of a drunk, or if my tattoos had some sort of sacral hidden meaning.

"The left arm," Kravets stated. He left a sketch for the left arm and even paid in advance.

"No," I answered and quickly went out the door.

No, no, no.

I was not going to go through that again.

I needed answers. Answers, not more riddles.

On the street, I threw the severed arm down the first gutter opening I came across.

WHEN I CAME INTO the *Charming Bacchante*, I was chilly, soaking, and hungry. There were blini and vareniki dancing before my eyes the whole way there. By the end of my journey, it even started clouding my vision a bit. In the cabaret, I asked them to make me a few sandwiches and an herbal tea. I took a nut pudding that caught my eye and walked up to Albert's apartment holding a tray laden with food.

The poet was working. Based on the sweeping movement of his arms, he was drawing, but when I arrived, he immediately put his notebook in the upper drawer of his desk and even locked it with a key.

I caught the aroma of women's perfume and couldn't resist a smirk:

"Am I to understand that your unknown beauty decided to pay a visit to this den of iniquity?"

"You don't understand the first thing about real feelings!" Albert waved it off and wondered caustically: "Are you alone today, or has your imaginary friend come along again?"

"You're missing him already?"

"Touché!" Albert Brandt threw up his hands and asked: "What have you brought?"

"Two sandwiches, some nut pudding..."

"News!" The poet interrupted me. "What is the news about Procrustes?"

I frowned, finished my glass of herbal infusion and advised him:

"Forget about Procrustes. You'd be better off writing an ode to the Sublime Electricity. Tesla and Edison are coming here for a visit."

"Tesla and Edison come and go. Procrustes remains."

"Procrustes died a long time ago."

Albert grew offended and turned to the window. I just shrugged my shoulders and started eating. I then took the emptied tray and put it in the bin, where the billiard ball I'd brought from the Chinese Quarter was still lying, and I articulated obligingly:

"By the way, Alexander Dyak was a huge help."

"How nice for you!" The poet grumbled, looking outside.

"Come off it!"

"Leopold, you're surprising me!" Albert exploded. "You say you know how fleeting inspiration can be! This isn't just some commissioned work. This is my heart's own bidding! I was having fun with the topic of Procrustes, but you're ruining everything. Your disbelief is sapping all my enthusiasm!"

I looked at the poet in sympathy, but didn't apologize.

"Albert, he's dead," I assured my friend and lay back on the ottoman. "And he's been dead for a long time."

"You can't know that for sure!"

"Yes, I can. Sometimes, I visit his grave. So I can say that the slab is right where it's always been. He's there, under two meters of dirt, Albert."

On hearing these words, the poet had a stroke. He spent some time batting his eyes in silence, then he walked up to the ottoman, hung over me and clarified:

"What did you say? You go to his grave?"

"Sure," I confirmed with artificial carelessness. "Procrustes was my father."

Albert pushed my legs off the couch, took a seat next to me and pursed his lips:

"If this is some kind of joke..."

"How could I be joking?" I sighed and stared at the ceiling.

"Enough playing around!" The poet objected. "The werebeast curse is transmitted genetically by the male line! It's a hereditary disease. Hereditary! But you, as far as I know, have never shown an inclination to howl at the full moon! How is that possible, huh?"

I shrugged my shoulders.

"I do not know."

"You don't know?"

"You don't think I've wracked my brains over this? I know one thing: I do not suffer from his disorder. I'd feel it."

"Maybe it's just waiting to come out? What if you're still in the latent period?"

"Albert, that is balderdash! The latent period ends in the teenage years. Anyone could tell you that. And I don't howl at the moon, I'm not afraid of silver, and my body doesn't heal over all wounds."

"I do not know; I do not know..."

"So you want me to be a werebeast that bad, huh?" I laughed uncontrollably. "Drop it! Maybe it's all the curse. My father changed very much after my mother died. He became different.

Nervous and anxious. It was like something broke inside him. We were always going from one place to the next. It felt like we were on the run. We never stayed anywhere for long. My father always thought he was being followed. He was connected with underground cells of Anarchists and Christians. He walked the very edge, and drank a lot. And sometimes, he flew off the handle."

"Killed people," the poet corrected me, no longer doubting what I was saying.

"No, flew off the handle," I shook my head. "He did business with dangerous people, and sometimes, these people thought they could put undue pressure on him. They were mistaken. And then we would have to move to a new place."

"Did you ever actually see him... kill?"

I nodded.

"Once, we were coming home late, and a gang of Egyptians tried to get the drop on us."

"And?"

"It took three days for a volunteer effort to find all the limbs strewn around the park," I frowned from the fairly unpleasant memories. "My dad, meanwhile, couldn't stop drinking for a week. He didn't like to kill, but he couldn't stop it when it came over him."

"But he never touched you?"

"No."

"How did he die?"

"As I said, he didn't know when to stop. He drank himself to death."

Albert stood from the ottoman and spent some time walking in silence around the apartment, thinking over what he'd heard. Then, he began to speak out loud.

"Anarchists, Christians, police, criminals. Dark streets, a child. That changes everything. That changes everything completely!"

He looked at me, as if seeing me for the first time and asked:

"Leo, I apologize, but I need to be alone for a bit."

Without another word, I got up from the ottoman, took my cloak and walked out the door. I was already near the stairs when Albert poked his nose out after me and shouted:

"Hold on! What are you doing tomorrow evening?"

"I have no idea," I answered. "Why?"

"Don't make any plans! I have two vouchers for the next showing of *Moon Circus*," the poet told me, and hid in his room.

My mind made up to figure out the details, I returned to his apartment but, when I glanced inside, Albert was already leaning over the table writing feverishly, from time to time dipping his quill in the inkwell.

Not wanting to distract the poet, I went down to the first floor, took a seat at the table farthest from the stage and, looking at the gray canal and raindrops falling from the sky, tried to figure out what had changed in me after my recent admission.

I had never before actually told anyone about that, and I didn't particularly enjoy remembering it.

Why did I tell Albert? For his poem? Nothing of the sort. For some reason, I felt like I needed to confess. But no matter how hard I tried to figure out why, I couldn't.

But then, Ramon Miro came in from outside and I had to think about something else.

"Ramon!" I waved at the squat man, calling him over to my table. "Take a seat!"

He walked into the bar and we were brought another pot of hot herbal infusion.

"Thank you," Ramon shivered, taking the cup. A small puddle quickly formed under the hook he'd just hung his soaked-through cloak on.

"What did you find out?" I asked my friend after he had taken a few sips, and was warming his shivering fingers on the hot cup.

Ramon frowned peevishly and admitted:

"Not much. I wasn't able to find the workshop where they made the fake, but my cousin promised to find out something about it."

"Are you sure the box was even made in Foundry Town?" I doubted.

"Ah, that's right!" The squat man slapped his palm on his forehead. "I totally forgot to say! There was a Judean they told me about getting information on aluminum goods. So finding the workshop is just a matter of time."

"Is anything known about the Judean?" I perked up my ears.

"They don't know who he is," Ramon sighed. "No one could even give a comprehensive description. His collar was raised, and his hat was low on his head. That's all they ever said. We need to find the craftsman he gave his order to. That guy will be able to describe him. And also, they say he had a noticeable burn on his cheek."

"The Judean?"

"Yes, on his cheek."

I took a deep sigh, tapped my fingers on the edge of the tabletop, then asked:

"Maybe it wasn't a burn, but a birthmark?"

"Do you have someone in mind with a birthmark on their face?"

"Yeah, Aaron what's-his-name... Malk!" I cursed out. "The manager's assistant! And he definitely had access to the bank's safe! At the very least on the day of the robbery!"

Ramon got up from the table, shook off his cloak and asked in a business-like manner:

"Will we take him ourselves?"

"Look at who's asking!" I exclaimed, not at all burning with the desire to share this information with the police. "There's somewhere we need to go first..."

WHEN I LEFT THE GUN STORE with the ten-caliber Winchester, Ramon, waiting for me in the carriage, had a drastically different facial expression.

"What's that all for, then?" He was taken aback.

I got out of the drizzle sprinkling down from the sky by going under the canvas top and ordered the cabby to drive to the Judean Quarter, then asked my friend:

"Is there a chance the werewolf is looking for the box?"

He frowned, but still admitted:

"Yes."

"If the werewolf is tracking the same person as we are, could we coincidentally end up at the same place where he is?"

Ramon threw himself back in the seat and admitted:

"We could."

"Guns don't hurt him, right?" I snorted and took the box of rounds Alexander Dyak had created from my briefcase. "It's important to note that this is not silver. Your mission will be to hold the werewolf at a distance for at least a few minutes while we wait for the poison to take effect."

"Will it work, though?" Ramon asked with doubt, loading bullet after bullet into the tube magazine under the barrel.

I showily loaded a clip of silver bullets in the Cerberus, and gave a meaningful smile:

"You just worry about hitting him. Sound good?"

"I hope it won't come to shooting," Ramon frowned.

"I'm actually hoping it will!"

IT WAS NO DIFFICULT TASK to find Aaron Malk's apartment. After getting the advance from Mr. Levinson, I had also asked him for a list of bank employees including everyone, regardless of whether they had survived the attempted robbery or not. Exposing inside men was the first thing they taught in police courses. In my early days, I'd thought that hard to justify. I hadn't ever even used it before, but now I was left only to thank my old instructors for pounding that information so deep into my brain.

In no particular hurry, the horses ran down the deserted streets. The carriage wheels splashed the puddles in every direction, both those that could only scare pedestrians, and those that would cover them with dirty water. By evening, the weather had cleared up. The low dark clouds had begun to leave the city, but together with twilight, a milky film of fog crawled over the city. The street lamps burned out orange spheres in it and were almost never very bright. Very little could be made out, even at a distance of a few dozen steps.

The feeling of the hunt came over us.

"I don't like this fog," Ramon muttered, getting out of the carriage. "I can't see a damn thing..."

I nodded and looked around cautiously. The street, lined with identical tenement buildings, stretched out along the very edge of the Judean Quarter. There was now a group of crooked-looking young boys staring intently at us as they leaned on a wall, sitting on the stoop under the front door overhang.

How must it have been for the very prosperous manager's assistant to return here night after night?

"He's probably got a fat old wife and ten kids," Ramon guessed. "All his money goes to clothes and food, so he rents an apartment in this hole. Or he has very old relatives who need expensive medicine. Or maybe..."

"Zip it," I demanded, walking up onto the

stoop and knocking at the locked door. I pulled the list of bank employees from my briefcase, led my finger down the list of residents and, just when a concierge looked outside at me, I read:

"Levinsky, Malik... Malk!" After that, I raised my eyes to the middle-aged doorman and asked: "Does an Aaron Malk live here?"

"Yes he does," the concierge confirmed.

"Is he at home?"

"No."

I looked expectantly at the man, but didn't get anything from him but that short 'no,' so I flared up:

"Am I gonna have to tweeze every single word out of you? When was he last here?"

"What seems to be the problem?" He perked up, taking a timid step backward down the corridor.

"We represent the Witstein Banking House!" I continued, not slowing my pace. "Have you heard of the Witstein Banking House?"

The concierge nodded.

"And are you aware of the recent events that took place at that respected establishment?"

And the concierge once again confirmed his knowledge with a miserly nod.

"Then you know who I am and why I am here."

The man frowned in annoyance:

"Mr. Levinson never should have done business with goys. It didn't lead to anything good."

"Aaron Malk," I reminded him. "When was the last time he was here?"

"I haven't seen him since yesterday."

Ramon and I exchanged pointed glances and I asked:

"And his relatives? Is there anyone we can speak with?"

"He lives alone."

"Then please lead us to his room. We want to make sure he really isn't home."

The concierge looked at me with unconcealed doubt, then I waved my list of bank employees before his face.

"Are you really gonna make us bother Mr. Witstein over this?"

"Just don't touch anything," he relented.

We walked up the creaky stairs to the third floor, and the concierge unlocked the door with his master key. Holding his Winchester before him, Ramon was first to cross the threshold. I groped for the Cerberus in my pocket and took a step in after him.

He wasn't in any of the rooms. However, in the air, there was a barely perceptible, lingering aroma that the two of us were well acquainted with.

Ramon pulled air into his nose and asked:
"Is that what I think it is?"

"Exactly," I nodded. "Check the trash bin," and turned to the doorman. "I hope having a goy go through his trash doesn't constitute a violation of your precepts."

"No," the concierge answered monosyllabically, clearly regretting having let us outsiders into this man's home.

Ramon took less than a minute, and after that, we parted ways with the sullen man and went outside.

"Did you find anything?" I asked on my way down from the stoop.

The hulking man showed me a small paper package with some smudged logograms on it.

"Opium?" I decided, in that his apartment smelled of the narcotic.

"Chinese," Ramon attested.

"Just don't tell me we're gonna have to poke our noses around the Chinese Quarter again!"

Ramon shrugged his hulking shoulders.

"If Aaron is still alive, he must be in an opium den there. I bet if we flash this paper around, we can find out which one."

"Should we ask the same constables?"

"Sure, we may as well start there."

"Let's go."

And we headed off in search of a cabby willing to take two gentlemen to the Chinese Quarter on this dank and rainy evening.

We did find one, of course. At times, money can perform true miracles.

IN THE RAINY WEATHER, the Chinese Quarter looked even shabbier than on clear days. And sure, there were slightly less beggars outside, and it wasn't smelling quite as strongly of scorched food, but the sidewalks were covered with water and there was filth floating all around. And there were no parades, streetlights, rickshaws, drum battles, or hordes of fun-lovers swarming the local bordellos and opium dens today either. The neighborhood had turned into a dirty shadow of itself.

It should be said that I spoke a bit too soon on the beggars, though. We just had to get out of the carriage before a crowd of the crippled poor quickly formed around us. Some were one-armed, some had no legs, and some were even rotting alive.

"Get out of here!" Ramon snapped in annoyance and stepped over to a noodle shop.

I hurried after him and quietly laughed:

"Don't let your fears out, friend."

"Get fucked!" The hulking man exclaimed, threw open the door and ducked into the snack shop. Soon, he came back out. Behind him there appeared a constable smelling of local cookery, the most senior in his division.

"Well?" He looked at us sullenly. "What is it this time?"

Ramon handed him the paper packaging. The constable spent some time looking at the symbols and even walked back to the window, then turned the piece of paper over to Ramon and declared frankly:

"These guys won't talk to you."

"How much will it cost?" I asked.

"That is the den of the Red Dragons," the policeman shook his head. "Act at your own peril. We've got our own work to do here."

"Could you just walk us there?" Ramon inquired.

The constable considered it, then nodded and popped back into the noodle shop. A few minutes later, his local underling came outside.

"Twenty francs!" The man announced as he walked.

"Ten," I extended him a rumpled bill.

The man did not refuse my money, but he did make a counteroffer:

"And five when we get there."

"Show us the way," I agreed.

The fog over the neighborhood was getting thicker. When we turned away from the lively street, the street noises quickly faded. All that remained was the splashing of water underfoot and the squelching of mud. Sometimes, it seemed we were walking through a rice paddy. It was important not to look closely, because there were some utterly disgusting things floating in the puddles. I personally preferred not to know what my boot soles were slipping around on.

It should also be said that I was not feeling up to this. While we wandered the labyrinth of narrow little streets, I was being tormented by the sensation that someone was prowling after us, looking out from around the corner, following us, and jumping from roof to roof. I was reminded of the werewolf, making me feel very unwell.

I undid the button on my Roth-Steyr holster and moved my Cerberus into my cloak pocket. I was getting ready to switch off the safety of the Mauser in my briefcase, but then we walked up to a two-story house with a snazzy banner with incomprehensible symbols interwoven with a great many red dragons.

Our escort immediately extended his hand and demanded:

"Five francs!"

I leaned on my cane, turned to Ramon and asked:

"What do you say?"

The hulking man looked at the slip of paper

he had and nodded:

"Looks like the right place."

"Five francs!" the he repeated, growing noticeably impatient. He didn't want to spend any more time here than he had to.

I took out my wallet, but before paying, I clarified from my partner in any case:

"Can we find our way back?"

"We can," Ramon confirmed confidently.

The man snatched the five and, in one moment, dissolved in the darkness as if he had never been with us at all.

"Look," my friend warned me, "if we do get lost, I'll never forgive you."

"I'm more worried about something else," Ramon snorted, flicking his Winchester down from his shoulder and heading into the opium den.

I sighed and hurried after him.

The conversation actually did promise to be fairly difficult. The Chinese Quarter, an opium den, triad territory – and two pernicious outsiders asking questions. An explosive mixture, even when you didn't consider the Winchester.

The Winchester in Ramon's hands was the very reason I entered the den first. I bowed, took a step into the low door, quietly stood up straight and looked around the smoky room. The great number of straw barriers between the booths threw me off, making it hard to tell the true size of the room, and also breaking up the meager lighting – the only kerosene lamp was on a table with a half dozen tattooed Chinese people playing Mah Jong at it.

One of the players looked at the sound of the door flying open and whistled:

"Here come the Pharaohs!"

When the others tore themselves from the game, I asked Ramon:

"Show them."

My associate, his Winchester lowered to the floor, calmly walked up to the table, placed the marked piece of paper he'd found in the trash can on the table, and took a step back.

"Just to avoid misunderstandings," I smiled, masking my nervousness with a smile, "was this sold by you?"

"What if it was?" The man who'd drawn everyone else's attention to us called back.

"Aaron Malk, a Judean with a red birthmark on his cheek," I then stated. We're looking for him."

The man exchanged glances with his gaming partners, then looked at Ramon's Winchester and shook his head:

"He's not here."

"Where should we look for him?"

This time, a dispute arose among the

bandits, but it was immediately broken up by a short man in a leather vest. He threw out a clipped phrase in Chinese, and when everyone else went quiet, smiled. Without any accent he then stated, aping me:

"In order to avoid misunderstandings, we do not talk to Pharaohs."

I did not deny our affiliation with the police. Considering these people didn't talk to police, they probably wouldn't hesitate to kill us if they discovered we were now mere private detectives. And I had absolutely no desire to get into a shooting match in the middle of the Chinese Quarter. For that very reason, I held back from threats.

"Mr. Malk robbed his employer and other important people. And important people don't like being robbed. Important people always return what's theirs."

"And why should we care about this?" sounded off in reply.

"There are some very important people who are quite angry right now, and money is no object to them. They want to punish the thief and get back what was stolen."

A bandit came out from behind the table and smiled, but it was no longer as friendly a smile as before.

"I repeat my question: why should we

care?"

"Today, no one is worried about what the thief spent his stolen goods on, but tomorrow, people are going to start asking unpleasant questions. Today, we might forget we came here. Tomorrow, this very place might be crawling with our colleagues."

"Cops running errands for fat cats?" The bandit frowned, his eyes narrowing.

"For important people," I corrected him and added pointedly: "Actually important people."

"Forget about this place!" He demanded.

"We will! Just tell us where to find the Judean."

The man turned to his henchmen, who had started vying to tell him something. Ramon and I just stood and waited, but I noticed how nervously my friend's finger was twitching near his trigger.

After hearing out his henchmen, the bandit smoothed out the piece of paper we set on the table and threw it into the corner, then turned and poked me with his finger:

"We're not giving the money back!"

"We're not after the money. We're after the Judean," I declared directly and repeated my question: "Where is he?"

"Second floor, the door opposite the stairs. Get him and get out. You have five minutes."

Ramon and I exchanged glances. He nodded and went first up the stairs. He stood at the top, and let me past into the room.

"And don't come back here ever again!" followed after us, then we heard laughter.

On the second floor, I took off my glasses and put them in my breast pocket. Then, pistol in hand, I stood outside the little room. Ramon, though, went further up the stairs, but immediately returned and told me:

"Up there's the attic," and pushed his way into the little room.

The door swung open with ease, and the smell of opium smoke flooded out. I crossed the threshold and immediately realized why the gangsters had agreed to give their moneyed client up to us: Aaron looked like death warmed over. It looked as if he had been smoking opium for two days in a row already, and very soon would have to be thrown out the door in any case.

We had simply been allowed to do a small favor to the caretakers.

"Clear," I informed my partner, stepping over the man, who was just lying there on a straw mat. I threw open the window, letting fresh air in from outside.

The intoxicating opium smoke had started making my head spin.

"Is it him?" Ramon asked, finding a place to

stand a bit further from the puddle of vomit on the floor. The squat man's Winchester was in the crease of his elbow, and he was looking cautiously through the cracked door into the hallway.

"It's Aaron Malk, in the flesh," I confirmed, crouching down.

"Is he alive?"

"He is breathing."

He was pale, and his skin had a bluish shade. His breathing was intermittent and his pupils were the size of a matchstick head. Those facts left us with no doubt that the manager's assistant had seriously overindulged on opium and it would be very difficult to bring him to his senses.

"Check his pockets," Ramon then advised me.

And I did but, beyond the wallet in his back pants pockets containing a few rumpled tenners and a handful of coins, I didn't find anything of value. I stuck the wallet in my briefcase, having made up my mind to study its contents more carefully later. Then I shook out the jacket that was lying on the floor, but there I also didn't find anything interesting.

"He doesn't have the box," I told my friend.

"No surprise there," he snorted.

I cursed out, picked up an earthenware

pitcher and poured its contents out on the Malk's head. He mumbled out something incoherent, and tried to push me away, but just kept lying on his back and breathing unevenly.

"It's already been five minutes," Ramon warned me.

"They can wait!" I cut him off, and perked my ears up at an incomprehensible rasping, but the sound wasn't coming from the corridor. It was coming from outside. "Watch the door," I asked my partner and set about rubbing the man's ears and cheeks in rage.

Malk resisted both stubbornly and drowsily, but gradually his gaze grew clearer and he began to get me in focus.

"No," Aaron said. "No! No! No!"

"A box with a lightning rune on top, remember it?" I shook him. "Answer me!"

Aaron Malk just smiled.

"I'll tear your head off!" I promised. "Why'd you change it out?"

"For money, why else?" Aaron licked his dried-out lips and then, unexpectedly soberly, asked: "Isn't it obvious?"

"Who paid you?"

But the momentary sobriety had already passed, and he just giggled in reply.

"Speak!" I snapped.

"So you can tear my head off?"

Aaron was overcome by a hysterical laughing fit. I gave him a few punches straight from the shoulder, but it didn't get better.

"It looks like we won't beat it from him," Ramon frowned. "So, we'll have to get him out of here."

"We will," I sighed, leaving my cane and starting to get him up on his legs. But he pushed me away and pressed his back to the wall.

"No," he turned his head, his back catching on the wall. "No! No! No!"

"Tell me who paid you," I decided to lead him to my answer, "and we'll leave you alone."

"Never!" Aaron sobbed. "Listen, I can pay you! I have a lot of money! Enough for everyone! We can all be rich!"

"You've got twenty francs in your wallet."

"No! I have ten thousand francs! On me!" Malk exclaimed, jerkily clutching his rumpled jacket to his chest. "But I'll get more still! I'll get as much as I ask for! Everything he has! Just don't get in the way! I'll share it with you! Three thousand, five, hell, even ten! We will be rich, just don't ask for a name! It's a secret! My secret!"

"You shouldn't smoke so much," Ramon sighed. "He definitely won't be with it until morning."

"Curses!" I swore out, sticking my briefcase

under my armpit and pulling Malk to me once again. Just then, though, I heard an obvious sound from behind my back:

"Pst!"

The countenance of the white-haired leprechaun flickered past the cracked door; Ramon hopped out into the hall and followed him with his Winchester, but the short albino's trail had already gone cold.

"Leave him!" I shouted and turned to Malk, and just then a dark figure crawled up onto the window sill.

Devil!

In one blistering jump, the werewolf had crossed the room. I put up my briefcase to block him, and a moment later, a powerful blow had knocked me off my feet and threw me into the far corner. Collapsed on the floor, I grabbed my Cerberus from my pocket. The werewolf deftly swung his knee, and my pistol flew down the hall. His clawed paw shot upward and, in the semi-dark of the room, a blinding spark came exploding from a gun barrel.

Blood spilled from the animal's head. The ten-caliber bullet tore through his crown and landed in a dividing wall. The Winchester's lever abruptly went down – clack! – and immediately came back up. The werewolf stumbled to the side, trying to get out of the line of fire, but

Ramon was tracking him with the barrel, following the animal's movement. He was left with no room to maneuver, and one of the improved ten caliber bullets went into his chest, broke out through a rib and hurtled the werewolf away into the far wall. He dug his claws into the window sill, stood up straight, and the next shot simply threw him outside. From below, we heard a weighty strike and the cracking of boards.

Ramon threw me a pair of steel handcuffs and went out into the corridor.

"Leo, catch up!" He shouted, running down the stairs.

"Stop!" I roared in pursuit, but my partner was already nowhere to be seen.

Curses! Malk was our target! Malk, not the werewolf!

I cursed, pulled my Roth-Steyr from the holster and leaned out the window, pistol in hand. The werewolf was lying on the earth as before. He was clearly visible from the second floor, and I managed to shoot almost an entire magazine at him before I heard an incomprehensible shuffling behind me. I turned around. Aaron Malk had woken up and was getting on all fours. He then darted out the door with unexpected agility. Having forgotten about the wounded werewolf all at once, I caught the escapee by the stairs. Without particularly restraining myself, I grabbed him by the scruff of his neck and handcuffed his right wrist to the thick balustrade of the strong-looking banister.

There, I also found my Cerberus, but the cartridge of rounds had flown out of it, and I didn't have time to find it. I snapped the top from my cane and rolled down the stairs to the first floor.

The men had all left, and no one was stopping me from jumping out the flung-wide back door with a cane in one hand and a Roth-Steyr in the other. By that time, the werewolf's trail had gone cold, and Ramon was prowling the alley, looking at the viscous drops of the werewolf's blood in the dirt.

"Ramon!" I called out to my partner and, at that very moment, a shadow that looked too dark stood up on the carriage-house roof. "Ramon, behind you!"

The shadow shot up into the air. Ramon turned in place, putting up his gun.

A shot thundered out. A long flame from the dual barrels lacerated the shadow and illuminated the spread-eagled werewolf mid-jump.

Miss! Both shots missed him!

Another bullet went flying, and the werewolf collapsed weightily on the earth a few steps from Ramon.

The lever on his Winchester gave a clank. A smoking shell flew onto the mud, but the animal had already managed to get up to Ramon and push the barrels skyward before another shot could ring out. The strike from his left paw, in comparison with previous ones, was markedly less powerful, and could even be called weak, but even so, Ramon was knocked off his feet. With a crack, he tore into the carriage-house, fell and froze motionless on the ground; streaks of blood were dripping down the walls.

Curses!

I jumped up from my place and lunged deep with my cane; the werewolf, with an unbelievably graceful pirouette for his body, started to dodge the strike, but a shot from my Roth-Steyr forced him to break step and the points of the electrodes caught his back and made him start chattering in electric convulsions.

The werewolf, howled, spun in place and then I, in a pitiful attempt to copy the dancing motion of a banderillero getting away from a wounded bull, dove under his splayed paw.

"If you let your opponent get to within slashing distance, you've wasted the last moments of your life for nothing," my father's admonition flashed in my mind, and at the last moment, the claws sped over my head; the werewolf lost balance and fell down on one knee.

The crackling of electric shocks went silent. I jumped back hurriedly and only there realized that I was unarmed. The cane's electric jar was out of power. I'd lost the cartridge for the Cerberus, and the slide stop on my unloaded Roth-Steyr was jammed.

So I unfolded my knife with a nervous smirk.

The titanium blade sparkled in the murk of the bleak night as an elegant strip of silver, but the werewolf had already started reeling, then fell snout-first in the mud.

And it wasn't just the effects of the electric shock: his wiry fur started falling out, denuding his skin to reveal that it was covered in boils and a web of deep cracks. His ribs started to shake, and a sharp cough tore itself from his lungs. His maw filled with a crimson foam, and when the animal fell onto his side, I could see his blood-shot eyes and a large number of bullet holes that hadn't fully covered themselves over.

"The Convent," the beast wheezed out, "will never leave it like this!..."

Then the werewolf lost consciousness, and his once-powerful body began to decay and fall apart before my very eyes.

The uranium bullets and his accelerated metabolism had brought this invulnerable creature to an end after all.

The animal now out of my mind, I tore off for Ramon. He had already come to and was even pressing a wound on his right shoulder, but based on the streams of blood whipping out between his fingers, his subclavian artery had been severed. He had just minutes left to live.

"How is he?" Ramon gasped hoarsely when I came near.

"Dead," I assured my partner, getting down on my haunches.

"I hope I can catch him on the way to hell and give him a kick in the ass..." the hulking man tried to laugh, but just clenched his teeth in pain.

"You'll live, don't even doubt it," I objected.

"Drop it, Leo..."

"It's true that they won't be able to save your arm," I continued, "it's hanging by a few shreds. They'll have to amputate. But it's better to live as a one-armed cripple than to be struck down in the prime of your life. You can keep working as a guard and..."

"No!" Ramon snapped as much as he had strength to.

His lurking fear of becoming a lame cripple burst out, and I grabbed onto the horror, set it alight with my *illustrious talent*, and stuck it back. The squat man gave a wail, arched his back and lost consciousness; the blood that had been shooting out between his jerkily clenched fingers stopped as if the wound closed up on its own. And that's actually what happened. Fears were my domain, after all...

I stood to my feet, blinked several times and shook my head, but it didn't get any better. My eyes were burning. Then I clipped my dark glasses onto my nose and returned to the werewolf. The animal was truly dead, and his partially decayed body made for a pitiable spectacle.

It won't be easy to prove that this is the beast that murdered Isaac Levinson.

And also, what the devil did he mean by "the Convent?"

I heard a cough behind me. I turned and it was Ramon, on his feet and limping toward me.

"You put in a lot of effort for me," he complained.

"Malk!" I suddenly remembered. "Ramon, after me!"

I grabbed the Winchester from the ground and ran up to the opium den. On my way, I pulled down on the lever and swung it back up, putting another bullet in the barrel. I was afraid the Red Dragons might be upset about the firefight in their establishment.

But no, the bandits still had yet to return to the smoke-spot. At the entrance, though, I found some agitated smokers who were still – or already? – able to walk.

I saw my Cerberus cartridge on the lowest stair and stuck it in my pocket. I then ran up to the second floor, and, on seeing the broken balustrade, fell into a moment of complete stupor.

Aaron Malk was gone.

But how? How had he done it?!

"Devil!" I cursed out.

"What are you talking about?" Ramon came up after me. His former weakness had already left him and his face had reacquired its normal reddish hue. He was also moving confidently as if he hadn't been just about to die a few minutes earlier.

And I started to feel ill. So much effort, and for what?

"Look!" Ramon suddenly pointed to a drop of blood. And another on the step above it. "He's in the attic!"

I held the Winchester at the ready and began walking up the stairs. Ramon pulled his Webley-Fosbery from his holster and set off behind me.

Aaron Malk really was hiding in the attic. He was sitting in the far corner, leaning on the slanted trusses. Just sitting and not moving.

He was finally and irreversibly dead.

"Opium does not lead to good things," Ramon sighed, lighting the way for me with a lighter.

I didn't answer and touched the dead man's cheek. It was very cold, as if he had died several hours ago. And under the collar of his shirt, on his pale skin, there were clear blue finger marks.

"He was murdered," I told my friend. "He was dragged here, interrogated and strangled. And it was no human that did it."

Ramon touched Malk's neck, rubbed his fingers on the cloak and took a step back.

"Dark matters," he decided.

"Dark as they come," I replied.

We walked down from the attic and I grabbed my torn up briefcase from the hutch, a scratched-up Mauser inside, and suggested:

"But what if we hadn't found him?"

"You mean at all?" Ramon clarified.

"We went into the room and found the werewolf. They definitely won't give us anything for the werewolf."

"Except money."

"Except money," I nodded. "I think the jaw impressions will confirm my theory."

"That would be nice," he sighed and headed down.

I followed after him, took a stool from

under the dice-game table and sat on it, giving my weary legs a rest.

"We should call the police," Ramon decided, "before the owners come back and throw us out."

"Let's send one of the neighbors," I suggested, reloading my Roth-Steyr. "Five francs per eye ought to do it. We'd better both stay here. I don't know what kind of beast killed the man, but whatever it is, it could still be nearby."

I placed the stool in such a way that I could see the stairs and both doors easily.

Ramon took the Winchester I'd set on the table and walked away to the exit.

"No matter who paid for your box, they have serious problems in store," he reassured me. "Before dying, he probably blurted out the name of his patron."

I just winced, not reproaching Ramon for running out to fight the werewolf.

What was the point now? Just to have a falling out?

And also, Aaron's body was giving off a whiff of something so horribly ghoulish that I didn't even have the slightest desire to meet face-to-face with his killer. Perhaps, Ramon had saved our lives with his poor judgement.

With a heavy sigh, I took Malk's wallet from my briefcase, opened it, and studied both bank notes in the light, then checked all the coins, one after the other.

"What are you doing?" Ramon asked in surprise after I stuck my knife into the wallet and started hacking it to shreds in my search for a hidden compartment.

"He said he had ten thousand francs on him."

"Opiated nonsense."

"Maybe yes, maybe no. I'll be back soon."

Pistol in hand, I walked up into the room on the second floor, took Malk's jacket and walked back down. I felt it, but didn't find anything suspicious, so I started ripping apart the seams.

"Leo, if you're feeling bored, we could play Mah Jong," Ramon joked.

"Very funny," I muttered and suddenly felt the rustling of a thin piece of paper under my fingers. Carefully, making sure not to tear it, I pulled it through a slit, took a look and froze, not believing my eyes.

Ramon came up close and whistled:

"A check for ten thousand francs! That's a hell of a stack of money!" But his joy didn't last long. He saw that it had been bounced and drew out his words in disappointment: "They paid him in phony money! And what trickster did that?"

I silently folded the check in half and put it in my own wallet.

"My uncle, the Count Kósice," I said, sweeping the dice onto the floor with an abrupt arm motion. "My very own uncle. Just think! Oh, I'll strangle him with my bare hands!"

"I'm afraid," Ramon shook his head, "someone else will get to him before you." He pointed up at the ceiling, reminding me of the strangled corpse.

"Nonsense!" I waved it off and got to my feet. "We just need to hurry, that's all!"

Outside, a piercing police siren rang out and Ramon sighed:

"This isn't gonna be easy."

I cursed and turned to the window. On its clouded glass, I could see the leprechaun drawing something that amused him from the other side. Tiny droplets of drizzle were constantly flowing down the glass, ruining his drawing, and he even stuck out his tongue in zeal.

"Hangman!" I suddenly realized. The small man was drawing a gallows with a rope and a person in the noose!

What a great omen!

The leprechaun noticed my confused gaze, threw his head into the noose, leaned it to the side, and started imitating pre-death convulsions.

I took the stool and threw it out the window with all my might.

My mood was bad enough as it was, and I

could be sure it would only get worse from here.

But a noose? Oh no, I've still got some kicking to do...

End of Book One

Want to be the first to know about our latest LitRPG, sci fi and fantasy titles from your favorite authors?

Subscribe to our NEW RELEASES newsletter:
http://eepurl.com/b7niIL

Thank you for reading *The Illustrious!*
If you like what you've read, check out other
LitRPG novels published by Magic Dome Books:

Dark Paladin LitRPG series by Vasily Mahanenko:
The Beginning
The Quest

**The Dark Herbalist LitRPG series
by Michael Atamanov:**
Video Game Plotline Tester
Stay on the Wing

The Neuro LitRPG series by Andrei Livadny:
The Crystal Sphere
The Curse of Rion Castle

**The Way of the Shaman LitRPG series
by Vasily Mahanenko:**
Survival Quest
The Kartoss Gambit
The Secret of the Dark Forest
The Phantom Castle
The Karmadont Chess Set
The Hour of Pain (a bonus short story)

Galactogon LitRPG series by Vasily Mahanenko:
Start the Game!

Phantom Server LitRPG series by Andrei Livadny:
Edge of Reality
The Outlaw
Black Sun

**Perimeter Defense LitRPG series by Michael
Atamanov:**
Sector Eight
Beyond Death
New Contract

In order to have new books of the series translated faster, we need your help and support! Please consider leaving a review or spread the word by recommending *The Illustrious* to your friends and posting the link on social media. The more people buy the book, the sooner we'll be able to make new translations available.

Thank you!

Till next time!

www.ingramcontent.com/pod-product-compliance
Lightning Source LLC
Chambersburg PA
CBHW071329020726
47502CB00001B/17